SURROUNDED

Longarm topped off the magazine of his Winchester as he allowed to himself that nobody lives forever. Like the Cheyenne say, one sunny day is as good a day to die as any. He knew a Cheyenne would be singing his death song by now. Sticking a cheroot between his teeth, he began to softly croon a ditty he'd learned back in Sunday school.

One of the rustlers picked up his voice in the wind and jeered, "Hymn-singing ain't gonna save you now!" He pegged a wild shot in Longarm's direction.

Aiming at the bandit's smoke, Longarm fired back and listened for the killer's howl of pain. The odds had just been dropped by one. Maybe he wouldn't have to sing that death song just yet....

TABOR EVANS

LONGARM
AND THE NAVAHO DRUMS

JOVE BOOKS, NEW YORK

LONGARM AND THE NAVAHO DRUMS

A Jove Book / published by arrangement with
the author

PRINTING HISTORY
Jove edition / August 1993

ISBN: 0-515-11164-3

Jove Books are published by The Berkley Publishing Group,
200 Madison Avenue, New York, New York 10016.
The name "JOVE" and the "J" logo
are trademarks belonging to Jove Publications, Inc.

PRINTED IN THE UNITED STATES OF AMERICA

10 9 8 7 6 5 4 3 2 1

LONGARM

AND THE
NAVAHO DRUMS

Chapter 1

A Spencer spat thrice among the rimrocks to empty two saddles a quarter mile down the canyon. The sergeant, sprawled bloody and brain-scattered in the dust near the remains of the guidon rider, might have known better. But their spanking-new second lieutenant thought it best to get the hell out of there, leaving behind his colors, his dead, and any chances for future promotion in an army commanded by General William Tecumseh Sherman.

The fair but ferocious old veteran was commanding it from Fort Leavenworth, west of the Mississippi, since neither Queen Victoria nor even that loco bastard Bismarck had scalped any U.S. citizens in recent memory. General Sherman's aides were allowed to sleep as late as reveille, and even grab some breakfast in the officer's mess as long as they didn't dawdle. So one April dawn the four of them found their gray but still ramrod-spry superior wide awake and pacing before a large-scale if largely inaccurate survey map of the Four Corners country when they joined him in his spartan quarters.

That poorly mapped and vast expanse of semi-arid stretch of the canyon-cut Colorado Plateau was named for the way white cartographers had decided the corners of Arizona, Colorado, New Mexico, and Utah should meet way out in the middle of canyonlands nobody important had ever seen. Other string-straight lines drawn across many an awesome bump ceded generous portions of the area to various Indian nations, some of whom might have been surprised.

The general jabbed at the wall map with a riding crop and no preamble. "Indian Affairs tells me the sniping incidents here, here, and there could have been overly subtle hints to the Great White Father from his Jicarilla, Navaho, or Ute children. I'm assuming Navaho for the same reasons I just take that quinine and get it over with when there's a fever going around. With the price of beef up and enlistments down, we need another Navaho war about as much as we need a toothache with a dose of clap combined."

The senior aide, a lieutenant colonel, felt obliged to speak up. "Begging the general's pardon, the Navaho have never risen since a pretty good irregular called Carson gave them a good spanking back in the sixties. It was the Ute who ambushed that cavalry column up along the White River just a summer or so back, and right now we've got everyone but a handful of Apache pretty well in line."

General Sherman looked disgusted and said, "You may call Victorio and at least four hundred bronco braves a *handful,* Colonel. I keep forgetting you've never been in the field against Apache, and what do you think Navaho might be, Pennsylvania Dutchmen?"

The lieutenant colonel sniffed uncertainly. "The general just pointed out I'm no Indian expert. But I'd hardly call Navaho Apache."

The older soldier smiled thinly. "At least you write with a fine Spencerian penmanship. Now listen tight and I'll try and keep things simple!"

Tapping the map where those four corners met near the San Juan Canyon, the old pro who'd fought Indians long before he'd taught Johnny Reb that war could be hell began. "Way back in what Mr. Lo calls his Shining Times, before any of *us* spoilsports got here, everything southwest of these four corners was inhabited by fairly live-and-let-live folk, from primitive wandering Diggers to Pueblo nations living way better than a heap of white homesteaders could be said to living today."

He tapped the map a tad to the north. "Then, about the time armored pests from the south marched north out of Mexico in search of more Indian gold, other strangers who called themselves Na-Déné or Déné or Diné started drifting down the west slope of the Shining Mountains from the north. Their caribou-hunting kin, way up in the tundra country of Canada, call themselves Déné too."

"You mean these mysterious newcomers didn't belong in the Southwest any more than the local Indians think we or the Mexicans do, sir?" asked a younger and hence more interested major.

General Sherman answered flatly, "Neither we nor the Mexicans in a more religious mood ever caused the original natives half as much trouble. Speaking a language no closer to most Pueblo dialects than English might be to, say, Turkish, and following medicines and customs as different, the newcomers were about as welcome in the Southwest as Attila and his Huns had been in early Europe, for many of the same reasons. Their various names for themselves all boil down to Human Beings. They lived by hunting Dini, meaning anything or anybody who wasn't one of *them*. Caribou running sort of scarce in our Great Southwest, they settled for hunting mule deer, bighorn, Zuni, Tanoan, Hopi, and such."

The lieutenant colonel gasped. "Good Lord, General, are you saying they were cannibals?"

General Sherman shrugged. "Depends on whom you ask. The Mohawk swear they never took more than a few ceremonial bites out of a brave captive, but Mohawk still translates as Man Eater from the Algonquin. Uto-Aztec-speaking Pueblos dubbed their new neighbors Apache, meaning Enemy. It didn't take the early Spanish, or us, too long to figure *all* of us had to be talking about the same mighty surly ridge-runners."

The major insisted, "But didn't the general just say Navaho is another word for Apache?"

General Sherman shook his head. "I hadn't finished. Whatever they were, they came down from the north in waves, anxious to get in on the easy pickings. The peaceful Pueblos were rich, by European peasant standards of the time. Even the desert-digging Paiute, Papago, and Pima had pretty women and nice baskets worth a real man's raiding. But after a time the once-harmless locals learned to fight back pretty good, as both we and the Mexicans found out on occasions *we* pushed our luck with 'em. And even when the Apache won, there were so many Apache that after a time the pickings tended to get slim. So some of the newcomers, the greater bulk, as word spread,

3

began to pick up good habits from the nations who'd been there long enough to know how to scratch a living from such a grand but unforgiving landscape. Captive Pueblos, and even some far more willing refugees who'd run off from Spanish missions, taught their erstwhile enemies to herd stock instead of butchering it on sight, or grow corn, squash, and beans instead of risking their lives to harvest it from the *nabaju,* or cultivated field, of an armed and dangerous neighbor."

The aides exchanged glances. Then one of them asked, "Then Navaho simply means cornfield, sir?"

The general shrugged. "They grow lots of squash too. As I understand it, the early Spanish learned to divide the really mean fighters into just plain enemy Apache and Los Apaches de los Nabajus, or the semi-civilized ones you might just be able to trade with. Any Apache who can manage loves to dress up like a Mexican, or what he thinks a Mexican ought to look like. The ones we now call Navaho are naturally dressed less silly. They know you're supposed to wear pants with those Basque shirts. Having flocks and produce to trade, they more recently turned to manufacture, their women weaving blankets even other Indians admire, while some of their men hammer out flashy but sort of handsome coin-silver baubles to swap for felt hats, firewater—and, I fear, Spencer repeaters."

Turning from his wall map, the old gray man in army blue moved toward his cluttered desk as he continued. "Be that as it may. I suspect I get the message some disgruntled Navaho has been trying to send us. You were right about the spanking Kit Carson gave the rascals back in '64, Colonel. I wish we had Carson with us right now. That man did understand the mind of Mr. Lo. But they just couldn't save him when he burst that blood vessel in his chest in the spring of '68."

The general looked away, far away, as he murmured, "It's sort of ironic, when you think about it. A month after the man who'd beat them down and rounded them up lay in his grave, Armijo, Delgadito, Manuelito, Herrero Grande, and seven other *ricos* signed a firm but fair peace treaty with me, in person, at Bosque Redondo. As Carson understood and as the title *rico* would indicate, the Apache we call Navaho set great store by their personal property. They felt crushed and castrated by the loss of their sheep herds, farm plots, and peach orchards in what they called Dinetah, over in the Four Corners. I told them truthfully it was costing the Great White Father more to keep them penned up at Bosque Redondo than it might be to let them go home to their old canyonlands and then hunt them down like mice and feed them to my cat if ever they beat those foolish war drums again!"

A young captain declared, "I'd say they must have thought the general meant it. They've never come out with other Apache since they agreed to the general's terms."

Sherman growled, "I *did* mean it. A man who'd go back on his word to anyone is a liar. A man who'd go back on his word to any Quill Indian is a menace to society."

Reaching for a wrinkled sheet of paper on his desk, the stern old soldier who'd once politely told a Confederate housewife that war was hell, just before he'd burned her house down, grumbled something about the Bureau of Indian Affairs as he waved his old copy of the long-forgotten contract, explaining in a louder tone, "Carson and his troops, red and white, hadn't left the Navaho much to go home to once they'd had their fill of Bosque Redondo. So a fair-minded Indian agent called Abe Norton asked us to grubstake the defeated *ricos* with enough seed, stock, and small change to start over back in Dinetah. Like a fool, I said I'd pass the request on. It's been more than ten years now. I suspect some of that surly sniping was intended to jog the Great White Father's memory."

"You mean they were screwed completely, sir?" blurted out the still-idealistic junior officer.

General Sherman grumbled, "Worse, from Mr. Lo's understanding. The failed lawyers we persist in electing to public office think in fine print few Indians or honest whites can grasp. The Navaho asked Norton to ask us if we'd replace the stock Carson had fed to his boys and the buzzards. They wouldn't have liked it, but they'd have forgotten it by now if we'd just said no dice. But the B.I.A. in its infinite wisdom sent them a fistful of silver and a few head of scrub stock from time to time."

Rummaging up another sheet of paper the general growled, as much to himself as anybody, "That drought we had the past seven summers in the west played hob with the scrub mutton stock we'd issued them to start over. When a Navaho means

5

to herd stock across semi-desert range, he's thinking about moving Churro sheep and Mancha goats aboard a Spanish barb pony. So it's not hard to imagine what they thought when the B.I.A. sent in some fat and thirsty Romney Marsh and Shropshire gummers. You pay less for sheep after they've worn down their last set of teeth."

Even cavalrymen could picture trying to raise toothless Eastern stock on mesquite and sage on a range where water holes could lay eighty miles apart. It was the lieutenant colonel who declared he could see what the Navaho might be pissed about.

General Sherman shrugged. "I wish I could say for sure those widely scattered snipers were Indian. I said I was assuming Navaho trouble because that would hurt us worse than anything else I can come up with at the moment. Victorio already has me playing musical chairs with not enough troops. I've sent most of the more experienced officers and men from Fort Defiance, in Navaho country, down to Fort Apache to keep an eye on Victorio's San Carlos cousins. I was planning on reinforcing the bare-bones cadre at Fort Defiance with newer officers and men who could use a little seasoning at a normally rugged but not *that* rugged post."

He glanced thoughtfully at his wall map some more as he stroked his close-cropped beard and added, "Interior has been working much better with War since Secretary Schurz took over from poor old Sam Grant's Indian Ring. I've been on the wire with Carl Schurz, and he seems willing to go along with a goodwill gesture if I can keep the costs down. There's this overly ambitious white stockman over near Durango, Colorado, near the Four Corners. I understand he's stuck with a lot of superannuated spring lamb and senile kid because he invested in a lot of Mex wool stock he could graze on such marginal range before he asked the local settlers and mining folk what they preferred to eat. Navaho don't butcher young and tender stock. So they sort of admire tough and stringy meat. Settlers tend to have their *own* stock, and mining men are paid better than most of our working class and eat accordingly."

The lieutenant colonel nodded understandingly and said, "I like the general's idea of a carrot-and-stick demonstration. Moving a strong miltary force into Navaho country along

6

with a generous gift of the hardy sorts of desert stock they admire."

"It will confuse the hell out of them if we're guessing wrong about the motive of those pinprick attacks on our routine patrols," General Sherman said. "Indians can get confused enough about us without any help. You're right about it looking like a carrot and a stick to you or me. We'd better have somebody who understands Mr. Lo's sometimes whimsical notions sound the *ricos* out as to just how they feel about all these sudden changes in their world."

He let go of his beard. "Carson and all too many of his ilk have ridden on to the happy hunting ground. Bill Cody's started his Wild West Show, John Clum is busy publishing his newspaper out in Tombstone, and Tom Jeffords doesn't want to work with us or the B.I.A. anymore. Do any of you gentlemen recall what they call that tall drink of water who scouted out Buffalo Horn's band during that more recent Shoshoni rising up by the south pass?"

The major sighed. "They call him Longarm, sir. Deputy U.S. Marshal Custis Long, who more usually rides for the Denver District Court and can always be a disciplinary problem."

General Sherman chuckled fondly. "I remember reading the report about him knocking that bird colonel on his ass. The bird colonel had it coming. Let's get on over to the telegraph room. I want this Longarm rascal waving some sticks and carrots for me."

Chapter 2

A week later, they had come to the end of an imperfect day in Durango and that afternoon gullywasher nobody had been praying for had finally blown over. Nothing else had gone right for him since he'd dropped off the damned train from Denver, so the man known to friend and foe alike as Longarm headed into town from the stockyards to see how wrong he might be able to go in a one-horse town he'd surely be stuck in for a spell.

The normally dusty street of Durango had been pounded by all that unusual weather for those parts to an ankle-deep morass of red clay, coal cinders, and horseshit. So Longarm was mighty glad he'd fresh-dubbed his old cavalry boots with a blend of tallow and beeswax, before changing to old denim jeans and jacket from his more usual three-piece suit, with just such uncertain trail conditions in mind.

He'd have been out on the damned trail west by this time if it had been up to him. He'd bucked like hell at the notion of playing nursemaid to a squadron of green troops and a thousand head of for-Gawd's-sake sheep. But seeing he couldn't get out of it, and seeing he was this damn close to those Four Damn Corners, he was far more anxious to just get it over with than he was to seek adventure and romance in dinky-damned Durango.

He'd been through Durango before. So he knew how tedious such a spanking-new railroad town could be. Durango had been built, fast and cheap, by the D&RG with a view to selling off a heap of marginal land the railroad had been granted to encourage some damned civilization down in this corner of

Colorado. Some of it was flat enough to consider plowing. Most of it sloped gentle enough for grazing. All of it lay more than a mile in the sky, in a part of the West where the rain clouds could be as flirtatious as a cat with a mouse.

At least they'd found an all-seasons creek they glorified as the Animas River, and there was coal to be dug for the locomotives as well. The hardrock mining didn't amount to much yet, but with any sort of non-agricultural payroll, a mess of truck and stock had to be grown within handy reach of a town. So since it was payday night, Longarm found the muddy streets and plank walks along Main Street more crowded than the last time he'd passed through.

Many a miner, nester, or stockman he passed cast sober looks at the tailored grips of the double-action .44-40 Colt Frontier riding cross-draw on his left hip. That was one disadvantage of a bolero-length denim jacket. Made a gent look sort of border *buscadero* when he was only trying to be sensible. Longarm had ridden six or eight years for the law, and just couldn't say who he might or might not meet up with, having put his share of owlhoot riders in jail or in the ground.

He'd been aiming for the Diamond Belle, recalling it as a place that served a local brew at a nickel a scuttle and a free lunch he hadn't been poisoned by last time. But the tinkle of an either out-of-tune or poorly played piano led him to the cavernous maw of the Blue Danube Dance Hall instead.

The barnlike interior was illuminated by paper lanterns casting a dull rainbow's worth of colored light through a haze of tobacco smoke that reeked of cheap perfume and sweat as well. The swirling crowd inside reminded him of that roller-skating palace he'd had a gunfight in that time in Fort Reno. Most of the menfolk were dressed in their work duds. The gals they'd paid to dance with were dressed more like schoolgirls at a Sunday-go-to-meeting-on-the-green, with summer-weight frocks hemmed to display more ankle than a full-grown schoomarm might have dared to, even at a Sunday-go-to-meeting-on-the-green.

Nobody was really on roller skates. They were swirling around and around like that because the piano, down at the far end, was making a game try at one of those fashionable waltz tunes by Johann Strauss.

Easing inside, Longarm crabbed sideways to the long bar running along a side wall. He snapped a quarter on the zinc top to order a beer when a plump barmaid in a limp linen pinafore asked him what he wanted. She said the two bits would just pay for the mighty foamy schooner she slid across the bar at him. A schooner holding less than half the beer a scuttle did, Longarm reached for one of his three-for-a-nickel cheroots, knowing he couldn't afford to drink fast at dance hall prices.

He felt safe lighting up with his back to the crowded dance floor, thanks to the big mirrors built into the back bar. Hence he shied like a bee-stung jackass and let go of the lit match to go for his gun when somebody too short for him to make out in the mirror made a sudden grab for his ass.

He managed not to throw down on the pretty little thing as he whirled. "Jesus H. Christ, don't never do that to anybody you don't know, ma'am!"

She looked up at him sort of hurt from her imposing height of no more than five feet two in her high-button heels. "I see I made a real impression on you that night in Leadville, Matthew. So what on earth are you doing down here in this hayseed town?"

Longarm knew his name wasn't Matthew. After that he had to study on whether he wanted to say so or not. The gal was a vapidly pretty blonde with a tasty-looking pair of cupcakes bulging the pleated bodice of her pale blue summer frock. He'd had many a high old time in Leadville over the years he'd been working out of nearby Denver, and the world was filled with vapidly pretty blond gals, but he figured he'd have remembered kissing one with such lush lips and a missing front tooth. The distant piano paused just long enough to remind him what he hoped he was doing in the Blue Danube. He smiled down wisfully at the less tempting temptation to say, "I fear you have me confounded with some other gent, ma'am. I have surely been to Leadville more than once, but I'd never forget a face like yours and—"

"Oh, come on, you can tell me," she said. "None of us who ever knew Faro Freddy would blame you for shooting from under the table like that when he accused you flat out. As I heard it, Faro Freddy was already reaching for his belly gun as he made that cruel remark about marked cards."

10

Longarm laughed incredulously. "Hold on. I did read about the recent demise of Faro Freddy Fuller in the *Rocky Mountain News,* and I'm glad to hear his pals think Monte Matt Gray was justified in terminating his one-man wave of destruction. But how could you possibly have me confounded with Monte Matt Gray?"

She peered up harder at his rugged but clean-cut features, now a mite shaded by the brim of his telescoped tobacco-brown Stetson. "Well, you certainly *look* like Matthew. And I wasn't as far away from him as this the night he declared his undying love for his little honey lamb. Don't you remember calling me your honey lamb upstairs in the Claredon House that night?"

Longarm whistled. "Monte Matt must have been lucky at cards too if he could afford the Claredon House in Leadville. But I remain your humble servant, Custis Long from West-by-God-Virginia, ma'am."

She sniffed and replied, "If you say so. I've been dancing a good two hours and it's about time for my supper break, Matthew. I got my own quarters just up the slope, and I doubt they'd be too upset if I took my own sweet time getting back."

He smiled wistfully as he replied, "That's the nicest thing anyone's said to me since I got off the train in a deluge this afternoon, ma'am. But tempted as I am, it would be taking advantage of your friendship with someone else entirely if I took you up on your kind offer."

She might have offered more. But then a surly cuss with frilly green garters on the sleeves of his seersucker shirt whispered in the blonde's shell-like ear and she sighed, "Don't go 'way." Then the bouncer herded her over to a grinning cowboy with his fists full of dance tickets.

Longarm finished lighting his cheroot and, after a puff or so, picked up his expensive beer schooner. That piano was playing a polka now. The crowd found it easier to keep time with the music now that most of the keys seemed to be getting hit more or less right. So the joint was literally jumping as all those mining boots and cowhand heels hit the planks in unison.

But this time Longarm wasn't surprised by the slightly shorter individual who sidled up beside him and declared,

"I heard you was in town. You've doubtless heard Durango ain't incorporated as a township yet. But I am still the law."

The cuss making the brag was about forty and dressed like, say, an undertaker or a railroad dick in coal-dust black. But not so many undertakers packed a brace of ivory-gripped Remingtons under their frock coats. Longarm surmised the guns were fancy-gripped to make sure they were noticed. The stranger had Longarm's undivided attention as he went on. "I am licensed by the D&RG and the State of Colorado to keep the peace within one mile of the tracks. Meanwhile, there ain't half that much law just off to the southwest if you'd care to just finish your beer and . . .what's so funny, Monte Matt?"

Longarm stopped laughing—it wasn't easy—and explained, "I owe an apology to a gal I suspected of just being out to augment her income. Do I really look that much like some tinhorn up Leadville way?"

The railroad dick firmly declared, "This ain't Leadville and we both know it, Monte Matt. I know Faro Freddy had an even meaner rep, and I'll not argue with that coroner's jury up in Leadville. But we both know Faro Freddy had kin who just might not care who started the fight their Freddy lost, and I don't want them squaring accounts with his killer here in my town."

"Please note where I'm packing my side arm as I reach for some damned identification," Longarm said, going for his wallet left-handed so the man could judge the innocent intentions of his gun hand as he did so.

Flipping his wallet open with one practiced hand, Longarm let the self-proclaimed local law see his federal badge and official identification. "I ride for Marshal Billy Vail out of Denver, and you have my word I'm not here in Durango to settle a thing with anybody you'd be worried about. The army and B.I.A. has me riding herd on some soldiers blue, some Mancha goats, and more damned Churro sheep than I ever thought possible. The stock and a brace of Mex Basque shepherds are over by the tracks, along with a couple of squads of mighty soggy soldiers in their leaky tents. All of us are waiting on the headquarters troop and some infernal newspaper reporter assigned to tag along and cover our expedition."

12

He took a weary drag on his cheroot and put his wallet away as he explained, "That's what they call delivering reinforcements to Fort Defiance and some decent stock closer to the middle of Dinetah, an expedition. I figured we'd follow the north rim of McElmo Canyon to avoid the South Ute Reserve, and then swing down along the San Juan past Hovenweep to—"

"You sure do *look* like Monte Matt Gray," the local lawman said, cutting in, apparently not half as interested in what sounded like a sort of tedious task to Longarm.

So Longarm insisted, "I can show you my identification some more if you like. I got plenty of time, Lord bless all tenderfoot reporters and officers who want to see their names in the newspapers. Custer used to chase Indians with his own tame press corps, and I'll bet they felt mighty awkward trying to write down all the names at Little Big Horn. I don't know what in blue thunder anyone expects to write about a herd of sheep moving down into Dinetah with a military escort, once I get them around the sometimes surly Ute without incident. They asked me to see if I could manage that because I arrested a crooked Ute agent one time and the Ute seemed thundergasted to be treated fair for a change."

The Durango dick grimaced and flatly stated, "I've yet to meet a Ute I'd turn my back on for one little second."

To which Longarm soberly replied, "I just said that. Ute do seem sullen at times. Of course, they say *we're* the ones who shit on *them* after they'd helped us chase heaps of *other* Indians out of all these mountains they used to feel they owned."

The Durango dick didn't want to hear just how Durango Township had wound up in white hands. He said, "Well, you sure could pass in better light for Monte Matt Gray, Deputy Long. So if I was you I'd watch out for strangers in back of me till they catch up with that *real* Monte Matt."

Longarm smiled thinly and said he always did, having made his own share of enemies who knew exactly who they wanted to backshoot. So they shook on it and parted friendly.

By this time the heroic head that barmaid had built in his beer had fallen to where it looked as if he'd already been sipping at it. So he just went on smoking till that same seersucker-shirted bouncer came up to him to declare, "Like

13

I just told Miss Ohio Olive, we like this dance hall dignified, and they do say Faro Freddy's kid brother is in town, Mister Gray."

So Longarm laughed again, although not half as loud, and confided, "I ain't Monte Matt and I'm getting tired of saying so. My name is Long, Custis Long, and I can prove it pleasant if I've been right in assuming your piano player bills herself as the one and original Miss Red Robin of Texas and too many other places to mention."

"You know Red Robin?" the bouncer asked dubiously.

Longarm managed to keep his tone polite as he replied he hardly ever lied just for practice. So the bouncer growled, "Grab your beer and follow me."

Longarm did. Behind them, a furtive-looking youth slipped into his empty slot at the bar to beckon the barmaid over, murmuring, "What happened? I gave you a whole half eagle to play a little joke on my old pal Monte."

The barmaid leaned closer to murmur back, "I did put those pills you gave me in his beer, damn it. What's the matter with you? You said they wouldn't hurt him but that they'd make anyone pee funny colors later. It's not later yet. Give the man time to find out if he needs to pee red, white, or blue, for land's sake."

Lem Fuller looked away as he muttered, "They said the . . . joke . . . would work faster than that. You're sure he really drank from the schooner you served him?"

"Who else would you expect to drink from it?" she demanded. Her eyes narrowed thoughtfully as she continued. "Say, what did I put in that drink if you expected to see results from the one or two sips he could have taken so far?"

But Lem Fuller was already moving away, a half eagle poorer and mad as a wet hen. But the night was still young and there was more than one way to settle the score all by himself, before Dad and Uncle Ralph got in from Leadville.

Dad had wired not to go up against such a gunslick all by his self now that they knew where Monte Matt was. But Dad hadn't said not to *kill* the son of a bitch who'd gut-shot poor Freddy!

Meanwhile, Longarm had followed the bouncer to the far end of a mighty long bar, where they could both gaze down in admiration at the lovely vision playing an upright piano sort of poorly.

The voluptuous piano player wearing fire-engine-red velveteen and upswept hair to match was neither a natural redhead nor, despite the way she was inclined to act around Longarm, a whore. For as she'd pointed out that time he'd arrested her down Texas way, a gal willing to screw for money wouldn't work such longer hours pounding a piano. Longarm, and doubtless many a boss who'd hired her, had figured sooner or later she'd learn to play better. Meanwhile, a right handsome fake redhead playing a piano badly had to have a piano just sitting there beat, so what the hell.

When the bouncer leaned over to growl in Red Robin's ear, she turned her cameo profile for a quick glance over her creamy bare shoulder, saw who he was talking about, and left a dance floor full of boots poised three-quarter-time to leap to her feet and charge around the stool. "Custis Long, you old asshole, what are you doing in the same room with me on your feet with your pants on?"

He figured she was showing off, and knew she aimed to kiss him in public, so he set the beer schooner on the end of the bar and got the lit cheroot from between his teeth just in time to keep Red Robin from putting it out with her tongue.

The bouncer didn't look too happy about her display of affection for another man. Longarm knew the poor cuss had tried, as any man would, and been turned down, as everyone Red Robin worked with always was. She was smart as hell about everything but telling the black keys from the white keys, even when she knew the tune.

Once she'd bussed Longarm good, Red Robin turned to the bouncer. "Would you tell the boss I'm taking my supper break a tad early, Wilbur?"

The bouncer said, "No, you ain't. You're going to get us both in trouble if you don't get back to your keyboard till old Dave gets in to spell you a set or two, ma'am. The boss told old Dave to get here around nine. How was he supposed to know you were fixing to elope with Prince Charming here?"

Then he turned to Longarm. "How's about it, Prince Charming? You want to let the little lady play some more or do you want to get her fired?"

15

Longarm said, "Don't get your bowels in an uproar, Wilbur. I was fixing to mosey on to the Diamond Belle for a spell in any case."

He saw Red Robin was fixing to cloud up and rain on the both of them, and quickly added, "I can get back before nine easy, all full of nickel beer and pig's knuckles, as easy as I can wait here at two bits a schooner and no free lunch."

So she agreed that made sense, but warned him she'd better not have to come looking for him. Then she sat back down and took up where she'd left off, smack on the second beat of a one-two-three waltz.

Longarm smiled at Wilbur, who just sighed, chagrined, and they each went their own way through the crowd. Longarm had made it to the door when the piano stopped again and he heard sounds of considerable dismay back the way he'd just come.

Getting back was tougher. Once he made it, he found a circle of Durango dancers surrounding a tragic little tableau on the sawdust-covered floor between Red Robin's upright and the end of the bar.

Red Robin was on her knees, oblivious of the sawdust on her lush velveteen skirts, as she held the gray head of a shabby old gent in her lap, crooning down to him as if he'd been a sick kid. He was surely one sick-looking old man. The bouncer, Wilbur, hunkered on the other side of the man, feeling for a pulse above that death grip the old drunk had on the handle of a beer schooner. Then Wilbur soberly said, "I think he's off to that big saloon in the sky with no more drinks to bum off nobody, ma'am!"

Longarm shot a thoughtful glance at the end of the bar where he'd left that expensive beer. The schooner wasn't there now. It would have been mean-spirited to accuse a dead man of helping himself to another man's drink, so Longarm didn't. A portly man who said he was a veterinarian pushed his way through the crowd to hunker down as well and fuss with the old dead man's chest a spell. Then he announced, "Looks like what's known to us in the profession as a myocardial infarction, or a heart attack in layman's lingo."

Wilbur declared, "Old Calvin here was inclined to fall down a lot. We always figured he was just a drunk."

16

The vet shrugged and said, "That couldn't have done wonders for his heart at his age. But as you just now said, the poor old bum will have no more worries. As coroner pro tem in these parts, I am writing this dolorous event up as death due to natural causes."

Chapter 3

There was nothing like a dead body on a dance floor to put a damper to the festive mood for a spell. By the time they'd hauled the old drunk's remains away and got a few couples dancing some more, Red Robin's relief player had drifted in. So Red Robin hauled Longarm off up the slope to her hired shack for a quick supper and maybe a longer after-supper smoke than usual.

They'd already established that Red Robin admired the color red. She'd picked a place with red and black wallpaper, and her bedroom faced a row of ore smelters belching scarlet fumes against a rusty overcast. But she'd still hung ruby sateen curtains over the glass—lest anyone peek in at a lady who liked to shave between her ivory thighs, she explained as she rustled up some flapjacks. So once they'd eaten and blown out the lamps, the place would have reminded a man of the lower depths of Hell if he hadn't been having himself a heavenly time.

Red Robin had explained she wanted to get on top right off, because she had to get back to the Blue Danube and play till one or so, once she'd steadied her nerves with a quickie or three. Red Robin could sure come fast, for a gal, if you let her get on top.

Longarm found it easy to come fast and hard with his old pal stripped to the buff, save for her high-button shoes of red kid and black silk stockings held halfway up those pale solid thighs with red frilly garters, as she sort of played stoop tag on his old organ-grinder, inspired to full erection by her sweet smile and big white bobbing breasts as it slid in and out of her

18

hairless but far from innocent opening. For as he'd assured her when first they'd met in Texas, after she'd thought she'd killed a man in Chicago with a gun, no woman with a pussy like hers would have to use a gun if she was out to get away with the perfect crime.

He naturally came first, but he was naturally in no position to disappoint a friend as Red Robin just kept bouncing Cossack-style till she suddenly sobbed, "Oh, shit, I wanted it to last longer!" Then she collapsed forward on his bare chest to throb wetly on his quivering shaft, crooning, "Lord love you, Custis, I can come with you without playing on my little pink banjo at all!"

He assured her he had no complaints about her screwing either, adding, "Do you want me to get dressed and carry you back to that dance hall now?"

She sighed and said, "I wish I didn't have to go, but a deal is a deal and I asked for an advance until next payday."

He asked if this wasn't payday night. She snuggled closer and said, "I blew the money I had coming this afternoon on new summer duds and a better hair coloring than I can manage on my own. So I needed more to live on till I leave for Silver City."

When he asked how soon that might be, she burrowed her turgid nipples into his bare chest and began to twitch her twat around his semi-sated shaft, assuring him, "Oh, we'll have almost a full week of this sweet screwing this time. I've always wondered how long it would take to get all I wanted of your horny donging, but up to now it's always seemed as if the fates were conspiring to part us, and just as we were getting down to the nice dirty stuff!"

He tongued her ear fondly and suggested, "That's likely why we've remained such nice dirty friends, honey. We agreed early on that I was a shiftless lover no sensible woman would waste a good time on, whilst you had a sort of tumbleweed existence ahead of you until you'd satisfied your own itchy ways."

He found himself moving too as he continued in as conversational a tone. "I've caught myself going home to my furnished digs in Denver to sleep alone, knowing full well a swell-looking gal with a feather bed was there for the taking, if

19

only I wanted to put up with a little nagging about my needing a haircut, smoking such stinky cheroots, or showing more interest in my durned old job than in her, sob, sob, sob."

Then, since they were both commencing to breathe sort of hard, he rolled Red Robin over on her back and hooked an elbow under each silk-stockinged knee to spread her thighs high, wide, and handsome as she demurely observed, "I know how annoying that can be. I'm always having some fool lover begging me to marry up with him and give up my musical career just because we've gone sixty-nine a few times. I don't know why some gents think a girl's in love with 'em just because she says she loves 'em when she's *coming* with 'em. What's she supposed to say, that she *hates* 'em? Right now I'm sure in love with you, or what you're doing to me at any rate. Do you promise not to propose if I get really mushy after a few more nights of this swell screwing, Custis?"

He started thrusting faster, deeper, as he assured her he'd likely be able to resist the temptation. "Ain't sure we have more nights than this to worry about, honey. I was supposed to be moving out earlier with a troop of cavalry and a herd of sheep and goats. Mostly sheep."

Red Robin hissed between gritted teeth, "Don't stop. That's just the way I like it. But Jesus H. Christ, can't you come up with a better excuse than that if you've got somebody else in mind for tomorrow night?"

He kept long-donging her the same way as he chuckled fondly down at the pretty face framed by a wild mop of dyed hair, both rendered hellfire red by the ruby light through her drapes, as he explained, between gasps of pleasure, why he and the U.S. Cav, of all people, had been ordered to herd sheep through the canyonlands of Dinetah.

She didn't ask what or where Dinetah was until she'd climaxed again, complaining he was either teasing her or killing her.

He came in her sweet shuddering insides, finally managed to get his wind back as he decided he might live after all, and when she asked a second time, explained, "Diné is what the folks we know as Navaho call themselves. They think of us as Dini, meaning inhuman critters, or Belagana, meaning white folks, when they mean to be more specific about who

20

they're sore at. They call the center of the world they know Dinetah. Lucky for us, they ain't as interested as their cousins we know as Apache in exploring other parts of their world. With Victorio and some of the lesser bronco leaders on the prod this spring, Washington is hoping to keep the Navaho where they are with some Churro and Mancha stock they were promised years ago. The soldiers are to beef up the garrison at Fort Defiance in case the plan don't work and the Navaho try to take it a second time. They almost took it the last time they tried."

She murmured, "Let me up before I get hot again. I have to go fuck with a piano. Why do you have to run off to Navaho country with all those sheep and soldiers just as we've met up again, damn it?"

He rolled off, reaching for his shirt and a smoke as he said soothingly, "Look on the bright side. We wouldn't have met up at all here in Durango if me and most of the outfit hadn't been delayed by some late-arriving officers and a dude reporter. I sure mean to thank those rascals for taking their time once they get here. As to *my* part in the plan, I'm supposed to help the soldiers avoid any needless fights over that Navaho herd."

Red Robin moved over to a washstand in the ruddy light to wash off a tad and perfume a lot as she asked, "How come? Seems to me that even if the Navaho mean to come out with the Apache, it would be awfully stupid of them to fight over a herd being delivered to them on a silver platter."

He sat up to get at his tobacco and matches right as he explained, "We've got to get all that stock past a mess of Ute first. Ute hate Navaho the way the French hate Prussians, even though the Utes were on the winning side most of the time. General Sherman fears, and I have to agree, some Utes may cotton to the notion of such a handsome gift to their blood enemies about the way an unreconstructed Rebel would cotton to the notion of his daughter eloping with a carpetbagger of Ethiopian descent who raises boll weevils as a hobby."

As she laughed at the picture Longarm lit his smoke and went on. "Ute don't think that much of sheep and goats either. They might want to stampede 'em over a rimrock, though, to keep their Navaho enemies from feeling prosperous. General Sherman heard I savvy Ho, which the Ute talk, and get along

21

with 'em better than most Saltu, which is what they call us. The general's wrong about me being all that fluent in any Indian dialect. But I'm not bad at the hand sign lingo they all seem to agree on. I mostly get along with Indians by trying to understand 'em. They know I don't. But they appreciate a good try, or mayhaps a good laugh."

Red Robin seemed to feel there was no call to bother with any underwear in warm weather or, for that matter, cold. Hence it took her less time to dress than it did to tidy up her hair again. As she was slipping on the rain cape she'd just worn up the slope, Longarm made a brave attempt to find his fool pants. But she told him she wasn't afraid of the alley cats between there and the back door of the Blue Danube, and added, "It's fixing to start raining some more and I don't want you catching your death in that cowboy suit, lover. You just lay back and get some more rest. You're going to need it when your horny baby comes back for more coming!"

So he swung his bare legs back aboard the rumpled bedding, and finished his smoke as she left to finish her chores down the slope at the dance hall.

He was glad he did when, just as he was snubbing out the smoked-down cheroot, he heard raindrops against the window-panes above the bed. He fumbled a flannel blanket over his naked body, and covered his head with an extra pillow as he heard the distant sound of a train whistle. It helped a mite when, a few minutes later, the night train came clanging and hissing into the nearby yards.

Longarm wondered idly whether those army officers and that dude reporter might have come in aboard that train. He decided he didn't care at this hour, muttering, "Let 'em find their own gals." He closed his eyes again and burrowed his head deeper into a good old gal's perfumed pillows.

He didn't remember falling asleep. One never did. But he knew he must have when he suddenly realized he wasn't in the Denver Public Library with no pants on after all, but somewhere a lot more private with a naked lady giving him a French lesson.

"Jesus, let's not waste a swell come!" he warned her bobbing head in the ruby gloom as he found himself really rising to the occasion.

22

Red Robin had been hoping he'd say that. As he rolled back in her love saddle she moaned, "Oh, yesss! It's been over three hours and it felt like forever, darling!"

He laughed and started moving in her faster, observing, "Felt more like a few minutes to me. I fear I might not have caught as much sleep as a man needs around you, Red Robin."

She moaned, "Oh, shut up and screw me hard!"

So he did, blissfully unaware of what else he'd avoided on such a raw and rainy night by lying dry and slugabed away from the center of town all that while.

For across the muddy street from the Blue Danube, a quartet of men who'd come in aboard that night train huddled cold and wet under the overhang of a storefront as the last of the Blue Danube cleanup crew padlocked the front doors and made their own dashes for drier parts. Ralph Fuller cursed and declared, as much to himself as the others, "If the son of a bitch was there at all this evening, we must have missed him in that stampede they held when the music stopped."

Nobody argued. Then young Lem and another Leadville loafer called Pancho came clomping along the planks to join them. Lem said, "I've a mind to rope and drag that lying bastard Wilbur!"

His Uncle Ralph said, "You mean that bouncer played you false? After you paid him a whole Union dollar to tell you which way the slippery son of a bitch went?"

Pancho said, "Hey, we got enough *hombres* here in Durango for to shoot, and let us be fair to this Wilbur, eh? He never said he was certain Monte Matt had made a deal for to meet that *puta* who plays such a bad piano. He only said he *thought* they were *muy amoroso*. He also said our Monte mentioned that Diamond Belle up the street, no?"

Lem Fuller spat, "He ain't there neither, you blind-ass Mex!" Then he turned to the others. "We waited around back, like I said we would after Wilbur told us their piano gal seemed to have a hankering for Monte Matt. There was nothing back there to stop the damn rain, and we almost drownded before that bitch come out the back door in her rain cape alone."

Ralph Fuller roared, "You let it go at that? It never crossed your mind they might have agreed to meet somewheres else

23

after she knocked off across the way?"

Lem Fuller replied defensively, "Well, of course it did, Uncle Ralph. That's how come me and Pancho followed the redhead clean to perdition through wind and rain. We trailed her to her bitty hired shack up the slope. She never met nobody. She just loped on home through the rain a mite faster than one might expect after watching her just sitting there most of the night."

Pancho said, "Was no lamps lit inside when we watched her unlock her front door and let herself in."

"The jasper could have been waiting for her in the dark, you know," observed another gunslick thoughtfully.

Lem Fuller snorted, "Give me credit for being at least as smart as a gnat. Pancho here said no man with blood in his veins would turn in for the night before a woman built like that one. But I guess I'm as suspicious as you are, Cousin Wallace. So when I spied lamplight coming out a side window, I hauled this easygoing greaser around for some Tom-peeping!"

"Ay, Chihuahua!" Pancho said. "*Que culo grande,* and her *melones* are not bad either!"

Lem Fuller sniggered. "We saw her bare-ass through the thin red curtains as she undressed for bed. I thought sure she'd spotted us grinning in at her when she turned our way. But she was only aiming for the bed, closer to the window. We could see her lift the covers and slide in bare-ass. Then she trimmed her lamp and it's a good thing she did, before I wound up raping Pancho!"

Pancho laughed and said, "Hey, not unless I get on top. Then, since the *mujer* was most obviously in bed alone, we went down and around to that Diamond Belle the bouncer had mentioned. Was one bartender and some drunks from the dance hall there. Lem is most sneaky talking to drunks."

Lem explained, "It ain't hard to say you're looking for an old pal who said he'd meet you there. The barkeep had no call to lie. So he was likely telling it true when he said nobody who could be described as Monte Matt Gray had been in all evening."

Ralph Fuller thought a spell before he decided. "Well, he has to be *somewheres* under a roof right now, and we're all likely to come down with the ague if we don't follow his example.

24

I vote we call it a day and start over in the morning."

It was Pancho who pointed out, "*Mierda,* such tinhorns are never out of bed before noon. And that *mujer* they call Petirroja inspires me for to seek shelter in a house of easy virtue I have heard of here in Durango!"

Chapter 4

So nobody anxious to gun Monte Matt Gray or any poor soul who looked like him was up and about when Longarm left Red Robin's place mighty drained of passion but full of black coffee and a heroic serving of fried eggs over mountain oysters.

The day had dawned sunny and crisp, but the streets were still muddy. First things coming first, Longarm went to say good morning to the trail stock he'd left in the livery near the rail yards. Most of the time he only hauled his saddle and such along when they sent him out in the field, picking up such horseflesh as he might need at the far end of an often tedious haul by rail. This time, suspecting he'd be on the trail a spell where picking up a fresh mount could be a chore, he'd picked out a pair of cow ponies he knew personally from the Lazy B over in the foothills to the west of Denver. The mare was a black Spanish barb with a speck of Morgan blood to smarten her stride. The other was a blue roan gelding mustang whose jug head and plow-horse hooves indicated a total lack of anyone ever giving a damn about his breeding. But a smart roper who stood a hand taller than your average cow pony could tote a big man or a light packsaddle as far as a man with a lick of sense might want to go in Dinetah with summer coming on.

Longarm made sure they'd both been watered and oated. Then he tipped the colored stable hand a dime when he discovered nobody had been at his possibles in the tack room overnight.

He left his McClellan and possibles to gather more dust for the moment, and headed over to the neat rows of tents, of various sizes, trying to dry out in the soggy vacant lot just upwind of the stockyards. As he approached he saw cavalry troopers, who'd of course been up before sunrise at this time of the year, up and at the pointless chores the army devises to keep bored troops out of the less seemly work they say the devil finds for idle hands. As a man who'd done some soldiering in his misspent youth, Longarm knew most of the troopers suspected their officers had been too drunk to jerk off when they'd come up with a lot of this bullshit.

Longarm asked a sergeant sharpening a saber whether their C.O. and that headquarters platoon was expected any damned time, say, this side of the first winter snows. The sergeant told him they'd come in the night before by train, accounting for those extra tents at the far end of the lot and those extra thirty-odd head of cavalry chestnuts across the way in the corral. But after that it turned out their captain, his adjutant, and that reporter from some big Eastern paper were still over at the Plata Palace Hotel. So Longarm got out of there before one of the doubtless disgruntled shavetails who'd spent the night with their troops in the rain could call him a sissy.

The stockyards being closer than that fancy hotel he recalled from an earlier stay in Durango, Longarm ambled on over to see how that stock intended for the Navaho had made out. He could tell a good spell before he could *see* any miserable critters how awful a thousand rain-soaked sheep and maybe five hundred goats got to smelling as they tried to dry out after a hell of a soaking.

Fifteen hundred such critters didn't take up two thirds as much space as that many cows, of course. But they still filled half a dozen pens along the tracks as they milled and bleated to be let out. Longarm could hardly blame them. Their sharp hooves sank deep as hell in the sepia mixture of rain-soaked dirt and sheep shit.

The boss Mex herder joined Longarm at the rail as soon as he spotted him there. The somewhat older man was actually a Basque, or what Spanish speakers pronounced as Vasco. His Spanish handle was Hernan. Basques didn't expect anyone to even try to pronounce their own tricky lingo, which they called Euska-ra. They claimed they were more honest than their Spanish or French neighbors because the devil had never

27

been able speak enough Euska-ra to lead any of them astray.

Speaking English, sort of, Hernan told Longarm, "We no can keep this *hato* here on this *mierda maldito* another *momento* if you wish any for to ever walk again! Churro *y* Mancha are both meant for to graze sun-baked *foraje* over dry and dusty range. A pig, or perhaps one of your gringo mutton breeds, can soak its hooves in mud like so without catching the hoof-rot, *pero* serious creatures such as you wish for Los Navajos to keep on sage and mesquite—"

Longarm cut in to say he'd see what he could do. "I never said I meant to grow old and gray in a one-horse town whilst an infernal troop commander gets around to commanding his damn troop."

Suiting actions to his muttering, Longarm returned to the livery, helped them saddle the black barb, and rode up to the Plata Palace at the more fashionable end of town.

Inside, he was told Captain Granville and his party had indeed checked in the night before, but that he'd left explicit instructions he was not to be disturbed before noon.

Longarm asked what room they were talking about, and when that didn't work, flashed his badge and laid a friendly .44-40 beside the register on the fancy marble countertop.

So a few minutes later he was politely pounding on the captain's door, despite the "Don't Disturb" sign hanging from the knob. When a surly sleepy voice demanded, "Go away, you son of a bitch!" Longarm used the passkey from downstairs less politely, announcing, "We're just not going to hit it off if you ever call me that again, Captain. My real title is U.S. Deputy Marshal Custis Long, and I have come to tell you we got to move that Navaho herd right now if we aim to dry their hooves hard enough to matter this side of sundown."

Longarm figured Captain Granville had to be the sort of jowly and pouty-faced cuss sitting up and scowling at him, since the other figure in the bed was coyly hiding under the covers. The asshole who'd just called a total stranger a son of a bitch complained, "We're not ready to move out! We're not even ready to get up yet, and when we do get up we're not about to go anywhere without a substantial warm meal! The food on that train was beastly and all in all, I've had a very hard night, Deputy Long."

28

Longarm smiled thinly down at the bulges in the bedding next to the bare-ass officer as he calmly replied, "I don't doubt that, Captain. Meanwhile, sheep don't drive much faster than a man can move afoot, and we'll want to let 'em graze some along the way. So I'll just tell them Mex boys to head 'em on out, and you and the rest of your outfit can catch up along the Hesperus Pass Trail, if you'd like to start most any time today. Doubt old Hernan can move 'em more than ten or fifteen miles by sundown if he drives 'em way harder than he ought to before they trail-harden some."

He started to leave. Captain Granville flared, "Hold on! I am the one giving the orders around here!"

So Longarm nodded and replied, "I never said beans about moving one soldier blue. I won't need you boys any more than you'll need me till we get into more serious country on the other side of that pass. If you don't want to tag along, I'd be the first to allow I can't make you. But them sheep can't make it anywhere with hoof-rot. So I'm heading 'em out before they get it, meaning right now."

"Don't you dare lay one hand on that stock entrusted to me and the U.S. Army!" the pudgy officer wailed, exposing more pale lard as he rose taller on his bare ass, winding up to lay down some law to a lawman who'd gotten mighty tired of taking military orders when he'd still had to take them.

So Longarm snapped back, "Listen tight, you simp. Your men may think you eat cucumbers and do other wonders, but General William T. asked for me personally to help you and that stock get through Dinetah alive and well. I can't get those dry country sheep and goats that damn far, even sick, unless we dry their muddy hooves out *poco tiempo*. So like I said, I'm moving 'em on out right now. If you'd rather register a formal complaint with General Sherman than just get up some time today, go right ahead. It don't make no never-mind to me whether I guide you or somebody sensible as far as Fort Defiance, and I somehow doubt the man who marched an army through Georgia will think I'm pushing you, or even the sheep, too hard!"

Then he turned on one heel and left, slamming the door behind him as he chose to ignore what the angry officer then called him. Had he let on he'd heard, he'd have had to go

29

back in there and pistol-whip the silly bastard.

He rode back to the stockyards instead, to tell Hernan he'd told the captain they were moving out ahead. He felt no call to confound the issue by mentioning what the asshole had said, and the Basque said he and his *muchachos* had been set to go since sunrise.

Seeing they knew far more about the critters than he'd ever likely want to, Longarm loped the barb back to the nearby livery and got his own self ready to do some serious traveling.

He took his time, knowing he had at least two weeks on a dusty trail with little or no chance of making up for anything a man might forget to bring along.

All his personal possibles, such as spare socks, soap, and more waterproof matches and ammunition than he usually packed, were just where he'd packed them in the saddlebags of his McClellan. He hauled out his Winchester saddle gun, and took it apart on a nearby tack bench to make certain it hadn't picked up a speck of rust since he'd left Denver with it. Then he reloaded it with sixteeen rounds of the same .44-40 Volcanic centerfires he'd picked up for both his six-gun and double derringer.

The popular .44-40 round was a tad underpowered for bigger game than human beings. But while it made for a soft-shooting rifle, a man really felt the kick when he fired it from a handgun. The U.S. Cav issued pistol ammunition with barely half the powder load and rifle ammunition backed by seventy grains. But while maybe it made for more scientific shooting under tranquil conditions, that hardly seemed to make up for the awkwardness of fumbling for the right .45 reloads in the middle of a more serious situation.

He checked his trail supplies again, and tipped the stable hands extra for filling his rubberized water bags with fresh-pumped *aqua pura* and a little vinegar to slow stagnation.

Then he led both saddled ponies over to the nearby smithy, to have a man who knew more about the subject assure him neither was fixing to throw a shoe on a rocky trail for at least two or three hundred rugged miles.

The smith told him the off-hind shoe of the blue roan could use a couple of extra nails. Longarm said that was why he'd asked, and told the old cuss to get cracking.

As the smith was securing the suspicious horseshoe, one of those second johns camped out in that muddy lot came running in. "Those Mexicans just lit out with all those sheep. They said you'd told 'em the rest of us would catch up later. Does the captain know anything about all this?"

Longarm smiled innocently at the officer and asked, "Do I look like a sheep thief, Lieutenant? Of course I told old Granville all about it. We had to get that dry country stock out of them muddy pens before they all caught hoof-rot. He said he'd be along no later than this afternoon, after he and his, ah, friend had eaten dinner."

The younger officer looked away and stiffly said, "I didn't hear that."

So Longarm said in a louder tone, "I said I found Granville in bed with someone in the hotel. He'll be there until high noon at least."

The lieutenant almost sobbed, "I didn't hear that either. I have never been one to question my superiors about their personal habits."

"Nor anything else in a peacetime army with Congress anxious to balance the federal budget, I'll bet," said Longarm dryly. So the second john went away. That had been Longarm's general intent.

After the smith assured him both ponies would drop dead before either would drop a damned shoe, Longarm settled up with him and remounted the black barb to lead the blue roan back out into what was shaping up a dazzling day under a cloudless cobalt sky.

The trampled stinking stock pens were empty of all but the lingering smell of the herd. Goat stink was far stronger and lasted far longer, but most cow folks insisted sheep smelled bad enough without a lick of help from a goat, or for that matter a polecat.

As Longarm rode out to the west he was doing so on pure faith. The blazing sun and thin thirsty air hadn't dried the rain-soaked trails out of town enough for even fifteen hundred head to raise dust above rooftop level. But as Longarm broke out of the west side of Durango, he spied the herd half a mile out. Old Hernan had sure moved them in the time he'd had to do so.

That old Basque and his boys were good. But of course Basques from Spain had invented sheepherding as it was practiced west of, say, Latitude 100. Neither old Hernan nor his helpers were playing Little Bo Peep with a herd that size. All three had Spanish riding mules under them, a bellwether or trained Judas goat out ahead of them, and a couple of dogs that looked like bastardly mixtures of sheep and wolves out to either flank.

It took far more riders to herd that many cows, of course. But thanks to the way sheep stayed bunched without anyone asking, one man and a dog could hold a thousand head of sheep on good range if he had no need to move them far and wide and sudden. But since General Sherman had ordered a forced march through Indian country, Hernan and the two younger sheepherders were earning their pay at the moment.

Both Churros and Manchas had been bred closer to their leaner and meaner Mediterranean cousins, the original wild stock mankind had commenced to tame way back in the time of the Good Book, if not earlier. So both the sheep and the goats out ahead were legged up a lot faster than most domestic breeds. Every now and again one of the critters, most often a goat, would make a break for it, not to stray from the herd as much as to get at something greener than, say, a mud-spattered thistle along the sides of the broad trail. A heap of other stock had passed through earlier, leaving trailside pickings that were mighty unappetizing, even for a goat.

Yet old Hernan and his crew were keeping them bunched so tight and moving them so fast that Longarm had to heel his own ponies to a trot in order to overtake them near the top of the first serious rise west of Durango.

It was just as well he did. The quartet of strange riders he saw blocking the trail just over the rise seemed to lose interest in mere Mexicans as they spied another Anglo, dressed cow, on his way to join in on one side or the other.

Old Hernan had naturally motioned his possibly hotter-tempered nephews or whatever to fan well out to the sides as he rode forward to see what the cowhands wanted, as if he didn't know.

Longarm knew. He handed the lead line of his pack pony to a younger Mex in passing before moving his barb in to join the fun at a thoughtful walk.

Folks back East, or off Australia way, raised sheep, goats, and cows on the same pasturage quite efficiently, with the cows cropping the grass, the sheep cropping broader-leaved weeds, and the goats trimming the hedgerows all around as they kept brush and the tougher weeds sheep didn't care for off the grass. The hatred both the Mex *vaquero* and the Anglo cowboy felt for sheep and the rival grazers who herded sheep on publicly owned open range had originated back in Old Spain, where both kinds of dry grazing had evolved, with lots of blood and slaughter.

The cow-herding *vaquero,* like the Spanish barb pony, the Hispano-Moorish longhorn, and a heap of cowboy notions, had been invented on the dry dusty plains of Andalusia in the sunny south of Spain, where dusky gents with Moorish grandmothers took their honor as Christian *caballeros* mighty seriously.

The Spanish style of sheepherding, suited more to raising wool on marginal range than mutton on green pastures, had been worked out in the somewhat greener but even rockier north of Spain, mostly by the mysterious Basques who'd been there way before anyone else and tended to suspect all strangers of the Evil Eye. The Spanish folks of Latin, Gothic, or Celtic descent were pretty sure the odd Vasco folk practiced witchcraft too. It was tough to tell when a neighbor talked so funny.

Nobody but poor folk ate mutton or beef in Spain. Save for fish on Friday, everyone preferred pork or chicken, and so Spanish sheep were mostly for wool, while Spanish cows were raised for hides and tallow, with wool the most profitable crop despite the swell rep of Cordovan leather and Castile soap.

Hence the tax-happy Spanish kings had tended to favor sheep on open range, or even across the cropland of small holders who had no pull at court. The crown-sanctioned Mesta, or herders' guild, had despoiled and overgrazed so much of Old Spain they'd turned a lot of farms and woodlots into stony desert lands. It was the seething hatred of the Spanish small-holder for the powerful Mesta that lay behind the mythology of the cowboy-sheepherder feud. Although neither your average cowboy nor your rare English-speaking sheepherder was as apt as Longarm to give a shit about ancient history or even common sense.

Longarm could see this as he rode within earshot and heard the burly apparent leader of the local stockmen declare, "We can see by your outfit that you ain't no sheep screwer. So how come you seem to be screwing with these sheep, cowboy?"

Longarm reined in to reply in a friendlier tone, "I've heard of screwing sheep. You'd be a better judge than me of what it feels like, next to your mother."

There came a collective hiss from the whole bunch, including old Hernan. But it was the husky cuss on the paint pony who told Longarm to take that back or fill his fist here and now.

So Longarm let them see how he could materialize a .44-40 out of thin air as he casually replied, "I don't usually show off this way for assholes I ain't really out to kill. But now that I seem to hold your undivided attention, listen tight."

Leaving the unwinking muzzle of his side arm trained in a don't-give-a-shit general direction, Longarm declared, "As you just now observed, I am not a sheepherder as a rule. I am not a cow screwer neither. I am U.S. Deputy Custis Long, and these critters are bound for the Navaho Reserve, a good week's drive the other side of you all, under the protection of the U.S. Government. They ain't about to bother you or any of your own stock. So don't bother them and we'll just be on our way. Head 'em on out, Hernan."

The old Basque explained in Spanish that their bellwether goat, trying to screw a sheep a ways back down the trail, wouldn't move through ponies blocking the way west. So Longarm passed this on, adding, "Let's get out of the way, gents. Don't you want to see the last of these stinky critters?"

The leader of the cow bunch took the straw Longarm had offered so graciously. He smiled uncertainly and declared, "Well, as long as you say they won't be ruining this corner of Colorado for cows. You're right about how funny they smell. What makes 'em smell like that?"

Longarm said, "Sheep shit and goat shit. Cows smell of cow shit and you smell of horseshit. I'm not going to ask you again to get the hell out of my way."

So they got out of his way. Most men would have.

Back in Durango, some harder men were far more determined to have it out with Longarm, or the man they thought he was. Faro Freddy's grim-faced father, who preferred stealing stock to dealing cards, and hence had more practice with a six-gun than his tinhorn son had displayed when he'd called another card player for cheating, was holding court at the Diamond Belle, knowing better than some how much other joints in Durango charged for a scuttle of beer.

Reporting in from his last sweep, young Lem Fuller announced, "An old boy I was drinking with last night says he saw the son of a bitch talking to them army men camped down by the stockyards. He ain't there now. But when I mentioned him as an old pal at the nearby smithy, they said Monte Matt, or somebody who sure described the same way, was in earlier having a pack pony reshod."

Old Dad Fuller sipped some thoughtful suds before he asked if they'd heard where the son of a bitch might be headed with a pack brute.

Lem answered, "Not exactly. The smith said he hadn't paid all that much attention over the noise of his own hammering, but he did recall Monte Matt jawing by the entrance with one of them army men. Lots of folk here in Durango say that cavalry squadron will be moving out against the Navaho directly, Dad. You reckon Monte Matt is planning on riding west with 'em?"

Dad Fuller shrugged and replied, "I don't know enough about the murderous bastard to say. He might have signed on as a scout or a scared traveler, hoping we'd never think to follow him into a fool Indian war. But to tell the truth, that don't sound like a gambling man who likely sits down to pee."

Staring soberly up at the others gathered around his table, the vindictive Dad Fuller decided, "All right. We can't waste time on wild geese, but we can keep a watch on that army camp easy enough. Pancho, I want you, Chuck, and Montana Slim there to circle that army bunch, and let us know the minute you see anyone who looks at all like Monte Matt."

Lem protested, "What about *me,* Dad?"

The grim-faced old owlhoot rider told him, "I want you to go sit in the lobby of that Plata Palace Hotel just up the way. You kids ain't the only ones who know how to ask casual questions in a strange town. Some of the officers who'll be leading that squadron against the Indians checked into that hotel when they got off the same train I did last night. Nobody's seen 'em check out. So why why don't you sit under a paper palm with the *Police Gazette* and let me know when they do. You don't have to be a college professor to tell a cavalry officer from, say, a whiskey drummer, you know."

Lem Fuller grinned and said, "Oh, I follow your drift, Dad. If old Monte Matt is tied in with them soldiers blue at all, he'll be near either their camp or that hotel when they're getting set to move on out."

It had been a statement rather than a question. So Dad Fuller only answered with a frosty undertaker's smile.

Chapter 5

Not wanting any more bull about sheep, they pushed the herd far harder than your average sheepherder, or sheep, might have thought possible. Longarm thought it looked like Hernan and his boys were driving a big fuzzy caterpillar, five or six head across and close to a quarter mile long, over hill and dale at infantry quickstep.

Longarm stayed out of it, riding point about a furlong ahead lest they meet up with more grass-hogging locals. The range rose higher and greener east of Durango, but tended to get lower and a bit more jagged-ass as one rode west toward the canyonlands of the Colorado Plateau, which was still more than a mile high. The ridges the trail kept crossing, which got steeper as they climbed, with longer, softer slopes beyond, hadn't been as heavily scalped of pit props and firewood a few hours out from the new settlement. But the juniper and piñon grew too spread out to offer shade along the trail, and as the morning wore on the sun overtook them to glare in their faces and bake the last rain out of the stony trail. So along about one in the afternoon, well clear of the unproven homestead claims clustered around Durango, they stopped to let the stock pick flowers and rest up.

Longarm cut back to the remuda of pack brutes, presided over in turn by Hernan's helpers, Mauro and Ramon. Young Ramon had brought up the rear with the pack brutes for the past hour, while Mauro and old Hernan had chased a dog up and down each flank of the herd aboard their own mounts. They were still off down the slope, making sure the herd would graze within the good forty acres of fresh greenup well clear of any brush or rocks Old Man Coyote had a mind to hunker behind. There was no way in hell even a ravenous coyote was going to pull down a grown sheep in broad-ass daylight with two dogs and four men watching, but Old Man Coyote liked to raise hell just for the fun of it, and a herd that size scattered from hell to breakfast was just disgusting to contemplate.

While Hernan and Mauro staked the bellwether goat mid-slope to show the rest of the herd where they were expected to linger, the bemused Longarm unsaddled both his ponies to let them get in on a good deal, hobbled but free to graze as they chose.

This close to May Day at this altitude, the grass was as green as it ever got in these parts, and the wildflowers were just fixing to bloom and hence as tasty as they could be to critters a whole lot bigger than any hummingbird or bumble-bee.

As Longarm turned both saddle blankets upside down to dry in the grass, a lonesome longhorn heifer came out of some juniper to join the sheep and goats spread out just a bit around the old nanny Hernan had trained to be bellwether. Further up-slope, young Ramon was building a coffee fire. Wanting to pull his own weight, Longarm moseyed back along the trail toward that clump of piñon they'd passed near the crest. Piñon shed lots of dry kindling and, in a pinch, a busted-off piñon branch would burn green, as full of pitch as the runty pines grew.

He saw that clump cast an inviting shade across a rocky outcrop just right for a sit-down smoke. So he sat down and lit up as he admired the scene below and worked on his second wind in this thin dry air.

The sunny slope wise old Hernan had chosen for a lunch break for the stock in his charge hadn't been overgrazed as yet by any sort of stock. So the different sorts of grazing critters spread across the pretty green carpet were making the most efficient use of the fodder Mother Nature had spread across her mountain meadow for them.

The mules, ponies, and that one cow were munching grass and the little clover mixed with it. The sheep were naturally cropping at the broader-leaved wildflowers, choosing the buds and greener tops when they had the choice. Longarm knew they'd go after the grass as well, as he'd seen on that sheep-mowed lawn around the state capitol in Denver. The Spanish goats seemed to go for weeds such as nettles, cockleburrs, and wild mustard by choice, likely enjoying a good chaw more than sheep. So, driven by Basques, or Navaho, instead of underpaid and hence underskilled help, such a mixed herd made a heap of sense on marginal range.

Sheep lore Longarm had never felt much call to remember was coming back to him as he finished his cheroot and got to gathering firewood in the pine-scented shade. He remembered what he'd heard from a pretty gal about never letting a herd of sheep hear the same church bells twice. They hadn't been acting all that religious in her sheep camp up the other side of the Divide that rainy night. But once you studied on it, you could see she'd meant you'd surely overgraze the range if you kept a herd on it two sabbaths in a row. It was also a good notion to move cows to fresh range every five or six days if they were getting no extra silage from you.

If anything, a hungry cow could do more damage to overgrazed range than anything but a rooting hog. For unlike sheep and goats, cows pulled grass up by the roots with their stronger muzzles when an ignorant or lazy stockman left them bunched too long on the same pasturage. But sometimes it was tough to convince an old boy of this when he was an unemployed farm hand riding for an absentee or even overseas land and cattle company. They did say some right notorious range wars had been inspired by European-held cattle baronies competing for grazing rights to open range the boards of directors had never seen. It was likely easier to order a foreman to burn out a rival brand than it would have been to do it yourself from an office in Scotland or a club in London.

He'd gathered about as much firewood as he could tote. So he was turning to carry it all down-slope to those sheepherders when there came such a pounding of oncoming hooves that he felt it best to let the firewood fall and go for his six-gun. But he held it down to his side politely as he waited to see what might happen next.

What happened next was a gal who seemed to feel she had to be at least a princess royal coming over the rise at full gallop riding sidesaddle on a handsome chestnut thoroughbred.

The gal was right handsome as well, with long hair that matched her mount pinned up under a silly black derby such as swells in the old Tidewater country back East rode to hounds under. She sat a sidesaddle well as anyone could in her long-skirted riding habit of Union blue. But when her dim-witted thoroughbred spied a mysterious stranger by the side of the trail and spooked, the princess royal, who'd never bothered to look where she was going, slipped ungracefully off her awkward saddle to land on one hip and demolish a good three yards of sagebrush and prickly poppy before a clump of springy soap weed full of needles brought her rolling and cussing to a dusty conclusion, flat on her back and staring slack-jawed at the sky above.

But as Longarm holstered his .44-40 and headed her way, she rose on one elbow to cry, "Never mind about *me*, you ass! Catch my *horse*!"

Longarm saw her spooked thoroughbred was tearing down to join the mules and ponies. So he told the gal, "Never mind your mount or my ass till we make sure *your* ass ain't broke, ma'am. That was a serious thump you just administered to Mother Earth with your, ah, maidenly anatomy. Don't try to get up just yet. Can you wiggle the toes in both boots?"

She frowned up at him as if he'd just asked her if that sky up yonder was blue. But as he hunkered down beside her she licked her lips less certainly and replied, "I'm not sure. My whole left, ah, limb seems to have gone to sleep. Perhaps if you would be so kind as to help me stretch my limb out straight in the grass . . ."

But he shook his head and replied, not unkindly, "It ain't grass. It's sage, and you landed awkward, no offense. A busted hip or a pinched sciatic nerve can feel the same at first. As the shock wears off we'll know more about it, like the old Sunday-go-to-meeting song says."

Down by the stock, old Hernan had cupped his hands to his mouth to wail up at them, "*Que pasa,* Señor Long?"

So Longarm yelled back in Spanish that they wanted some pigging string and at least two blankets up where they were *poco tiempo.*

The fallen horsewoman asked, "Where's my hat and what did you just tell those Mexicans about me?"

He pointed with his chin at her upside-down derby in a clump of nearby prickly poppy. "I never said nothing dirty, and I ain't sure a Basque is a true Mex, ma'am. I asked 'em to fetch us some padding to brace your knees just so, and some pigging string to sort of hogtie you till we see how you feel as more feeling comes back to you."

"Oh, are you a doctor?" she demanded dubiously.

"Nope. I'd be Deputy U.S. Marshal Custis Long, and Lord knows how we'll ever get you to the nearest sawbones back in Durango if you're really busted. Meanwhile, it's sure to be a whole lot tougher if you get to thrashing in pain to compound yourself a fracture, if you ain't already. Do you reckon a lady in your position would know if she was bleeding under those thick skirts?"

The raven-headed gal stared with wide hazel eyes at him as she replied, "I think so. It's starting to go pins and needles, whether that's good or bad. I'm George Weatherford, of the *Washington Globe,* by the way."

Longarm smiled thinly and said, "Howdy, George. I've read your stuff about Mr. Lo, the Poor Indian. I reckon it's to be expected from anyone writing for an opposition paper, but to tell the pure truth, I had you down as a bit more masculine, despite the sentimental way you write about noble savages."

She sniffed and explained, "It's not easy to be accepted as any sort of reporter in a man's world and . . . What are you doing to the hem of my habit, you fresh thing!"

He went on gingerly raising it as he told her soothingly, "Making sure you ain't compounded, ma'am. Don't get yourself het up over my neighborly intentions, Miss George. Anyone can see you're wearing underdrawers, and fortunately, they're such thin white muslin it would show if you'd sustained yourself a compound fracture down yonder."

Then he lowered the blue hem of her habit to her pigskin-booted ankles, adding, "Since you didn't, we'll say no more about it."

The young newspaperwoman blushed becomingly as she primly gasped, "I should think not! I'll have you know I'm not accustomed to having strange gentlemen peering up under my skirts!"

They both wound up smiling a mite after he'd said, "Aw, I ain't so strange and I never claimed to be no gentleman. How's it feel now, Miss George?"

She concentrated on her numbed toes a moment before she told him, "Awful. All pins and needles from my toes to parts I'd just as soon not mention. But I don't seem to be in any actual pain, and yes, I can move my toes and bend both ankles now."

He said, "*Bueno.* But take it easy whilst we make more certain." By this time Hernan had joined them, taking in the scene before he actually hunkered down beside Longarm to quietly ask, "*La cadera ó musio?*"

Longarm said, "Neither, Lord willing and the creeks don't rise." But he still placed the wadded blankets under her upraised knees as he warned her, "Don't try to straighten her out till you get a mite more feeling. We got plenty of time. I take it you rode on ahead of that Captain Granville and his snails, Miss George?"

She sighed. "I did indeed. He seemed upset by your suggestion they catch up with you in some mountain pass ahead. As you see, I had no trouble overtaking you. But then, I was mounted on a decent horse and not hauling any wagons after me."

"Thunder on the mountain!" Longarm shouted. "You say those soldiers blue had planned on hauling *wagons* through the canyonlands of the Four Corners, and worse yet, Dinetah?"

She sat up straighter. "They're not *planning* on it. They were *doing* it when last I left them a few hours back. I haven't seen anything up to now that a light army spring wagon would have trouble getting around or over. But you were so right about a bunch that seemed in no hurry to get anywhere in a hurry."

Longarm exchanged knowing glances with the old sheepherder as he muttered, more or less to the both of them, "You just can't get where Granville has orders to go with any sort of wheeled vehicle. I can think of a dozen places this side of the Navaho line where the trail hairpins down one canyon wall and up the other, no wider than a schoolmarm's hips and feeling even narrower to folks riding single file and trying not to look down. What might our gallant captain be out to deliver to Fort Defiance in all that rolling stock, ma'am?"

42

She said she didn't know, adding, "I don't think the War Department shares the editorial slant of the *Globe*. When I asked if the army meant to bombard the poor Navaho with shrapnel, as it did the Comanche, they told me not to be silly."

Longarm sighed. "Had you been with Kit Carson at Adobe Walls that time, you'd have likely been glad for those field guns that tipped the balance, Miss George. But let's not argue about Indian policy till we see whether you'll be riding on another mile with this murderous expedition of livestock. I want you to see if you can straighten your left knee now. Slower than old Granville seems to march to meet the foe."

She took a deep breath and made a gallant little try. Then she sighed with relief and declared, "I can move my, ah, joints without any pain. Could I do that if I'd broken anything?"

He said, "Not if you'd busted anything important, ma'am. What say us gents pick you up and carry you down for some coffee and a softer seat in real grass?"

She said she was sure she could walk now, and proved it when Longarm and Hernan gently lifted her to her feet by taking a few steps with ever-growing confidence. Then they let go and saw she was likely to live after all.

Longarm started to head back to his firewood. But Hernan said he'd fetch it, the friendly old cuss, and let Longarm help the still-unsteady newspaper gal down the grassy slope.

As she tidied her hair and pinned her derby back atop it, George Weatherford recalled her position with the *Washington Globe* and asked Longarm, "Are you sure that's only six hundred sheep down there? I could swear it was more."

Longarm nodded amiably. "It's more like fifteen hundred and some of 'em are goats, ma'am. Who told you we had no more than six hundred head to issue Mr. Lo this trip?"

"My editor sensed a story when someone at the War Department mentioned a squadron of cavalry herding a brigade of sheep to the Navaho Reservation in the hope of keeping them there while their Apache cousins rebelled against mistreatment."

"Back up and let's study on what you just said," Longarm told her. "You and your paper might have been right in calling the tender mercies of Grant's Indian Ring mistreatment. But for all his picky notions about Maryland Rye and courtroom dress codes, old President Hayes ain't been mistreating no Apache. All but a handful of younger *ricos* have been behaving their fool selves this spring so far. Victorio and his horse thieves have been raiding for the usual reasons horse thieves raid. They want the horses. They ain't above carrying off any pretty gals they meet along the way either. But are you and your paper suggesting the B.I.A. ought to give even a noble savage all the ponies and love slaves he wants free?"

As they got closer to the herd she quietly admitted, "I'm afraid someone opposed to the current Administration, however rightly, got a little carried away about this belated atonement to the Navaho. But why would any army official, working for the very government at fault, describe that big herd as a mere brigade? A brigade is six hundred, as in that poem about the Light Brigade, right?"

Longarm laughed in dawning understanding. As he steered her by one elbow toward the little fire where Ramon had started the pot, he gently explained, "I was too young for *that* war, but I do recall that poem. I reckon that Noble Six Hundred was called a Light Brigade because it was way under strength. Your regular brigade, in *our* army leastways, is made up of at least two regiments, adding up to twelve hundred or more, depending on how much artillery, scouting, and other service units you got tagging along. So when that unnamed army official described yonder herd as a brigade, he wasn't as far off the numbers as you and your editor figured."

He helped her down to a graceful perch on a cushion of bunchgrass and hunkered between her and Ramon as he sighed and went on. "As for *atonement,* the Indians are lucky you and your paper ain't the only ones in Washington who feel sorry for them. I'll allow the Navaho have lived by the terms of the peace they made with us back in '68. But I'll be whipped with snakes if I can recall any Indian ever *atoning* or even allowing he was *sorry* in any of the Na-Déné dialects."

He muttered in Spanish about the coffee, and when Ramon told him water took its own damned time to boil, Longarm reached for some cheroots, asking the gal if she smoked.

George hesitated, then dimpled and confided, "I suppose it would be silly to call it smoking in public way out here in these hills."

Then she spoiled it all by remarking, just after he'd passed out a nickel's worth of cheroots, "The poor Indians have the excuse of their own ignorance. What justification did those mean army men have for butchering the Navaho stock in Canyon de Chelly or all those poor Cheyenne ponies on the Washita?"

Longarm lit her smoke anyway, and quietly explained. "Carson and Custer likely thought it kinder to slaughter the Indian stock than it might have been to slaughter the Indians, ma'am. Neither the Navaho nor Cheyenne would still be in any position to complain about either campaign today if both hadn't worked so well with a minimum of human bloodshed. Chivington and his Third Colorado never shot too many Cheyenne ponies at Sand Creek, remember? But there was surely a scandal about all the Cheyenne men, women, and children they cut down while being less cruel to animals."

That reminded him nobody had chored her lathered mount, and anyway, it made more sense to dig postholes than it did to argue on Indian policy with a white gal from Washington. So he muttered something about horse sweat and boiling water as he rose to his considerable height to amble toward the remuda, where that beautiful but dumb thoroughbred was grazing with its reins on the ground near the more safely hobbled riding stock.

The bigger brute eyed Longarm warily as he approached, but went on picking flowers as Longarm calmly murmured, "Don't you dare shy off up no hill from a friend unless you just love saddle sores, you bird-brained show pony."

Then he had a big foot planted on a rein, and it didn't matter how much the throughbred spooked when Longarm bent over to gather some firmer control from the grass. He only had to jerk the bit a couple of times and punch the fool horse in the muzzle once before the big dumb chestnut decided it was safer to just calm down.

Once it did, Longarm removed the hobbles someone had been smart enough to latigo to the off-side of that side-saddle. He was mildly surprised to find no saddle gun to go with them,

45

nor the bedroll any overnight traveler carried across the flaps of his or her saddlebags. He didn't look inside the lady's saddlebags as he uncinched her side saddle to set it in the grass upside down. Her blue felt saddle pad was sweat-soaked even worse. So he spread it atop a clump of rabbitbrush to let the thin dry air get at both sides.

Once he had the brute barebacked and securely hobbled, Longarm removed its bridle so it could chew better with no bit in the way. As he draped the bridle over some soap weed he muttered to both himself and her mount, "Lots of folk who worry about hurting the feelings of Mr. Lo, the Poor Indian, don't seem to care what they shove in a pony's mouth, do they? Someone likely told her that spade bit would offer a woman's wrists the leverage it might take to master a saddle-broke grizzly. We both know she can't ride for shit."

The thoroughbred just chomped gratefully on some of the blue-eyed grass, which was really more like garden chives, running wild all over Colorado in the greenup time. That needlessly cruel spade bit told Longarm more than the inane saddle did.

Her particular sidesaddle was the type they built lopsided on a flat English saddletree. Some earlier spoilsports, noting how enthusiastic some young gals seemed about riding astride, had guessed the hidden motives of at least some of them. It wouldn't have taken a college degree in male and female anatomy. For as any young boy discovered the first time he rode astride at a trot, the ridge of most any sort of saddle gave male balls one hell of a thumping unless one carried most of one's weight in the stirrups Tex-Mex-style, or posted clean clear of the saddle as it rose the way they tried to teach in the Cav or at fox-hunting clubs.

Young gals had no problem riding tomboy-style astride. But some doubtless dirty-minded elders had realized just what it might feel like to a sweet little thing with a wide-spread twat to get pounded the same way at a brisk trot as their brothers did.

Riding sidesaddle was aimed at preventing unexpected orgasms on the part of schoolmarms on their way to church. There was only one stirrup on the near or left side. A properly skirted lady was supposed to mount more or less like a man.

46

But instead of forking her right leg over and settling down on her clit, she hooked her off-leg over a sort of leather banana growing out of the near swells, and lowered just the right cheek of her ass to the top of her mount, where it felt more as if she was getting a lop-sided spanking if she chose to ride at a mile-eating but bone-jarring trot.

Longarm knew most of the trip ahead would be ridden at a walk because most any horse or mule could amble at the speed a sheep or goat could maintain for any length of time. But old George hadn't kept her seat or even landed on her feet up yonder when her mount had shied without really bucking.

He was still thinking about that when the newspaper gal almost got him to shy by announcing, closer behind him than he'd expected, "That Ramon says the coffee will be ready any minute. Thank you for being so kind to Crusader. I'm afraid it simply slipped my mind that he'd been saddled and bridled all morning."

When Longarm turned to see her standing there with no obvious signs of recent injuries, he smiled down at her. "It was my pleasure, Miss George. I'm pleased to see you back on your pretty feet, which brings us to the subject of falling on your, ah, derriere. Didn't anybody warn you this expedition was headed into some seriously disturbed country? There's hairpin bends ahead where a fall from an insecure seat could last quite a spell before one landed, say, two or three thousand feet below."

She shrugged and pouted, "Pooh, I guess I can ride my Crusader anywhere a herd of sheep and a baggage train can go."

He said, "I also noticed the spade bit. Noticed how much it helped when your chestnut slid out from under you too. The sheep will be driven single-file along parts of the trail. The goats will be even more surefooted. Those spring wagons ain't about to make it, and I take it any bedding you brought West has been loaded aboard one of them?"

She nodded thoughtfully. "Captain Granville must know what he'd doing, if they've put him in charge of the whole troop."

To which Longarm could only reply, "I don't care if they've put him in command of a whole brigade, Miss George. When and if Granville catches up with us, you'd better have all your important possibles latigoed to that saddle. Mark my

47

words, them wagons will never make her much farther than Hovenweep, if they manage to make her that far!"

She declared, "I have too much baggage to pack aboard Crusader with the rest of me. What's a hovenweep?"

He got them started back toward the Basques around the little coffee fire as he explained. "Ain't sure just how to translate from the Ute dialect, but I know what's there. Four or more Indian ghost towns. Long-deserted cliff dwellings the Utes feel uneasy about, though they're not quite as scared of such places as the Navaho. For a fee, a Ute might lead you up into one of the Hovenweep ruins and wait outside as you poke about for pottery and worse. The professors who argue about old ruins are still arguing about who might have built cliff dwellings up canyons too dry for any Indians of today. There's said to be as many or more further south in the canyons of Dinetah, but Navaho are just scared so skinny of ghosts that you can't get all that many to even *talk* about ghost towns they might or might not know about."

By this time they were back by the fire. As he helped her to a seat on a bunchgrass tussock Longarm added with a thin smile, "It's sort of funny how some Indians feel about ghosts, soon as you study on how some glory in manufacturing them from living enemies they don't seem at all afraid of."

He hunkered down across from her. As Ramon handed them both tin cups of bile-black coffee, brewed with plenty of grounds to make up for the way water boiled at high altitude, he got back to her main question and his concerns for her safety, saying, "Suffice it to say, you don't build cliff dwellings in country laid out like the Washington Mall, Miss George. Hovenweep's nigh smack on the Colorado-Utah line, or less than a tenth the distance to Fort Defiance. Many a cliff we got to get up or down in Dinetah will make those up around Hovenweep look sissy. We're going to have to work out a more sensible way for a lady to ride if we can't talk her into turning back whilst she's ahead."

By this time Ramon was dishing out their light dinner of *refritos* rolled in tortillas. The Eastern gal regarded her repast dubiously as she insisted, "You caught me by surprise up there atop the hill. I'll have you know I've ridden to hounds over many a fence back in Tidewater, Virginia. What on earth is this? It bears a disturbing resemblance to you-know-what wrapped in damp pasteboard."

Longarm smiled. "Tastes at least a mite better, ma'am. The brown mush ain't what it looks like. It's baked, mashed, and more recently fried frijoles, or kidney beans. That handy wrapping is white corn bread baked unleavened, like they baked bread in the Old Testament."

She was a good sport about it, once they'd convinced her to try a chaw. Lots of Anglo folks expected Mex grub to be full of peppers, and a heap of it was, when it wasn't sort of tasteless. Like many an Anglo who admired hot tamales or chili con carne, Longarm found some of the blander Hispanic notions hardly worth the trouble, not to mention the enthusiasm lots of Spanish-speaking folks showed for such traditions as unseasoned *refritos* or chicken baked in bittersweet chocolate.

It would have been impolite to discuss how good or bad such grub could get, at least in front of a kid who'd cooked it and might savvy enough English to feel insulted. So Longarm glanced up at the clear sky to remark, "Those soldiers blue better get a move on if they're intent on joining us here." He turned to old Hernan to ask how long a trail break he generally gave his critters.

The Basque seemed pleased by Longarm's confidence in an older man's sheep savvy. He replied, "In God's truth is better for both ourselves and *la manada* for to keep them a little tired until each *criatura* knows its position on the move. As you know, we have no *coreros,* I mean lambs, for to slow us down. But this *manada* is intended for breeding, and you know how goats and even sheep get if one does not keep them too hungry and too tired for to think about romance, no?"

Longarm didn't think it best to mention what a goat was up to with a sheep in the distance behind George Weatherford's back. Like the sheepherders, he knew nothing good nor bad was going to come of a little fun between species. But he surely didn't want to see more such nonsense. So he nodded and asked Hernan if he thought a few more hours along the trail might steady the critters a mite by sundown.

The courtly old Basque must not have wanted the Anglo *señorita* asking why that fool goat out yonder seemed to think he could ride a sheep like that. For he muttered in his own odd lingo to Ramon, and then as Ramon ran off to make the same strangled noises at Mauro and their dogs, Hernan gravely poured the last of the coffee over the dying embers of their little fire and announced, "We may be able to pasture for the night up in Hesperus Pass, where the night winds and distant howls might serve to keep them bunched tight for us. Should it not be possible to move them that far, at least they will be less, ah, restless after a good stiff drive, no?"

That fool goat had finished by the time the three of them were on their own hind legs. Stories about wicked country kids having their wicked ways with critters didn't extend to male goats and gals, despite all that bullshit about devil worship, because goats, like all horned critters, screwed as fast as any other herbivores in a world infested with carnivores. Longarm had it on good authority that four-legged female critters got an unusual thrill out of being donged by a meat-eating sheep dog, or sheepherder, who'd evolved to screw far longer than any horny grazing critter. So when you studied on it, that standard army punishment for the seduction of, say, the regimental mascot was likely a mite harsh for such a silly offense.

As Hernan and his boys went about their own chores, Longarm led the newspaper gal over to the remuda, and let her watch as he got her thoroughbred and his two ponies ready to move on. Since he'd spent so much of the day on the black barb, he loaded her with the lighter packsaddle this time, and switched his McClellan to the blue roan. When the gal asked what the roan's name was and Longarm replied he just called it a blue roan, she observed she could see it was sort of slate blue, but allowed she'd never been too clear as to why some pastel shades of horse were called roans while others were not. He had to grin as he remarked, "I can't wait to tell the boys back at the Lazy B this here gelding got this shade from pastel chalk. He's a roan because, when you look close, you see what looks like an even shade of solid color is really two kinds of hair, mixed like salt and pepper. It's the white hairs mingled with almost black hairs that adds up to the overall blue roan shade, see?"

She dimpled and replied, "I do now. My Crusader here only has one shade of reddish brown hairs, right?"

"Save for the white blaze betwixt his eyes," Longarm agreed, as he glanced around to see how their companions were doing. Hernan and his *muchachos* were good. They were almost ready to move out as well. Longarm told the spunky but hopelessly out-of-place young reporter, "The two of us can ride five times faster or more than a sheep can be driven, and there's still plenty of light, Miss George. You feel up to some real riding?"

She asked archly, "Why, Deputy Long, whatever are you suggesting? Just in case I take you up on it, I wish you'd quit calling me Miss George. George Weatherford is my pen name, for obvious reasons. But naturally my mother never named me George. It's really Grace, and what's so funny?"

He said, "Nothing, Miss Grace. Everyone looks awkward falling off a horse. As to what I was suggesting, I thought you might like me to carry you back to that main party, seeing your bedding and all is with the soldiers blue and Lord only knows what lies ahead of us this side of sundown."

She pouted, "I don't want to turn back. I've already seen what's back that way. I was sent out here to report on anything exciting a body might see."

"Let me help you mount up," he said with a weary smile, barely able to resist a remark about other pesky females in the newspaper game that he'd met in his time, Lord love 'em. They all seemed cut from the same nosy self-confident mold, no matter what they were built like. There sure seemed to be far more of them since those Brontë sisters had scandalized the neighbors by publishing whole books in their own names just before the war. But he'd suspected for some time that the newspaper syndicates were hiring so many gal reporters in hopes of getting the same number of words for far less money. Male reporters willing to work as hard as female reporters all seemed to wind up famous and expensive, like old Mark Twain, Bret Harte, and such. So seeing he couldn't get rid of such an ambitious sass, he boosted her up on her sidesaddle and mounted the blue roan. Then he grudgingly hauled out his derringer, detached it from his watch chain, and heeled his mount closer to her own as he grumbled, "Seeing you chose to ride off into the great unknown without even a blanket to call your own, you'd best put this belly gun somewhere you can get it back out in a hurry. Don't thumb that safety that could be taken for a hammer till you're ready to shoot, and hang on when you do. It's overloaded a mite for a derringer."

She stared down thunderstruck at the wicked little weapon and demanded, "What on earth might I need with a gun, good sir?"

He said, "Call me Custis. I don't *know* what you might need with a gun, Miss Grace. Didn't you just hear me say we were headed into the great unknown?"

Chapter 6

Another rider was even more concerned as he rode west into Durango from the east after many a worried hour in the saddle. Like Longarm, for the same reasons, he had his dusty hat telescoped in the Colorado style and packed his side arm on his left hip in a cross-draw rig. Normally a fancier dresser, he now rode into Durango clad in dusty denim aboard a dusty cordovan gelding, with a cocked Winchester across his knees and a wary eye out for any unusual moves by anyone in the nearly deserted sunbaked area near the rail yards and that livery he remembered from last time he'd been there.

Hoping he'd ridden far enough, the worried rider dismounted on the far side of the sunny street from the livery and eyed the gaping black entrance thoughtfully for a time as he held his Winchester in a desperately innocent manner. A nearby railroad worker, leaning on a shovel handle after scooping up more than enough sheep shit for the time being, called out, "What's the matter, Deputy? Wouldn't them old army boys let you choose the sheep of your dreams?"

The sardonic worker with a drinker's nose would never even guess how close he'd come to dying on the spot as Monte Matt Gray spun into a wider stance, noted there was nobody there but some asshole armed with no more than a shovel, and quietly said, "Were you talking to *me*, friend?"

The yard worker blinked, peered harder, and said, "I thought I was. At first glance I took you for someone else entire. But as

I gaze on you more intent, I see you're just the same general type, no offense. Had you mixed up with another tall dark drink of water wearing a heavy mustache and thin jeans. Sorry I pestered you over nothing."

Monte Matt nodded graciously and lowered the muzzle of his loaded and cocked Winchester a shade as he prepared to lead his tired pony across to the livery. Then he turned back to the yard worker and casually asked, "You say you had me mixed up with a local *lawman* just now?"

The yard worker shook his head. "I never said no such thing. Had you mixed up with a federal deputy marshal called Long. Talked to him earlier, just up the way, about all the shitty sheep we had in these here pens. He said he meant to help the U.S. Army herd 'em over through the Four Corners to bestow upon the shiftless Navaho. Ain't that a bitch?"

Monte Matt smiled knowingly. "That's the army for you. Reckon they feel that if they don't feed 'em they'll wind up with nobody to fight. You say this Deputy Long who sort of looks like me rode out to the west with 'em?"

The older man had watched three troops and a baggage train of eight spring wagons light out just after noon. Now he said thoughtfully, "I ain't sure enough to bet all my money, if that's what you mean. But he told me he was with that bunch, that bunch is gone, and I ain't seen him since. They'd likely know for sure at yon livery across the way. Deputy Long was keeping two ponies there. If he's still in town, they'd still be in town, right?"

Monte Matt thanked the shit scooper for the sensible advice and led his cordovan across the way to take it. But when the hostler, who knew Longarm's full name, said he was pretty sure U.S. Deputy Marshal Custis Long had ridden out a few hours *ahead* of the army column, the wily gambling man decided not to leave his own mount at that particular livery after all. He got back aboard it and walked it across town to another livery he recalled from earlier and less tense times in Durango.

Dismounting again, the man on the run from the Fuller clan told the younger stable boy in charge, "I'd be U.S. Deputy Custis Long and I'll likely be in town at least a week on government business. So I'll thank you to turn this old pal

54

of mine out back to graze, once you've watered, oated, and rubbed him down good, hear?"

The kid was in no position to argue. He'd heard the talk about the mushrooming town of Durango seeking to incorporate itself as a new county seat. So it stood to reason there'd be all sorts of government bullshit going on, and it was impolite to ask for cash in advance when you knew a customer had a steady job.

Monte Matt, for his own part, saw no need to pay the fool kid to board a fool pony that had belonged to another cuss to begin with. He meant to steal another horse and be well on his way before anyone got to really wondering about such a nondescript cow pony in a livery paddock with others. An experienced horse thief never stole a mount that could be identified from more than a few paces away. Seeing that that yard worker hadn't been too sure about his own appearance from a few paces off, Monte Matt felt no call to seek that two-bits-a-night place he'd had in mind. For as soon as a slick gentleman of fortune studied on it, it seemed dumb to economize with another man's credit. It made more sense to stride bold as brass to that new Plata Palace with his saddlebags and sign in for a corner room as U.S. Deputy Custis Long.

So that was what Monte Matt Gray did, grinning like a shit-eating dog as soon as he shut and bolted the door behind him, feeling free to relax his jangled nerves for the first time since he'd lit out of Leadville on another man's mount. So far, it had only cost him that one thin dime he'd had to tip the bellboy for showing him the way up to his room on the top floor.

Draping his saddlebags over the brass bed rails, and tossing his hat and guns on the chenille spread for now, the man with a faint resemblance to Longarm strode to the window to grin down at all the hats that never looked up from down yonder. He felt downright safe up there, and meant to stay that way for now. He'd have his meals sent up from the kitchen, as long as some asshole called Custis Long would be getting the bills for all this service later.

The pace old Hernan was setting for the Navaho stock, as the afternoon sun got really serious, involved about an hour's worth of forced marching, at least for a sheep, followed by no more than a five-minute break to let them inhale some wind and eat some weeds as they rested just enough to keep from dropping on the move. Neither the goats, dogs, nor riding and packing stock got tired enough at Hernan's pace to lose all sense of fun. So both dogs and the herder stuck with the chore during alternate trailbreaks had some fun with the few fool goats who seemed to want to go into business on their own.

George Weatherford was too Victorian to even stare hard at those Churro ewes who, having failed to lamb that spring, were coming into heat and sort of advertising their willingness to get screwed by most anybody.

"Why are so many of those sheep such funny colors if this is supposed to be a prize herd of thoroughbred breeding stock?" asked George Weatherford as they sat their ponies side by side, pretending not to notice that sorrel Mancha trying to mount a Churro ewe who didn't seem quite ready yet.

It took Longarm a moment to grasp her meaning. Once he did he chuckled and replied, "Your mount is a thoroughbred. Them goats are more or less purebred Spanish Manchas, whilst the Churro is a more recent Mex breed developed for rough grazing under less certain skies than even a true Spanish Merino can safely abide."

Seeing Hernan didn't mean to stay there all that long, he held off on reaching for that chocolate in his saddlebag and continued to explain. "All them fuzzy cream-wooled critters are Churro sheep, Miss George—I mean Grace. The ones with more horn and less hair are Mancha goats. We're delivering that many goats because goats make better eating and we don't want any Navaho hunting off their reserve for deer, as anyone might after eating too much mutton. Navaho never butcher a sheep until it's dying of old age, and the Churro is not a mutton breed to begin with."

"Then it's the goats who come in all those different colors?"

He nodded. "The Spanish breeders never worried all that much about the coats of critters they don't shear for wool in Spain. A Mancha can give fair milk and slaughter to fair meat on a diet that would starve a cow, even if cows climbed rocks that good. A B.I.A. man who knows something about Navaho weaving said they'd be happier with a wide range of natural colors. Unlike the Spanish, who scrape the hair off cow and goat hides and just keep the tanned leather, Navaho weavers mix colored goat hair in with their wool as they spin it to produce colored yarns. They brew up vegetable dyes as well, of course. But for some blankets they feel the medicine is a lot stronger if the stripes of cream, rust, slate, and such are just natural. You can tell the older, more traditional weavings by such natural colors and more simple designs. As I understand it, some of the older Navaho who look back to their Shining Times feel it's a mite dangerous to try for *too* pretty a blanket, and naturally, no Navaho in his or her right mind would try to weave a *perfect* rug or basket."

She didn't ask why. Lots of folks who waxed sentimental over Lo, the Poor Indian never seemed to ask all that many questions about him. Meanwhile, Hernan gave one of those odd Basque whistles and, as a man who asked questions, Longarm knew they were fixing to get it on down the trail. So he said so, adding, "You'd best stay back here with the bulk of the herd out in front of you. Meanwhile, I'd best scout a mite further ahead as the sun gets lower and the ridges get higher. We had us a little discussion about sheep with some cowboys a spell back, just before you joined us, and from here it looks like that rise beyond the next one could be crested with high chaparral."

"I'm coming with you. I want to see," she said. When he tried to tell her how dumb that sounded, she just kept right on fussing until, the herd starting to move again, Longarm suddenly decided, "You're right about it being a free country, but you may never speak to me again if I get you killed."

Neither one of them could speak as they loped past the herd with Longarm shouting a terse explanation to Hernan in passing.

Longarm set the same serious gait over the next bald rise, but reined in to a more wary walk as they reached the bottom of the grassy draw for a sober stare up through all those branches the sun was glaring back through. He muttered, half to himself, "Them lodgepoles and junipers are too skinny for anything serious to hunker behind. But I surely wish there wasn't all that infernal piñon growing smack up to the trail on both sides."

She asked if he meant those shrubby little crab apple trees.

He nodded but said, "They ain't crab apples. They're a scrubby sort of pine that grows about the same way. I don't see nobody in amid that tangle. On the other hand, if I was lying in wait for a sucker up yonder, he wouldn't see *me*. So we'd best scout that clump cavalry-style. I want you to keep to my far side as we follow this draw north a ways, hear?"

She asked why, of course, as he turned them off the dusty trail to ride up the grassy vale. He drew his saddle gun, levered a round in the chamber, and braced it across his thighs to trot with his left hand holding the reins, as usual, while his right hand held his Winchester's muzzle casually trained to their west. The brunette drew the derringer he'd given her and sort of sobbed as she bounced on her sidesaddle, "Won't anyone lurking amid those bush trees be able to guess our intent to move up the slope to the north of them?"

Longarm answered, "Sure they will, unless they're mighty stupid. But they'll have to break cover to do anything about it and . . . Well, speaking of the devil, what do you know!"

"My God!" gasped the girl as she too spotted the bunch moving through the trees along the ridge to their left. "There must be a hundred of them, and what could they want with us?"

Longarm snapped, "I make it two dozen, and let's not hang around to find out what they want. *Vamanos,* over the rise to our east, and don't spare the horses!"

So they didn't, and by the time they were halfway up the bare slope to their east a long ragged-ass line of whooping riders was tearing down through the trees of the higher slope to the west.

As Longarm and the girl crested the bald rise, Longarm reined in to shout, "Keep going and warn Hernan! Then do exactly as he tells you! What are you slowing down for, girl? Are you looking forward to being gang-raped? Get that pretty ass out of here *pronto!*"

She did. Longarm didn't stare after her all that hard. He was too busy dismounting at full gallop to land atop the ridge

58

on one hip and roll into a prone position with his Winchester trained back the way he'd just come. He let the oncoming skirmish line have three rounds of rapid fire to let them know how rapid he could fire, and as he'd hoped, a dozen saddles emptied as if by magic.

Their ponies, like his own, had sense enough to clear the field of fire as soon as they heard some firing. Longarm had naturally rolled away from his own gunsmoke by the time all those excited sons of bitches proceeeded to empty their own guns into where they thought he might be.

Longarm held his own fire till a familiar figure half rose from the knee-high grazing down the slope to shout, "Follow me, boys!"

Some did, the other way, once Longarm spun the silly bastard around with a .44-40 round in one arm and another dusting up his boot heels to keep him going that way, back down the damned slope.

Longarm didn't nail any of the others who rose, seeing they were rising the right way. Hoping they were simply unusually bird-brained cowboys, he didn't want to turn this nonsense into a real blood feud by killing anyone who didn't really need some killing.

He began to see somebody smarter than the one he'd winged might need some killing when, once out of range, the sons of bitches got together for a terse council of war and then— damn some military training one of 'em must have had— commenced to spread out in both directions, afoot, with the obvious intent of moving up high from both directions, out of range, to creep along the ridge at him like the jaws of some ragged-ass tongs.

Standard military field tactics were annoying as well as obvious. They got to be standard by working so annoyingly well. On a way the hell smaller scale, they had him in the same fix Custer had likely been annoyed to find himself in at Little Big Horn. There was just no way to defend an open position atop a grassy rise from a two-pronged attack by far superior numbers.

Having refought the Battle of Little Big Horn over many a beer with many an old army man, Longarm had long since agreed the best move poor old George Armstrong Custer could have made the minute he found himself staring down off Last Stand Ridge would have been an all-out retreat at full gallop.

Longarm had no idea where his blue roan had galloped without him by now. He figured he had even less time than Custer had had to get out from between the jaws of that two-pronged attack before those determined bastards could get themselves into position. But it sure hurt like hell to fire a couple more rounds to freeze everybody, and then crawfish on his belly through the weeds under the cover of his own gunsmoke. For while he figured he could likely make it back to his own side, though out of breath, there was simply no way four men and a girl were going to keep the miserable shits from scattering the herd. And then what was General Sherman going to say about a stupid asshole who'd talked poor innocent sheepherders into herding their defenseless sheep so far out ahead of the army escort he'd provided with just such bullshit as this in mind!

Longarm stopped crawfishing, and proceeded to top off the magazine of his Winchester with spare rounds of .44-40 as he muttered, "Well, nobody lives forever, and like the Cheyenne say, one sunny day is as good a day to die as any. At least I won't have to read all the mean things they're going to write about me in that *Washington Globe* and likely the *Denver Post*!"

He knew a Cheyenne would be singing his death song by now. Since he didn't know any such songs he settled for sticking an unlit cheroot between his teeth, lest he offer an easy target with tobacco smoke, and proceeded to softly croon:

Farther along, we'll know more about it,
Farther along, we'll understand why,
Cheer up, my brother, walk in the sunshine,
We'll understand this, all, by and by!

Off in the distance, some other kid who'd been forced to go to Sunday school shouted, "Hymn-singing ain't gonna save you now, you sheep-screwing son of a bitch!"

Longarm had already peeled off his Stetson to make his head a smaller target in the tall weeds all about. Yelling into it lest they guess just where he might be at the moment, Longarm sweetly inquired, "Is that what this is all about? Why didn't you just *ask* if you wanted to screw a sheep? We got half a dozen in heat, and far be it from me to fight a gun duel over the good name of any woolly lady you desire!"

It worked. The outraged cow lover pegged a wild shot and let out a swell howl when Longarm fired at his smoke puff and then got himself somewhere else.

A more distant voice commanded, "Hold your fire, damn your eyes! Can't you see what he's trying to do! Stick to the plan and we'll do him right!"

Longarm had been afraid someone would say something that mean. The son of a bitch had obviously led at least a platoon in the war. Likely wearing butternut gray under General Hood, judging from that Texican accent.

Longarm didn't try to draw him out by yelling endearments down the slope at him. That worked best on hot heads with green horns, and tended to give the cooler ones a line on where you were yourself. Trying to put himself in that Texican's head, Longarm realized anyone moving in on an armed and invisible enemy always had to avoid moving in too fast or too slow. Hoping he could get them to move in too fast, Longarm just lay low when some anxious cuss to his south called out a mighty mean suggestion about his mamma. So that gave him a better line on how wide the jaws of their two-pronged crawling advance might be.

He flinched, rolled, and almost threw down on some grass stems swaying a whole lot closer before he recognized the voice softly calling, "*A donde estar, Brazo Largo?*"

Seeing that had to be young Mauro, and seeing Brazo Largo was as close to Longarm as Spanish got, Longarm called back even softer, "*Aqui, pero silencio, pendejo!*"

As the young Mex Basque joined him belly down in the greenery, Longarm noted the Yellowboy .44-40 the kid had hauled in after him with approval. He whispered in Spanish, "I'm sorry I called you that, but this seems neither the time nor the place to give away any positions."

As if to make Longarm's point, that same crude rascal bawled out, "Are you still there, sheep lover? I thought I told you to go home and fuck your mother for a change!"

Mauro savvied enough Anglo to growl, *"Comé mierda!"* and lever a round into the chamber of his Yellowboy.

Longarm warned, "Don't let them draw you out. Hold your fire now that you're ready to fire after all this time. How many rounds do you have to work with in that antique?"

Mauro said he'd loaded the tubular magazine of his carbine with six or eight rounds. He didn't sound at all ashamed. Half as many rounds as a saddle gun would take had likely seemed enough to any sheepherder worried about no more than Old Man Coyote. Longarm was glad the kid's gun was a Yellowboy at least. That was the nickname of an earlier-model Winchester, made more or less along the original improvements on the basic Henry patent, although with lots of yellow brass where Longarm's more modern Model '73 was stronger tool steel. The Yellowboy's softer brass vitals wouldn't rust whether a kid took care of his gun or pissed in it regularly.

Speaking terser Spanish than your average Mex, Longarm explained their fix to Mauro, then asked how the others with the herd might be making out.

Mauro explained how old Hernan had forted up with Ramon and just the riding stock on higher ground to the east, after sending that newspaper *mujer* and her racehorse even further east for help at a full gallop.

When Longarm agreed that had been as smart as anything else he could think of, Mauro added that the dogs, controlled at some distance by whistles, could control the herd as long as nobody got too noisy. Longarm said he was a mite puzzled about that as well.

He said he agreed the *pendejos* creeping all about them would find it simple to just leave all the armed humans the hell alone and simply circle around, out of rifle range, to do whatever they damned well wanted to the helpless stock.

Chewing thoughtfully on the soggy unlit cheroot, Longarm decided, "At least one of them sounds as if he knows his dismount drill. I've already winged one of his followers, and I let them know I'd done so with a repeater. From the way they still seem to want to play this game, they have to be riding for someone with a permanent mailing address not too far from here."

Mauro suggested, "If they know those sheep and goats are

government property, and that all of us are working for the government, I think they must know it could go very hard for them if they ran off with that herd and left even one of us alive to tell the Army and the Indian Bureau what they had done, no?"

Longarm nodded his bare head and reached for his nearby hat. "I know of at least two big cattle outfits down to the southwest that switched to sheep during that dry spell we had in the late '70s, and of course lots of your own Mexican outfits have been running goats with cows from the beginning. On the other hand, that very herd was up for sale locally just a few weeks back, with the owner anxious to entertain almost any offer."

Mauro said, "I know. He lost money on the forced sale. On the other hand, the government did give him *something* for each and every head. There are still at least fifteen hundred head. So what if he wished to pay even less for them. Perhaps the price of just a few bullets?"

Longarm whistled softly. "You could show a handsome profit on a herd that size at two bits a head, assuming you'd paid nothing at all for them. I suspect that must be what makes stock stealing so tempting out on open range."

Someone else shouted a suggestion that sounded silly from yet another direction. So Longarm muttered, "We could both be right or wrong about what they want with the herd. It's obvious as hell they want us, or me at least. They don't know you're up here with me. If they were planning to bypass me and go after the others, or even the herd, they'd have done so by this time. So what are you waiting for, a farewell kiss?"

The young Mex Basque calmly replied, "I am not that sort of a man. I do not run from a good fight either."

Longarm grimaced and insisted, "Shit, this is not going to be a good fight, Mauro. If they don't rush this position before sundown they'll rush it after dark, and there's no point in letting them have two for the price of one."

Mauro asked, "Why don't we both slip away while there is still time, then? The cowards are hanging too far back to notice, eh?"

Longarm sighed. "Somebody has to hold 'em here. As long

as I do, they might not feel free to move in on Hernan and the herd."

Mauro started to ask a dumb question. But he was learning fast, and anyone could see how Longarm's field tactics were complicating whatever the other side thought it was up to. The kid smiled shyly and announced, "With you covering our field of fire to the north and me covering it to the south, I fail to see how they can get us without us getting a lot of them, no?"

Longarm nodded grudgingly. "I'd say the one with a Texican accent has already figured that out, not even knowing you're backing my play, Don Quixote. He's almost surely waiting for dark, and look how low and red the sun over yonder is already!"

Mauro sounded cheerful, considering, as he decided they had over an hour before it would get really dark. Longarm said, "They won't wait for full dark if they know their basic infantry tactics. Dawn or dusk, when the light is tricky, is best for frontal attacks on uncertain enemy positions. You need broad daylight to sight a rifle. So when they come at us, almost surely late in the gloaming, just aim as if you were pointing the thumb of your left hand at the nearest blurs in turn. Your gun muzzle will follow the thumb of the hand closest to it, if it follows any directions at all."

Mauro thanked him gravely for the advice and suggested, "What if we spread out more, so one of us can hit them from the side as they charge the other one?"

Longarm shook his head and gently explained, "It's better not to try to play chess when the name of the game is checkers. Our only chance of living through their first few charges calls for them to be more confused than us. Firefights are always confusing. That's why I prefer to fight alone when the odds are less one-sided. You'll never hear this said at West Point, but the art of war is a matter of childish simplicity, complicated by the natural panic of any adult who's ever attended a funeral. I've often suspected that's why so many great generals have been such boobs and idiots at everything else. U.S. Grant was a terrible President for the same reasons he was a brilliant leader, they said, at Shiloh. Not having half the imagination it took to get as rattled as the smarter soldiers all around him, old Grant just made all the

64

simple moves it took to win until he'd won a mighty messy fight."

Mauro sounded unconvinced. He insisted they'd kill more of their unknown assailants if they worked out some tricky cross fire while they had the time.

Longarm said just as firmly, "Firing back-to-back from this close together, we'll be much more likely to hit someone else instead of one another once things get really hot. Is this the first time you've been in a real gunfight, Mauro?"

The kid pointed out he hadn't been in any yet, as he tossed in a very rude remark about the glorious sunset to their west.

Longarm said, "Never mind that and pay attention. You don't have to worry about your gunsmoke in a twilight gunfight. But they will throw lead at your muzzle flashes. So while we want to stay fairly close together we still want to . . . No, this is not going to work, my friend! I'll do better by myself up here when I don't have to worry about who I'm shooting at. I could tell you a sad story about a rattled gunslick called Hickok and a deputy who came up behind him at exactly the wrong time and place. But why don't you just slide down the far side of this rise, and we'll talk about all the things that can go wrong in a gunfight later."

Mauro insisted stubbornly, "You shall not be able to talk to anyone about anything if they kill you. I am staying to cover your back and make that more difficult for the sons of a defrocked nun and a leprous man with festering boils on his penis!"

Longarm had to smile at the picture, even as he repeated his sensible demands to a green gunfighter who'd likely just be in his way—that is, if the attackers were still coming.

Mauro considered that too, observing, "It seems very quiet out there now. We would not have seen it if they'd decided to pull back or go around, no?"

Longarm said, "We'd have heard it. They've been taking orders from their elected or self-appointed leader. Be quiet and let me hear him too when he orders any serious moves."

Then, as if to prove his point, before it was clear how

Mauro might have taken that last order, someone off to the north ordered a general assault with a ferocious rebel yell. So Longarm snapped, "Hold your fire till you've got a target against that lavender sky, and then shift at least twice your own width before you fire again."

Before the kid could answer Longarm spied somebody hulking one hell of a heap closer than he'd expected, and blew the son of a bitch back down the slope as, behind him, Mauro let loose with that Yellowboy a lot, shouting something Longarm couldn't make out above the rattle of small-arms fire coming from all directions. Then the fool kid had rolled half on top of him, gasping and jerking like a gal trying to screw on top. So Longarm rolled out from under the sex-mad or brain-shot cuss, rolled twice more, and fired up into another odd hulk, inspiring someone to wail, "Oh, Sweet Jesus! I've been shot in the balls and I'm dying fast, I hope!"

Longarm didn't take time out to mourn poor Mauro as he rolled back over the kid's limp sprawl while somebody shot the weed cover to tossed salad where he'd just been. The next time he looked up, a big black hat fluttered like a bat between him and the first bright evening star. So Longarm fired and rolled some more, to fetch up in the better cover of a runoff gully down the steeper eastern slope of the rise. He lay doggo for the moment as someone else called out, "We got him! Over this way with half his fool face blown off! I wish he'd taken longer to die, after what he just done to Pecos and poor Mormon Jack!"

Another voice close enough to make Longarm's heart skip called back, "Are you sure, Red? I could have swore I was chasing some-damned-body over this way. Who's got a light?"

That Texican accent answered, bless every twang, "Never mind all that and let a man listen to the evening breezes, damn it! I could swear I heard a distant bugle just now!"

So everyone stopped breathing, including Longarm, and damned if that didn't sound like a tinny cavalry call to advance in a line of skirmish! Good old George had made it forth and back, sidesaddle, with the help she'd been sent to seek!

That other obvious veteran of one army or another called out to his own followers, "*Vamanos, muchachos!* We've gunned the smart-ass the boss sent us to gun, and this child ain't

66

about to shoot it out with the U.S. Cav for what the Flying W pays him!"

Nobody argued. Longarm just lay doggo in the dirt as he listened to them lighting out. After a while he heard hoofbeats leaving to the west and hoofbeats coming from the east. There wasn't so much as a cricket chirping in the trampled and shot-up weeds atop the bald rise. So Longarm pounded a thigh with a frustrated fist, hard enough to hurt. But it didn't help at all. So he got up and commenced running toward the oncoming cavalry in hopes there might be a chance in hell of cutting trail before dawn.

Chapter 7

Some said General U. S. Grant had been a lazy self-indulgent cuss at heart, who'd won all those battles with brutal directness so he could get back to his more serious drinking. The more imaginative Confederate General A. S. Johnston had managed to get killed in the opening skirmishes at Shiloh while old Grant had been soaking his head in a tavern miles away. So he'd naturally won the battle, once they had him on his horse, just by ordering his rattled junior officers to make the usual damned moves by the usual damned book. When a badly mauled division commander told Grant they'd marched into a clever Confederate trap, old Grant had just chewed his old cigar and told him not to whimper like that because the book said it was plain impossible for a smaller army to trap a bigger army.

So those surprised and shot-up Union troops had just turned back and proceeded to hammer it out with buttstock and bayonet until the bigger bunch won, just as old Grant and the book said they would as long as they didn't mess up completely.

Captain T. J. Granville, as they met again on the far slope of the draw, seemed to have heard all about Butcher Grant's sure and simple approach to army life and taken every lesson to heart. For by the time Longarm trotted into the night camp they were in the process of setting up, they already had night pickets out a good hundred yards all around to challenge a winded civilian.

Longarm said he didn't know their damn password and didn't care about their damn countersign. But they'd been expecting to spot his familiar figure looming out of the moonlight at them. So they let him through, and even told him where to find their damn captain, as Longarm put it. From the way the two nearest followers of old Granville laughed, Longarm sensed he'd hit a nail on a head that he hadn't been aiming at that hard.

He didn't care about Granville's personal habits. Fighting Joe Hooker, commanding the Army of the Potomac, wouldn't have bestowed his name for all time on all those camp followers if he hadn't lost so often. Nobody had called him Screwing Joe instead of Fighting Joe Hooker until after Chancellorsville. Longarm wasn't ready to fault old Granville for forting up for the night on high ground until he heard what the captain meant to do about those sons of bitches who'd just murdered one federal employee in the sincere belief they were murdering a badge-packing federal lawman.

To no great surprise, he found Granville seated at a fire way too big for an early Colorado evening in May. Good old George—or was she still Grace in front of all these soldiers blue?—spotted Longarm coming through the confusion of an outfit making bivouac and sprang up to dash over, sobbing, "Oh, Custis, we've been so worried about you!"

He didn't grab hold of her, although he sensed she might not have gotten sore if he had, as he smiled wearily down at her to say she sure rode good for a gal, sidesaddle and all.

Before she could answer, they were joined by old Hernan and young Ramon. So Longarm told Hernan in English, "They got Mauro. I made sure there was nothing that could be done for him before I came down off yonder ridge. I'm more sorry than I can say. If it's any comfort, Mauro got at least two of them. The others lit out with their bodies but I heard 'em jawing. I suspect Mauro winged at least another one he didn't kill entire."

"My nephew was of the Raza Euska-ra," said Hernan simply in Spanish, and even the Eastern gal followed his drift when the old sheepherder added, "None of them would have escaped with their lives if it had been broad daylight. You say his body still lies over on that other ridge, Brazo Largo?"

Longarm nodded soberly and said, "That's only one of the things we'd best cut the captain in on. So let's do it."

They tagged along, of course, as he circled the big fire to join the captain on the far side. In point of fact, Longarm just stood there like a kid sent to see the headmaster because the fat-assed pretty boy was seated on the tongue of his army ambulance, a spring wagon somewhat smaller and more squared off than a covered prairie schooner, and there was no place else to sit.

Granville didn't seem to care as he pointed up at Longarm. "You should have waited for us. We were only a few hours behind you and making up the time at our own faster pace when Miss Weatherford rode in to tell us you'd led these poor Mexicans and the government herd into some sort of ambush."

Longarm could only reply, "You're right. I should have waited. I wasn't expecting any trouble this close to civilization, and I've just told Hernan and Ramon here how sorry I was. Let's talk about a military funeral and what sort of an ambush that might have been."

Before Granville got around to answering, a couple of his troopers came out of the surrounding darkness with folding canvas camp chairs for the lady and, apparently, their senior civilian guest. Longarm murmured in Spanish for the older Hernan to sit down as Granville stiffly said, "We'll naturally bury anybody who rates a military burial by the book. Who are we talking about and what was so unusual about a ragtag band of cowboys rawhiding sheepherders? Hernan, here, has already told us about the trouble you had with that bunch earlier."

Longarm said he was sorry he was still a mite rattled, and took time, however tersely, to bring the captain and some other officers drifting in up to date on events since he'd sent Miss Weatherford down off that rise to the west at full gallop.

Then he fished out a cheroot, lit up to allow himself time to organize his head a mite, and continued. "I thought it was the usual grudge over beef and mutton myself, at first. Now I don't know why push came to such a shove. It seems obvious that first bunch went home to get a little more help. From remarks I overheard, they knew who I was. Hernan's smart nephew, Mauro, was the one who pointed out they'd have simply gone around us if it had been the *stock* they were after."

A first john, even softer-looking than his somewhat older and bigger captain, said he'd heard cowboys had no use for

70

sheep at all. Longarm resisted the impulse to ask whether they'd taught him that at West Point or V.M.I. He nodded politely and said, "Whether they've any use for wool products or not, they were after me, as a paid-up federal agent. I heard their leader say so."

"Meaning what?" Granville demanded.

It was a good question.

Longarm blew smoke out both nostrils as he shrugged and replied, "I ain't sure. But as a general rule, I've discovered gents who send hired guns after any sort of lawman have revenge or some other sort of lawbreaking in mind. That same leader, who sounded like Texas and could have red hair or a florid complexion to go with his nickname of Red, made mention of an outfit called the Flying W. That couldn't be too old a brand in such recently settled country. The town we all recall from recent memory as Durango was deep inside a far bigger Ute reserve a short spell back."

He let fly more smoke. "Don't ever massacre your B.I.A. agent, however annoying, if you don't want the Great White Father opening up more of your treaty lands to white settlement."

Grace Weatherford, likely thinking like George, asked sweetly whether he considered the Battle of Milk River a massacre.

He said, "Nope. Milk River was an ambush, ma'am. It was at *White* River the Utes massacred Agent Nathan Meeker and a mess of unarmed male employees. They didn't massacre Meeker's wife, daughter, and an in-law just visiting. They only raped the three of 'em, a lot, and the army managed to rescue them from their romantic adventure after abusing Mr. Lo some more. But could we get back to all the Ute lands thrown open as a result of all that earlier strife?"

She asked if he didn't mean that earlier excuse to steal more land from Lo, the Poor Indian. He said, "Not now, George. For even as we rehash how come this corner of Colorado was converted to open range, those white killers we just brushed with can't be more than a few country miles from here, heading for that Flying W spread under the mistaken notion they just gunned a federal agent as directed by the owner, ramrod, or whatever of that same registered brand!"

71

Granville sniffed and interjected, "If you heard aright, and if those riders were off a lawful spread and not some canyon hideout used by stock thieves, you mean."

Longarm didn't want to waste time arguing. He said, "You could send a courier back to Durango to ask if anyone there knows more than any of us about that brand, couldn't you, Captain?"

Granville answered simply, "I could, but I don't intend to. My orders were to get these replacements and that Navaho herd to their proper destinations in the Arizona Territory. No person or persons unknown has done a thing to prevent my carrying out those orders so far."

Longarm blinked incredulously. "Have you been at the after-supper brandy before supper, Captain? I thought I just now told you we tangled with a couple of dozen riders just across the way, and even as we speak, a kid employed by the United States government is likely a mite stiff by this time!"

Granville turned to the first john to murmur, "See to that for me, will you, Mr. Compten?" Then, as his adjutant moved off to do so, Granville told Longarm calmly, "Supper should be ready within the hour. I'm afraid we don't have any brandy to offer you, but if you'd rather ride back to Durango yourself, I'm sure you'd be able to overtake us in no time. You were right about how slowly sheep or even goats can be driven."

Longarm didn't answer. He saw old Hernan had risen to chase after that first john with Ramon, and knowing why, he just muttered, *"Ay que pendejo!"* and went after the sheepherders. He hadn't gone far when he heard that pretty but sort of pesky newspaper gal calling after him, "Where are you going? Can I come too?"

So he called back, "No. That's an order," and he'd meant it. For whether she'd understood his Spanish or not, he meant to call that asshole an asshole more directly as soon as there was no mixed company around, and in any case, there was no need to expose an old boy's blown-out brains to a gal.

That adjutant had heard another legend about old U. S. Grant, it seemed. For less than fifty yards from the fire he shouted for his duty sergeant, and once that portly individual materialized from between two other wagons to hit a brace, the first john told him to form a burial detail and that these civilians, meaning Longarm and the surviving Mex Basques, would show them who they were fixing to bury by the book.

Then he spun on one heel to go back and admire his captain and likely Miss Weatherford some more. So Longarm told the noncom where they'd all meet later, and legged it over to where his Mex Basque pals said they'd piled his recovered saddle and possibles.

They stuck with him. So that was how things were when old Grace or George caught up with him as he was putting his Winchester back in its boot. She asked, "Oh, are you putting that away for now because you won't need it with all those soldiers coming along with us, Custis?"

He growled, "I ain't putting it away exactly. Having crossed yon good-sized draw mounted up and afoot, I stand firmly convinced that riding that far beats walking after all the exercise I've already had. I told you that you couldn't come. I thought I'd told you why as I explained how Mauro bought God's little acre earlier. If you can't picture what a Big Fifty rifle does to a human skull, just take my word it's a mighty disgusting sight."

She gulped, but gamely replied, "I can take it. I'm supposed to. I'm a newspaper reporter, not the silly girl you seem to want me to be, Custis."

He straightened up, saddle braced on his hip, chuckled down fondly at her, and said, "I never wanted you to be anything at all out here where the going can get even rougher. But I ain't trying to low-rate the hair on your doubtless pretty chest, Miss George. It's old Mauro's feelings we got to consider."

She said, "Call me Grace, and how can poor Mauro feel anything if he was shot in the head with a . . . big what?"

"Big Fifty. Buffalo rifle throwing a slug half an inch in diameter, until it hits with considerable force. I'll be proud to help you put such details down on paper afterwards, Miss Grace. But if you were laying up on yon rise all waxen and slack-jawed, with half your pretty face blown away, would you want a whole mess of gentlefolk remembering you that way?"

She gulped again and softly said, "Oh, I thought it was only *my* feelings you were worried about. I'm sorry, Custis. It's just that you can be so considerate one minute and so, well, rustic the next."

"It was your notion to imply I was being needlessly mean to old Mr. Lo back yonder, and there's just no nicer way to imply a white survivor got raped. Why don't you go have some supper, and I can help you spell Mauro's name later on."

She didn't argue. The Mex Basques picked up their own saddles, and followed as Longarm headed down-slope to where all the riding stock, including the blue roan, which had wandered back on its own, was being casually guarded by a trooper seated on a water bucket. He allowed it was likely all right for them to ride off on their own mounts.

As they saddled up old Hernan sighed and said, "Mauro would have been pleased you mentioned no more than his mutilated face to *la mujer linda,* El Brazo Largo."

Longarm shrugged. Then he said, "I had no call to mention the way a brain-shot man can shit and piss his pants. Did you?"

Chapter 8

The moon was still low and less than a quarter full. So Mauro stunk more disgustingly than he looked as they dismounted downwind of him atop the bald rise. Once they'd tethered their mounts to soap weeds and got a bit closer, Longarm could see how the gang had mixed *him* up with a sheepherder. It would have been a chore to make out the dead boy's face in detail if all of it had still been there. By dim moonlight the messed-up parts looked more inky than gory, though you could see one eye socket, cheek, and ear had been blown away by that soft-heavy buffalo round.

Ramon found Mauro's Yellowboy and emptied his dead pal's pockets—for the next of kin, he said—as Longarm circled around for sign with no luck. He'd already heard the bastards lighting off afoot for the mounts they'd doubtless hid amid the trees even further west. Hoofprints would be far easier to read, although not by such shitty light. So he figured he'd best wait for some dawn on the subject before he decided whether to locate that mysterious Flying W by trailing across open range or going all the way back to Durango.

Never having served in any army, the two Mex Basques couldn't see what was holding up that army burial detail. So Longarm, seeing he doubtless had the time, told them a second legend involving a notoriously drunk and famous general.

It was said that once he'd started winning more battles than a heap of doubtless tidier Union generals and been promoted

75

to a much higher position, old U. S. Grant had noticed he'd need a far bigger staff. So being an old soldier as well as an old drunk, he'd come up with a childishly simple but good enough way to separate a good aide-de-camp from an officious asshole.

When interviewing a bright-eyed and bushy-tailed junior officer, old red-eyed Grant had simply asked how he'd go about erecting a fifty-foot flagstaff in the middle of the parade ground out front. Lots of applicants tended to ask where they were supposed to get such a considerable amount of timber, or whether the general wanted it sanded and whitewashed or not. So he'd naturally sent them back where they kept such poor souls.

He didn't want a junior officer who assured a general with self-confidence that he'd gather together a work detail and see to all the details personally.

Assuring the general you'd fill out all the proper work orders and assign the task to the post engineer qualified a new officer as maybe a quartermaster down the line. But to serve on the general's staff and share his tobacco and liquor with him, you had to tell him you'd just step outside, grab the first sergeant in sight, and tell him the general wanted a fifty-foot flagstaff standing in the dead center of that damned parade ground by the next mess call.

Longarm wasn't sure either Mex Basque really understood old army yarns retold in Border Mex. But by the time he'd explained the point some more, they heard a mounted squad coming up the dark slope to join them, and sure enough, that duty sergeant had saddled a kid corporal with the grim chore.

You didn't get to be a corporal in the peacetime army by saying you didn't know how to carry out any orders they gave you. Hence it took Longarm a few minutes to surmise the kid had never commanded a burial detail before. But any soldier knew how to dig a hole, and so once their corporal had put two of the troopers to work at that, a few yards away from the moonlit cadaver, Longarm took the kid aside and confided, as if man-to-man, "I can see you've carried out a full ceremony in your day, Corporal. But seeing this dead civilian's kin might want his body somewheres else later, would you mind if I was to make a few suggestions?"

76

The young corporal allowed he stood ready to do most anything but drop his pants and bend over. "I've took part in this sort of shit as private on the firing squad back East. But to tell the truth, I let the chaplain and the sergeant of the guard worry about the small print, sir."

Longarm said, "You don't have to sir me. I never made it that high in my misspent youth. The army budget we got today won't pay for more than one regimental chaplain, and we both know how busy the sergeants must be right now. But seeing as you asked, four feet down ought to be deep enough. There's no sensible call for a grave wide enough for the usual coffin either. But it might be a neighborly gesture to wrap him in something that rots slower than the rest of him."

The kid looked relieved and confided, "I brung along a waterproof tarpaulin with that in mind, sir."

Longarm let the second "sir" go, seeing the kid was doubtless so used to sirring anybody he didn't get to boss, and told him such a swell cover was just what he'd had in mind. "They may just leave him be. Mexican folks are more philosophic about dead kinfolk. But I don't know as much about Mex Basques."

He got out a couple of cheroots as he added more confidently, "In either case that canvas ought to hold him together at least a few seasons. I'll see if I can get old Hernan to say a few kind words over the poor cuss in their own lingo. I see they let us have more than enough hands up here. But I don't see anybody with a bugle."

The corporal said, "I asked. They told me even white civilians hardly rated taps and a rifle salute."

Longarm flatly stated, "A Basque is white as you or me and even if he'd been an Eskimo, he was riding for the U.S. government when he was killed in action, damn it!"

The corporal gulped and replied, "I never come up here to argue about that with anybody, sir. It ain't for me to say how fancy we're supposed to dispose of the Spanish gentleman."

Longarm said, "His pals may not notice if we settle for a rifle salute. You boys did bring your carbines this far out of bivouac, I hope?"

The kid said they had, but that he didn't know whether they'd approve of expending a four-gun volley over a greaser.

Longarm said, "Don't you ever call any dead pal of mine a greaser again. I don't mean to tell you that twice, and I never said we were fixing to fire one volley over anybody. A proper respect to a fallen comrade calls for *three* four-gun volleys. Are you saying your boys can't manage that with repeating carbines, Corporal?"

The kid shook his head and replied, "Nosir, but that's twelve whole rounds of .45-70 under discussion, and you should have heard what they said about that canvas back there!"

Longarm handed the kid one of the three-for-a-nickel smokes and lit it for him. "I'll pay your ordnance officer for the damned brass, seeing they pay me so lavishly next to you boys."

He lit his own smoke and shook the match out as he continued in a firmer tone. "Seeing that's settled, you'd best form your honor guard and tell them how you want that carried out. I'll have a word with old Hernan about Basque religious notions."

So a few minutes later they had young Mauro wrapped up in canvas and down in the shallow grave they'd dug for him. Then old Hernan, hat in hand, stood near the north end of the hole saying nice things in Euska-ra that nobody but Ramon could understand about a dead boy none of the rest of them had ever really known. Longarm figured old Hernan wouldn't lie to the Lord anymore than he lied to the law, and so far Longarm had never caught the old gent in any whoppers.

When Hernan finally wound down and tossed a fistful of dust in to get on with it, that kid corporal, having made up his mind to do things by the book or not at all, did the book proud by sending a dead civilian off with a spit-and-polish expenditure of .45-70s.

As they were filling in the grave with their entrenching spades, Longarm explained why it might be best if he talked to the captain about all that distant gunplay first, and mounted up to beat everyone else back to bivouac. But as he rode in and asked the squirt on night duty as officer of the day, he was told Captain Granville had already retired to his fancy spring wagon.

That didn't mean the muley cuss was asleep this early. So once he'd seen to his mount and spread his own bedroll on the ground near the south end of the quiet camp, he moseyed back to have a word with old Granville lest that kid corporal catch a needless reprimand.

But Longarm and the captain never got to say good night after all. Because just as Longarm was fixing to rap politely on the moonlit cover of the captain's headquarters ambulance, he heard Granville on the other side of the canvas moaning, "Oh, yeah, take it all the way to the roots and let me come deep inside you, honey!"

"Honey" seemed agreeable to the passionate request, judging from the soft moans and creaking springs of the boxy wagon. So Longarm eased away in the dark before anyone else came along to suspect him of eavesdropping. But on his way back to his own bedding he met up with that young officer of the day again. So he offered the poor shavetail a smoke, and this gave him a chance to casually ask if he could have somehow missed another lady traveling with the column.

The shavetail got his own cheroot going before he answered in an open enough way. "I don't know where you got that idea, Deputy Long. That Miss Weatherford from the *Washington Globe* is the only woman I know of within miles, and isn't that worry enough, riding into Lord only knows what between here and Fort Defiance?"

Longarm agreed it sure was, and went on back to his own lonesome bedding, snorting smoke and muttering to himself about the boundless perfidy of the unfair sex and the total stupidity of his own.

But as he stripped down to his underwear in the dark, seated atop his bedding on the unforgiving ground, he reflected that things might well have gone even worse.

For had he not made the mistake of treating old George as if she'd been a lady, he might have wound up going sloppy seconds to that lard-assed T. J. Granville before he'd realized who that had been in bed with the captain back in Durango less than twenty-four hours before!

79

Turning in so confounded and pissed, Longarm didn't realize he'd missed that late supper until he woke up later, before dawn, too hungry to notice his raging erection.

There wasn't much a man could do on an open campground about a raging erection without looking silly. But he'd thought to pack a few chaws of chocolate and smoked buffalo tongue in with his canned emergency grub. So he rummaged in his saddlebags, and had the edge off his cravings—for food—by the time the clear sky to their east was pearling light enough to make out the inky horizon over that way.

By the time he'd dressed and strapped on his gun rig, it was light enough to catch young Ramon jacking off in a nearby bedroll. But it seemed more polite to just amble the other way through the slumbering camp till, sure enough, he found the sergeant of the guard and half a dozen groggy privates sharing coffee around a small night fire. It would have been impolite to ask where the officer of the day jacked off at this hour. So after he'd hunkered down for a tin cup of shitty army coffee and taken time to explain what he was going to do, Longarm went back to the remuda, saddled the black barb this time, and rode back to where he and Mauro had shot it out with those mysterious riders the evening before.

By the time he could see the sort of croquet mallet Mauro's Mex Basque pals had improvised from a green juniper limb to indicate something more important than trail trash under all that loose dirt, a bugle back in camp was sounding reveille. Longarm found a dozen or so spent rounds, mostly .44-40 either side could have fired. Then it was light enough to see colors and so, seeing spatters of dried blood but nothing else of interest where he and Mauro had shot it out with the bastards, Longarm rode further west to scout that higher wooded ridge the ambushers had been skulking in earlier.

There was far more sign up there amid the thicker cover. He could smell more shit, horse and human, than he could make out hither and yon among the bunched groves of juniper or piñon. The cold ashes of a fair-sized campfire down the more open far slope told him they'd been lying in wait a spell before he and that camp-following newspaper gal had almost ridden into their ambush.

Spotting where someone had mounted in a hurry amid the trees, Longarm muttered, "Well, at least I kept her pure for her soldier blue. How come you rode *that* way, you total asshole?"

One rider, rattled by a gunfight and spooked by oncoming bugles, might have lit out most any old way. But after Longarm had scouted out eight or ten other southbound beelines along the timbered rise, he reined in to light a thoughtful smoke and study some.

The east-west trail they'd all been following out of Durango ran just north of the South Ute Reserve on purpose. By this late in the game, rightly or wrongly, almost all the Ute who'd once considered the western half of Colorado their own to keep and cherish had been marched clean across the Green River and beyond. Those few Ute who hadn't been chased clean out of Colorado yet were naturally far more worried about the Saltu or strangers than that crazy old Chief Colorow had been when he'd engineered the Meeker massacre.

But for the moment the bands just to the south, since they'd sided with Kit Carson and other Saltu against their old Navaho and Jicarilla Apache enemies, and since they still constituted a buffer against them, were supposed to be left the hell alone. The federal government had forbidden even the Colorado National Guard, under federal authority now since that Confederate Army had been based on Southern state militias, to set foot or hoof across that nearby reservation line, on pain of federal arrest by the ever truculent and sometimes bloodthirsty Ute Agency Police.

So why would a whole flock of white-ass roughnecks be riding due south into pissed-off Indian country when they couldn't even seem to get along with Mex Basques? Or an Anglo lawman they'd likely known by name?

Longarm followed the easy although tangled trail at a walk as the sun peeled over the eastern ridges to shed yet more light on the subject. The ground-hugging rays of sunlight made tracking a chore so simple that a good tracker had to be a mite suspicious. But when he circled wide in search of less obvious sign, he failed to find so much as a scuffed-over pebble or a freshly busted stem. When some early-rising flies drew his attention to blood spatters keeping pace with the hoofprints of a loping pony, Longarm decided that the old boy had been riding rag-doll limp across a saddle. Nobody bleeding that good could sit his mount at that pace without a heap of help. Other hoofprints punched through the crusted dust of the recent rain agreed the whole bunch had been riding fast and close together, as if more anxious to put some distance between themselves and that army bugle than to hide the way they'd headed.

Longarm felt no call to be unduly modest about his own tracking skills as long as he was alone on the trail. Anyone who'd known he was riding with that army column would have likely heard the troopers were green to these parts. But nobody with any training was supposed to be *that* green, and even if the ambushers felt sure they'd nailed the only real tracker in the bunch, they were still leaving a whole lot of tracks. A determined schoolmarm would have been able to trace their headlong flight along the crest of this wooded ridge. A lot of the tree-shaded surface was bare sand, smoothed fresh to show lizard tracks, for Pete's sake, by the recent wet spell. Longarm didn't even have to rein in for a closer look as he rode over a patch where a loping pony had cut across the earlier spoor of a bobcat tracking a lame deer fawn.

"They never split up, circled, or even wavered as they rode this way through the night," he told his own pony, heeling it to a somewhat faster slow trot. "They knew nobody would be on their trail any earlier than right about now. That means they figured it wouldn't matter even if I was a whole squadron. So just what in the hell might I be riding into alone?"

He didn't slow down as he thoughtfully hauled out his saddle gun and levered a round in the chamber. His Winchester '73 would lob a 200-grain .44 slug twice as far with the same 40-grain powder charge as his .44-40 six-gun. But that was still this side of 600 yards with the point of aim twice the height of the rascal you were out to hit. So he figured it was safe to trot along a thinly wooded ridge where a rider could likely see what lay a quarter mile or more ahead. Any lawman who worried all that much about scope-sighted buffalo rifles had no business tracking owlhoot riders in any damned case.

But he did rein in among some fluttering fresh-leafed aspen when he came to a stretch of slickrock where he lost the trail.

The route ahead was dominated by an ominous hogback of red sandstone thrust up into the morning sunlight like a giant stone lean-to.

Bracing the butt of his saddle gun on his right thigh so the muzzle could proceed him like the lance of a knight of old, Longarm told his barb, "A total asshole might just hold his breath and ask you to take him across all that bare-ass rock ahead. I doubt anyone would make a stand over yonder either. But the graveyards are full of lawmen shot by assholes who outsmarted 'em by acting sort of stupid. So let's show our imaginary drygulcher why that's a good place to ambush a greenhorn but a piss-poor place to ambush anyone smart as us!"

The pony didn't argue. What they did, of course, involved about a furlong retreat into the sparse timber, followed by a quarter-mile-wide detour through the the stirrup-high cover at a lower level to the east, where the slope was steeper.

Longarm knew anyone holed up amid the big rusty slabs of sandstone above would see what he was up to, of course. There was just no getting around that lots of times in mounted field tactics. He was giving any sneak the choice of staying put among the rocks of that isolated outcrop, and possibly getting pinned until those soldiers blue came along, or running that ridge while there was still time to do it.

But nobody had been laying in wait for anybody after all. Longarm made certain by backtracking once he'd cut the trail of the gang again amid more timber to the south of the outcrop. Those same graveyards were full of lawmen who'd taken things like *that* for granted too.

"Those old boys never stopped to consider killing me more than that one time last night," he confided to his horse as he reined in amid some contorted stone pine atop another high although softer rise for a thoughtful examination of the wide-open view ahead.

The day was breaking sunny and crystal clear, with the horizon to the south meeting the cobalt blue bowl of the sky unblemished by smoke or dust. Reading his mental map of the Four Corners country, he declared aloud to his pony, "They stuck together and beelined due south into the South Ute Reserve."

That was something for a lone rider to study on. A dozen or more white riders could get in enough trouble not far ahead if they'd dropped in uninvited. The highly pissed-off and well-mounted South Ute were always accusing Colorado riders, with good reason, of yet another land grab.

Although over a hundred miles long and averaging better than fifteen miles across, the Ute Strip running east along the southern border of Colorado from the Four Corners was a pathetic sliver next to the original hunting grounds of a proud but bewildered nation. Allowed just that little scrap of their original range as reward for their keeping faith with the Great White Father, the South Ute knew their bitter enemies to the south and west had wound up with much larger reserves, and that even their renegade cousins, the North Ute, had been granted more than ten times as much range, new range or not, on the far side of the Utah line. So had it been up to Longarm, Washington would be sending presents to the Ute, not the Navaho, right about now!

But it wasn't up to him, and even though some Ute knew Longarm as Saltu Ka Saltu, or the stranger who is not a stranger, Longarm had to allow that Little Big Eyes, Secretary Carl Schurz of the Interior Department, was making a certain amount of stern sense with his current Indian policy.

Aside from being brave and decent, by the standards of their traditional Indian enemies, the Ute just didn't have much going for them in a white man's world.

Their traditional Pueblo enemies, whether they'd admit it or not, were if anything better off now that the U.S. government had occupied the Southwest and told both the Hispanic missionaries and Indian raiders to leave them the hell alone. Both Mex and Anglo neighbors understood what an Indian who lived in a fixed place and grew crops in a fenced-in field was up to, and vice versa. So save for the few occasions Mex or Anglo officials had mistaken the calm ways of the Pueblo for weakness and gotten too officious, the Pueblo had managed to get along tolerably well in their changing world, taking up a few useful notions from their Mex or Anglo neighbors, but for the most part clinging to their old ways in their old hometowns. Taos, still occupied by Tanoan Pueblo, was the oldest still-inhabited town anywhere in These United States.

The Navaho, for all their recent hell-raising, had of course gotten halfway as "civilized" as the Pueblo, from the white man's point of view. But the poor benighted Ute wouldn't have known what to do with that herd of sheep and goats if it had been addressed to them. So it hadn't been. Trying to turn Ute into agriculturists had gotten poor old Agent Meeker up at White River killed for all his pains. The Ute admired horses. There was just no giving a Ute more horses than he felt the need for. Like other Horse Indians, he liked guns too. After that, he just wanted the Saltu to leave him the hell alone and let him worry about who was going to feed him, his family, and his horses, whether they wanted to or not.

Nat Meeker had tried to show the North Ute how to grow spuds in a mountain meadow. They'd gone loco when they saw white men plowing up grass they'd grazed their ponies on since they'd stolen the first colt from their Arapaho enemies. White men still tended to go loco at the thought of the Ute wasting all that high range on such childish notions. Longarm had found that, all in all, it was best to leave the Ute be whenever possible.

This seemed one such time. Pondering the matter long enough to smoke down one cheroot, Longarm wheeled his barb around to head back the way they'd come, muttering, "If those old boys are in good with the Indian Police, I can find out later where they might have wound up."

On a brighter note, he knew that a large party of Saltu riding uninvited across the rugged South Ute Strip would doubtless wind up under arrest, if they were very lucky, and his pals in the Indian Police wouldn't even have to be asked. They always turned white men they took alive over to the nearest white-run courts.

And so, humming "Farther Along," Longarm dropped down the west side of that north-south rise to aim for the westbound trail at a forty-five-degree angle. For he assumed even a sluga-bed such as old Captain Granville would have moved on by this late in the morning, and Longarm's unstudied trigonometry put the show on the road well west of that foiled ambush to his north by now.

He didn't want to consider how late a man might linger in bed come morning with anything half as tempting as that sweetly two-faced newspaper gal. He figured if he intersected the trail a tad ahead of the column, he'd still be better off than hitting it both late and downwind. Coming up from behind could make for some dusty, shitty riding after a cavalry squadron, a wagon train, and all those goats and sheep had churned up the same narrow trail with the sun glaring down so severely.

As he rode along in the thin dry breezes he decided he could have used a more serious hat. Laugh as one might at the tall floppy sombrero of the dry-range Mex, there was a heap to be said for hat brims that shade one's whole upper body, and that tall crown let a heap of sweaty heat rise shaded from a rider's scalp. "Sombrero" derived from the Spanish word for shade, which was *sombra,* although a sweet-screwing *señorita* who'd studied lots of Hispanic historical shit had once assured him the famous Mex sombrero was a North African notion, introduced to the first of the old-time *vaqueros* or buckaroos by Moorish cowboys, who fancied an even floppier sombrero woven more loosely from palm leaves.

The Stetson Buckeye was as close to the shadier sombrero as even a Texas rider felt he needed to survive in more northern climes than, say, Chihuaha. As a lawman who spent more time in less wild surroundings than a Texas trail drive, Longarm had long favored a plain old J. B.—the original Stetson Plainsman with its medium crown telescoped High Plains or Colorado-style—because it was a pain in the ass to have your hat blow off in the middle of a chase, and some asshole in Denver was always asking where you were from if your damned old hat wasn't Colorado-crushed.

That morning, walking his mount at a sensible but mighty sunny pace, Longarm removed his Stetson long enough to punch the crown out as high as it would go. Wiping the sweatband with a kerchief before he put it back on helped a bit, and despite the baking sun, he felt there was no danger in smoking as he rode along. For the open range all around was green as it ever got in these parts. The thrifty roots of those plants Professor Darwin said one ought to plant down this way were still sucking plenty of water from soil that wasn't likely to stay that way through the end of May.

Meanwhile, despite the harsh sunlight, or maybe because of it, the Four Corners country sure looked swell. It was tough to picture the hills and dales he kept crossing all summer-killed and straw-matting gray when an Oriental rug of short-lived flowers was smiling up at him right now. But this wasn't the first time Longarm had ridden this range. So when he reined in and dismounted to rest and graze his barb in the shade of some stone pine, he told it, while stomping some to get more blood in his legs after all that riding, "Eat all that blue-eyed grass you've a mind to and see if I care what your breath smells like. It'll all be dried down to bitty bulbs in no time. See them unusual columbines up yonder by that thunderbolted cedar?"

The barb went on cropping wild onions as Longarm explained. "I know you thought columbines were supposed to bloom more blue. I never even knew them flame-colored flowers were columbines till this educated lady who'd studied botany explained how some old columbines down here in the southwest corner of Colorado had learned to bloom red and yellow, on less water, than their sissy blue relations up in the greener mountain meadows."

He plucked a sulfur flower to chew its pungent stem as he mused aloud. "I forget why that botany gal said so many flowers grew red or yellow on marginal range. We were going at it dog-style when the topic of her floral collection came up. Jesus H. Christ, it ain't halfway to noon and how come I keep harking back to pussies of the past? It's getting too blamed *hot* for pussy, even if I knew of a likely one within many a dry dusty mile!"

That was no lie, unless one aimed to count a bawd claimed by another cuss as pussy. Longarm didn't. As a lawman he knew all too well what trouble such rivalry could lead to among *friends,* and he hadn't thought much of T. J. Granville even before he'd overheard him with that newspaper gal in camp.

Trying not to think about that two-faced newspaper gal in bed with *any* man was about as easy as not thinking about a dead pal at his funeral. So he sipped some canteen water, filled his hat with more for his pony to enjoy a few sips, and said, "Let's get it on up to that trail, honey. I don't know about you, but I'd surely enjoy a sit-down dinner in some shade come high noon out this way."

Chapter 9

The black barb was in no position to argue. Longarm let her walk up-slope, and trotted her down at a mile-eating but comfortable enough pace she could maintain an hour at a time, with only short trail breaks on the increasingly rare occasions they came across any shade.

The range they were riding now was still lush by the standards of the Four Corners country. But Longarm had worked with cows often enough to spot where more than a few had been grazing this side of April Fool's Day. Given their druthers, cows cleaned out clover and the richer grasses first, leaving tougher or more bitter growth for a later pass if they wound up stuck with it. There was enough in the way of unplucked flowers and even bland but tasteless cheat grass to read as a fair-sized herd being moved at a fair pace, neither all that long ago nor all that recently if he was any judge of dried cow pies.

A cow could shit going any damned direction. So it took Longarm a while to come upon a sandy wash some cows, and steel-shod cowponies, had crossed much earlier headed the other way.

Reining in on the next rise, Longarm stared soberly south for a spell at nothing much as he muttered, "All right. Somebody drove some cows, say a hundred or so head, toward that same Ute Agency a week or more before somebody killed Mauro instead of me and lit out in the same general direction.

"But that don't mean the two are connected. That's a mighty tolerable strip of mighty empty country. So sticking with what we see around these parts, all we know for certain is that the

Ute may or may not be riding shod ponies this spring. Whether Indian or not, a herd that size don't add up to a raid either we or the War Department would have heard about. So let's read it as a modest beef drive to, let's say, the trading post at Red Wash, and let the B.I.A. concern itself with distributing the fresh meat."

He knew the Ute weren't really all that interested in *raising* anything but ponies, cur dogs, and kids. The B.I.A. simply gave them cows from time to time so they'd shut up about all the antelope, deer, and elk they'd had to stuff their fool selves with in their Shining Times. It was tough, Longarm felt, but that was the way this old world was. As old Professor Darwin said, men or beasts changed their ways to fit their changing world or they went the ways of the dodo bird, the Mandan, the Mohegan, and such. He was sorry he'd never get to see one of those comical dodo birds in the flesh, and old-timers who'd known them said the Mandan, and maybe even the Mohegan, had been as decent as Mr. Lo usually got. But that was the way things worked. He'd met old-time white folks who couldn't change, and some of them had been right neighborly, till a well-meaning stranger tried to get them to change their ways. It seemed a shame so many quick-witted sons of bitches, red or white, seemed to be doing so well in a world that just didn't have as much room for courtly old Dixie belles, California grandees, clipper-ship skippers, or Cheyenne Crooked Lancers. At the rate this old world was changing, Longarm suspected, there could come a day when lawmen such as himself might be considered obstacles to further progress. Sometimes he suspected that was why Mother Nature had invented death. For old mountain men still carrying on about the real West they'd known were enough of a pain in the ass, and how would it be if there were still folks around who thought their old cave was good enough and that nobody but a sissy would bother to *cook* a blamed meal?

He knew why he was thinking about cooked meals when he sniffed a second or third time and decided that either he was suffering from a new sort of mirage, with his nose, or somebody was really brewing genuine Arbuckle Brand close enough to matter.

90

Reining in, Longarm wet a finger and tested the faint breezes. When he saw the tempting smell was coming from a bit to the left of his chosen route, he chose to ride that way instead, although at a cautious walk up the rise to his west. For while a man who'd pass on mid-morning coffee was one sort of fool, a man who'd bust over a rise blind was another.

Aiming for a clump of piñon on the crest, Longarm gazed down from the handy cover on a sort of sorry scene. A paint pony lay unsaddled and dead just south of a lonesome-looking young squirt hunkered over a small fire in a sandy wash below. That coffee Longarm could smell better from up here was brewing in an old enameled pot. The squirt's saddlebags lay mighty flat across the bedroll he'd removed from his double-rigger roper but left rolled. The squirt wore a Schofield .45 thumb-buster on one blue-jeaned hip. So Longarm let fly a loud howdy at a safe distance. Sure enough, the squirt was up, gun drawn, but holding it politely on the far side of that fire as Longarm broke cover to walk his pony in, calling, "I'd be Deputy U.S. Marshal Custis Long on his way to the Navaho Reserve with no warrants on anyone I know of under such a big white sombrero. What happened to your mount, pard?"

The squirt called back in a surprising voice, "My own damn fault. I was riding him too fast for the dawn light and he put a hoof down wrong and busted his near fore-cannon. Shot him soon as I was back up on my own feet, of course. I'd be Nancy Slade and I was bound for Durango from Red Wash. How far do you figure I got to walk now?"

Longarm felt better about that girlish voice, now that she'd owned up to being the genuine article. But it wouldn't have been a decent way to treat a lady if he'd come right out and grinned down at her outrageous costume and sort of interesting build. So he just told her, "Way too far to walk, Miss Nancy. But you can ride her in less than two full days, pushing some. I'm with a good-sized government outfit, out ahead an hour's ride or so. So why don't we finish off that coffee with some canned goods I just so happen to have on me, and then I can ride you and your own saddle postern as far north as the trail we're both looking for."

She confessed she'd been getting mighty hungry since the last she'd seen of her own trail supplies. So Longarm let her open some beans and tomato preserves as he tethered his barb and relieved it of its sweaty saddle for a spell.

As they washed down the cold canned snacks with hot black coffee, the boyishly dressed young gal, an ash-blonde under her oversized Stetson, turned out to be the daughter of some B.I.A. folks stationed down near Red Wash in the Ute Reserve. He didn't ask her why she'd been in such a hurry to get to Durango. He was more interested in folks riding the other way. He was pleased to hear she knew all about that cow sign he'd read earlier. She confirmed his guess about a beef herd purchased by the B.I.A. and already distributed among the Ute to the south. Then she shook him up some more by adding that the agency at Red Wash bought lots of beef, at a good price, from the Flying W.

Swallowing too fast so he could get the words out sooner, he said, "Hold on, Miss Nancy. You say you've heard of this Flying W outfit?"

She seemed unconcerned as she demurely replied, "Everyone in these parts has. They've been grazing the new open range just north of here since our poor Ute Nation was forced to cede it to Colorado. Their brand is a well-known W with a bitty angel wing to either side. But why are we jawing about a perfectly ordinary cattle operation, Deputy Long?"

Longarm said, "My friends call me Custis. You find me this far off the ordinary trail west because just last night some Flying W riders shot a pal of mine and tried their best to shoot *me*. I'm on my way back to my own outfit after trailing 'em about as far as the Ute Strip you just left. So now it's your turn, Miss Nancy."

She said, "*My* friends call me Nan, Custis. After that you can call me totally confused. I know some Flying W riders to talk to, from a time or two we coffeed and caked them after they'd delivered Indian beef. The ones I've met hardly struck me as the sorts you'd expect to see in trouble with the law. Who told you the rascals you met up with were off the Flying W?"

To which Longarm could only answer tersely, "*They* did, and I never met up with 'em. They were laying in wait for

92

me, by name. As they left me for dead by mistake, I heard one mention getting back to the Flying W so they could brag to their boss on killing me."

She washed down some beans as she studied the dying coals of her thrifty little cookfire. Longarm admired folks who studied on what they had to say before they said it. So she sounded convincing when she finally observed, "They must have been trying to fool any survivors. At the worst they were talking about some other crook who only *rides* for the Flying W. The respectable widow woman who owns and operates the spread has a heap of riders on her payroll, and you know how saddle tramps come and go."

She could see he still had a thoughtful eyebrow raised. So she insisted, "I've never met her myself. But I know the Widow Donovan by rep and as I just said, she's respected in these parts by red or white. Moved her operation out this way from the Front Ranges after her man, old Kevin Donovan, chased a calf under a low branch and stove in his chest, oh, a couple of years ago, I reckon."

Longarm nodded thoughtfully. "Year before last. I read about it in the *Rocky Mountain News* and agreed it was a sort of ironic way for an old-timer who'd ridden with Captain Goodnight against Comanche and Cheyenne to die."

He washed down the last of his own beans and said, "I can't see any sensible reason for Kevin Donovan's kin to be at feud with me or any other lawman. He had a well-established rep, and I'll take your word he'd have married up with a lady as honest. So let's try her another way. Before I brushed with those riders so seriously I'd had words with an earlier bunch, maybe at least some of the same. It was one of those dumb discussions about cows versus sheep on a public thoroughfare across government-owned open range. So naturally I won, without hurting more than maybe a few feelings. How do you like a bullyboy I backed down riding back to his line camp or whatever to gather a bigger bunch and lay for me further along?"

She poured the dregs of her cup on the dying coals and finished her snack with the last of her tomato preserves before she asked, still frowning thoughtfully, what a U.S. deputy marshal had been up to with a herd of dad-blamed sheep.

So he told her he'd tell her the whole story along the way, and got started as the two of them kicked dirt over the fire and empty cans before he resaddled the one mount they had to work with.

General George Brinton McClellan had made up for his piss-poor showing at Antietam by designing the damned fine army saddle named after him. Rougher on the rider than it was on his mount, thanks to the way its tree cleared and ventilated the mount's spine, it was favored by Longarm and other thoughtful riders because of how much further it might carry a man and his possibles in a pinch. The fussy worrier who'd designed and redesigned such an all-purpose saddle had provided it with twice as many brass fittings as your average cavalryman would ever use for attaching extra shit to his general issue. So it was simple to latigo Nan's roping saddle, by its horn, bottom side out, to the off-rim of his cantle, where it would ride securely enough, however clumsily, with his bedroll and off-saddlebag keeping it from punching his mount in the floating ribs if they wanted to trot some. He naturally tied her heavy wood stirrups to her horn and draped her bridle over the whole shebang.

That allowed the shapely but lightly built Nan to sit sidesaddle postern despite her jeans, with both her high-heeled boots hanging down the near side. To make up for her having no stirrup to hold her half-ass atop his bedroll, she just grabbed hold of him around the waist as they lit out at an easy walk. It sure was odd how well a man could tell, without looking, and even without perfume, when it was a woman instead of a man that close to him.

It didn't take long to bring a gal dressed so cow up to date on his recent misadventures with sheep and goats meant for the Navaho a good ways on. She agreed that that first encounter sounded dumb, and suggested nobody high on the totem pole of a good-sized beef operation would mount an all-out war against the federal government to avenge the honor of a backed-down range bully.

She made him admire both their brains more when she pointed out how any paid assassins expecting him, by his name and hence his rep, would doubtless have known what sort of mission he'd been sent on. She said, "If they knew

94

those army riders were with you, they surely knew about those sheep, and knew they were only headed through, right?"

Longarm had already figured that out. He nodded thoughtfully, staring east despite the early sun-dazzle, in hopes of spotting at least some distant dust as he replied. "I don't think they were worried about that Navaho stock. They did gun a sheepherder, thinking he was me. But then they ran off, hugging their fool selves for being so slick, without even stopping to pet a sheepdog. So I suspect somebody in that first bunch told somebody higher they'd had trouble with me personally, and the rest you know."

She hugged him tighter, just long enough to shift her weight on her less-secure perch, as she said, "Neither one of us knows too much then. Did you tell that first bunch who you were, or did they act like they already knew?"

He thought, nodded, and replied, "I follow your drift. I said who I was. I didn't much get into other details. I just told 'em to get out of our way and . . . Right, the higher power they reported to didn't *care* what I was doing with them sheep. It was the notion of me, a federal lawman with a rep for being nosy, headed . . . All right, where?"

She seemed confused. He asked, by way of explanation, "Have you heard anything about that Flying W outfit having any dealings with other Indian agencies, Miss Nan?"

She shrugged. It felt swell against his denim-clad back. "Other than the two Ute agencies I know more about? I'm not ready to bet my fair white body on it, but why would the Widow Donovan want to drive her beef any further than she has to? Don't all B.I.A. agents pay about the same price?"

"They're supposed to, based on the latest quotations on the Chicago Board, although back in the bad old days of President Grant and the Indian Ring I caught me a few old boys playing fast and loose with the books. How's a poor benighted Indian supposed to know prime beef and top-grade wheat flour from sowbelly and cornmeal? Did you just say there were two agencies, two separate agencies, down where you just come from?"

She explained, "The strip still held by the South Ute runs more than a hundred miles east to west. So it's administered as if it was two reservations side by side."

95

He nodded. "That leaves no Ute family more than about twenty-five miles to ride whenever they want to pick up some trade goods or register another complaint with the Great White Father. It's tougher to crook Indians when they have more than one trading post to shop at. Let's talk about beef. When that nice old widow woman delivers beef on the hoof down yonder, do the Ute get to butcher the stock themselves, or does some swell Saltu take the critters apart so the meat can be parceled out neatly weighed and wrapped, with each and every head accounted for in the B.I.A. books?"

She giggled and said, "My heavens, you do have a suspicious nature, don't you? Now that you've shown me the primrose path, I see how easy it would be to lose a side of beef here or even a live steer there. But I'm afraid the Indians sign for live beef at our western or mountain Ute Agency. Lord only knows what a Horse Indian might or might not do with a beef critter once he gets it back to his own band. But I fail to see how any white folks involved could fiddle with the figures for fun and profit."

"How about resale?" he asked. "Jicarilla, Navaho, and even Hopi would rather eat beef than rabbit, and if some ration-hogging Ute were to fatten up a yearling or more to sell later at a better price to . . . Yeah, I see what you mean."

She laughed lightly. "Why would other Indians raised to hate every Ute buy beef from a Ute at a higher price than their own agents can purchase on the open market? You don't know the Ute very well if you think they care enough about cattle to run some sort of sneaky feedlot operation, and even if they did, weren't those riders who gunned that friend of yours a mite whiter than he was?"

Longarm said, "Mauro was a Basque. But you're likely right about most of that gang being more Saltu than Ute. You'd have heard if anyone in this corner of Colorado had been missing beef that might just have sort of intermingled with that bigger Flying W herd?"

She laughed incredulously. "We'd have heard if any outfit was missing washing off their clothesline! This range has only just been opened up to whites, and you know how some folks a tad new to Indian neighbors accuse them of stealing them blind whether they're missing anything or not."

96

"Wasn't worried about Indian crooks just yet," he pointed out. "Just trying to figure out what those white crooks were afraid I'd find out. It's the sort of trouble I've tripped over in the past. There is nothing like a guilty conscience to bring on a serious case of the sneaks, and there's been many a time I'd have just ridden through if some mean-spirited scoundrel hadn't assumed I was after him and inspired me to wonder what in thunder we could be fighting about!"

She said she believed him, saying he'd surely make *her* proddy if she had any secret sins worth a killing.

So that got them back on the subject of why she'd been riding in such a hurry to as dull a town as Durango. She sighed and said it was a dull story. But he said he wanted to hear it anyway.

He was sorry he had by the time they finally made it to that east-west trail to find they'd beaten the infernal main party by way more than planned. For she'd been right about how tedious it was to hear, once again, how bored a young spinster gal could get, not getting any younger, at a remote Indian agency where kindly but correct elder white folks viewed all the single young gents for miles with less favor than Queen Victoria was said to view her Hindu guests at Buckingham Palace.

He told her all about that as they reined in under some fluttering trailside aspen to tether the barb in the dappled shade. For it was a more interesting tale than her story about a coming birthday. Everybody made it to twenty-five if they were lucky, and it sure sounded as if she'd saved up enough to make it to a school chum in Denver. But lots of folks who busted a gut trying to act like Queen Victoria seemed to think the poor old gal never ate grub or breathed air like more natural human folk.

So as he was unsaddling the barb while Nan watered it, he told her what this English tourist gal had related to him about a fancy supper Queen Victoria had invited lots of high-toned folk to.

It had been some time after Disraeli had proclaimed her the Empress of India. So she'd been a good sport and invited a bunch of those maharajas and their maharanis over for a good feed. But since some Hindu folks had sort of dark

97

complexions, a high-toned lady-in-waiting had declared that she for one would just as soon not sit at table with a bunch of niggers.

Nan said there were white ladies like that down at Red Wash in the Ute Strip, and asked how Queen Victoria dealt with such feelings at her court.

Longarm chuckled. "They say she told her ladies-in-waiting they could join her and her guests at table or go bloody hungry for a fortnight, because her subjects of the Hindu persuasion wouldn't be headed back to Hindustan for a couple of weeks."

Nan giggled and said Buckingham Palace didn't sound half as dull as Red Wash.

Meanwhile, Longarm couldn't see any movement at all to the damned east, even with his eyes shaded.

He decided, "The troopers have to wait on the herd, and I told you how old Hernan lost his best assistant sheepherder last night. The range seems to be getting drier as we trend westward too, and you know how stubborn all grazing stock can act about leaving the green pastures behind to traipse after Moses into the wilderness."

She said she thought the green pastures lay *beyond* the wilderness in the Good Book. He just as dryly pointed out how few if any sheep could quote chapter and verse that well.

He admired the skylark laugh she had. He admired her even more when she tossed her big sombrero on the flower-spangled grass all around and let her unbound ash-blond hair fall free before she just tossed herself after her hat to sprawl gracefully in the inviting shade, smiling up at him in a shyly inviting way.

When she yawned in a kittenish way and allowed she could surely do with forty cool winks after all that riding across that sunbaked range, Longarm knew she was inviting even more than she might have intended this time of the year in an aspen grove.

Bending over their grounded saddles he soberly warned, "Forty winks is one thing. Tick fever is another, and wood ticks go with aspen shade the way skeeters go with swamps."

He unlashed his own bedroll as he added, "Seeing you rode off in quest of adventure without any bedding, we'd

98

best spread mine atop that grass for you."

She dimpled up at him. "Why, Custis, whatever are you suggesting?"

There was no doubting the suggestive twinkle in her hazel eyes. But he still explained, in a desperately innocent voice, how a tired lady could lie atop the blankets with only the thin rain tarp over her so any bugs in the brush would have to really work at pestering her.

She sat up to smile at him sort of knowingly as he unrolled his bedding in the shade right next to her. Then she slipped right in, atop the blankets as he'd suggested, and proceeded to get undressed as she coyly asked how the two of them were ever going to fit in there side by side.

Longarm got back to his feet and reached for a cheroot as he studied on his answer. The pretty little thing smelled clean, and she'd already bitched that she hadn't been getting any at all recently.

It seemed obvious as hell she'd had enough at some stage in her young life to know what she was missing and to want some, a lot, right now.

Longarm muttered something about her getting some rest while he stood guard against Victorio or somebody, and turned his back to light his damned smoke and take a quick leak on the far side of some sticker brush. The brambles were in bloom, so it was too early to say what kind of berries they'd be offering in a month or more. He didn't want any damned berries. But considering one form of sweets he just couldn't get at was supposed to distract his old organ-grinder as he shook the dew off it and stuffed it back in his jeans.

He knew there was likely time, this surely was a swell place for some sweet slap and tickle, and the lady in question seemed to want what he wanted even more than he wanted it, and he wanted it a lot.

After that a man had to consider the awesome responsibilities of pronging an unattached young female who seemed stuck with a restless nature, a passionate body, and no carefully thought-out plans for the future.

Longarm looked in the mirror when he shaved, and so there were times he failed to see what all the fuss was about. But many a gal more worldly than young Nan Slade had carried on silly as hell when the time had come for him to get it on down the road. Longarm liked womankind too much to consider himself a love-'em-and-leave-'em sly dog. But his tumbleweed job and the thought of leaving a young widow precluded lingering romance. So he told them that, up front, and a heap of them seemed to understand this was only for the moment. Then the moment passed and they commenced to weep and wail and tear their hair as a poor boy was only trying to haul up his damned pants.

So he moseyed out on the sunlit trail lest that pretty little thing in the shade call out an open invitation no man could refuse, unless he stood ready to let a female call him a sissy. But the sun had made it clean past noon and the day was shaping up a real scorcher. So he finished his smoke, and was fixing to go back under the trees and take his chances when he spied a bitty mushroom of dust sprouting over a rise to the east and muttered, "It's about time."

It still seemed to take a million years, and it was even hot in the shade by the time Longarm made out a single rider in blue astride that tall bay thoroughbred. So he figured that newspaper gal had loaned her mount to a scout, if not a sweetheart. It seemed a tad more reasonable that Captain Granville had sent someone ahead to look for Longarm. Longarm hoped the asshole hadn't stayed put all this time waiting for him to get back.

Slipping off his light denim jacket, which was too damned much for this heat in any case, Longarm moved back out into the sunlight to wave the paler lining as a signal. Then he ducked back in under such shade as there still was, with the sun so high, and tossed the jacket and his sweaty hat aside, calling out to the gal stretched on the grass in his bedroll, "Company coming, ma'am. You may as well get dressed again so we can talk to the army about getting you on to Durango."

She seemed sort of pissed, despite his friendly tone, as she sat up in his bedroll, careless as hell about that top tarp. So she was sitting there bare-chested, just starting to shrug on her mannish shirt, when George or Grace Weatherford rode in, ducking her head under some low branches, and gasped, "Oh, Custis! I thought I'd find you alone in here!"

Longarm was hardly unaware of the irony of the dumb scene, and he was sort of enjoying it as he calmly replied, "Howdy, George. Miss Nancy Slade here had a sleepless night as well. But I see there wasn't as much time for her to rest up here as we figured."

By now the ash-blonde had covered her tits enough to matter, but Longarm was sure she was wriggling into her jeans so obviously to let another gal surmise she'd had them off under that tarp.

The newspaper gal smiled down at them both, colder than a well-digger's socks, and sweetly said she was charmed, she was sure. Then she hauled out the double derringer Longarm had given her the night before.

She didn't aim it at anybody. She told Longarm, "That nice old Señor Hernan has let me use poor Mauro's stock saddle, and as you see, the dead boy's saddle gun. So I won't be needing this toy anymore, Custis."

Longarm took it. The toylike belly gun had come in mighty handy on earlier occasions. As he picked up his jacket to put the gun back on his watch chain he answered amiably, "That Winchester Yellowboy is a handy weapon, and I'm glad to see you've switched to riding way more practical. Where'd you get those trim-fitting cavalry britches? They seem a mite small for Captain Granville, don't they?"

You had to admire a bawd who could stare you right in the eye as she demanded, "What are you talking about? That nice quartermaster sergeant found me an extra pair of army pants meant for a soldier about my size."

He put the jacket back on, but left his hat on the grass to cool some more as he smiled thinly and replied, "Well, they do say they select smaller recruits for the cav because light loads are easier on the horses. You'd know better than me how trim our gallant captain might be around the hips."

She flared her nostrils down at them both and spun her thoroughbred away as she snapped, "I'd better ride back and tell him what you've been up to all this time!"

Longarm couldn't resist calling after her, "We took plenty of time for breakfast earlier."

As the fancy-dressed brunette galloped off, the more roughly put-together blonde slid only partway out of his bedroll, with

101

some of her buttons yet to be fastened, as she thoughtfully smiled up at Longarm and demanded, "Do you really want that stuck-up priss to go on thinking what she's surely thinking about you and me?"

Longarm shrugged and said he didn't care. "That captain you just heard me mention tends to rile me too."

Nan said, "Oh? You mean you suspect this annoying officer is competing with you for that snooty brunette's favors?"

Longarm smiled thinly. "Nope. I know for a fact she likes him best. But that ain't why I don't like him. I mean that ain't the only reason."

She naturally wanted to hear more. But next to a kiss-and-tell, there was nobody Longarm had more contempt for than a grown man who mean-mouthed a gal for screwing somebody else. So he just told Nancy Slade she'd best finish dressing.

But he couldn't help feeling a mite tickled about that newspaper gal suspecting him of screwing another gal who was so pretty.

Chapter 10

By the time the head of that government column showed up, it was too hot to screw Helen of Troy if she'd been there stripped to the buff and begging for it.

Longarm thought he'd told Nan Slade what a pompous pain in the neck Captain Granville could be. Longarm saw he'd undershot the mark by yards when Granville took one look at the inviting but not so big patch of shade under the aspen and declared he and his headquarters staff would have their afternoon coffee in the trailside glade.

Why they had to haul their tarp-shaded spring wagons in there at the expense of not a few saplings eluded Longarm, although he'd long since learned there seemed to be three ways one might go about doing most anything—the right way, the wrong way, and the army way.

The army way was getting them cross-country about as fast as a cripple might make it without his crutches. Although Longarm had to take Granville's word when the gallant leader said those Mex Basques were having a tough time moving that herd short-handed.

Old George must have been off sulking someplace as Granville and his young adjutant compared notes with Longarm and Nan Slade just off the trail. When Longarm explained how the gal had lost her own pony and needed a remount to get her pretty self on in to Durango, Captain Granville smiled at the boyishly dressed but shapely ash-blonde in a way that reminded Longarm of some dirty growling in a wagon. Then he explained reluctantly, "We'd be only too happy to give you a lift to that trading post on the McElmo, Miss Slade. But I fear I'm just not authorized to issue you a government mount for *keeps*."

When Nan began to piss and moan about Durango being the other way entirely, Longarm cut in soothingly. "That trading post to the west would be days out of the lady's way at the rate we're moving, Captain. But what if she was to leave, say, a mule from the remuda at the livery in Durango till I got back there my own self along with Hernan and Ramon?"

Before he could even talk about forwarding that mule to the nearest army remount station, the captain said, "Why don't you or those Mexicans loan her a mount if you're feeling so generous?"

Nan snapped, "Are you calling me a horse thief, Captain?"

Before Granville had to answer, Longarm spoke up. "Fair is fair and the man has a point, Miss Nan. Every time *I* commandeer a cavalry mount the army writes it up in triplicate, and every time I fail to return that mount on or about their set date, they seem to hold them a general court-martial, if not a congressional investigation."

Nan sniffed, "I'm not known as a horse thief or even a big fibber in these parts, damn it!"

Granville smiled down at her and assured her she could borrow his watch and other personal belongings, as far as he was concerned. When she replied she didn't need a durned old watch half as much as she needed a *horse,* Longarm told her, "We got us some riding stock coming that the army don't own, Miss Nan, and it's too blamed hot for serious riding right now in any case."

The two officers crawfished off, muttering about coffee, to let Longarm have all the fun of calming Nan down and explaining. She'd gone all proddy and stayed that way as soon as Granville had made mention of that trading post on the McElmo. So even as Longarm was working out the way she could board a borrowed mount in Durango before boarding her train, he was drawing mental lines across the fuzzy mental map he had of the Four Corners country.

No white man had a really detailed overview of a vast and still partly unexplored expanse of mighty crumpled terrain. But knowing where most of the more prominent features stood in relation to one another, Longarm decided Nan's tale of riding north from Red Wash in a hurry made way more sense than her fleeing the McElmo canyonlands to the west did. He wasn't sure you could *get* clean around to the way she'd been coming from in any reasonable time if you started from where this trail swung perilously close to some considerable drops. So her distaste for riding a full day out of her way, at the pace of walking sheep, was likely no more than the natural impatience of a pretty gal with better things to do in the opposite direction. He knew he could ask, once they got to the McElmo, whether anyone as pretty had done anything wicked there. Since the trading post would still be just inside the Colorado line, it wouldn't be a federal worry if old Nan had emptied the till or worse.

An enlisted trooper came over to tell them they'd been invited to have coffee and cake with the captain. So they followed the kid through the ruined aspen glade to where, sure enough, old Granville and Grace Weatherford were sort of holding court, seated side by side in folding canvas camp chairs alongside that spring wagon with such squeaky springs.

The newspaper gal looked as if butter wouldn't melt in her mouth as enlisted orderlies rustled up less-imposing ammunition crates for Longarm and Nan to sit on. That might have seemed more fair had the newspaper gal still been wearing skirts. Longarm managed not to stare at the fly of the cavalry breeches she filled out in such a female way. A couple of junior officers joined them, sitting on the grass, as yet another pair of orderlies dealt out mess trays of shortbread and scones with tin cups of coffee. Nan said she understood when the captain explained they'd eaten their noon dinner earlier. So the captain added, "We don't normally travel at such a leisurely pace, but as you see, those infernal sheep haven't even made it as far as we have yet."

One of the shavetails muttered mockingly that he'd be over-aged in grade by the time they reached Fort Defiance, and used that as an excuse to turn to Nan and ask, "Does this right-angled march around Robin Hood's Barn make sense to a native of these parts such as yourself, Miss Slade?"

Nan shrugged and replied, "Deputy Long here tells me your aim is to escort that Navaho herd somewhere near that trading post run by the Hubbels before you report in to Fort Defiance, right?"

The second john nodded, but complained, "I've been study-ing my survey chart. Both that trading post in the center of the Navaho Reserve and our final destination lay almost due southwest out of Durango. So what I don't understand is what's preventing us from beelining cross-country at about a forty-five-degree angle?"

The rough-riding Nan exchanged glances with Longarm. It was her country. So he let her tell it. She said, "We call 'em the Chuska Mountains where they slope a lot, and the Defiance Plateau where the rimrocks loom level above the sage flats the Navaho farm and graze most. A Navaho could likely move a modest herd of sheep and goats as you suggest, if his Ute enemies let him. That mostly unmapped higher ground of which you speak is a maze of canyon passages, and all sorts of Indians have always wriggled through where none of us would even try to go."

Longarm chimed in. "Kit Carson had Utes who knew the canyonlands scouting for him that time. That's how come he managed to surprise Delgadito and Herrero Grande in Canyon de Chelly back in '64. They figured none of us dumb Belagana had ever heard of their secret hideouts in the unmapped Chuska Mountains, and they were right. Carson never would have caught up with 'em there if his Ute scouts hadn't been fighting those old boys a heap longer. Carson marching in on Canyon de Chelly so unexpected sort of took the heart out of them particular Na-Déné raiders. I reckon it would be sort of the way Abe Lincoln might have felt had he woke up one morn-ing to find old Robert E. Lee in bed with him at the White House."

Everyone there had to chuckle at the picture. Despite her barely hidden contempt for Nan Slade and any man who'd kiss her, there was enough Reporter George in the real Grace Weatherford for her to paste an uncertain smile across her pretty face and ask Longarm, "Could you tell me why the Navaho use so much Spanish if they speak this mysterious Na-Whatever, Custis?"

Longarm nodded easily. "Call it common courtesy, rude as some of 'em sometimes act toward the rest of us, red or white. I think I told you before how unrelated the Na-Déné, Apache, Navaho, or whatever are to all the other folks in these parts. Before us English-speaking folks got here, less than thirty-five years back, Spanish-speaking missionaries, traders, slave raiders, and such had been teaching their own lingo as a sort of trade jargon for more than two hundred years. Whether the Indians *liked* the folk they called *nakaih* or not, the Spanish baby talk they all knew beat trying to learn Tanoan, Hopi, Ute, or whatever every time you wanted to court a gal or trade with somebody too tough to fight. Translating your Indian name into Spanish serves two purposes to their way of thinking. It tells your enemy more about you than if you just made sounds he didn't savvy, and after that, it gets you out of telling anyone your true spirit name."

Another junior officer, doubtless anxious to show off, declared he'd read about that in Custer's Field Instructions on Horse Indians. Longarm felt no need to jump in as he pontificated, "Indians aren't named the way more advanced folks are. When an Indian's born his parents name him the way you'd name a pet, just to have something to call him. Once he's big enough to play with other kids, he gets another name, regardless of his parents' wishes."

Longarm couldn't resist asking dryly, "You mean them savages give one another *nicknames*?"

The shavetail seemed oblivious to the amused expressions of both ladies present as he gushed on. "You might call it that. Custer wrote that once a warrior proves himself by counting coup in battle, they give him a more formal name, whether it sounds like a nickname to us or not. But meanwhile, somewhere along the line in some dream or secret inspiration, our Indian finds a *secret* name, known only to himself and his totems, or spirits."

The newspaper gal had set aside her tray and cup to rummage out a pencil and notepad. When she shot Longarm a questioning look, he nodded and silently mouthed, "Close enough."

She jotted in shorthand, then said aloud, "I didn't know the late General Custer was still considered an authority on Indians."

Granville said, "Lieutenant colonel, ma'am. That was his permanent rank. He was breveted or made a temporary major general during the war."

She looked so confounded now that Longarm felt obliged to horn in. "They did things like that during wartime, ma'am. Going by some who served with him, he rated his brevet promotion at a time old Abe was having a time finding generals who wanted to fight. Old George Custer was what you might call a fighting fool, and I've read some of his writings on Indian fighting. I find his views sort of interesting, in view of what happened to him the summer of '76."

"You mean he knew what he was doing?" she asked uncertainly.

Longarm didn't sound any more certain as he calmly replied, "I wasn't there. But ain't it funny how folks who profess to admire the Noble Savage prefer to call Custer a blithering idiot, as if there could be no other explanation for one squadron of the Seventh Cav getting licked fair and square by superior numbers?"

"Well put, sir!" gasped Captain Granville, staring wide-eyed at a damn civilian willing to give the army an even shake. It didn't make Longarm respect him a lick more. Custer had been out on point for Terry, who never seemed to get blamed for *putting* him there, and by definition one side or the other comes out on top in every battle. Granville was in full command here, and acting sort of dumb without help from higher up the chain of command.

Having finished his cake, and not really wanting to rehash the Battle of Little Bighorn again, Longarm finished his coffee, said something about slowpoke sheepherders, and rose to amble back to the trail. Nan came with him. The afternoon glare made it feel as if he'd opened the fire door of a steam furnace, but sure enough, wavering in the heat waves atop the next rise to the east, came the bellwether goat and old Hernan with the head of that long slow fuzzy caterpillar.

Longarm and Nan waited as the old Basque took his time. In fairness to the captain hogging the shade behind them, Longarm had to admit a man, a boy, and two dogs really took time to get fifteen hundred head of stock an infernally short distance.

The army riders who'd been trailing behind the herd, upon seeing there was a trail break ahead, piled off atop that other rise to catch such breeze as there might be while Hernan and

Ramon spread the herd to graze as they drifted them down into the wide weedy draw.

An army rider loped on in to report to the captain. Longarm was too polite to do more than point at the nearby trees. The other riders were of course spread out along the sunnier slopes to rest their mounts and sunbathe at the same time.

When Longarm saw Ramon moving the mounted remuda to the east-facing and hence slightly shadier slope, he told Nan to stay put, and moved down afoot to see about that mount she needed.

Hernan asked if he'd killed any of the *ladrones* who'd murdered poor Mauro. Longarm was sorry he hadn't lied when, once they moved on to a lady's problems in the here and now, the old Basque seemed to think he was *loco en la cabeza*.

"For why should I trust a *mujer* I do not know with a *caballo*?" demanded the dusty old man, ignoring the approaching Nan Slade, but switching to Spanish as he added, "For that matter, why should you trust her? Have any of us ever seen her before? How do you know she was not riding with that bunch who ambushed us last night?"

Longarm said, "I'm pretty sure they were all men. She says she was riding the other way, from the Ute Strip. Even if she's lying, why would a woman, alone, split off from a big gang and head back to meet up with the law?"

Hernan said, "Maybe she did not know you were following them so close. Maybe she was simply looking for *el rapto supremo*, eh?"

By this time Nan had come down the slope far enough to smile sweetly up at the mounted Basque and say, *"Estas lleno de mierda, viejo!"*

So all three of them laughed. But even though he was a good sport about being told he was full of shit, old Hernan commenced to give her a real argument instead of the one damned mount she really needed.

So Longarm said, "Hold on, both of you. I got another way to skin this cat."

Pointing along the slope at the remuda Ramon was watching closer than the sheep or even goats, Longarm told Nan, "See that big blue roan nibbling that rabbitbrush? He ought to carry

109

you into Durango with no trouble and a heap faster than he got this far west."

She nodded soberly and said, "Now that's a nice-looking horse, Custis. What do you want for him?"

He said, "He ain't for sale. They know him, and me, at the livery near the rail yards. If you leave him there when you buy that train ticket to Denver, he'll doubtless be there when and if I ever get my fool self back from Dinetah."

She stared up at him in wonder. "What will you do if he's not, Custis?"

To which Longarm could only reply soberly, "I'll have to allow I misjudged you. In the meantime I ain't caught you lying or stealing yet, and you just said you didn't want to ride any further west with us."

Nan hesitated and said, "I'm almost tempted. This old Vasco may have had a point as to why I just left home for good. But then I'd only be in the way of that fancy brunette, right?"

Longarm laughed incredulously and said, "Lord love you, come on along if you're feeling horny! For there's nothing like that going on betwixt me and that newspaper gal, Miss Nan."

She said, "Really? Nothing at all? Another woman can usually tell and you could have fooled *me*. But alas, I've still got that train to catch and . . ."

"Go on back to where you left your saddle and bridle," Longarm told her. "No sense the both of us risking sunstroke. I'll just borrow a throw rope and lead him on over. If I were you I'd let him cool some too, and head for Durango around four or so to get in most of your riding during the cool shade of evening."

She stood on tiptoe to impulsively kiss him before she scampered off, laughing like a mean little kid.

As he turned to old Hernan, the Basque said, "I was listening. Go after her, *pendejo*, and cool your overheated head. Let me worry about that fine *caballo* you are never going to see again."

Longarm said, "Look, we don't want to drag her kicking and screaming the way she just don't want to go, do we?"

Hernan shrugged. "It might be more fun than losing a valuable mount to a stranger. Are you sure you did not get

110

any of that, El Brazo Largo? It seems to me you are willing to do more than most men would for someone who means nothing to them."

Longarm started to ask what that poor cuss in the Good Book had meant to the Good Samaritan. But he never did. The old Basque had a cross hanging from his neck, and likely argued religion far slicker than a country boy from West-by-God-Virginia.

Chapter 11

Folks who hadn't spent much time under the sunny skies preferred by Spanish-speaking folk tended to dismiss *la siesta* as yet another lazy greaser notion. Longarm had learned to go along with *la siesta* on sunbaked range, in the summertime leastways. For the Anglo ways of dividing up a workday weren't the only ways a workday could be divided, and it seemed just plain dumb to do much of anything under a Four Corners summer sun when it was over a hundred degrees in the shade.

It didn't matter whether Captain Granville had adapted to local customs or figured some things out for his lazy self, as long as he declared they'd be moving on around four that afternoon in hopes of making up the lost time by moonlight.

But Nancy Slade refused to wait past three, insisting the sun would be at her back by then and not a whole lot cooler whether she lost another few hours or not.

So Longarm helped her cinch her own saddle on his big blue roan, but made her refill all her canteens from an army water bag, whether she was right about all those water holes she knew between there and Durango or not. It was true water weighed eight pounds a gallon, but the blue roan was a big old brute, and one water hole dried earlier than a traveler might have planned had made many a traveler wish he or she had packed along an extra hundred pounds or so.

When she shyly asked what that livery in Durango was likely to ask when she dropped the roan off in town, Longarm tore a leaf out of his notebook, licked the tip of an indelible pencil he packed for more official matters, and block-printed clear instructions for the owners of the livery to wire the Lazy B their horse was on its way home and then send Old Blue by rail, charged to the Denver District Court in his own name and badge number.

When the boyishly decked-out blonde asked whether he might not be sticking his neck out for her, Longarm shrugged and said, "They allow me travel expenses, and shipping this mount on home ought to save us way more than it would cost to board him Lord knows how long in any livery. There has to be a quicker way to move this outfit all the way to Dinetah. But at twice the pace we've been setting it could be a month or more before I made her back to Durango, and once I do, what would I need this fool roan for?"

She agreed that train they both meant to take on over the Divide to Denver had horseback beat by at least two weeks. So they shook on it, and would have parted that way if she hadn't suddenly blubbered up and buried her head in his chest. "God bless you, Custis Long. You're the only man I've met since I've had tits who seemed willing to do this much for me without *grabbing* my tits!"

He patted her back and said, "Aw, mush, don't go making me out some kind of saint or sissy, honey. I'd be proud to grab your tits for you under less trying conditions. But there's times a lady needs a grabbing and there's times she just needs a boost aboard her saddle."

She kissed him instead. Then he had her mounted up, and gave the blue roan a slap on its big rump to send it on its way before it tried to kiss him too.

Nan rode off, likely out of his life, not looking back. Longarm watched from the edge of the aspen grove, then turned to go find more shade.

That was when he saw Grace Weatherford staring at him hidden by brush from the waist up between two pale aspen trunks. She'd likely been in that waist-high scrub cedar with her army britches down. He didn't ask what she was doing there. The brunette's face was sort of pale in the dappled shade as she licked her lips and said, "Oh, Custis, can you ever forgive me for misjudging you? All this time you were simply being a gentleman and I thought . . ."

He felt his ears burning as he could only reply, "Watch out

113

who you call a sissy. At least you never caught me eavesdropping."

She protested. "I wasn't trying to overhear your conversation with that other woman. Sometimes things just happen, ah, naturally."

He managed not to grin as he nodded and told her, "You just go on and act natural there, ma'am. I got other chores to tend."

He didn't ask why she was blushing so red as he turned away from her. They both knew. Folks who aped the stiff manners of old Queen Victoria had their work cut out for them in a world where plumbing was still an inexact science. But it was easy enough to pretend no properly brought-up folk ever had to shit, as long as nobody ever mentioned the possibility or asked what anyone was headed into the bushes for.

When he asked a trooper, he was told Captain Granville was in his headquarters ambulance and didn't want to be disturbed. He'd met gals who didn't want to use the chamber pot under the bunk in broad daylight as well. It was funny how some gals who begged for it dog-style liked to pretend they had no assholes.

He was watering his black barb, over by Hernan's remuda on the shady although exposed eastern edge of the glade, when the old Basque caught up with him there to confide, "Is impossible for to herd so many head any faster with only one *ayudante,* even if those *ladrones* had murdered Ramon instead of Mauro."

Longarm dryly replied, "I noticed. Ramon can ride the far flank from you to keep the critters lined up along the trail or he can bring up the rear with all this riding stock. He can't do both. If you're asking me to volunteer for some sheepherding, I'd be willing to try anything, as the old maid said when she took her broomstick to bed, but they want me out on point, scouting for such bullshit as we ran into last night."

Hernan nodded and said, "Ramon can ride flank better than I could teach any *novicio* between here and those Apache de Nabajú. But what must any *caballero Anglo* be taught about riding drag while managing this remuda for me, eh?"

Longarm said he'd ask the captain about that, adding he didn't think many cavalry troopers were likely to volunteer

114

for riding drag behind fifteen hundred head of anything.

He was right. When Captain Granville came out of his wagon a good spell later, Longarm had to explain it twice before the pouty-looking officer seemed to grasp his intent. But once Granville saw it might mean moving at least as fast as lovers might stroll, it was a good thing nobody in the army got to talk back. The captain told his adjutant to see to it. The adjutant told a platoon leader to see to it. So the shavetail told a sergeant and it got seen to. A corporal and his eight-man squad were told to report to Hernan for further instructions, and when the corporal sullenly asked if he was supposed to take orders from a greaser, he was told he'd take orders from a Chinaman, in Chinese, if the captain wanted him to and he still wanted his damn stripes.

Longarm borrowed a cordovan mare from Hernan to rest his jaded black barb, but sat his fresh mount on the ridge a spell as the outfit moved on, around four-thirty, to see how things might be going behind him before he rode out on point some more.

Fifteen hundred head of sheep and goats sure took a while getting over a rise in a column of fours with Hernan, Ramon, and their sheepdogs moving up and down on either flank to keep them out of all that tempting shade.

Most of the thirty-odd-man third platoon hung well back to let the trail dust settle some between themselves and the woolly asses of the last trotting sheep. That corporal's squad riding drag were perforce required to stay close enough to herd stragglers ahead of them as they led the eighteen ponies, pack and spare, of the remuda.

All nine drag riders had naturally covered their faces below their squinted eyes with their faded yellow cavalry bandanas. Their gray hats and summer blues were already so dusty they seemed about the same shade of nothing much. One of the men was cussing fit to bust in German. You couldn't tell who, and Longarm didn't savvy much of that lingo. But he could follow the unhappy trooper's drift. For he'd been stuck with riding drag when first he'd come West after the war.

It was a chore that needed to be done. But a chore that sent many a kid home to Mamma after he'd run off out West to become a cowboy—and riding drag behind cows was *nicer*.

A big herd of anything dropped tons of shit in fine dry dust, and churned it all up to rising fumes and drifting-down dust for a drag rider to enjoy, whether the afternoon sun and western breezes were in his face or not. So Longarm could see why that old boy kept calling out *"Zum Teufel!" "Schafscheisse!"* sounded enough like sheep shit for Longarm to get the drift.

He chuckled and wheeled his mount to cut through the aspens well clear of the herd. He could still smell it, deep in the leafy shade. So he could feel for the poor kids riding drag, but what the hell, they'd joined up to savor the American Wild West, right?

A poorly kept secret of the U.S. Army at the moment was how few U.S. citizens it managed to enlist in peacetime. With a ranch hand making at least a dollar a day, and a mining man making three times that much, it was tough to convince any semi-literate native-born American he'd be better off fighting Indians or painting rocks white at thirteen dollars a month, which was really a pissy ten dollars in base pay, with an additional three dollars' uniform allowance you were supposed to spend on passing inspection without your ass hanging out.

So save for career officers and a few senior noncoms, most of the American-born soldiers blue were "Buffalo Soldiers" in colored outfits such as the 4th or 10th Cavalries. Most of the white enlisted men who'd died with Fetterman or Custer had been immigrants recruited on the docks as they'd gotten off the boats with neither a grubstake nor a better job to go to. Trooper Martin, the last white man who'd ever seen Custer alive, had been an Italian greenhorn, born Giovanni Martini, whose English had been so suspect that they'd garbled the message he'd carried through the Indians from Custer, even though the brave greenhorn had had it right.

Bursting back out in the sunlight, Longarm rode west through low chaparral well clear of the column till he passed the forward guidon, fluttering red and more salmon than white in the late afternoon sun, and swung over to hit the trail a couple of furlongs ahead of the rest of the outfit.

The sun was still hot as it glowered redly in his eyes from above the purple skyline to the west. The sky above was a cloudless Dutch-tile blue at this hour and altitude. He figured they had four to six hours of visibility ahead of them. It took

116

more clouds than they had to work with to fashion much of a sunset or add up to much gloaming after the sun was all the way down. But with any luck the moon would be up by the time it got too dark for even the horses to make out a trail this clear.

It made more sense, riding at a low sun, to gaze off across the rolling range in other directions where you could at least see what lay out yonder amid the sage, cheat, and wildflowers.

There seemed a bit fewer of the latter now. Spring flowers who knew Changing Woman's fickle ways in these parts had long ago learned to sprout from mummified seeds, grow fast, blossom, and go to seed in the time they might have between wet spells. But the tougher blooms such as tar weed and prickly poppy were still grinning up at him from either side of the trail, and the bumblebees and hover flies were out buzzing again as the afternoon began to cool down to just plain hot.

A roadrunner broke cover to run along the trail just out ahead of Longarm, glancing back at him from time to time over where its fool shoulder would have been if overgrown cuckoo birds had shoulders.

Longarm didn't care. He'd met roadrunners before, and knew why the gawky chicken-sized critter was acting that way. A roadrunner didn't run down the road ahead of a team or a rider because it was out to play some taunting game of tag. Before humankind and its own stock had come along, the roadrunner had likely scampered along ahead of deer, antelope, or those impossible critters the professors kept digging up out this way. For the roadrunner's real game was to run along on its light tippy-toes to spot the smaller and more shy critters that big old heavy stompers seldom noticed.

It was early for snakes, lizards, and such to be moving about. Mice and voles never moved at all when it was light out, if they felt they didn't have to. But when that roadrunner up ahead suddenly darted into some soap weed, to emerge a hundred yards on with something wildly wriggling in its daggerlike bill, Longarm knew at least one night-creeping critter had mistaken the hoofbeats under him for the real danger out this way.

Longarm was sitting his borrowed cordovan at a brisk walk.

117

So when he heard trotting hoofbeats overtaking him, he turned in the saddle instead of dashing off to get eaten by a road-runner.

It was that newspaper gal, astride with Mauro's Yellowboy across her thighs as if she was scouting for Cheyenne. So Longarm had no call to rein in, and sure enough, she caught up in no time and reined to a walk beside him, panting, "I didn't know you were out this way until I spied you from that rise a quarter mile back. What are we looking for this evening, Custis?"

Longarm almost smiled before he recalled some panting and groaning wagon springs and growled, "*We* ain't looking for anything. If *I* don't ride into more trouble this side of that trading post near the rim of McElmo Canyon, we ought to make her there sometime before midnight, if we can keep your gallant captain moving at this pace."

She said she'd suggest the same to old Granville.

He said, "Do that. It might help, coming from you. Naturally, we all want to stop for supper around Snake Time, which only runs about an hour after sundown at this altitude this time of the year. So by the time Changing Woman sends her little diamondback mousers back to their dens for the night, the moon should be up and—"

"Who on earth is Changing Woman?" the nosey newspaper gal asked.

Longarm smiled sheepishly. "I try to think like the nation I'm scouting when I'm scouting any Indians, and the ones we're delivering that herd to have a nice old haunt they call Istsa Natlehi, meaning Changing Woman. The Apache nations further south know her as White Painted Woman. But she seems a good old gal in any case. Lots of other Indian haunts demand presents and still play mean tricks on mortals from time to time. But Changing Woman asks nothing and gives everything, albeit all in her own good time."

Grace asked, "You mean she's supposed to be some sort of nature goddess? Why do they call her Changing Woman?"

He made a sweeping gesture with his free hand and replied, "Look around you. A day or so ago this range was a flower-spangled kelly green. Right now it's already going to straw in patches, and in no time at all a stranger passing through

118

would swear it had never rained out this way for many a year. The Navaho hold that Changing Woman made all life spring into being from nothing, changing it as she saw fit to suit her mysterious pattern for the web of nature. So we've got to go along with the simple fact that nothing alive can be the same as it was a day ago or a day ahead. Istsa Natlehi and her constant changes are the only hope of this world. For once all changes stop the world and everything in it will be dead, the way all of us get the day we stop changing, see?"

Grace repressed a shudder and declared, "I'm not sure I share the enthusiasm you seem to feel for this Indian goddess. Is she supposed to be pretty?"

Longarm could only shrug. "Depends on how she's feeling at the moment, I reckon. The Indians say she's a smiling young maiden in the greenup time, a nurturing motherly figure at harvest time, or a hungry old hag in times of want or fever. I reckon she's a lot like Mark Twain said New England weather was. Whenever you just can't stand it, you only have to wait a few minutes."

The pretty brunette laughed. He liked the way she laughed, damn it. He'd doubtless enjoy the way she moaned and groaned if only that had been his own dong moaning and groaning her like that.

The memory reminded him of less alluring Indian haunts, and since he didn't want to picture female images of any kind he looked away and said, "They believe in Old Man Coyote, the same as other nations, and tell droll tales of Begochidi, a trickster haunt who makes Old Man Coyote look sort of stuffy."

She asked how to translate Begochidi into English for her newspaper readers. He said, "They'd never allow you to print that, ma'am."

She blinked, laughed, and insisted, "Oh, come on, you can tell *me,* can't you?"

He smiled thinly, but resisted the impulse. He knew for a fact that Queen Victoria and Lemonade Lucy Hayes, the First Lady back in Washington, had been screwed enough to moan and groan in their younger days. But that didn't mean a man who'd never screwed either had any right to talk dirty to them. So he told the expectant newspaper gal she'd have to take his word that Begochidi meant something downright sassy in Na-Déné.

She naturally insisted, adding, "I'm not exactly the blushing schoolgirl you seem to be taking me for, Custis."

To which he could only reply, staring off across the sage flat they were crossing now, "I never said you were. I ain't *that* dumb. Let's say Begochidi creeps about invisibly till he spies some Indian in an indelicate or mayhaps anxious pose. Picture a young gal bent over her laundry, or an anxious hunter drawing a bead on an elk at barely possible range. That's when Begochidi suddenly grabs them from behind indelicately and yells *Bego! Bego! Bego!* inside their skulls."

He had to chuckle at the picture too as he quietly added, "I've been assured a shock like that could unsettle a body for quite some time."

Grace marveled, "It certainly would unsettle *me*! You're saying *Bego, Bego* means somethings like gotcha?"

He said that was close enough. He felt no call to go into that other favorite stunt of Begochidi. A gal might think him sort of queer-headed if he told her how Begochidi liked to sneak up behind a bare-assed buck screwing away at another man's woman so he could grab him by the balls and screw him in the ass to make him yell and give himself away. But when she demanded more details for her readers Longarm said, "Well, they say that should a Navaho gal act the wallflower at a corn harvest dance, old Begochidi will grab her from behind to make her squeal and start dancing like anything, all red-faced and covering up with her crossed arms."

"Oh? Then Begochidi means something like titty grabber?" the cool-looking brunette demanded mighty coolly.

Longarm said tits were close enough, and growled, "You'd best rein in and wait for the others here, ma'am. We both know what happened the last time we rode up a wooded rise around this time of the day, and there's high chaparral along the crest ahead."

She asked, "Couldn't you sort of scout those bushes and wave me on to rejoin you if it's safe?"

He shrugged. "I could. I don't want to. When a man rides on ahead alone, it generally means he'd like to be alone."

She didn't rein in. Keeping her thoroughbred abreast of his

less-imposing mount, she demanded, "What have I done to make you so cool to me, Custis? I know it's me you're annoyed with. You were almost lovey-dovey with that shabby blonde back there, and you even profess to admire Indian earth mothers!"

He resisted that temptation as well. Life was too short to waste any of it listening to two-faced females, and he'd fibbed some his own self about slap and tickle he hadn't seen as another gal's damn beeswax.

He assured himself she had as much right as anyone to relieve that old itch with anyone handy, whether that pouty pretty-boy with captain's bars was his cup of tea or not. For Lord only knows what a certain widow woman back in Denver would have said or done to him if she'd known for certain about him and that China doll from that chop-suey joint on Curtis Street. So he just heeled his cordovan into an uphill lope in hopes this other temptation would take the hint.

She didn't, and mounted on a thoroughbred, she'd be able to keep up with him, he knew, no matter what he did this side of silly.

Nobody lay in ambush amid the dwarf cedar and soap weed atop the rise. So they reined in to admire the view ahead.

The low sun made golden bangles of the springwater ponds that still survived amid acres of green sedge grass spread across the flats ahead. When Grace clapped her hands and said, "Oh, it's so beautiful, Custis!" Longarm grumbled, "Yep. Why don't you ride back and tell your gallant captain we've found more water and grazing than we'll ever need for a supper break."

She shot him an odd look and demanded, "Why do you keep calling Captain Granville *my* gallant anything, Custis? Surely you don't think there's anything going on between me and that . . . sort of silly man?"

Longarm hadn't been brought up to call a lady a liar if he didn't have to, whether she was a lady or not. So he simply shrugged and declared, "Ain't none of my beeswax how silly anybody else might get. If you don't aim to tell 'em I reckon I'd better."

But naturally, she tagged along like an infernal kid sister on a thoroughbred when Longarm loped his slower pony back

121

the other way. So his only consolation was that she couldn't bend a man's ear at full gallop.

That gave him time to think about both her faces in more privacy. He'd gone back to his widow woman up on Capitol Hill more than once after a fling with something else, sometimes something not as pretty, who'd somehow aroused his curious cock.

Fair was fair, and doubtless cunts had as great a right to feel curious as cocks did. He'd heard of females experimenting even wilder than men might dare with objects animal, vegetable, or mineral that might just serve to relieve that old devil itch, and it wasn't as if Captain Granville was deformed, or even downright repulsive—to a gal, at any rate.

So how come the gal seemed to be trying to butter *him* up right now instead? He knew she was. He'd studied the unfair sex enough to know that whenever a poor innocent cuss got around to wondering how much a pretty gal might like him, she'd generally planted the notion in his fool head herself.

It was true a total asshole could convince his fool self a gal who found him pathetic was madly in love with him. But when a grown man who'd written a gal off as unavailable found himself wondering whether she was available, she was letting him know she was available.

But Longarm just kept loping. For whether the pretty little thing had decided to change her luck or not, she was the sort of woman men fought over, and damn it, whether he could whip Granville's ass or not in a fair fight, the pudgy bastard had a whole troop of the U.S. Cav to back his play.

Chapter 12

A whole troop of cavalry consumed an awesome amount of water, even when it didn't have fifteen hundred extra head of stock in tow. So more than one of those golden spangles got turned into a mere mud puddle by the time the outfit had refilled all canteens and water bags and watered all that thirsty stock.

Longarm had expected Granville to declare a supper break on the slightly higher near slope of the wide well-watered draw. But when he saw the enlisted men pitching their tents as if for an overnight bivouac he went hunting for the captain to ask why.

He found Granville seated in that same folding chair near his fancy spring wagon, smoking a fancy cigar as he waited for his supper to be served. Grace Weatherford didn't seem to be using the other chair nearby, so Longarm sat down and reached for a less impressive smoke as he said, "I figure we can't be more than eight or ten miles from that McElmo trading post, Captain. If we were to forge on after giving the moon time to rise and the snakes to settle down..."

"We'd never make it before midnight," Granville said. "I've been going over our government survey charts as well, and they show more than one narrow side canyon twisting across what a fool might take for gently rolling to dead flat range this side of that really nasty drop just north of that trading post."

Longarm insisted, "I know all about the sneaky sidewindings of the Four Corners canyonlands, Captain. I've been out this way before. Meanwhile the *trail* we've followed all this way out of Durango has been surveyed by the same gov-

123

ernment and figures to be well lit by the waxing moon this evening. I've hardly ever followed a trail laid out by white men straight off a cliff, have you?"

Granville answered dryly, "Not so far, and I don't intend to start. The weather hasn't heated up enough to make riding after dark in uncertain surroundings worth the risk. Thanks to your suggestion about detailing some of my men to herding sheep, we've been moving a a lot faster. But I mean to go on playing it safe, and anyhow, what difference does it make if we get as far as that trading post tonight or early enough tomorrow? There's nothing we're likely to need at an out-of-the-way trading post in the business of swapping red ribbons and such for Indian . . . baskets?"

Longarm said, "The Ute trade more in horses and hides than anything else. I understand more whites than Indians save themselves a ride into Durango or up toward Cortez by shopping at McElmo, and naturally, it's the only post office for a hard day's ride in any direction. What I'm sort of anxious to shop for there is information. Next to small-town barbershops, there ain't nothing like a trailside trading post to catch up on all the gossip for miles around."

He lit his cheroot before explaining. "Folks ride in from miles all around to set a spell before riding on. I don't know about you, but I'm sort of curious about those jaspers who shot Mauro and tried for me by name."

Granville asked whether Longarm really expected anyone at the trading post up ahead to tell him what they knew, if they knew anything.

Longarm blew a thoughtful purple smoke ring in the fading light of the golden gloaming. "I'm a lawman. I'm used to asking sneaky questions. If those drygulchers weren't directly off that local spread they mentioned, they might still be known as wild-ass bullies off some other. Old boys don't suddenly take a grand notion to ride all over their home range like a pack of mad dogs. You ask around, say, Clay County, Missouri, and everyone will tell you the James, Younger, and Miller boys were a mess of wild young assholes before they ever got up the nerve to aim serious at anyone."

He savored another drag on his cheroot. "Those assholes aimed serious as hell at Mauro less than a hard day's ride from here. I've already been assured by one local rider, that blond gal Nancy, that the Flying W outfit they mentioned belongs to a well-known old widow woman with a decent local rep. I'd feel better about that if I heard somebody else say the same about that outfit."

Granville cocked a brow and removed the cigar from his pink wet lips to whistle softly and ask if Longarm suspected that strange gal from the Ute Strip of serious lying.

Longarm shrugged and looked the officer in the eye. "Women have lied to me in the past, and I don't doubt a few will lie to me some more before I'm done. Nancy Slade's story works good enough, until and unless I get someone to tell me another that works better. You're sure you and your boys don't have just a few more country miles left in you after supper, Captain?"

Granville shook his head, but said, "You can ride on ahead for all I care. Eight miles is less than a full hour at any kind of a lope. It would take us more than two hours on the damned trail after we managed to break camp and get started again after, say, nine."

Fair was fair. So Longarm sighed and decided, "Might take even longer for the ground to get too cool for snake bellies, after a day like we just had. You'd still get there before midnight."

"To what avail?" Granville demanded, sticking the cigar back in his moist mouth. "Why on earth would they be waiting up for us that late at even an army post? Have they been informed we were coming?"

It was a good question. Longarm got to his feet, saying, "You got a point there, Captain. Might be interesting at that if I was to ride on ahead and surprise anyone scouting this outfit. The bastards who killed Mauro might still think it was me they killed."

Not wanting to ride into anything half so uncertain on an empty gut, Longarm said he meant to put away some grub and plenty of coffee before he borrowed a fresh mount. Then he went scouting for Hernan to see if the old Basque had such a critter to lend a pal.

He found Hernan and young Ramon boiling there own grub down-slope from the far bigger army mess detail. Hernan said to go on and pick any *caballo* he fancied, as long as meant to ride it no farther than, say, the mail stop at Vado.

When the old herder explained sort of sullenly that he and Ramon were hardly of a mind to go much farther than Vado, Longarm consulted his mental picture of the canyonlands ahead and shot back, *"Por que, viejo?* You agreed to herd all that stock clean down to the middle of Dinetah, and unless I'm lost you're talking about that wide spot in the trail where the trail meets the San Juan, just inside Utah Territory and way the hell this side of where they want us to deliver that stock!"

Hernan said stubbornly, "Is far enough for us to travel with *cabrones rudo* who despise us and threaten to screw our sheep!"

Longarm sighed and muttered, *"Ay, mierditas!* Are we talking about that Arkansas corporal or an Alamano *pendejo* who doesn't talk any more like an Anglo than you?"

Hernan said, "All of them. They do not seem to like anything about us, our stock, or our country. So, at Vado, you should have no trouble finding Navaho herders willing to go on with you, and perhaps they will not understand English as well as Ramon and myself."

Longarm suggested, "I'll have a word with the first sergeant. I ain't sure what we might or might not find along the north fringes of Dinetah, *viejo.*"

Hernan insisted, "You ought to be able to find Navaho, and are not those sheep and goats intended for Los Apaches de Nabajú? Do not worry. We shall remain with the herd, if not the *soldados pendejo,* until such time as you can find someone else for them to treat with so much *falta de respeto!*"

Longarm could see the older man was too pissed to talk sense to at the moment, and *mañana* would be not only another day but at least two days short of any showdown either way at Vado. So he moseyed back up the slope to see if supper was being served, and maybe kill another bird with an after-supper smoke with that first sergeant.

Supper was bully-beef and fried spuds. Army coffee was always strong but dreadful. He forced down enough extra for night riding, and asked about their first sergeant till he caught up with him, sharing some suspicious-smelling coffee with their troop clerk as they perched like big-ass birds on a wagon tongue a ways off from the greenhorns who didn't rate any after-supper sour mash.

Longarm offered them both smokes to get things started. Once he had the first sergeant on the subject of the next day's march, he said they'd doubtless do better if only some of the boys would leave off hazing those surviving sheepherders.

He explained, "They're in mourning to begin with, and Basques instead of regular Mexicans after that. Basques are a sort of proud and proddy breed from the highlands in the north of Spain. Get a Basque really pissed and he's inclined to make an Irish drunk in an English whorehouse sound polite. We wouldn't want anyone riding with us on a detour to Fist City now, would we?"

The first sergeant smiled up owlishly. "Why not? I'll put my money on old Arkansas Brown against any damn greaser born of mortal woman or, shit, sheep!"

Longarm saw they'd both been drinking more and longer than he'd thought. But at least he knew where the trouble was coming from now. He'd have felt better if it had been that German trooper. A noncom on good terms with his first sergeant could be another fish to fry.

He let the stupid bastards keep the cheroots anyway, and cut back through the bivouac to do it the dirty way, by going over a few heads. He'd hated it, in his own army days, when some shit had gone direct to the officers instead of just telling him he'd screwed up again.

By this time the sun had finished setting and the stars were winking on above him in a deep purple sky. But he still thought it seemed awesomely early when another sergeant he asked said Captain Granville had already turned in.

There was no way even a lazy bastard could have fallen sound asleep that early, and that shit about hazing Hernan and Ramon had to be nipped in the bud. So Longarm strode on to Granville's damned spring wagon. Son of a bitch if they weren't going at it again in there, without waiting for the rest of the outfit to quiet down for the night!

So Longarm never disturbed the horny troop commander as he stood there in the gloom just long enough to hear Granville moaning, "Oh, yess! Suck my nuts dry and swallow every drop of it, baby!"

Longarm strode away scowling as he muttered, "Aw, shit
I never meant to French-kiss her in any case, knowing I'd be
going sloppy seconds to that wet-mouthed slob!"

Then he singled out a chestnut gelding with a blaze and
matched stockings, and saddled up and rode before he wound
up threatening anyone with bodily harm.

He was still pissed, more at himself for feeling so pissed
about a flirt he'd never really fooled with, when he spot
ted lamplight out ahead after a forty-minute lope along the
starlit trail.

Naturally, at least a half-dozen cur dogs commenced to
bark at him before anyone inside could hear his approaching
hoofbeats. So there was no call to fire a warning shot as
he just rode on in like he owned the trading post near the
McElmo Rim.

A front door opened before he reined in to dismount in
their dooryard and lead his mount closer, calling out, "Howdy
Sorry to disturb you so late, but you know how it is on a
strange trail."

The old jasper lounging in the doorway with a friendly smile
and a Greener Ten Gauge replied, "I sure do. Only been out
this way a couple of summers myself. Name's Abrams, Ike
Abrams, and we're open for any business as comes our way
at any hours, Mister . . . ?"

"Call me Dickerson," Longarm replied. It was at least an
easy name to remember, seeing it belonged to one of the
federal judges he rode for back in Denver. He continued in
a more truthful vein, "I'm on my way to the Navaho Reserve
on B.I.A. business. Lost a pony this side of Durango. Left my
packsaddle and such with some army men a ways to the east
Knowing you all were in business up this way, I was hoping
you'd be able to sell me at least a jackass to carry me on
down to, say, Ganado."

The trader quieted his growling yard dogs as Longarm
tethered his mount out front. Abrams allowed they'd already
supped but that his womenfolk could likely rustle something
up.

Longarm said he'd just eaten with the army as he followed
the hospitable trader inside. He was sizing up the others seated
around the small stove in the center of the cluttered trading

128

post, and vice versa, as Ike Abrams insisted, "Coffee and cake never killed a man, and I wouldn't want you to say I was stingy just because I skinned you on a horse deal."

Everyone chuckled. Such talk was expected of a man with horseflesh to discuss. Just as a stockman invited to sup with a neighbor was supposed to say it felt nice to eat some of his own beef for a change.

There were three other men and two women present as Abrams showed Longarm to an empty bentwood seat near the unlit stove. Such central fixtures tended to form the focal point in country stores whether lit or not. Longarm knew that come, say, Halloween, that bitty stove would be glowing red hot and still not helping all that much at that altitude in such uncertain country.

The white woman lounging against a counter was somewhat older than the sullen young Indian or breed gal she obviously got to boss around. She told the dusky serving gal, in Spanish, to get cracking with that damned *café con tortas*. She hadn't waited for the trader to tell her. Longarm wasn't surprised to learn she was his wife.

The men already seated seemed to be another old geezer dressed more cow, a younger sidekick dressed the same, and a fat harelipped kid Abrams introduced as his nephew and all-around helper out from Saint Lou to learn Indian trading.

When Longarm asked what the local Indians had to swap, the kid pointed at a bale of smoke-cured hides in a nearby corner and said he'd just got them off some Ute for an old muzzle-loading Hawken .58 and a sack of brown sugar.

The older stockman, who seemed to be called Pop Waldo, laughed and opined that Indians had no head for business. "They think we make brown sugar out of bee honey taking all that trouble, and most any old gun has a bow and arrow beat for shooting from horseback, I reckon."

The harelip sneered, not a pretty sight, and observed that the shiftless redskins were getting the better part of the bargain, seeing the white taxpayers gave them all those free cows to skin out as they saw fit.

Longarm said he'd thought they looked a mite big for elk hides, and casually asked Pop Waldo whether he got a good price for his stock from the B.I.A.

129

The old cowman shook his head wistfully and replied, "The Widow Donovan has this government contract to feed the South Ute beef on the hoof. They say she inherited it from her man, a well-connected Rock Solid Republican with pals in high places. So you might say she gets to set the price of beef in these parts."

Longarm said he found that last part a mite confusing. So Pop Waldo explained. "The Widow Donovan's herd can only drop so many calves up around the headwaters of the La Plata. So she's been known to flesh out a drive down to the Ute Strip with yearlings riz by others. Opinion is divided as to whether she pays her neighbors a neighborly price or not."

Longarm cautiously asked if they were talking about hard bargaining or free and easy roping. Mrs. Abrams must not have cared. She went in the back to cuss that Indian gal pretty good in her bad Spanish as Pop Waldo declared, "Ain't been no stock stealing down this way since the range was opened up. Everyone knows everyone knows everyone else so far, and being knowed to your neighbors as a cow thief can take years off your life."

Longarm tried, "I was told this Widow Donovan was decent enough by another lady. Nancy Slade from Red Wash to the south?"

The locals exchanged thoughtful glances. The harelip said, "Red Wash is smack dab in the middle of the Mountain Ute Agency."

Ike Abrams nodded. "There's a white agency carpenter and his old woman answering to the name of Slade on or about Red Wash. Marvin Slade, his name is. Don't know her'n. He sent a Ute boy up this way one time to buy some hardware off us. I disremember just what he needed for some shed he was building for the Indian trade school down yonder. But he never tried to beat us down on the price. So I reckon he's all right."

Longarm said, "I was given to understand Miss Nancy was a daughter of the family. You don't know her?"

Abrams shrugged. "Wouldn't know her if she walked in through that door behind you. Why should I? Don't they have their own trading posts, more than one, down to the Utah Strip? That deal I cut with her father was an emergency, now that

130

I study back on it. He needed door locks. Said the licensed agency trader didn't stock none because Indians hardly ever want any locks."

Longarm was saved having to answer his seemingly innocent questions when that young Indian gal came out from the back with a heavy load of coffee and cakes on a fair-sized tray. He was more curious about her nation than any reasons Nan Slade might have had for not wanting to be seen around here by folks who didn't seem to know her. The Indian gal wore her shiny black hair pinned up, like a white gal's, and the hand-me-down Mother Hubbard she wore didn't offer any clues to her nation either, although old Begochidi sure would be likely to grab for those heroic tits under that thin red-checked calico the first chance he got, if she had any Na-Déné blood in her at all.

Mrs. Abrams had naturally sent her out with coffee and cake for all around. As their Indian servant dealt him a tin plate of chocolate cake and a thick china mug of coffee, he started to thank her in the Spanish he knew she savvied. Then he thanked her in English for the same reasons he'd introduced himself as some kin to Federal Judge Dickerson of the Denver District Court.

When the gal just looked through him with her big sloe eyes, Ike Abrams called out, "Cindy don't speak English, Mr. Dickerson. We got her off some Ute already speaking Border Mex. She says she ain't Apache, but it sounds like Apache. She calls herself Ashy-patches or whatever."

Longarm considered Absaroka, or what others tended to describe as Crow Indians. It worked as well as or better than Apache as soon as one studied the nations the Ute had on their shit list.

He didn't suggest it aloud. As the Indian gal served the harelip and turned back his way, he raised his free hand as if to tilt his hat back, and just sort of fanned his brow with fingers spread wider than some might have found natural before he sort of covered a yawn politely with the same stiff hand.

In the universal sign lingo most Indian nations used, he'd just indicated he wanted to ask some question as privately as possible.

He knew she'd followed his drift when she drifted over to a

far corner as if waiting in the shadows for further orders from old Ike or her boss lady. Nobody but Longarm had as clean a view of her as she quietly reached up to grab herself by either shoulder before she brought her arms down in front of her, wrists crossed, to sort of snap them apart.

Universal sign was universal because it was simple as baby talk. So it wasn't too clear whether she meant she'd been taken prisoner and escaped or wanted him to know she was a prisoner aiming to bust loose as soon as she could.

He wasn't as free to sign to her. So he didn't. He went on eating cake and jawing with the other white men. Cindy, if that was her name, raised a fist to her own forehead to let him know he'd guessed right about her being Absaroka, likely off the Crow Reserve just north of the Colorado line. Absaroka and Ute had fought so long and mean they'd almost learned to admire one another. Capturing an Absaroka gal alive would have counted as quite a coup to some Ute a spell back. It was at least five years since Ute had been allowed to be so frisky with a nation that had sided with the Great White Father as well.

He asked anyone who aimed to answer whether that Widow Donovan raised any sheep up her way. As the harelip laughed in a sort of disturbing way and Pop Waldo choked on his coffee, Longarm saw his chance to sort of fool with his mustache in a way that asked Cindy if she was being abused right now.

The Indian gal placed two fingers to her breastbone and sort of drummed at her heart with them in turn. In sign this indicated a feeling of having two hearts, or feeling sort of confused as to how one was supposed to answer.

Mention of sheep had inspired a turn to the conversation that made Longarm feel glad the only white woman there who spoke English was out of the room. But there was a lot to be said for sheepherder jokes when a man who'd heard most of them was trying to carry on a conversation with somebody else. For nobody was paying any attention to him as he signaled the floor beside his chair and asked if she needed any help.

Cindy's sloe eyes sort of glowed in the gloom as she held out a cupped palm as if to examine it, and then laid the index finger of her other hand in it, meaning she wanted to go someplace else with somebody else, likely him.

The young hand seemed interested in his reaction to a joke he'd doubtless heard a lot himself. So Longarm had to pretend he gave a shit as Pop Waldo went on and on about a man coming West after the war to hire on as a sheepherder.

Longarm knew the old-timer was winding up for the big finish, so while the others were hanging on Pop's every word, Longarm raised a stiff pair of fingers to assure her they were pals. Then he had to risk pointing the index fingers of both hands at the cold stove to indicate "future," and then touch his fingertips and thumbs together just long enough to let her know he meant they'd be meeting together some time in the future.

In that far corner, Cindy raised her right trigger finger and then rocked a balled fist, thumb extended, to indicate that yes, she understood him. So Longarm felt free to join in the laughter as Pop Waldo wound up.

Longarm told the one about the sheepherder counting off his herd in the morning as "Eight, nine, ten—good morning, sweetheart—twelve, thirteen, fourteen . . ." as Mrs. Abrams came out to ask what they were all laughing about. So Longarm suggested they get back to the subject of that pack brute he wanted to buy.

Abrams said, "It's too dark out to argue horseflesh right now, Mr. Dickerson. Were you in a hurry to fall in a canyon tonight?"

When Longarm said he hadn't given the matter much thought, the old trader said, "*Bueno*. We can put you up for the night atop that pile of hides with some fairly new army blankets, or you could spread your bedroll in the hayloft around to the back if you got a bedroll with you."

Longarm dryly observed he always depended on hotel accommodations in such settled country. So they settled on that hayloft, even though he'd have liked to leaf through that whole pile of hides, reading the brands that would still be visible. A man trying to think on his feet had to go with the current when it was carrying him at all sensibly, and a late-night conversation in a barn would likely be a heap less public. It would have sounded odd to ask the older couple

133

where they meant to bed down later. But he somehow doubted they slept in their barn.

Like most lawmen, he'd found folks with guilty knowledge were far more likely to let some slip when you didn't make them feel guilty. So he polished off a second helping and let others do most of the talking as he asked just enough to establish they were either as dumb as himself about night-riding gunslicks or too slick to trick into allowing they'd ever heard a thing an outsider might be able to use.

Ike Abrams said he didn't know, and Pop Waldo said that widow gal who ran the Flying W had perhaps a dozen regular hands, hiring twice that many temporary hands whenever she needed to move enough beef to matter. Pop nodded at his hired hand and sounded casual as an innocent cuss was supposed to when he volunteered, "Bucky here has worked a few roundups for the Flying W. Ain't that so, Bucky?"

The hand nodded as innocently and replied, "Spring before last. Told Widow Donovan I was busy last fall. She pays extra help the way she pay for extra beef stock, cheap. I may not be pretty but I guess I'm white at least, and you can't get a good Mex roper for no four bits a day now that the price of beef's so high back East."

Pop Waldo nodded, but grudgingly admitted, "She's a smart old gal when it comes to milking turnips. After I'd calculated to the penny how much it would cost me to peddle my yearly increase as close as the damned Denver market, she was able to show me I was making just a few cents more a head selling direct to her."

He sighed. "A few cents adds up to dollars when a man has enough beef on the hoof to sell and the infernal railroad acts as if they were riding your cows in Pullman cars!"

The hired hand insisted, "She's still awfully cheap, if you ask me. Everybody knows she gets more for those cows than she pays any of her neighbors when she drives 'em down to the durned old B.I.A."

Ike Abrams laughed. "Hell, Bucky, that's just the way business is supposed to be. Nobody buys dear and sells cheap if they have the brains of a gnat. Anybody who don't want to sell to such a sly old gal can always pay the freight over the mountains to higher prices, right?"

Bucky insisted sullenly, "She's cheap, and it's not fair for her to sell to the B.I.A. so exclusive. I'll bet she bribes them old Indian agents good to keep the rest of us out of the game!"

Longarm was in no position to argue. It would have been dumb to brag on the times he'd arrested government officials, high and low, for bending the rules just as Bucky had suggested.

But why would anyone enjoying a personal edge with B.I.A. beef-purchasing agents want to raise such a pointless ruckus over sheep that were only passing through?

Mrs. Abrams came back out to order the Indian gal to bed, saying she'd pour the last of the coffee. Pop Waldo took the hint as well as the coffee, allowing he and the boy had best be getting on home before their own women came looking for them.

Longarm pressed his luck to say, "I heard someone off the Flying W has been having trouble with sheep men. Rider called Red? I wasn't paying much attention when they were talking about it at the barbershop in Durango the other day."

The locals exchanged puzzled looks. Pop Waldo said nobody he knew of was raising sheep within miles. "Navaho graze a heap of sheep and goats about a week's drive to the southwest. Heard the Indian Agency was sending 'em some more. Navaho don't have what it takes to herd cows. You know a Flying W called Red, Bucky?"

The hand shook his head and replied, "Not off the Flying W. There's Big Red over to the Rocking T and Little Red off the Triple H, but . . . Oh, there's an old boy called Fat Red, rides for that contract drover Peterson in Durango."

Pop Waldo snorted and said, "That's *Pearson* as hires on for outfits who don't have the manpower to drive their own market herds to the rail yards, Bucky. The man was asking about proddy Reds at feud with sheepherders."

Bucky shrugged, and said he didn't know anybody at feud with sheepherders on a range nobody seemed to be grazing sheep on all that much.

Longarm tried, "I think I passed that government herd you just mentioned, Pop. Had them soldiers blue riding with 'em.

135

You reckon anyone betwixt here and the Navaho line are likely to start up with 'em?"

The old cow man polished off his mug of coffee and set it aside as he marveled, "Take on an army backed by Uncle Sam and the Bureau of Land Management just because they're keeping company with sheep none of us have to worry about ever seeing again? I suspect you ain't never tried to negotiate grazing rights on federal land, old son. Cow folk being crowded desperate on overgrazed range might risk a range war. But the range all around is so undergrazed it ain't all been *explored*! What kind of a fool would pick a fight for no good reason with the army or even the Indians?"

Ike Abrams nodded. "We still have enough trouble with unreconstructed Ute, who don't cotton to sheep any more than the rest of us. Be silly to start up with them half-patch Navaho for no reason, as Pop just said."

Bucky offered, "I've heard them half-patch and all-nasty Navaho drygulched some army men this very spring. I say praise the Lord for raising 'em so far away, and this child for one ain't about to pick a fight with 'em about their chosen career in the wool trade!"

Ike Abrams said, "Having 'em herding sheep beats having 'em raiding everybody, red or white, for miles around. I got some well-made Navaho saddle blankets in trade off a Ute last fall. Sold 'em, for real money, to the first cowhands as laid eyes on 'em. So far as I care, the more sheep them half-patch Navaho have to keep 'em out of mischief the better!"

Pop Waldo agreed and got to his feet to thank Mrs. Abrams for her swell coffee and cake.

Abrams told Longarm he'd show him the way to his hayloft, long as they were all on their blamed feet in any case. So within less than half an hour Longarm found himself alone in the barn, atop his bedding spread across half-cured hay. The horseflesh stabled just below him didn't smell much sweeter than the sort of mildewed sour shortgrass hay, cut too early and not tedded long enough in the sun before lofting. Those professors who worried about bugs said the kind that pickled silage when you stored it green was the same as the kind that turned raw cabbage to sauerkraut when the Dutch folks packed it away in stoneware pots. Sauerkraut was much better to eat with sausages than it was to sleep on.

Longarm was tempted to slip down the ladder, saddle up, and ride on back to rejoin the government column in their night bivouac. He wasn't really sleepy yet, and as musty as the damned hay was, it was still mighty risky to smoke in any damned hayloft!

But he'd signed to that Cindy that they'd get together later, and it wasn't all that much later when you considered those yard dogs and a spry old cuss who didn't look too old to screw at all before he called it a night. So Longarm decided he'd better wait a spell.

Chapter 13

Waiting was one of the worst chores that went with packing any sort of badge. But like other serious hunters, a lawman just had to steel himself to wait, and wait, and then wait just five minutes longer than lesser mortals could abide.

Indians tended to have more patience than your average crook. So waiting for an Indian was a total pain in the ass, and Longarm had figured for certain the blamed Absaroka gal was sound asleep in the damned trading post when he suddenly made out the outline of her head and shoulders in the almost total darkness. For she hadn't made as much noise as your average grass snake moving out of the trading post, across a yard watched by dogs, and up a rickety-ass ladder.

As she joined him atop his bedding, he could see she had on a white cotton night shift. When he started to address her in Spanish, Cindy softly laughed and confided in fair English, "Sometimes it is best to let people think you are not able to understand them. Are you the one my people call Wasichu Wastey? You fit the description of a good fighter who talks straight and never twists what was agreed on the way so many other Wasichu try to."

Longarm answered not unkindly, "They say a Wasichu beaver trapper called Jedediah Smith once thought he had an understanding with the Absaroka up north of here. Smith had given his red brothers a lot of good things and taken an Indian wife. They told him he had permission to hunt and trap among them. He thought they were straight talkers."

She murmured, "That was all so long ago, in the Shining Times before I was born."

138

But he persisted sternly. "The Absaroka—he called them Crow—raided Smith's camp while he was out on his trap line. They raped and murdered his young Indian wife. They robbed his camp. Then they spoiled everything they didn't want to carry away, just as a wolverine spoils anything it doesn't want to eat by tearing it apart and pissing on it."

"You are Wasichu Wastey," she sighed. "Your own people call you Longarm. Everyone agrees you have a good heart, but that you don't let anybody shit you."

To which he could only reply with a modest chuckle, "Never mind about me. I ain't the one in trouble. Tell me about an Absaroka gal who claims somebody captured her."

The barely visible but interestingly scented mystery woman told him, "My Absaroka name is Sintehaska. I matured earlier than some of the other children I grew up with. So Ute raiders took me alive to use as a grown woman is used before they killed me. One of the Ute men liked the way I resisted him. Maybe I liked him more than the first ones who'd raped me, after I'd learned the way raping went."

Longarm suggested, "We'd have to be talking at least ten summers ago, before the Ute up around Crow country had been resettled closer to, say, this side of the White River?"

She said, "It was just after the big fight you Wasichu had with Mahpiua Luta along that army road you built across his hunting grounds when I was little."

Longarm nodded soberly. "Red Cloud's war over that dumb Bozeman Trail in the late '60s. Your nation sided with my nation at the time, since a chance to kill a Lakota was always a chance to kill a Lakota. But where do even North Ute come into a brawl taking place up Montana way?"

She said, "Oh, Wasichu Wastey, I was just a little girl, living with my own band just north of the south pass. The Ute never liked the Lakota any more than the rest of us. They just saw a chance to hit other old enemies while the soldiers were so busy with Mahpiua Luta, so they did. After a while the Ute warrior I didn't hate so much was killed in a fight with Jicarilla. But by then the others had forgotten I belonged to an enemy nation. They were having enough trouble with you Saltu, as they say Wasichu. There were times even I had to agree your people were really shitting

139

on them. But I was glad when my Ute husband's family sold me to the Abramses last summer. They ask more of me. But I don't have to worry about either old person suddenly remembering an old grudge and throwing something at me. Will you take me with you when you ride on, Wasichu Wastey? I know how to cook in the Wasichu fashion, and if you would like me to show you, I am really good at screwing!"

He tried not to laugh too loud—it wasn't easy—and confided that his closer friends called him Custis. But when she proceeded to roll atop him, hoisting her thin night shift, he felt obliged to warn her, "I won't be riding anywheres near Crow country, which is now a mite farther off than you remember, Cindy."

She sat astride him, bare thighs spread, and commenced to fumble with the buttons down the front of his jeans as she asked where her own folks might have settled since last she'd seen them.

He said, "The Absaroka wound up with lots of reserve up around the Little Big Horn, including the battlefield you must have heard about whilst you were residing with the Ute. I reckon you could call the Big Horn Crow Reserve spoils of war, seeing your nation helped my nation take that range away from the Lakota, buffalo, and such."

She sort of pouted, "Hear me, those dry plains are not the really good hunting grounds we had in our Shining Times. You people screwed the Ute after they'd helped you fight the Navaho too, and . . . *Heya!* Do you really expect to screw me with what I just found here, you *Tatonka Wasichu?*"

Since it was already in her tight, and she was already moving up and down like a kid on a merry-go-round and enjoying it, he felt no call to apologize for the heroic boner inspired by her sneaky brown hands after it had already been teased by white blondes and brunettes.

He just shot his wad up into her the first time as the two of them conspired to get rid of his duds and her night shift without stopping.

Then he was on top, buck naked, with an elbow hooked under either tawny knee as he tried to get her to open wide and say *"Heyaaah!"*

She did, rotating in a literally screwing motion as she moved up and down to meet his thrusts, and he was thrusting hard as hell toward the last as she clawed his back with her nails and panted in his face like a puppy fixing to howl.

He blew back in her open mouth the same way. For as Jedediah Smith had doubtless noticed, gals from most of the Horse nations found that as romantic as white gals found kissing French-style.

He had her calling him Custis by the time she was back on top to finish the way her breed preferred, squatting on her bare heels to lean forward and brush her naked nipples across his face as she sort of screwed and sucked at the same time with her muscular innards, bless every slithery bounce.

Old Cindy's tits dangled bigger than most, although her Indian name could translate as either "big tail" or "high tail." It was hard to say which fit as she moved her fair-sized brown butt high and low while sort of gumming him the length of his shaft with her amazing love maw.

He came again, and might have gone soft, for all either of them could tell with her old ring-dang-doo gripping it so friendly. He reached down between them to strum her old banjo and help her come when she started panting more desperately than a puppy dog.

It worked, and she thanked him profusely as she lay shuddering atop his naked flesh to mingle her love sweat with his. Then she purred, "That was very kind of you, Wasichu Wastey. Not many men seem to care if a woman enjoys it as much or not."

He grumbled, "I told you my pals call me Custis, and why did you want to do it at all seeing you're still feeling so formal?"

She bit down tenderly with her warm wet insides. "I wanted you to like me. Women always screw men to get them to like them. It's the best way to get a man to do what you want him to do for you."

He said he'd noticed that and felt no call for romantic objections; fair was fair and her sort of primitive view was likely less dishonest than those of some who sipped tea with a pinkie raised. Because once you got down to it, what was the difference, save for her price, between a gal who wanted three

141

dollars to take it three ways and a far more snooty one who figured the least a man owed her for a few good screws was food, clothes, and lodging for the rest of her natural life, with flowers, books, and candy thrown in—unless a man aimed to hear a lot of pissing and moaning about the better catches she'd passed up for such a worthless brute.

He figured he owed it to this more honest friendly screwer to warn her, before they got hot again, where he was really headed and with whom.

Cindy didn't seem to mind soldiers blue, or even sheep, but she didn't seem to really cotton to the notion of riding deep into the canyonlands of Dinetah with anybody.

Toying with the damp hairs on his chest while she continued to let him soak inside her, Cindy pouted, "I'd rather go back to the Ute than fall into the hands of Navaho. They are crazy people, *witko*! At least Ute *think* a bit like Absaroka, once you learn their new words for things. But I have tried to talk to Navaho captives, in the Spanish my Ute husband taught me for trading. Even when Navaho speak Spanish as well as you do, they say *witko* things!"

He didn't answer as he caressed her big firm ass. For whether he agreed in full with her or not, he followed her drift. That anthropology gal who'd had a somewhat smaller bare ass had explained, one night when they were just drifting like this, how most of the other nations of so-called Indians seemed distantly related, speaking different tongues and following different spirits a lot of different ways, yet sharing at least some common notions of sentence structure and the logical views of their world that went with them.

Indians as different in lingo and custom as, say, Zuni farmers and Arapaho buffalo hunters were still about as closely related, way back in the Old World where all folks had started out, as, say, the various Aryan folks of Europe, save for Basques, Finns, Hungarians, and other such mysterious outsiders. Folks who spoke English, Spanish, or even Hindu, for Gawd's sake, were said to share a heap of root words and original notions. That anthropology gal had pointed out that all the old Aryan tribes had used about the same words for "mother" and their magical number, "three." But more important, they'd doubtless had similar notions of right and wrong

142

as they wandered into Europe way back when. Egyptians, Assyrians, and such had prayed to funny gods with funny heads, save for the Good Book folk, who'd come up with a whole new notion that made more sense. Yet all the Aryan folk, in their pagan days before they had the Good Book, had prayed to gods that had a lot in common, despite all the odd names they'd had. Brahma, Dagda, Odin, Jupiter, and Zeus had all been father gods who lived with mother gods and all their baby gods somewhere in the sky, and they'd *getcha* if you broke their rules, some of which the Good Book frowned upon nowadays.

The folks now known as American Indians had started out with other gods, as Longarm's kind persisted in calling notions that weren't what white folks pictured when they said "god," "spirit," "ghost," or even "medicine," although "medicine" seemed close. The morals that went with the medicines of Indian folks were skewed a mite from the white man's way of thinking. A lot of innocent blood had been spilled, by both sides, trying to come to a meeting of equally certain minds, until, over the years, most whites and most Indians had learned to halfway follow one another's drift.

The Na-Déné-speaking Apache or Navaho were different, the way old Hernan and other Basques were different from regular Aryan Spanish-speaking folk.

Starting from some different part of the Old World with a whole different way of talking and thinking, the way Hungarians had sort of drifted into Eastern Europe talking and thinking like half-ass Turks, the Na-Déné had always bewildered the other nations they met up with as much as they'd fussed and feuded with them.

Their odd lingo was likely only the start of it. Longarm had found most other nations followed the same sign lingo, and they all seemed to string their words and hence their thoughts along the same lines. But where Cindy's Sioux-Hokan-speaking folk would say *"tashunka sapa"* or "horse black" for a black horse, and *"tashunka Wasichu"* or "horse American" for, say, a cavalry mount they stole, a Navaho would have to know whether the horse was present or absent and doing what, before he'd tell you what he *called* the dad-blamed critter.

It got more complicated when you tried to pin a Na-Déné-speaker down on right or wrong. At last count, they had over a hundred gods, holy people, guiding spirits, or medicines. They said it was none of your damned Belagana business if you pressed them too tight on that, and if you pressed for the exact meaning of Belagana, it came back more as *tl'ohya'gai,* meaning a white man they were *more* pissed at.

One Chiricahua Apache, which they called *teiji,* had finally decided their secret passwords for Longarm's kind translated as something between "white eyes" and "white streaks in the grass." She and Longarm had been screwing at the time, so she'd likely been honest. And they had odder notions than the names they gave things.

He told Cindy, "Another Indian pal once assured me, at a time much like this, that her words for stranger, enemy, or somebody smarter were about the same. So you might not get along as well over yonder in Dinetah as you did amongst the Ute. Have these white folks you've been working for been torturing you, aside from asking you to work?"

She began to move just enough to keep things feeling friendly as she replied. "I had to work harder when I was a captive of the Ute. White folks have a lot of labor-saving devices, starting with soap. But I miss the many-colored grasses of the foothills where I grew up. Sour cherries grew in almost every draw, and when the men came back from the buffalo plains to the east, we ate fat cow until the grease ran down our chins and we had to go outside and throw up so we could eat some more!"

He tightened his ass muscles to find he could get it up again, enough for her to feel and respond to leastways, as he told her, "There may not be enough buff left to consume 'em so wastefully, but there's still some up around the Big Horn Reserve, and the Bureau's been trying to teach your nation to raise cows our way."

She planted a heel closer to his bare hips on either side and began to move in a more teasing fashion, tightening on his growing erection on each slow upstroke, as she protested in a more or less conversational tone, "I've heard bad things about our new home where the Lakota killed Pahuska and all his soldiers. It was better where we roamed in our Shining Times, where the High Plains met the Shining Mountains.

Hear me, Wasichu Wastey, my people fought those Lakota on your side, just as my Ute husband's people fought Navaho and Apache on your side. Why do you people always screw people who help you screw your enemies?"

He asked if she wanted to stop.

Cindy laughed like a mean little kid and started bouncing faster as she insisted, "I wasn't talking about *this* kind of screwing. You *know* how you screwed your Ute and Absaroka friends out of as much as you took from your enemies!"

He said he was sorry as hell, and they were too busy screwing in a friendlier way to argue about Indian policy for a spell.

When they finally got back down from the stars, to find they'd somehow wound up in another corner of the loft with straws stuck all over them, he kissed her good, rolled off, and said with a sigh, "I sure could do with a shower, or better yet a swim, right now."

She said she doubted anyone would notice, at this hour, if they took a dip in the stock tank down the slope a ways. So they climbed down from the hayloft bare-ass.

Cindy said the yard dogs wouldn't bark at him seeing he was with someone who fed them, and she was right as the two of them strolled naked through the moonlight. But Cindy seemed surprised, once she could see him better, to see he was carrying his Winchester.

She asked, "What's wrong? Do you suspect me of leading you into an ambush, Wasichu Wastey?"

He chuckled fondly and replied, "I could tell you a tale about needing a gun suddenly as I was swimming in a stock tank on another occasion, but it might make you jealous."

She didn't press the matter. When they got to the big round tank of coopered cedar at the base of a sunflower windmill, he just leaned his saddle gun against the outside and climbed in with Cindy, to find the water was just fine.

They swished around without splashing, lest they awaken folks who might not understand. Thanks to the sun shining down into the tank all day, the water was warmer than the cool night air. When Cindy shivered and said she feared catching a chill, it seemed only natural to hold the poor little gal against him, and the slippery feeling of their wet clean bodies naturally

145

led to other natural feelings. So they found that he could keep them both close enough to the sort of slimy wall of the tank by holding on to its rim as Cindy wrapped her tawny arms and legs around him under the surface. Wet tits in the moonlight sure served to inspire a man who'd thought he'd had enough. He learned he hadn't once they got it back in her half soft, and it felt odd as hell when the base of it felt alternately pleasant shocks of cool water and warm pussy.

"Don't take it out," she pleaded once they'd both come in such a comfortable position. So he said he'd try, but all too soon, alas, the combination of cool water and satisfaction puckered him to where she sort of spit the poor thing out like a melon seed.

She said she didn't care, and demanded he just hold her that way forever and forever, till the end of time.

He kissed her eyelids. He didn't think she'd want to hear about Changing Woman, since old Istsa Natlehi wasn't a haunt of her own nation, but he still told her, "Nothing stays the way it is forever, honey. You're younger than I am and you're already starting to talk like an old lady wanting things the way they are, or were, because she ain't got all that much to look forward to."

Cindy sniffed and insisted, "I *do* wish things could go back to being the way they were before you Wasichu came and made our world so different! In our Shining Times we rode free across our endless hunting grounds and ate fat cow till it made us sick!"

He softly suggested, "You're recalling times that might not have been so grand to the long-ago folks stuck with living in 'em. To begin with, none of you Horse nations would have had any *horses* if it hadn't been for my kind bringing 'em across the main ocean in the beginning of your Shining Times. After that, nobody rode all that endlessly before they ran into others claiming the same hunting grounds as their very own. The Arapaho say your nation took all that so-called Crow country away from them. You fought on our side after the Lakota and Cheyenne took so much of it away from *you*."

"Then you Wasichu took all of it, all, away from every-body!" she cried bitterly.

146

"Bullshit," he said. "That Big Horn Crow Reserve you're pissing and moaning about covers better than three thousand square miles of well-watered and part-timbered shortgrass range a heap of my kind would kill for. Nations that fought us have been given reserves big enough to qualify as states back East as well. How much land did you Absaroka set aside for the Arapaho when you'd licked 'em fair and square? What do you figure the Lakota or Cheyenne would have ceded to you after they'd finished with your way smaller nation."

She hugged him closer and pleaded, "Don't be cross with me. I was talking about your people, not you!"

He said, "I know. I'm supposed to understand that my kind of folks are the villains of a naturally peaceable world and the only snakes in a natural Garden of Eden inhabited by noble savages and happy-go-lucky cannibals. You just told me yourself how pure-ass Indians murdered your little playmates and carried you off as a prize of war, Cindy. You can stay here with folks who treat you tolerable. You can go into town and find a better job, or you can let me stake you to a train ride to the Big Horn Agency and the government handouts us murderous Wasichu taxpayers torture your poor nation with. There is just no way in Heaven or Hell to turn back the clock to the way things never really were."

She insisted she didn't want to return to her own people and live worse than trash whites on miserly B.I.A. allotments.

He suggested they get out and warm up under his blankets back in in the hayloft. She went along with that up to a point. But as Longarm slid into his bedding, Cindy sat atop the covers, hauling her night shift back on as she pouted, "If you really cared for me you'd take me with you in the morning. You don't mean to stay among the *witko* Navaho forever, do you?"

He said, "Nope. Just long enough to abuse 'em with a herd of prime breeding stock. They'll doubtless bitch we should have sent more. When you were living with the Ute the B.I.A. never sent you enough free beef to eat until you threw up, right?"

She said, "They *owed* my husband's band fat cows for all the help the Ute gave Rope Thrower and his bluecoats at Canyon de Chelly!"

147

She smoothed the white cotton over the thighs she was kneeling on as she bitched, "You Wasichu are all alike. You get us to do everything you want and then you toss us aside like chicken bones!"

He knew better. He still found himself muttering, "Sure we do, and for the record, there are white kids all across this land trying to get to sleep on empty stomachs because they got to get up and go to work in a coal mine or cotton mill come morning. I never said this world was easy, or even fair, for your kind, my kind, or any kind. But your Ute in-laws could have done worse. Maybe somebody in Washington *did* cite Kit Carson's Ute scouts when they were figuring out what to do about the White River Massacre and other childish fits us civilized folk are supposed to sympathize with."

"You don't understand," she said.

So he replied, "Why is it always *us* stuck with understanding folks who openly hate our guts? Have any of *you* ever lost a wink of sleep over white folks trying to get by on starvation wages and tough shit if Ma gets sick or Pa loses his job? Ain't no B.I.A. looking out for white greenhorns getting off the boats back East with no jobs in sight and even a worse grasp of the lingo than most Indians have by now. If you don't want your pie without cheese, got out and *earn* some damned cheese, girl!"

She blinked and asked him what on earth *cheese* had to do with a tight-fisted Indian policy.

Longarm chuckled sheepishly and explained, "Dumb story I was told by a church lady. Pretty little thing with chestnut hair and cornflower eyes and . . . that's another story. The one she told me involves a charity church supper given for a bunch of war orphans a few years back. She was still a kid herself at the time, so her folks had made her give up an afternoon of summertime play so's she could dish out chicken, mashed potatoes, and such whipped up by the ladies of her parish for the poor starving orphans."

Cindy nodded and said, "Everyone should feed hungry children."

Longarm said, "Everyone had been, for some time, it would seem. Came time for dessert, this young blue-eyed kid was serving fresh-baked pie her mamma and the other ladies had

148

spent hours baking. But as she was serving a generous slice to a snot-nosed kid who'd already stuffed his fool self, he asked where the cheese was. He was used to having a wedge of tangy cheese with apple pie back at the orphanage."

Longarm smiled fondly at the memory of hurt cornflower eyes as he continued. "When this sweet little gal in a fresh-starched summer frock told the starving orphan she just didn't have any cheese to go with his pie, he yelled, 'Aw, shit, pie without cheese!' and threw it smack in her face. It still bothered her years later. Yet she was still doing charity work at the time. I swear that for all the shit my kind has been accused of handing out, there ain't nobody takes as much back when they don't really have to."

She said she didn't understand what some blue-eyed Wasichu who served pie without cheese had to do with her.

He said he hadn't expected her to follow his drift, and asked if she aimed to get under the covers with him or not.

She wistfully said she wanted to, but figured she'd better get on back to the house before she got fired, seeing he wasn't willing to let her tag along with fifteen hundred head of stock and a troop of cavalry on the prod for Indian trouble.

He couldn't tell whether they'd parted friendly or not. One minute she was there and the next she was gone, as silent as, well, an Indian in the tricky light.

But next morning, serving flapjacks to him and Ike Abrams in the house, Cindy seemed friendly as your average cigar-store Indian. So after coffee, he followed the trader back out to the barn to talk about horseflesh.

Old Ike was sharp. Longarm did his best to seem dubious about a six-year-old buckskin gelding with a cayuse jug-head and likely the surefootedness that went with such bloodlines. But old Ike still wanted thirty dollars for him.

Longarm knew he could doubtless re-sell such a pony for forty closer to civilization once all this canyon country bullshit was over and done with. He still felt obliged to protest, "That's a heap to ask for a pony that don't even come with a cunt, Ike. Even if it had one, I only want to ride on top when it ain't packing my trail possibles for me."

Ike swore he'd taught that fine buckskin to suck cock and whistle the "Battle Hymn of the Republic" while standing on just his two hind legs. But in the end he let Longarm beat him down to twenty, and that was still way more than he'd paid for it in trade goods.

He only told Longarm this after they'd slapped palms on the deal and Longarm was counting out the money. But Longarm took it in good humor and confided, "I may have been holding back on you a mite, old son. Seeing you're bound to find out any minute in any case, I may as well tell you an army column will be coming along sometime this morning. I mean to wait here, if it's all the same with you, and I mean to ride on with 'em after."

The old trader smiled thinly and said, "I was wondering last night what you might be doing out this way all by your lonesome."

Longarm said, "You and the ladies were mighty hospitable to such a mysterious stranger, Ike. I may as well tell you, this late in the game, I rode in under false colors. I'm really U.S. Deputy Marshal Custis Long, attached to that army relief column on its way to the southwest with that Navaho stock we were speculating about last night."

Ike Abrams nodded and said, "I know. Cindy told us all about it as soon as she come in the house after midnight, Longarm."

A big gray cat got up, turned around twice, and lay back down in Longarm's breakfast as he considered how much damage he'd done his own fool self, decided it was survivable, and said with a sheepish smile, "Perfidy, thy name is Woman, and Damn Fool, thy name is Man. For she *told* me she was out to get on the good side of me, and when will we ever learn?"

Ike Abrams chuckled and said, "When we're too old to get it up, I reckon. They got an advantage on us, not having the hard brainless cock we've got to contend with."

He saw Longarm was still sort of flushed, so he added in a soothing tone, "It was two to one against you and your poor mortal flesh, kid. My Molly was the one who had the suspicions of the tales you told. I confess I didn't give a shit. I wish Molly would suspect *me* of something and send such a devoted servant after me to find out what I'd been up to. I've thought about it. But I know she'd tell my Molly no matter what I offered her to keep her mouth shut. The two of 'em carry on in Spanish for hours at a time, and sometimes I suspect the two of 'em are plotting against me!"

Fair was fair, and the Absaroka gal had already played him false. So he quietly asked if old Ike knew their Indian gal spoke perfectly understandable English.

Ike spoiled his fun by answering, "Well, sure she does. How did you think *I* get her to do anything around here? My Molly used to have some Mex help, and so she and old Cindy like to sort of play a little game with others. It's surprising what you can find out about folks if you don't mind them thinking you're not as sharp as they'd like to think they are."

Longarm had to laugh. He said, "You'd make a good lawman, Ike. I let folks take me for an idjit now and again, albeit last night I'd say I was an idjit for real. I've been strung along like so before by good-looking gals I thought I was outsmarting. But I never seem to learn, and you must think I was dumb as hell, right?"

To which the old trader could only reply, in a sincerely wistful way, "Oh, I don't know. At least you got some of that sassy red ass, which is a lot more than *this* poor old horny cuss can say!"

Chapter 14

By noon the sky was overcast, heat lightning was flashing off to the northwest, and the cavalry was nowhere in sight. Skies in the Four Corners country could get like that in the spring, and an outfit bossed by a self-indulgent slugabed could be most anywhere.

Longarm took advantage of the delay to openly ask Ike Abrams for a closer look at those hides he'd bought off the Ute. The agreeable trader said why not, and allowed they'd be serving hash with peas and carrots for noon dinner.

All but a few of the cowhides bore the by-now-familiar brand of the Widow Donovan. Some had fresher Flying W brands imposed on older brands of original owners. But they'd already told him the old gal with the inside track fleshed out her own stock with that of others. It was traditional to slap a trail brand, superseding earlier ones, on a herd being driven to market. It was more important, according to Ike, that nobody in this corner of Colorado had reported missing enough stock to matter. Longarm still copied the disparate brands on a sheet of notepaper, in case he got the chance to compare notes in Durango on his way back. He agreed those few hides that bore no brands at all had most likely been peeled off mavericks.

Such willful ways went with grazing Tex-Mex longhorns on marginal open range. The beef breed most favored by Western stockmen had this independent nature to go with its ability to survive in country that would kill your average cow. So from time to time an old she-cow would stray way the hell off to drop a calf and raise it as wild as a deer.

By long-established custom and legal precedent in most Western courts, critters running wild with no brand or earmarks could be claimed by the first human being they met up with on open range. White hands were inclined to rope and brand them. Indians, as the maverick hides amid the others would indicate, were more prone to treat mavericks as a sort of sissy variety of buffalo. Had the Ute to the south been more willing to learn the ways of the Saltu cowman the B.I.A. wouldn't be issuing white-raised beef on the hoof to the poor abused wards of the government.

Longarm tallied the unmarked hides in with the others, meaning to mention that later to somebody in the B.I.A. For that Widow Donovan would hardly be delivering unbranded beef to the white Ute agents down yonder with any hopes of being paid for it. He explained to Ike Abrams, "Only way you get mavericks in any numbers is by paying poor attention to cows in considerable numbers. Yet you say the Ute butcher and skin out their government beef as soon as it's allotted to 'em?"

Ike Abrams said, "*I* never said shit. I've never been there when the band leaders rode in to pick up their beef on the hoof. Pop Waldo and other white cowmen around here allow they'd never hire any Ute help for a market drive. So there's no great mystery here. Must be heaps of stray beef living wild as elk up many a canyon down that way by now. I agree it's a sloppy way to run things, but when did the B.I.A. ever run things right?"

He got no argument from Longarm on that. Things had improved a lot under the current reform Administration of President Hayes, and in truth a lot of the wild and woolly bullshit poor old Grant and his Indian Ring would never live down had been inspired by Indians as mean and selfish as the political hacks appointed by Grant to rob everyone, red, white, or blue. But the real fly in the ointment was the way folks back East who'd never seen an Indian tried to set a new "Indian policy" every time their bunch won an election.

As a peace officer who failed to gladly suffer fools of any race, and favored most any Indian policy as long as it was fair and above all *consistent,* Longarm knew how dumb it would be to stray far from his assigned mission to the Navaho to pry into likely minor mismanagement among the South Ute. A local beef baroness with political pull and an unfair edge with the B.I.A. purchasing agents was likely to be considered business as usual when he reported it.

If he reported it. In his time he'd made some good arrests and made the charges stick. But most times, charging a political hack with gross irregularity was a waste of time. Unless he stumbled over something far more crooked than political favoritism, he'd be in much the same position as a Denver foot patrolman reporting lewd behavior in the houses of ill repute run by old Ruth Jacobs, Madam Emma Gould, and other pillars of the local political machine.

The simple fact that erstwhile elk hunters living off the Interior Department might be mismanaging stock they'd never had to pay for was hardly apt to inspire any congressional investigation. So by later that morning, as the glowering skies threatened to rain fire and salt, and that hash with peas and carrots began to sound more reasonable, Longarm had about put aside such side issues.

It was well he had, for before noon dinner could be served that government column came in, guidons fluttering and bugle blowing a trail stop. Then Captain Granville rode into the dooryard with that newspaper gal, old George or whatever, to sternly warn Ike Abrams he'd report any price-gouging of his troopers, which seemed reasonable. Then he warned Longarm he'd place him on report if ever he rode on so far ahead without asking permission again.

That didn't sound reasonable. Longarm said so, knowing the two of them were doubtless influenced by the partly female audience. Molly Abrams and the dusky Cindy had naturally come out front to listen in, and the newspaper gal was sitting her thoroughbred close enough to take in every word as Longarm quietly suggested the captain hang some crepe on his nose if his brain was really that dead.

Captain Granville may have been even more worried about looking like a fool in front of womankind. He said he wasn't accustomed to being addressed that way.

Longarm knew at least two of the ladies already had him down as fool, and he didn't care what a gal who'd suck

154

Granville off thought of anyone. So he just said, not unkindly, "Don't push me and I won't push back then. I rode on to do some scouting. That's what they told me to do for this column. Lord knows, it would be run way different if I'd been told to *run* it, and I ain't about to peel potatoes or polish no brass!"

Granville must have followed his drift. As he started to dismount he stiffly announced, "We're only staying here long enough to let those blasted sheep and my third platoon catch up. We don't need any trail supplies, but as I said, my men may shop for any personal luxuries a man drawing less than four bits a day can afford."

Ike Abrams said he followed the captain's drift, and told his wife and Cindy to shove dinner on the back of the stove till business got slow again.

Longarm had his own business to take care of. He saddled the buckskin to see how they'd get along, and leading the pony he'd borrowed off old Hernan, backtracked three quarters of a mile along the trail until he met up with his Basque pals and the government herd they were noon-grazing in a wide flat-bottomed draw full of peppergrass. Which was really a dry-land cousin to watercress, and tasty enough to serve as salad greens in many a Western hotel.

It had much the same effect on sheep as love grass had on cows. So there was just no moving the woolly grazers off that peppergrass till they'd eaten enough to build up some nice tangy cuds to chew while they enjoyed the scenery further west.

Hernan agreed the new pony looked tough enough for the country ahead, and asked if Longarm would mind leading his own mount back to those *pendejos de la segunda* who were supposed to be managing the remuda on drag.

Longarm didn't ask why a sheepherder was dismissing members of the U.S. Cav as second-rate assholes. He didn't have the time. He rode through the peppergrass around the unruly herd to meet up the third platoon's shavetail, headed the other way.

They both reined in. Longarm told the young squirt what was going on up ahead at the trading post. The shavetail said he meant to ride forward and jaw with his captain. He asked

Longarm to tell his own noncoms they'd doubtless have plenty of time to buy fresh plug or smoking tobacco when and if they ever got that far, at the rate your average sheep moved. "I honestly think they back up three steps every time they shit, and sheep shit a lot."

Longarm saw his chance to ask if the lieutenant had noticed any friction between his men and the surviving Mex Basques.

The shavetail started to just shake his head. Then he said, "Nothing serious. You know how troopers tend to gripe about everything and tease everybody. That younger greaser, Ramon, has a short fuse he'd going to have to learn to control if he wants to get along with white boys."

Longarm said, "Ramon's a Basque. They claim to have been there when other white folks moved into Europe from parts unknown. They may be full of shit. But that's what they hold, and they hold it sort of tight. I've talked to them about maybe acting a mite too proud and proddy about rawhiding doubtless meant in fun. Could I get you to talk to at least one of your noncoms about pushing his luck with folks who may not share his sense of humor?"

The shavetail looked annoyed and said, "If you're talking about Corporal Brown, the first sergeant's already mentioned your complaints about his harmless teasing. Brown's a good soldier. I'll not put him on report for simply joshing with an overly sensitive greaser!"

"Basque," Longarm corrected. "You're right about some of 'em being mighty sensitive. Regular Mexicans don't mess with anyone they call a Vasco unless they're really ready for a fight."

The shavetail blinked in disbelief and sneered, "A fight between that skinny little Ramon and Moose Brown? Now that would be a sight to see!"

Longarm said, "No, it wouldn't. Ramon packs a Winchester Yellowboy with sixteen rounds of .44-40 in its magazine. As any Mexican will tell you, and as I just said, you don't mess with Los Vascos unless you're serious enough to see somebody die. They don't view a fight as a sporting event, the way some of us might. They try not to get in fights. When they do they figure it's best to finish their man off, because there's just no way in hell a Basque can *lose* and be a sport

156

about it. Did I mention Ramon's Winchester? Oh, yeah, they say knife-throwing is a popular indoor sport in the saloons of certain parts of Spain."

The shavetail blustered that any Mex who killed a man in army blue would hang by the neck until dead, dead, dead. So Longarm just nodded and rode on. There were army officers you could talk to, and there were others there was no sense wasting wind on.

He found Hernan's remuda and the thirty-odd mounts of the third platoon hobbled to crop peppergrass under the casual eye of a mounted horse guard. Peppergrass likely tasted about as good to ponies as watercress tasted to people, so the ponies were acting more sensible than the prancy goats or gorging sheep. He found the men of the third platoon around the cookfire up the far slope.

He reined in, and tethered his own stock to a handy stone pine for the moment as he told the platoon sergeant where their shavetail had gone and why. Then he contributed some jerked venison from a saddlebag to the mulligan pot they had simmering.

He didn't have to ask which of the three corporals had to be Moose Brown. The regular from Arkansas was not only a head taller than anyone else, but had to say, "Aw, now ain't that fancy?" when Longarm said that was jerked deer meat, not kindling wood, he was putting in the pot.

Someone else suggested it might be best to let the whole mess strew a spell longer. Longarm nodded at the hulking noncom on the far side of the fire and mildly asked, "Would you like to take a little walk with me, Corporal Brown? I got something to say to you in private."

Brown moved around the fire like flowing lava, and stood so close a less experienced civilian might have taken an instinctive step to his rear. But Longarm stood his ground. He didn't understand the way a born bully thought any more than he liked the breed. But over the years he'd learned to anticipate their instinctive tries for dominance the way he'd learned to sense when a pony was fixing to buck or a cur dog to snap. So just as it seemed they were about to bump their chests together, Longarm snapped, like a riding crop talking sense to a half-broke colt, "Don't try it, friend. I said I wanted to

157

keep it private. It might well be in your own best interests to go along with me on that."

Brown was a tad taller and a lot heavier across the upper body than Longarm, who'd been described as a moose himself by lesser mortals. But it was Brown who stepped back, since somebody had to if they were ever going anywhere else, as he mockingly replied, "Well, if you say so, Deputy Long Johns, as long as it's distinctly understood I'm the one who gets to play the daddy, not the mommy."

More than one of the others laughed. Longarm knew why. Aside from being their squad leader, Brown had been working on keeping them scared shit of him. Some of them would have doubtless laughed like hell if he'd said mean things about their mothers, and knowing the breed, Longarm suspected Brown likely had.

As soon as they were far enough from the fire to be out of earshot, Longarm stopped suddenly and spun so that Brown had to make an effort to stop in time. For two could play at such schoolyard games, and while Longarm didn't share the sick need to dominate other men just to be doing it, a lawman had to know how it was done. A little judicious bullying could have pistol-whipping or worse beat by miles when the suspect was only an asshole.

Brown tried to recover his lost ground by growling, "I'll bet I know what this is about, Deputy Long Johns. I heard about you going over my head to the first sergeant. How come you're so sweet on that sheepherding greaser, Deputy Long Johns? Does he screw better than all them pretty young sheep?"

Longarm said soberly, "It was dumb of me to go behind your back to old boys you have the Indian sign on. It might have made you feel you had the Indian sign on me. I'm telling you privately you don't, because I don't want to argue the point in front of your squad. They say you're a good soldier, despite your peculiar sense of humor."

"I ain't a *good* soldier!" Brown shouted. "I'm the *best* soldier in this whole damn outfit! Ain't an officer in it as don't sit down to piss, and I've been under fire twice!"

Longarm said soothingly, "I'm sure you've seen wonders and eaten cucumbers. I heard the outfit was sort of green.

158

That's how come I want you to help me carry out my mission, which, as I see it—"

"Since when do noncommissioned officers of the United States Army help damn civilians do shit?" the burly Brown cut in.

Seeing a soothing tone didn't seem to be getting him anywhere, Longarm replied with more barb, "Don't need your help shitting, and my federal station is that of a U.S. deputy marshal assigned to see that government herd and any other dumb brutes through to where a U.S. Army general wants 'em all to wind up!"

Corporal Brown struck like lightning.

Longarm was fast in his own right. But he'd hardly expected any unarmed fool to throw a sucker punch at a grown man wearing a .44-40 on his hip. So even though he tried to roll with the punch, it knocked him out from under his hat and sat him down hard in a spiny clump of soap weed Brown had likely had in mind for him.

The needlelike jabs in the ass through jeans and underdrawers didn't hurt as much as his jaw as Longarm did a backward somersault down-slope to come up spitting dry grass with six-gun in hand.

"My side arm's with my saddle!" the born bully yelled in mingled protest and taunt as others rose, behind him, to catch any stray rounds with their own fool faces. Brown continued in a jeering tone, "What are you going to do with that pissoliver, sheep screwer? You aim to gun a poor helpless boy like me in front of witnesses?"

Longarm ignored the throbbing in his jaw as he smiled thinly up at his tormentor and replied in an admiring tone, "You're good, Brown. I'll bet you had all the little boys and girls scared shitless you'd be waiting for 'em after school."

Then he holstered his six-gun, unbuckled his gun rig, and tossed it into some dry rabbitbrush as he lightly observed, "I reckon you were counting on my not wanting to hang for dealing with you as you doubtless deserve. But there's no law saying a man can't hit a sucker puncher back with his own bare knuckles, right?"

"Oh, Lord, we're going to have us a Bonny Reel!" chortled a trooper too far up-slope to worry about either of them. A second ass-kisser yelled, "You can do it, Arkansas! Knock his sassy block off!"

So Brown tried. He had to, once he saw his latest victim didn't aim to back him down gracefully at gunpoint. Longarm had his own doubts as to the wisdom of carrying this bullshit any further as he saw Brown moving in the way real boxers were taught to, by professionals teaching the science in a real gym.

In the way he knew a sudden mountain wind shift could mean dry lightning, without really having to understand why, Longarm knew a boy born a bully either learned to be more reasonable or learned to fight like hell by the time he grew as big as this big son of a bitch. So with some misgivings and damn little choice, Longarm put his own dukes up left-handed.

Longarm was not left-handed. As a rule he fought right-handed, whether bare-knuckled or meaner, for the same reasons even a lot of natural left-handers did. Facing your opponent with your left toes aimed at his center of gravity and your left forearm raised as a sort of shield, you were less open to the instinctive right swings of the natural brawler or the right hooks of a well-trained left-hander. He knew Brown had been trained to throw left hooks and jabs in hopes of getting inside the guard of right-handers, in hopes of opening his victim up for a Sunday punch with his cocked right fist.

By extending his own right arm as if it was his natural guard, Longarm hoped to make Brown pause long enough to think. Not an easy task for his kind. Brown bulled in without much study, sure of his superior bulk and doubtless encouraged by memories of all the other poor souls he'd beaten the shit out of.

So he wasn't expecting Longarm's right jab, thrown with the full strength of a right cross, from an unfamiliar angle. Brown caught it with his left elbow, of course. It still made his funny bone tingle like hell. Then he was more concerned with the left cross he just knew a natural left-hander was going to follow up with. So he was open to the right hook Longarm threw instead. It exploded against the bigger man's left ear to fill his head with freight-train noises and his eyes with spinning stars. Then Longarm threw that round-house left Brown had

160

been worrying about too early, and the effects on Brown's wide-open face were severely messy.

Having landed a hard left to the bridge of the bully's nose, Longarm switched his lead foot to the left and danced a trip-hammer series of left jabs into the wide-open Brown as he finished their fight right-handed.

It didn't last long after that. Brown was so blinded by pain and confusion he kept throwing counterpunches aimed at stopping a left-handed attack, all the while blubbering threats and curses as he kept getting hit hard.

Then he was down and somebody was yelling, "Stomp him, Deputy! Stomp him good if you want to live!"

Longarm did no such thing, of course. His jaw was only numb by now, and he'd clean forgotten those soap weed spines through his jeans as it seemed more important right now just to breathe.

So he was standing there, fists bunched but lowered, as he panted for his second wind and waited to see what Brown meant to do or say next.

Brown didn't say anything, unless you wanted to count guttural growls and slobbering moans. But what he *did* next involved an eight-inch barlow knife gripped low for some upward ripping as the downed but hardly out Corporal Brown rolled back to his feet to move back in on Longarm, wary as a wolverine out to snatch the bait from a bear trap.

So Longarm muttered, "Aw, shit, this has gone far enough," and drew his double derringer, still attached to one end of his watch chain. "I've just established I can lick you fair, you dumb bastard. Put that damn knife away or I'll kill you and we'll just say no more about it."

Being a born bully who'd survived well into manhood, Brown somehow knew Longarm meant it. So he stopped where he was, but protested his knife was no fair match for a damn gun.

Longarm smiled amiably and replied, "That's why I pulled it on you. I ain't as fond of bleeding as you seem to be, Arkansas. If you want to fistfight some more, I reckon I'm game for that. If you're talking about finishing one another off with weapons, well, the man being picked on has his choice of weapons. You can look it up. You'll find it in that Code Duello some other

161

fighting fools made up and put down on paper in French."

Corporal Brown had to grin through busted-up lips as he gamely replied he didn't savvy French, but didn't aim to go against the rules if Longarm was sure that was how they'd been put down.

So Longarm moved back to gather up his hat and gun rig as others helped the battered Brown back to the cookfire.

By the time Longarm had offered Brown a leadfoil tube of zinc white in sulfurated oil from his saddlebag, the mulligan and weak coffee were about ready.

So Longarm got to have a sensible talk with Corporal Brown after all, as they ate together a tad apart from the others on a patch of cushiony mountain campions.

Still bleeding some through the thick coating of soothing cut ointment, Brown seemed able to see now how important it was to keep those Mexicans screwing with the sheep till they could be delivered, the way General Sherman said. When Brown said he was still sure he could lick Longarm and both his greaser pals after a little rest and a chance to consider what he'd done wrong just now, Longarm confided, "Young Ramon may look sort of prissy next to you and me, Arkansas. But I may have saved your life just now. For the last thing you ever want to do is pull a knife on any Basque. That's what both them sheepherders are, and Basques sort of invented knife-fighting. You ever read that long poetic *Chanson de Roland* when you were in school, pard?"

Brown protested, "Shit, no. You was the one quoting French at us just now."

Longarm chuckled. "They got it set in English, and I was sure a fighting fool like you would be up on the subject. Old Roland was one of them armor-plated knights, riding for old King Charlemagne at a mountain pass called Roncesvalles. That's up in the Basque country betwixt France and Spain."

Brown said, "I've seen pictures of them armor-plated riders. I never seen one in the flesh, though."

Longarm said, "Neither had the Basque folks who lived up yonder in them hills and hollows. It might have been jake with them if old Charlemagne had asked their permit to march his army through their range. But being a king, he likely didn't feel he had to. Poor old Roland was the one who wound up

162

a heap like Custer at Little Big Horn when pissed-off Basque mountaineers came boiling out of the rocks all about. They gave him and his rear guard such a one-sided licking that later, when they set it all to music, they gave the credit to the Moors, saying there'd been twice as many of 'em."

He fished out two after-stew smokes as he explained, "Moors had armor-plated cavalry and a ferocious rep. So that beat explaining how sheepskin-armored kids with quarterstaves and throwing knives kicked the liver and lights out of all them French knights, see?"

Brown felt his puffed upper lip and said he'd smoke such a fancy cheroot later. Then he asked, "Are you saying them two sheepherders we've only been having a little fun with could be kin to a bunch of good old boys who taught them fancy Frenchmen not to mess with 'em?"

When Longarm allowed he was, Brown croaked, "Well, shit, how was I supposed to know they weren't just plain old greasers? You got to admire a country boy who won't take shit off Fancy Dans who think their shit don't stink, just because they went to some Fancy Dan college."

Putting the cheroot away under his dusty blood-flecked summer tunic, Brown grumbled, "Ain't an officer in this outfit who's ever heard a shot fired in anger, for all their West Point diplomas that won't mean shit when Mr. Lo comes at 'em hollering for hair! I told you I fought Shoshoni up to the South Pass the last time they riz under Buffalo Horn, didn't I?"

Longarm nodded soberly. "That was a good scare while it lasted."

He felt no need to brag that he'd been there as well. And even the official records preferred to describe Buffalo Horn's hostiles as Shoshoni rather than Bannock, likely for the same reasons Basques were called Moors in that *Song of Roland*.

After he'd had more mulligan and weak coffee than he'd really wanted, Longarm gathered up his two ponies and led them all the way down to the remuda. Old Hernan joined him as he was switching his McClellan to the rested-up black barb and packsaddles to the new buckskin, who deserved a rest from carrying him.

The old Basque pointed up at the soldiers in the distance with his grizzled chin and softly asked, "What was that all about, El Brazo Largo? From down here it looked like a fight."

Longarm said, "It was. Don't tell Ramon, lest he feel insulted, but I don't reckon he'll have as much trouble with Corporal Brown now."

Hernan nodded soberly and declared, "You are right. He is young and young men are inclined to feel insulted more easily than older men think wise. But what if this Corporal Brown starts teasing the boy again, perhaps when he recovers a bit?"

Longarm sighed and soberly replied, "I reckon someone will just have to kill him then. For there are stupid sons of bitches you can knock some sense into and there are others you can't."

Chapter 15

The wind shifted and it started to rain. By the time Longarm had hauled out his black slicker and cussed it on, the lightning bolts cracking all about had scattered the goats, bunched the sheep, and made the remuda hard to handle. So Longarm saddled the black barb and mounted up to give the whistling sheepherders and their barking dogs a hand.

Goats spooked a lot like cows, save for being smaller and prone to turn on a dime. So Longarm and his pretty good cutting pony had their work cut out for them, and they were mighty thankful for some help from old Bilbo, a black and tan mutt who just loved to snap at goat muzzles.

By the time they had the soggy herd back in one bawling millstone, the rain had let up and, though the sky stayed dark enough, afternoon sun was getting through the overcast to make Longarm regret his choice in raingear. For while the New England-made yellow oilskins favored by most range riders could make a lawman stand out at an easy rifle range, they were a hell of a lot lighter than his vulcanized poplin version.

He'd dismounted to spread the sticky garment smoothly over some dwarf cedar when he spied that shavetail coming back with company. He had to grudgingly concede that newspaper gal sat a horse well as the two of them came down the wet slope to the west at a fast lope.

They swung around the herd, ignoring the mounted Basque on that side, to rein in close to Longarm. The young officer asked, "What on earth have you all been doing back here? Captain Granville has already moved on, lest man and beast alike come down with the ague by just standing about all afternoon wet and shivering!"

Longarm replied agreeably, "Yonder stock will doubtless dry out faster, or at least they won't stiffen up, if we head 'em on out. I'll see if Hernan feels they've had their fill of peppergrass for now."

The platoon-leading squirt said in that case he'd ride on and get his men mounted up and ready to ride. Longarm expected the gal to go on with him, seeing she seemed to admire officers so much.

When she stayed put, he smiled up at her uncertainly and calmly demanded, "Is there something I can do for you, George, seeing your gallant captain's busy?"

She looked confused, the way gals always did when they wanted a man to disbelieve what he knew, and replied, "I rode back with the lieutenant because you and this tribute to the Navaho seem to be the real story, Custis."

He regathered his still-damp slicker as he growled, "Don't you dare put down one word about anyone offering *tribute,* George. Kit Carson licked the Navaho fair and square, and it's the *losing* side as gets to pay *tribute* to the *winning* side. This here stock is a generous peace offering to a nation sensible enough to stay friends with us Belagana during times of temptation."

She demanded in a schoolmarm tone, "Don't you mean the Great White Father remembered overdue treaty provisions after his Navaho children gave his soldiers blue a good scare earlier this spring?"

Longarm lashed his loosely rolled raingear atop his saddlebags behind his bedroll as he grunted, "That too. Albeit only Changing Woman could tell us what inspired that outbreak of sniping, if she was in the habit of explaining. I keep saying they don't see things exactly the same as us, or even other Indians, but nobody listens."

He swung up into his saddle, adding, "At least I know how little I know about the plans of mice, men, and Changing Woman. Fetterman and Custer were more sure than me about Indians. All I know is that it's best to do more than *guess* at what's making that noise in the cellar before you tear down the steps without a light."

166

He didn't invite her, but she tagged along as he loped over to old Hernan and asked if he thought the herd was about ready to move on. When the older man said he'd try and went whistling after Ramon, the newspaper gal asked, "Why didn't you tell him the captain *ordered* all of us to move on?"

He cocked a thoughtful brow at her and asked, "Are you in the U.S. Army, George? I was wondering why you took orders so good. Hernan and Ramon ain't. I just got through straightening out some of the army about that, I hope. Aside from being proud and proddy, those two professional sheepherders are in position to herd fast or slow as they danged well please, no matter who orders 'em to do what. As a hand more familiar with herding cows, resentful or enthusiastic, I doubt I could prove whether they were messing up deliberately should they choose to lose that herd completely among the canyon maze we're depending on them to move 'em through."

She seemed smart enough to grasp that, smiling in sudden understanding as she said, "In other words, you believe in riding fast as possible with a gentle hand on the reins."

Then she asked, "May I ask why I seem to be the exception to your easy riding, Custis?"

He couldn't help saying he hadn't been the one riding her.

She insisted innocently, "Yes, you have. You've been cold as ice to me of late, and I just don't understand you at all. You seem so free and easy with everyone else, save for perhaps the captain when he gets a little silly."

"You'd know better than me about how silly he can get," Longarm almost blurted out like a jealous school kid, even as he told himself, or tried to, it was none of his beeswax why such a refined-looking young beauty would want to suck off such a pompous lard-ass. He managed not to blurt out anything childish about having shot it out with more Indians than her gallant captain had ever looked at from the window of a passing train. He shut up to let her have her say.

Which was: "You treat those Mexicans as if they were old friends, and you've even a wistful smile for that pagan goddess Changing Woman. Yet whenever I try to talk to you, you make me feel as if I was a bug on a pin you were examining with a lens, but not too much interest."

167

He assured her she was more interesting than your average bug, and swung his mount to ride on as he saw the Basques and their dogs had the bellwether moving again.

She tagged along, even though he was riding away from her gallant captain for the moment. He stood in the stirrups and waved at the drag riders, sitting their own ponies uncertainly off to the east.

They savvied his cavalry hand signals and fanned out as he wanted. Up the slope behind them he saw that shavetail had his platoon about ready to ride rear guard. So he spun his barb to lope wide of the herd the other way, with that infernal brunette loping after him to shout, "Where . . . are . . . we . . . going . . . now?" as her pretty butt got a slower pounding than it was likely used to, the pudgy son of a bitch.

As they topped the rise Longarm reined in for the moment, pointed at the distant smoke rising from the Abrams trading post, and swung back over to the trail through the stirrup-high wet sage without further comment. She sure asked a lot of questions for a sass who thought she knew all the answers.

Thanks to that recent rainsquall, the sign read sort of funny on the storm-smoothed trail ahead. Had he been breaking in a green deputy, he'd have explained why it read only two ponies appeared to have moved east along that trail in recent memory, the rain having wiped away the sign of two cavalry platoons and a wagon train that had been over it just an hour or so earlier.

He didn't say anything to the pretty pest riding beside him. It hardly seemed likely she'd ever be called upon to read sign for her *Washington Globe*. But when she asked him what he was pouting about now, he relented and tried to make light of it as he said he'd been thinking about getting those wagons past Hovenweep.

He hadn't, but he knew no pretty female could stand the thought of a man she didn't give a shit about not giving a shit about her.

If he wasn't careful she'd start trying even harder to give him a hard-on, just for practice. Although more than once he'd convinced a snooty sass she just had to have him, seeing he didn't seem to just have to have her.

In this case, since he sure as shit *didn't* want the captain's play-pretty, he tried to sound more friendly as they rode along, with her asking most of the questions about the flora and fauna they encountered along the trail. He believed her when she said she'd never known the columbines grew red and yellow instead of blue on this side of the Continental Divide. But he knew she was just making conversation as she declared a jackrabbit they flushed a monster. For he knew they had rabbits back where she'd grown up.

Glancing back from time to time, he saw Hernan and Ramon had the herd moving pretty good on full bellies under a cool spring overcast. That saved them stopping as they rode past the Abrams trading post again, although he felt obliged to wave at old Ike and the two ladies watching from the front steps.

As they rode on, he casually declared anyone from the third platoon who needed to shop back there could catch up easily enough since they were moving no more than three miles an hour.

The brunette said, "That Indian girl back there is very attractive. You say you spent the night there, Custis?"

He couldn't help growling, "Sure I did. It was a lot of fun. So how was *your* night, George?"

She sounded innocent as hell, considering, when she answered him she'd had a little trouble getting to sleep in her wagon. When she sheepishly added she was probably just a dude gal who'd spent way too many nights in feather beds, he muttered, "Reckon it depends a lot on who's on top."

He was sorry he had when she gasped, "Oh!" in a small hurt voice and fell silent, even though that was some improvement, and even though he knew some men would have come right out and said what they thought of a teasing cocksucker with such disgusting tastes in cocks.

He felt no call to comment on the torn-up state of the trail ahead, now that they'd overtaken sign left by her captain and the others since that rain. But after close to an hour's silent riding they came to a fork in the trail. Whereupon Longarm muttered, "What the hell?" and reined in to reach back in a saddlebag. The newspaper gal asked what was wrong, adding, "There doesn't seem to be any mystery here. Even I can see they took the fork to the right."

Glancing up at the overcast sky, he muttered, "I could be wrong. We'd best let my old army compass decide."

He got the brass instrument out, saw what was magnetic north at a glance, and held it up to sight the azimuth of some snowcapped peaks far to the northeast before he snorted in disgust and asked nobody in particular, "Don't they issue even one compass to a whole troop of cavalry bound for strange canyon country?"

The second time she asked what was wrong he explained, "The trail your gallant captain chose seems wider and more traveled because it's a cattle trail, leading in toward Durango from Lord knows where. I reckon Granville and his veterans don't worry about wagon ruts when they're traveling in the company of wagons."

The brunette proved she was smart about some things by nodding and saying, "I see what you mean, Custis. That other trail to the left has those two deep grooves, as if lots of steel-rimmed wheels must have gone *that* way instead of . . . where, Custis?"

To which the only truthful reply was: "I don't know. Back there at the trading post they assured me wagons could roll at least as far west as Hovenweep Canyon. I didn't ask what lay up yonder, off any survey map I've ever seen. It all looks fairly level from here, but the drainage, a heap of drainage for millions of years, runs towards the McElmo to the south of us."

He swung his mount to face the fork in the trail as he heard whistles and the tinny clanking of the bellwether overtaking them. When Hernan spotted them and rode forward to see what was up, Longarm called out, "*El capitan es perdido!* The rest of you follow this trail that goes somewhere, and I'll overtake the *pendejo* and turn him around before he leads his column over a cliff!"

He nodded to the newspaper gal and added, "Stay here and pass it on to that shavetail bringing up the rear, George. I got some riding to do if we're all to eat supper in one bunch this evening."

He lit out at a lope he figured the barb could sustain, knowing the riders ahead would be moving slower in consideration of those sheep and goats they thought they were leading somewhere.

170

He hadn't ridden far when he heard the blasted hoofbeats of that big thoroughbred overtaking him, and sure enough, it was that pesky newspaper gal, cutting across the gentle bends in the false trail to overtake him.

He reined to a walk, calling, "Don't leave the trail in canyon country, girl. Trails sometimes bend in these parts, with a mile-deep slit in mind!"

She quickly got back on the trail. He didn't ask why she was in such a hurry to get back to her gallant captain. He said, "If you're riding with me, listen tight. They call the formation under us the Navaho Sandstone or Pumpkin Rock because it's sort of orange and carved up artistically by Changing Woman and many a falling raindrop, however rare they might fall in a given year. The Indians call it crawling into the pumpkin when it's done on purpose, and falling into the pumpkin when it's a fatal accident. Either way, think of what seems the solid ground we're riding across as all sliced up, sometimes only inches across but deep enough to kill you if you fall in. The folks who laid out this cattle trail wouldn't want that to happen, even to a cow. So let's ride, but stay the hell out of that innocent-looking chaparral to either side, hear?"

She said she understood, and the cattle trail was wide enough for them to ride side by side most of the time. He set a pace her faster mount could manage, despite it's not having the wind of a cow pony.

They were both as surprised, a few miles on, when they topped a slight rise to see the trail ahead seem to vanish in the middle of nowhere.

He slowed to a walk, warning, "Stay back. I reckon I see what's going on. But you never know for certain in canyon country."

He saw it was going to be all right as, approaching the rim, they could see how the cattle trail ran through a break in the rimrock at a sharp angle to lead down a gently sloping canyon wall to the narrow but flat sandy bottom. Taking the lead, Longarm marveled, "Old Granville must really enjoy nights in his spring wagon if he risked it on a ledge this narrow!"

The captain had, they saw, when they read all the easy sign an army column leaves in damp sand while making a hairpin turn. Longarm chuckled and told the brunette, "They figured it out without our help. Even a greenhorn could see how this canyon narrows up the other way, and someone likely broke out a compass at last."

She said, "I don't see any other trail leading *down* this canyon, Custis."

He said, "Of course you don't. Where were you when all that rain came down this afternoon, George? What your gallant captain and all them cows in the past got to treat as a trail, betwixt rains, is more like what you might call a river bottom at other times. The newer sign's so easy to read because the party ahead is moving over a sort of clean slate. Outlaws and Indian raiders like to confound their oppressors by hitting and running just before they figure it might rain. Let's go. Your gallant captain will doubtless cut across the sign of Hernan and the others on the right trail now. For it has to cross this watercourse as it widens out, one hopes, where it has to join the McElmo to the south."

They rode after the column, over a wide soft surface, save for occasional clumps of brush in the lee of immovable boulders and a narrow braided creek of purling water left over from that last rainsquall. He found himself explaining how the Pueblos farmed some of these canyons, where conditions were just right. She actually seemed to care as he said, "Growing crops in the narrower cuts through the pumpkin can be tricky. Some years you get no water at all for your blue corn, pinto beans, or squash. Other times, like this spring, you may get too much. We seem to be coming out of that dry spell that added to the other discontents of the Grant Administration. But let's hope it's rained all it means to today. We wouldn't want to find your gallant captain drowned with all his soldiers blue, you know."

She demanded, "Why do you keep calling Captain Granville my gallant anything in that sarcastic tone? Are you still suggesting I could be sweet on the rather pompous thing?"

Longarm shrugged and declared with conviction, "You're sure a good sport if you don't even *like* him, George."

She wound up to ask him what he meant by that. Then they'd rounded a bend and she glanced up to gasp, "Oooh, what in the world is all that, Custis?"

"Cliff dwelling," he replied laconically as they rode closer to what was more a village, or at least a fair-sized hamlet, built into an overhang of orange rock, say, thirty feet up the cliff.

Waving his free hand at the cluster of free-stone flat-roofed cubes and tubular towers he said, "Nobody lives that way no more. The Indians say these out-of-the-way cliff dwellings were built way back when by Anasazi or Hohokum, depending on whether you ask Na-Déné or the Hopi, who might be their remote descendants. You can't get the Hopi or other Pueblos to bet on that."

He saw where Granville and the others had reined in to send a couple of scouts up into the ruins afoot before riding on. He told her, "White men are more curious about cliff dwellings than Indians. That's likely why you still find prayer sticks, pots, and even dead Indians in some of the back rooms. Pueblos hold it's disrespectful to pester what translates as the Used Up People. The Navaho, calling 'em Ancient Strangers, Ancient Wise Ones, or Ancient Enemies in their own sort of flexible lingo, are just plain scared of whoever they were. All Na-Déné-speakers are scared of dead folk they haven't killed themselves. They say dead folk can turn into Chindi, which is like what we call a haunt, only worse."

She asked if they could go on up and sort of explore the ruins. He'd been a kid once. But it was getting late, and the riders out ahead of them had already made sure there was nothing up there worth a grown man's worry. So he was about to say no. Then he cocked an ear and decided, "We'd better see if we can work our mounts at least as high as that brush ledge halfway up to them ruins."

The brunette eyed the steep rock pile he was pointing at with a look of uncertainty as she protested, "That's crazy, Custis! My poor Crusader is a thoroughbred, not a mountain goat!"

Longarm snapped, "He ain't a sea lion neither. Didn't you just hear that thunder higher up? Get off and get up them rocks whilst I see what I can do with these ponies!"

He sounded like he meant it. They both heard more thunder as she dismounted and scampered up the rocks in a way that reminded a man she was a well-built female wearing tight cavalry britches.

173

Getting their mounts to scale the heights took longer. He led his smarter cow pony up first, in hopes the beautiful but dumb Crusader would see he wasn't really trying to hang horses by the neck until they were dead, dead, dead.

The newspaper gal had paused at the ledge midway, where crack willow and box elder had gained a purchase for their roots in a sideways crevice. So he handed her the barb's reins and slid back down for her mount as she wailed, "That was hardly gallant of you, and I'll never speak to you again if you drown my Crusader!"

He didn't, although he had to bloody the fool thoroughbred's mouth with the bit before he had it up beside the barb. He nodded at the fine job she'd made of tethering his mount to some stout box elder, and returned the favor by securing her spooked and wild-eyed mount too far from the barb to bite, or vice versa. His female companion stood clinging to a willow, facing the canyon on the fairly wide ledge. So she was the one who gasped, "Oh, my God!" as she saw what had been chasing them down the canyon.

Longarm turned to regard the churning waist-deep sudden flood of brown water in a calmer manner, observing, "Told you that was thunder we just heard. It won't be so bad lower down, where the water will have more room to fan out. That's likely why the modern Pueblo build on flatter ground."

She asked how long he thought they'd be marooned up there in the middle of nowhere.

He glanced at the overcast sky. It didn't tell him anything for certain. He said, "We ain't marooned in the middle of nowhere. We're waiting out a thunderstorm in what other folks used to call home."

It began to rain where they were. It was coming down fire and salt out in the open, but they found themselves behind a silvery veil as the downpour cascaded off the overhanging sandstone above.

The newspaper gal glanced back up into the gloom at the haunted-looking ruins and said, "Anasazi, you called them? I can see why they built here. Could we go on up and look around?"

He said, "Sure. We ain't Indians. But watch where you grab hold climbing, and if you smell vinegar, stop. Ain't nobody

174

brewing vinegar in these parts, but that's what vinegaroons smell like. Opinion seems divided on whether they're real scorpions or not. When you don't know what a strange man or critter may or may not do, it's best to just live and let live. Vinegaroons won't come at you as long as you let 'em be."

They didn't meet any scorpions, true or false, as they worked on up the steeper slickrock above the brush ledge. Longarm found himself explaining that the ancient cliff dwellers had braced log ladders in the tougher parts, but pulled them up when they were expecting unpleasant company. He added, "You can see for yourself how even a kid from the ruins above could clobber you good with rocks if you were somebody he was sore at. Meanwhile, as you see, there's no way to shoot back with a short bow and climb that steep a slope at the same time."

He realized he was talking so much because he was staring her smack in the crotch as she wriggled and slithered up ahead of him. Thanks to all that recent riding a distinctly female odor hung musky and, damn it, alluring in the moist air between his face and her twat. So when she made it over the edge above and turned on hands and knees to give him a helping hand, he ignored it, growling, "I'm all right. Just get out of my way, George."

She did, looking more puzzled than pained. Then she was on her feet to scamper on up to the ruins like a curious kid, shouting out, "Ooh, these walls seem ever so much higher and thicker once you're this close to them, Custis!"

He got to his own feet to follow, curious in his own right. He hardly ever got to arrest extinct folks. But who could pass up such a chance to explore haunted houses, a whole village of them?

So they explored, moving from one musty empty chamber to another in a vain attempt to guess what any particular one had been used for. The floors would have sloped had not the ancient builders dumped a lot of clay-bound pebbles over the original bedrock they'd put all this hard work on top of. They found occasional terra-cotta shards, but no unbroken pottery. Longarm figured that meant that the old-timers had moved away peaceably, with plenty of time to pack, or that he and the captain's play-pretty weren't the first whites who'd ever climbed up there.

When she asked about the absence of pottery for readers of the *Washington Globe,* he told her, "We know your gallant captain sent at least one scout up here earlier. Pot-hunting whites usually take way longer to strip one of these ruins this totally. Indians consider it bad medicine to own anything that might have been dear to a Chindi when he or she was alive. Maybe the folks who used to live up here took all their valuables with 'em whilst they were still alive. Let's look around some more."

They did. Longarm was the one who found a narrow opening into the low atticlike space where the overhang came down to join the flatter bedrock behind the back walls of the dwellings to form storage bins or whatever. It was dark and stunk of bat shit. He struck a waterproof Mex match made of candle wax, and felt the hair on the back of his neck tingle as he soberly murmured, "Sorry to disturb you, sir or madam as the case may have been."

The articulated skeleton bundled in a mighty moldy turkey-feather robe just lay there on its side, grinning hollow-eyed and gape-jawed back up at him as the match flickered out.

Longarm struck another, explaining, "I ain't out to invade your personal privacy. I just want to . . . Don't come in here, George!"

But she already had, gasping, "Oh, my God, how horrible!"

He shook the match out, saying, "Sometimes they mummify really spooky in the drier canyons. White folks have been up here ahead of us."

As they ducked back outside he explained. "Whoever that was in there, he or she would have been laid to rest with at least a few pots or baskets of grub for their trip to the spirit world. No kin would have disturbed such belongings. No strange Indian would want to. Yet that long-gone cliff dweller lay there without so much as a shell bead to call his or her own. Cowhands, most likely. When it ain't a river, this canyon seems to serve as a cow path up to that higher level."

She followed as he moved on, explaining half to himself how the Four Corners country was laid out in a series of more or less flat levels that varied in altitude like the stories of some vast building, or perhaps like those rice terraces he'd seen in picture books about the Orient. He said, "As I follow the geology of these parts, George, once upon a million years ago it was all the bottom of a swampy inland sea, with all sorts of mud spreading out flat in layers that hardened to different kinds of rock. So once Changing Woman lifted it all up a mile or so, and commenced to carve at it with time and patient weather, each maze of canyons cut down to the harder layers, and then spread out to form a whole new level of range, which started to gully in turn until its frayed edges fanned out at a still lower level and . . . Suffice it to say, there's a monstrous expanse of arid range off to the west called Monument Valley, which is really sort of the basement of this here canyon, with rocks such as this canyon's walls standing all about like tombstones clean to the horizon. Ain't that a bitch?"

She glanced out a window slit at the falling rain as she allowed it all seemed awfully complicated. He was too modest to say that was likely why General Sherman had wanted him to ride with the outfit.

They found a large beehive-shaped chamber where someone before them had built a fire, a big one, in the center of the circular clay floor. Longarm said, "White men. No Indian would build that big a fire indoors, even in wintertime."

He spied a glint of blue glass near the freestone wall, and moved over to pick it up and hold it to the light, saying, "What did I tell you? This here's a medicine bottle."

He moved outside with it to see if he could make out the lettering molded into the small thick bottom of the six-ounce bottle. There was a lot number and the name of the New Jersey glassblower who'd made it. But no indication as to what the bottle might have been meant to contain. He grimaced and said, "Must have had a paper label that's long gone. Seen a bottle like this in a lady's medicine cabinet one time. Wouldn't have been polite to ask her what she used it for."

The newspaper gal asked to see it, held it high, and assured him in a sort of flustered voice that it didn't seem like the bottles a lady bought for female complaints or . . . hygienic reasons.

177

He almost said he'd already figured that. But he didn't want to get into how an unmarried man might have learned so much about female hygiene. He took it back and said he'd find out later.

She laughed incredulously. "What on earth might it possibly matter, Custis? Who cares what some saddle tramp had in a bitty bottle he left behind as worthless?"

Longarm shrugged. "Might have been a she. Told you the last time I saw a bottle like this it was in a lady's medicine cabinet. The more I think about it, the less I see why cow folk of any gender should be herding cows through here."

Pointing with the blue bottle at the veil of rainwater between them and the open canyon, he continued. "The climate or at least the drainage must have been different, a heap different, when the folks who built these ruins built 'em."

She sighed and said, "It's all so sad, after all the work they put in, to think of how the advance of civilization spoiled it all for them."

He blinked, frowned, and declared, "George, you ain't been listening. The folks who built these cliff dwellings moved out of the canyons a good time before Columbus took that wrong turn to India! Civilization didn't spoil their way of life. They *were* civilized folk, trying to get by despite less-civilized neighbors. Wandering hunters and gatherers don't understand property rights as settled farm folks do."

She looked puzzled. "Where could anyone farm around this godforsaken part of the world?"

He said, "I'm sure the Lord and Changing Woman have changed it around some, George. The farm folks would have grown their corn, beans, squash, and peppers on that canyon floor out yonder, doubtless with enough tobacco to see 'em through in the ceremonies we can only guess about today. There ain't no way to farm this canyon or many another now. Like I said, Changing Woman's messed up the drainage. Canyons carry ever more runoff as they grown longer and deeper further up. Or maybe the old cliff dwellers we'll never really know *did* grow crops, some years, on almost impossible croplands. Maybe they had to because they were way outnumbered by more savage folk. Then maybe they grew to bigger bands, or learned to fight better, so they moved out of these narrow canyons to farm more sensible fields, or *nabajus,* around those way bigger pueblos such as Taos or Black Mesa, and maybe they never really got to be extinct at all."

She frowned thoughtfully. "That's not nearly as good a story as a lost race of mysterious cliff dwellers. But are you out to convince me their modern descendants wouldn't have been better off today if Columbus hadn't taken that wrong turn?"

He shrugged. "If the dog hadn't stopped to sniff he might have caught the rabbit, or been caught by the dogcatcher. *If* is an uncertain word by definition, George. I like Hopi and such the way they are. Hopi means Peaceable Folk, and they try to live up to their handle. But have you ever considered what might have happened over this way if Columbus had never arrived?"

She stated in a positive manner, "The American Indian would have been ever so much better off!"

He shook his head. "You mean *some* of 'em would have been better off, whilst others might have wound up in an awful fix. I know we're supposed to be the meanest folks on Earth, George. But did you ever hear of the Aztec customs of ripping living hearts out or peeling naked gals alive so the priests could dance about inside their skins? Columbus was doubtless a religious fanatic, a slave raider, or worse. But he still met up with cannibal Caribs who'd been eating the Arawak men and carrying off Arawak women before the first white man came along to ask 'em to stop. Mohawk means Man Eater, you know. But why not stick with the more gentle conquering nations, no worse than, say, the Romans, Vikings, or Huns back in our old countries. Do you really think Indian nations that gloried in warfare as their natural calling would have left peaceable Hopi or harmless Paiute alone if we'd never come along to change their happy way of life?"

She ventured, "We'll never know. We *did* come along and we *did* change their way of life, Custis!"

He gave up, not up to mentioning the quaint Bannock custom of riding down Paiute just for practice, without pausing for so much as a scalp lock since no coup could be counted on mere Diggers.

He fished out his watch, consulted the sky outside as well, and told her, "We may as well study on a fire. Fortunately,

179

I packed some emergency rations in my saddlebags. That's what they call being caught short on the trail without your pack pony, an emergency."

She stared uncertainly up through the rain, asking, "Are you saying we could be stuck up here past suppertime?"

He started for the drop-off as he replied, "Might be stuck here longer if that blasted rain don't let up. But don't worry, George. Your gallant captain and the others will be waiting this out on high ground somewheres ahead. He won't ride on without you."

She said, "There you go with that guff about my gallant captain again, and how many times do I have to tell you that my friends all call me Grace?"

He said, "Stay here and I'll slide down and get some grub and our bedrolls, George."

He would have too had she thought to pack along her bedding atop her own saddlebags. He unlashed his own, and improvised a tote from his slicker for the canned goods from his saddlebags.

The two ponies were not where he'd have chosen to leave critters he was at all fond of. But they could get at puddled runoff and green leaves if they put any effort into either. So he told them both how sorry he was and gathered up some firewood, green branches being a tad thicker than dry, before he threw his bedroll up ahead of him and hauled firewood and grub after him in his slicker.

When he rejoined the brunette on the ledge above, she hadn't made any move toward his tightly rolled bedding. She regarded it dubiously and announced, "You seem to be taking a lot for granted, whether we're stuck here for the night or not, Custis."

He smiled thinly and replied, "No, I ain't, George. This rain may let up. Then again, it might not, and I'm not about to climb down over that slickrock in the dark."

She said, "That's not what I meant. We only seem to have that one bedroll between us."

To which he could only reply, "It ain't my fault you left your own bedding in your rolling love nest, George. I wasn't expecting company when I rolled my own this morning. Let's see about getting that fire started inside, and farther along, like

180

e old song says, we'll know more about it."

He toted his load inside that same beehive chamber, figuring spot one white man had built a fire in was likely a good lace to get another going. The brunette watched from the oorway as he spread shredded bark atop a crumpled square f notepaper, bit the slugs off two .44-40 rounds, and salted e kindling with black powder, observing, "This is wasteful s well as lazy. But damp as both the air and this kindling is, might save in matches what I'm losing in ammunition."

She didn't seem to care. She said, "Custis, I know I may eem a woman of the world to you. I'm not going to pretend ɔ be a virgin to such an obvious man of the world, but eally . . ."

"I thought we weren't supposed to take too much for ɡranted," he grumbled as he broke up some stouter branches vith his strong hands and reached for his matches. "I don't now what gives you gals the right to assume every poor ucker that looks at you is just dying to slobber all over you. Ain't we allowed any say in such matters? I mean, come on, ɪe *fair,* George!"

She laughed despite herself and said, "Why do I feel some nvisible hand is going to reach out and go *Bego! Bego!* where ι girl sits down?"

He grunted. "Guilty conscience, most likely. They say Ƀegochidi mostly haunts those working hardest to preserve ɦeir dignity and hide their silly sides from the rest of the vorld."

He struck a match and applied it to his gunpowder. There :ame a bright flash and a man-sized mushroom of white ɪmoke. Then, for a minute, he was sure it wasn't going to vork as he knelt on hands and knees to puff at the few ɡlowing sparks in there until, just as he was about to start ɔver, a feeble flicker of flame winked up at him and began ɔ grow.

Settling back on his haunches, Longarm reached for a can ɔf tomato preserves, and began to slit it with the can-opener ɒlade of his pocketknife, saying, "If we share these tomatoes :old, we'll cut our appetites a mite and have a can to boil ɪome coffee in."

She said you couldn't make coffee that way.

He assured her, "I never said it would be *good* coffee George. I said it would be coffee. I generally pack along Arbuckle Brand, made for the cow trade specially to brew sort of primitive. You don't have to drink none if you don' want. But I meant to stay wide awake tonight whether here there, or anywheres."

She gulped and softly murmured, "Let's hope the rain let up before dark, then. For Lord only knows what sort of trou ble Begochidi could cause a poor girl around here before morning!"

Chapter 16

The rain let up just after sundown, to be replaced with pitch-black clammy darkness as the sky above stayed overcast while, down below, the canyon floor still ran with inky floodwater.

So along about midnight an uneasy brunette awoke with a start in Longarm's bedroll to ask where she was and what was going on.

Longarm growled, "I went to check our mounts again and gather us more firewood. Go back to sleep."

Being a woman, she propped herself up on one elbow instead, and watched as Longarm piled box-elder branches on the hot coals of their half-dead night fire. He'd chosen box elder over willow because it burned longer, if only you could set it on fire.

It wasn't easy. He'd tried for dead branches, but thanks to all the rain they'd had of late, the bark at least was still damp as a clapped whore's crotch.

It gave off more smoke and steam than further light on the subject for a time. But he knew it would dry enough to burn before the coals of the earlier greenwood went out completely. Meanwhile, the heavy smoke just billowed on up through the six- or eight-foot opening at the top of their beehive to stream up and around the curve of the overhang in a manner that caused no concern on such a dark night, even in Indian country. So Longarm moved over to seat himself against the circular freestone wall as the gal in his bedroll stared thoughtfully at him through the ruby light.

After an awkward silence, she licked her lips and shyly asked him, "Wouldn't we both be much more comfortable

183

under these covers—provided, of course, you promised to behave?"

He growled, "Stuff a sock in it and go back to sleep. You know that even if we did manage to fall asleep in such a ridiculous position, we'd only wake up screwing."

She gasped, "Oh! How dare you use that word around me!"

He grimaced and said, "All right. I take it back. We'd wake up in a state of fornication. I've made such deals with gals in my time. I even meant to sleep with 'em platonic on at least a few occasions. As you doubtless know, the parts of us below the waist don't always go along with the rest of us, or even with common sense. Let the brain go to sleep and the old ring-dang-doo will just naturally take over."

She didn't answer for a long time. He thought she might have dozed off as he'd suggested. Then she confided, in a small sad voice, "I lost my virginity that way. I was sleeping over at a school chum's house, and I never knew she was that kind of a girl until, suddenly, in the middle of the night, I was that kind of a girl too. I *wanted* us to stop. I knew it was awfully wicked if not downright crazy to go that far with another girl. But then we'd gone too far to turn back, and damn her, it felt so good to climax that way!"

The smoke was thinning, although if anything it seemed darker with the fresh wood refusing to blaze up as it dried out. Longarm told her, "I was wondering where you'd developed such tastes. Couldn't we sort of keep past sins to ourselves, George? I ain't no papist priest, and even if I was it would likely give me a hard-on picturing young gals going sixty-nine without a pal of my own to ease the pain."

She gasped, "Heavens! I've never done anything like *that* with any other woman. We just sort of, you know, played with one another under the covers while we kissed and said silly things."

He growled, "Well, feel free to play with yourself and quit saying such funny things, George. I know you only want to know whether I'd like to screw you. Gals always want to know that. Even when they don't give a damn or find the man downright repulsive. There's something in the female makeup

184

hat seems to feel way better once it knows it's wanted."

He reached for a smoke as he continued. "Consider yourself wanted, if it'll shut you up and let you get some rest. We may have some hard riding ahead come morning, if I ever get them ponies back down off this canyon wall."

She sounded like she was crying. He didn't ask why. Women tended to give off such sobbing sounds when they wanted a man to jaw with them some more.

He lit his cheroot and tossed the wax match stem into the nearby fire. It flared brightly and went out, of course, but it did seem as if the smoke was rising cleaner in the ruby gloom. Anyway, the air in there wasn't cold enough to keep a man from catching a bit of watchful rest at least.

Thanks to the black coffee and strong tobacco he was smoking, he figured he could tough it out till it was light enough to ride on with all this temptation.

He blew a thoughtful smoke ring at the glowing coals as he idly wondered why she was working so hard at it. For all his bullshit, old Casanova had been right about the effects of talking to a whore as if she were a lady and treating a lady as if she were a whore. He figured it was likely the novelty. He'd found it usually worked. So how come this camp-following cocksucker seemed so intrigued by a man who'd been treating her like, well, a camp-following cocksucker?

He'd have been treating her more like a lady, or at least a pal, had he wanted sloppy seconds and likely harsh words from her soldier blue. He'd been treating her like what she was because he'd seldom met such a gal who didn't ask to be paid extra when a man talked man-to-man about what she might have to offer.

From the bedding on the far side of the fire the sultry brunette suddenly demanded, "Is that why you've been so mean to me? You somehow suspected I liked girls?"

He laughed in surprise and replied in a friendlier tone than he'd intended, "Now *that* would be about the last thing anyone who really knew you would accuse you of, George!"

Then he blew more smoke and added in a more thoughtful tone, "Come to study on it, though, I have heard lots of soiled doves do get their real pleasures that way after work, when they feel no pressures to please mere men."

185

She protested, "What gives you the right to call me that kind of a girl, damn you and your superior smiles!"

He considered, nodded, and said soothingly, "I reckon soiled dove is too harsh a description for what one might call an adventuress, out for a good story come what may, and not really charging cold cash for . . . such favors."

She sat bolt upright, eyes blazing redly in the dim light and proud breast heaving under her summer-weight bodice as she demanded, "What lying bastard in the U.S. Cavalry claims I've even kissed him for any reason at all, dad blast him?"

Longarm blew smoke out both nostrils, sighed, and said, "Aw, lay down and quit lying, George. Ain't nobody but me knows what's been going on betwixt you and the captain, and your secret's safe with me."

"What secret?" she demanded so wildly it seemed to inspire bright flickers of flame to spring up between them as she almost screamed, "I'd screw my horse before I'd let that repulsive man even hold my hand! Who in God's name told you I was having an affair with Captain Granville, Custis?"

She sure sounded convincing. But he was used to dealing with good liars. Being lied to went with the badge. So he just shrugged and answered soothingly, "Maybe it was some other gal he was having so much fun with in his spring wagon more than once. Anyone can see we've got lots of gals tagging along with us out here."

She blinked, laughed hysterically, and snapped, "You big idiot! You mean you didn't know about Captain Granville and his baby-faced adjutant? It's the talk of their whole troop! I overheard it without even trying, tending my own . . . natural business during a trail break on our first day out on the trail!"

Longarm stared dubiously across the round chamber as the light kept getting better. She seemed to have no trouble meeting his level gaze, but any good liar could manage that. He finally said, "I dunno, George. It's true I've spent more time riding point and at least some of the troopers seem to find me a mite abrasive. But I heard what I heard, and you just now admitted you could be persuaded to act sort of familiar with members of your own gender."

She said, "Good grief, that was years ago, and if you must know, I found out soon after it felt ever so much better with a boy! Are you saying I'm just accusing Captain Granville of being a queer because I'm that way myself?"

He smiled thinly and replied that the thought had occurred to him. He added, "Any fireman can tell you tales of firebugs sounding the first alarm, George. I've lost track of the cow thieves who've told on cow-thieving neighbors, sometimes telling me true, albeit I've had more than one suspect grab others for me out of thin air. All I can say for certain is that *somebody* has sure been going at it hot as hell with Granville in that spring wagon!"

She almost popped a button, opening her blue bodice to expose a tasty-looking pair of bare tits in the firelight as she glared gypsy-wild and sobbed, "Does this look like the body of a queer, you goddamned fool?"

To which he could only reply, "Yep. Arrested a gal like that one time trying to pass for a banker's sweetheart, and no offense, she was built like a brick shithouse and talked more feminine than many another gal."

The very feminine brunette rolled up on her knees to unbutton and lower her army britches, exposing one mighty feminine torso as she knelt there half-undressed and taunted, "Come over here and find out just how much I like women, if you're *man* enough, Custis Long!"

So he did, even as what was left of his common sense tried to tell him it was better to be safe than sorry. The fire was blazing brightly by the time they were both watching it go in and out of her as he took her dog-style atop the bedding and their rumpled duds. But he didn't know whether to buy her wild story or not until later, after a more romantic finish and a shared smoke, when he asked her to play him a tune on his French horn and get it hard for him some more.

Kissing his bare chest, she began to fondle him down yonder, but softly pleaded, "Please don't ask me to do that, darling. I know a lot of respectable married couples do things like that, but maybe I just haven't had enough experience. One of my previous lovers even made me commit a crime against nature, and I never spoke to him again. Call me a big silly if you will. But it hurt and I hated it."

He reached out with his free hand to snub their cheroot on the the bare clay as he softly marveled, "Well, if you're

187

fibbing you're good at it and you like old Granville better."

She bit his chest, not hard enough to draw blood, and gave him a good hard squeeze down yonder as she said, "Bastard! How can you say that after making me come with this in me twice?"

He kissed the part in her raven hair. "You got me half convinced. That other gal, if it was a gal, seemed to be taking it from Granville in the mouth. If it was the adjutant, then he was also taking it up the . . . way you say you found sort of painful."

She snuggled even closer, saying, "I felt degraded too. Why do you men work so hard to get at a girl's vagina if you really like it better other places, darling?"

He chuckled, reached down to rock the little man in the boat for her, and said, "Grass always seems greener on the far side of such fences, I reckon. Maybe we just want to own all of a gal totally. Or there ain't no sensible reason. The way we carry on might look silly to a salmon or black widow spider, and why would anyone with a lick of real sense ever want to go to this much trouble to begin with?"

She began to stroke him skillfully, for such an inexperienced young thing, as she purred, "Do you want me to quit and just let this poor thing ponder the true purpose of the universe, dear?"

He began to stroke her faster too as he assured her, "That old organ-grinder ain't got a brain in its head high as you seem to be raising it, kitten. But speaking of common sense, can't you see how much smarter it would be if all of us just jacked off every time we felt such tingles?"

She was breathing faster too as she managed to reply in the same objective tone, "Would you really want to live in a world where nobody did anything they didn't really *have* to, darling?"

He rolled atop her and let her guide his fresh erection where they both wanted it, without his asking, as he assured her, "Hell, no. I'd be out of a job, and this sure feels better than anything either of us could do by hand. So Powder River and let her buck!"

But he still knew he was going to feel a lot better about all this once he found out for sure about Captain Granville and that adjutant. For he could be in a hell of a fix if she was fibbing!

Despite their late start they got a reasonable amount of sleep. Next morning, in the cold gray light of reason, she naturally accused him of having planned his curious seduction of a poor curious newspaper reporter from the beginning. So he let her have her own way, which seemed to be with her on top, once they'd polished off the last of their cold coffee and she'd decided to forgive him just this once.

He warned her he hadn't packed his emergency rations with two riders in mind. So she agreed they'd best get dressed and see about catching up with the others.

It wasn't easy, even after they'd worked their mounts down to the canyon floor and grazed them some up a box canyon that hadn't been scoured clean by all that floodwater.

She accused him of being lost after they'd ridden half the day through an ever more confounding maze. He explained he wasn't lost. He knew he was working his way southwest through the canyonlands of the Four Corners country. It was a damned old government column he was confused about.

Thanks to the recent gully-washers, any sign left by anyone within the past twenty-four hours or more had been obliterated. He'd already told her how canyons running together in a braided pattern could turn into more like a monument-studded plain. But the sun was out again, and he knew the even deeper canyonlands of the McElmo had to run not too far to the south. She was still saying they ought to stop somewhere and ask directions when he decided, "We've crossed the trail. I mean we've crossed where it used to run. The ripple marks all around are telling a tale of water that was really running last night. I doubt the old boys who blazed that old trail were figuring on bobbing down the McElmo on rafts."

He reined in and swung them around, although not to retrace their double line of hoofprints across the pristine sand. He pointed off to the west between two massive buttes of sandstone and said, "We got to work our way to higher ground before we swing north in search of sign. Ain't no sign to search for where all that water just ran."

She said she was in no position to argue, and asked why anyone had ever blazed a trail through such horrid country to begin with.

He replied, "Aw, it ain't so horrid if you admire scenery a mite on the stark side, George. Most white riders headed west through the Four Corners are prospectors or carrying the mail to Mormon settlements along the north bank of the San Juan River. Everything south of that is Dinetah, or that big Navaho Reserve we're headed for. We'll find a good crossing somewhere this side of where the Chinlé Valley runs due north into the San Juan. The plan is to herd all that stock due south up the Chinlé, to where the Navaho *ricos* may see fit to take 'em off our hands. With luck we may get rid of the fuzzy pests by the time we get to the big bend of the Chinlé, and I'll be free to ride on to Fort Defiance with you all."

She dimpled across at him and said, "Ooh, *bego bego.* What's the big difference between a *rico* and a chief, and why would either refuse a handsome gift right on his reservation line, darling?"

Longarm looked pained and said, "No *rico* has the authority, or the nerve, to grab fifteen hundred head of treaty stock for himself. We're the ones who confuse heaps of Indians and Indian treaties by deciding who's a chief, a medicine man, and so on. Folks with neither Webster's Dictionary nor a written constitution ain't as clear as us about such matters. If I'm pronouncing it right, a Navaho who seems to have good medicine, or *alil,* is called a man of respect, or *xastin,* unless he's admired enough to be listened to, which makes him a *xastoi. Rico,* or Mex for high-toned, seemed closer in meaning to a squaw man and good scrapper called Kit Carson when he hammered out a treaty with a bunch of 'em back in '68."

She said she'd heard Indian chiefs ruled more by persuasion than actual authority.

He said, "It's more complicated than that. Those one ought to listen to Navaho-style divide into *xastoi* with *bixo,* or wisdom, and *biji,* which translate more like spirit rapping. So which *xastoi* a Navaho might listen to at a given time depends on what sort of a problem he's faced with. He'd want the advice of a smart raider if planning a raid, a good deer hunter if he was off to hunt deer, or a gent who'd memorized all five

190

hundred or so chanting ways if he was having trouble with a toothache or other witchcraft."

The sandy range they were riding now had been smoothed by rain but not scoured by floodwater. So he swung them north, past those two rock formations, as he explained, "The current tribal leaders, spiritual as well as temporal, will doubtless have to wave their prayer sticks at the sky, paint with colored sand on the ground, and whang away on their chanting drums a spell as they work out just how many head of stock each *rico* and his band might rate. Like I said, I'm hoping for an early resolution this side of where the army column has to fork off toward Fort Defiance on the Navaho-Ute line. For there's a good twenty-five thousand square miles to Dinetah, and that sure gives 'em plenty of opportunity to inconvenience a wayfaring Belagana!"

She said, "I'm just beginning to get a sense of how big the country feels out this way. Back in Washington I was given to understand the poor Indians had been shoved into little worthless corners of the West."

He smiled thinly and replied, "Lots of Indians would agree with you. Uncle Sam has still ceded the average Indian way more land than any homesteader is allowed to claim after paying a filing fee. Some Indians wound up stuck with less desirable reserves than others, the same as some white settlers wound up with good or bad claims. Dinetah is not only bigger than my whole home state of West-by-God-Virginia, but the original hunting ground they chose for themselves, at the expense of less ferocious Indians. But that ain't saying they won't bellyache for more in newspapers such as your own."

She demurely stated she wasn't as sure what she'd report about a mission that seemed more complicated than she'd expected.

Longarm suddenly laughed and pointed ahead, where the westbound trail ran only a little blurred by all that heavy rain. He chortled, "See how the third platoon fanned out to herd them woollies to higher ground at a trot, George? They've been making way better time than I thought. Hernan must have convinced the captain that wasn't distant chanting drums they kept hearing down among these canyons."

191

She said the least a gentleman could do would be to call a lady by her right name after all that *bego bego* she'd put up with. So he tried Grace a few times, and settled for honey. He doubted she'd go for pard.

They followed the clear-to-read trail another few miles before they came to a watered grassy side canyon and turned up it a ways to water, graze, and rest their jaded mounts while they caught up on some more *bego bego* under the shade of an old piñon tree.

When she asked him whether it meant titty-titty or pussy-pussy, he said he wasn't sure. They'd told him Begochidi grabbed gals both ways from behind, and he showed her what he meant as they went at it dog-style as well as bare-ass in some vanilla-scented love grass.

Later, as they shared a smoke in the sun-dappled shade while the unsaddled ponies cropped contentedly, Grace snuggled closer to sigh and murmur, "I'll just never forgive those drum-banging Navaho if you don't go all the way with me to Fort Defiance. Do you suppose we'll be able to share a real bed in a private bedroom there, dear?"

He grinned at the picture and assured her, "Not hardly. You'll be invited to stay at the post commandant's as an honored guest, and they'll expect you to spell their names right. But getting back to civilization from there won't be half as complicated, honey. Uncle Sam sent us through all these canyons from the northeast because that was where both the bargain stock and reinforcement for Fort Defiance were to begin with. Once you reach the fort you'll find it's only a good day's ride by a southeast post road to Gallup, New Mexico, and points east."

She said she'd wait for him at Fort Defiance if he got hung up with those sheep and dad-blasted Indians.

He didn't answer. He knew how she'd feel after a day or so in a dull frontier post with a story to file for her Eastern paper. He got rid of the smoked-down cheroot and said, "We'd best get dressed and ride on if we expect to catch up with the outfit by suppertime."

She wanted to screw some more while they had this Garden of Eden all to themselves, so sure enough, it was well after sundown when they finally rode into Captain Granville's

192

bivouac. They had to eat their army rations cold. But she said she didn't mind, and he figured it had been worth it as well.

The outfit had pulled off the beaten path into yet another side canyon, this one boxed at the upper end to form a natural corral for all the stock. The officer of the day told them the captain had retired for the night.

Longarm had already noticed there were no spring wagons parked within sight. When he asked about that, the junior officer explained the captain had sent them back, escorted by most of his headquarters and service platoon, to catch up as best they could on the longer but far safer way around, down the far side of all those incredible bumps in this particular road.

Longarm mildly observed he'd thought they might get at least as far west as Hovenweep with the wagons, but he didn't rub it in. The gal he'd made it so far west with took him aside to ask where she could possibly sleep, now that they'd sent all her bedding back over the Continental Divide in that dad-blasted wagon.

He calmed her down by leading her still further aside, with their ponies, and unlashing the bedroll she'd already helped him warm up. "I'll find out what they did with your baggage. I doubt even Granville would be dumb enough to send it on for you by way of Gallup, New Mexico Territory!"

He spread the roll out on a patch of soft dry sand where some knee-high sticker bush grew between them and the main camp. He told her to make herself comfortable there while he scouted some.

She said they could never go dog-style right in the middle of an army bivouac. He told her to think more romantic thoughts, and left to see what he could see dark as it was getting.

He didn't actually catch Captain Granville and his adjutant in a bedroll together. A smirking immigrant, doubtless chosen for a piss-poor ability to gossip in English, turned Longarm back with a garbled explanation about long days in the saddle.

He got further confirmation when he finally found Hernan and young Ramon muttering in Basque around their own fire up the canyon past the horses. Hernan said everyone knew the captain was a boy-buggering *fregado,* now that he and his *mariposa* had no place for to hide their *habito tonto.*

Then he said, "We are not concerned with such childish *mierda,* El Brazo Largo. I have already told you we do not wish for to go on past the reservation line with these *cabrones pendejo.* Now I tell you we may not go that far. A man is a man, and you do not treat him as if he was a small boy if you wish him for to be your friend, *comprende*?"

Longarm thought he did. He grimaced and growled, "I told that asshole Brown to quit riding you. Are you saying I got to whup his ass for him some more, Hernan?"

The old sheepherder shook his head and said, "The corporal no longer speaks to us. His squad, some of them at least, have been inspired for to treat us with mocking respect. You are familiar, of course, with the childish game of Tu Madre?"

Longarm nodded. Everyone who'd spent any time at all along the border knew that one. Tu Madre, or Your Mother, was an exercise in smiling sarcasm and veiled threat, with the loser being the one who showed he was the least bit annoyed without showing the gumption to really go for blood.

A typical exchange might go, "They say the open mouth draws flies, my talkative and extremely brave friend. Might that have been a woman of my family I just heard you mention?"

The answer, unless you wanted to just say *"Tu madre!"* and go for your gun, would be something more delicately nasty, such as: "But how could I make disrespectful mention of any woman you could be related to? I don't know any of their names. I try to stay away from the sort of houses such beauties no doubt would work in."

Longarm doubted anyone in the U.S. Cav would have refined snide politeness to that point. But even as he assured the pissed Basques he'd look into it, he knew he'd be in for a fistfight with a feather mattress if he took it up with Brown or his superiors again. But with any luck he might keep Hernan and Ramon from lighting out for at least a few more miles.

Chapter 17

They lasted as far as the stop at Butter Wash, about half a dozen miles short of the Navaho trading post near the mouth of the Chinlé on the far side of the San Juan. Longarm had thought he had Hernan convinced he was trying. He had spent time riding along with them and the herd to see if he could catch any drag riders hazing Ramon or even a nanny goat. But naturally nobody had said or done a thing, unless you wanted to count a wise-ass smirk on a rider's dusty face as a thing worth a pistol-whipping.

So one evening the two Basques put the herd on fair forage up a box canyon running into Butter Wash, and the next morning neither they nor any more horses than they'd started out with seemed to be there anymore.

Captain Granville wanted to send an arresting party after such horse-thieving sons of bitches. Longarm managed to convince him they all were in enough trouble.

He had a tougher time convincing his amorous newspaper gal she didn't really need to tag along as he rode the other way for help. He said, "You'll soon be seeing more blessed Indians than you might want to. They're mighty curious about all us Belagana, and some of 'em may not have ever seen a white gal before. I want to talk to some of 'em more man-to-man before they get to gawking and paying no heed to my foolish chatter, see?"

She did. So he saddled the buckskin and rode, first across the ominously high brown swirls of the rain-fed San Juan, and then along the south bank through cane and willow, past many an oversized chess piece of weathered rock, till he

195

spied smoke rising above a treetop just as he was starting to wonder.

It wasn't clear whether anyone lived full-time in the cluster of hogans situated on a rise near the junction of the Chinle and bigger San Juan, or whether they just gathered there from time to time for trade or ceremonies. The two tended to blur together among folks who spoke the Na-Déné dialects.

A hogan was sort of what an Eskimo might make instead of a regular igloo if he was forced to build with timbers, sod, and mud. He'd seen some built neater, with octagonal walls, where the Indians had been able to steal railroad ties. But no railroad ran within weeks of this bunch, so they were built rounder, closer to the earth, and likely a lot more like the original hogan from somewhere up Canada way.

The dogs noticed him and the buckskin first, of course. A stranger knowing less about Na-Déné customs might have expected to get devoured alive by the snarling, snapping yellow curs. But Longarm just steadied his mount and soothed, "Easy, Buck. Them *letcai* mutts know well as we do what happens to a really mean dog around Navaho. They eat ponies that annoy them too. It's the *sheep* they really *value*, see?"

A fat old Navaho gal came out of a hogan to see what the dogs were fussing about, blinked in astonishment at Longarm, and squatted down in the dust to hoist her layers of pleated cotton skirts and scoop gritty dust up her crotch as she yelled in mortal terror.

That brought other Indians and a breed dressed more white outside to regard Longarm more calmly as he rode on in. A younger Navaho gal yelled at the older fat gal. Then she called out to Longarm, "Gordita thinks you wish to rape her. I just told her I think you must be with those blue sleeves we have been expecting. I hope you will not make a liar out of me, Belagana."

He refrained from saying the fat old gal sure flattered herself as he rode past her to dismount by the far prettier one. She seemed to be in charge of translating, in both Na-Déné and Spanish, as he told her who he was and let her introduce him all around. The trader seemed to be a Mex. Longarm felt no call to let anyone there know he spoke some Spanish just yet. The trader didn't seem capable of plotting against anyone

196

n the pretty little thing's native lingo, and a man just never new till he knew folks better.

The Navaho gal, dressed in a maroon velveteen blouse and many a yard of gathered red calico skirting, all held at her rim waist by a handsome concho belt of coin silver, said e might as well call her Charladora because he'd never be ble to pronounce her Na-Déné name, which meant about the ame thing.

Charladora was Spanish for Chatterbox. He didn't need an xplanation. With her help he explained about the sheep and goats a half-dozen miles away, with nobody but a bunch of unskilled blue sleeves to herd them across the San Juan and up he Chinlé to wherever their *ricos* wanted to distribute them.

An older but still virile Navaho with just a hint of gray in is long black bob spoke Spanish, likely in consideration of heir Mex trader, as he told Charladora, "I know about the reaty gift they have only now remembered we were promised, many summers ago, by the rope thrower who had a real woman nd a straight tongue. They have been chanting about this to he south, just this side of Ganado. I think we should do two hings. I think we should send a swift rider to tell the *xastoi* ve are helping these Belagana. I think we should help these Belagana herd the sheep and goats to Ganado. Does anyone ere have a better idea?"

Nobody did. Old Gordita even offered to help as soon as she washed her gritty cunt out in the nearby river. Longarm wouldn't have known that if they hadn't told the trader that n Spanish. It wasn't true that Indians had no sense of fun. Longarm managed not to join in the laughter. But it wasn't easy.

The trader stayed behind, along with more than half the Indians. So the ones who mounted up to ride with Longarm, Charladora, and the helpful *rico*—she said his Spanish name was Lobo Ladrono or Thieving Wolf—felt no call to commu- nicate anymore in Spanish.

Knowing only a few words of their mighty complicated lingo, he decided to come clean with them and allow he spoke enough Spanish to get by. They seemed to think that was mighty droll as well. But after they'd finished laughing at him, the few who spoke Spanish switched to it so he'd be able to follow their drift. It wasn't true the Apache de Nabajú had poor manners, no matter what Hopi, Zuni, and such might say. Their manners were just different from those of most everyone else on Earth. The fact that they had unusual *morals* didn' keep them from being *polite* to anyone they weren't in the process of robbing, torturing, or killing at the moment.

Like all defeated warrior nations, from Napoleon's Empire on back to Attila's Huns, they'd worked out a view of the world allowing they were the victims of big bullies, only fighting to protect their womenfolk and manly honor. So even though Longarm hadn't asked, old Thieving Wolf proceeded to fill him in on that misunderstanding back in the late '60s.

Longarm let him rattle on until he got to the part about Indians only learning to scalp from wicked Belagana, who'd brought the habit over from their old country.

Knowing it was useless to point out neither Jesus nor the wives of King Henry VIII had been scalped by white folks out to do them dirty, he just said, "That's interesting. I never knew the story of Changing Woman and the Hero Twins was one my own ancestors made up."

Thieving Wolf blinked owlishly Longarm's way from aboard his own paint and demanded, "Who told you that? Changing Woman is Diné, Diné, Diné! Not even our Chiji cousins pronounce Istsa Natlehi as beautifully as we do! Who told you she and her sons, the Hero Twins, were Diyini—Holy People of your *own* Blessing Way, Belagana?"

Longarm smiled back at the *rico* on the small paint. "You did, just now, when you said only my nation took scalps in the Grandfather Times when the Diyini were putting this old world together. The way I heard it, the Hero Twins killed most of the Nayé or monsters who would have made it impossible for us human beings to live."

Thieving Wolf nodded brusquely and said, "That is true. Our Changing Woman sent her Hero Twins, fathered by Shining Sun, to rid the world of most bad things. They spared *some* bad things, such as Pain and Old Age, to keep the human race from growing soft. But they killed the really *bad* ones, such as Big Monster, who can still be seen as what you Belagana call Mount Taylor. You call the corpse of Tall Monster Ship Rock. The Hero Twins killed all the really bad ones, all!"

198

"And carried their scalps back to Changing Woman," said Longarm with a knowing smile. "Making her and her brave boys Belagana, like me."

There came a stunned moment of silence. Then Charladora, riding to their rear on a red roan, laughed like hell and called out, "I know who this one is now, *Xastoi*. The Nakaih call him Brazo Largo, and our Nodaha enemies call him Saltu Ka Saltu. They say he talks with one tongue. But it is best to talk the same way to him. He has fought good fights and feels no shame about winning or losing."

She switched to English to add, "He was only shitting you because he thought you rode for the B.I.A., Longarm. We always shit our agent at Fort Defiance because he gives us more when we make him feel bad. We are very good at that. Your people have given us more than they have given any other nation because we tell better stories."

Longarm replied in Spanish to keep Thieving Wolf in the picture as he said, "Your Hopi and Zuni neighbors would be the first to agree with you on that, Charladora. You probably know you're getting a good many sheep and goats to keep you from joining Victorio in his raiding for stock this summer."

Thieving Wolf laughed boyishly and opined, "Victorio is a fool who seems anxious to get himself killed over nothing, nothing. As you just said, Little Big Eyes of the B.I.A. will give any band of any nation many good things, without any fighting, if they know how to beg from you Belagana. We learned this long ago, losing many young men and all our sheep to Rope Thrower Carson and his Nodaha scouts. We were beaten so badly it made your people feel they had done something wrong. So we agreed to forgive them and they made us richer than we were before."

Waving his free hand expansively at the harshly beautiful scenery all around, the older man continued. "All of this is ours, forever. We no longer have to fight anybody for it, and only you Belagana pay taxes on land you think you own. Our Chija cousins have never learned how to deal with you Belagana. They keep fighting you and getting killed. We found out a long time ago that you are strong, too strong to fight, but very stupid, with a childish desire for our blankets

199

and silverwork. How far did you say your friends are holding our sheep for us?"

Longarm waved at the riverside brush ahead and said, "Upstream and across, near Butter Wash. I don't think we ought to take all the others who seem to be following us into that army bivouac. I think we should take just a few of your young men who know how to herd sheep, and ask all those women and children back there to wait on this side of the San Juan."

Charladora protested, "We are not on the warpath this spring. We are allowed to leave our reservation on peaceful business. Ask Little Big Eyes if you don't believe me!"

Longarm smiled back at her over his shoulder and said, "I thought you just said you weren't going to shit me anymore, Charladora. You can come along as translator. But you know why I don't want any other Diné gals amidst them innocent blue sleeves before I talk to 'em, and I have spoken on that!"

She laughed innocently and replied, "We keep forgetting. Most of you are so stupid. The fight with Rope Thrower was before I was old enough to understand. But I heard my elders speaking as we were being marched across the mountains to Bosque Redondo. They could not understand how anyone so stupid could have beaten them. Rope Thrower knew a little about us. But most of you knew nothing, nothing, and most of your blue sleeves would die in just a few days if they were left alone on range the Paiute find easy. But it doesn't seem to matter. You have many blue sleeves, many, and you have plenty of those cans and jars to feed men too stupid to forage for themselves."

Longarm agreed it was sure a caution how the U.S. Army just kept winning. He didn't want to encourage a possible enemy by offering his own true feelings about a peacetime army suffering through draconian budget cuts from a President who refused to serve strong liquor at White House suppers.

They reached the spot where he'd forded the San Juan coming the other way. Charladora called out in her own lingo, and despite some bitching and wailing only a quartet of young Navaho tagged along as Longarm, the one pretty gal, and old Thieving Wolf braved the current.

But even so, they created quite a stir when they rode into the army bivouac. Longarm introduced the Indians to Captain Granville and a handful of officers and noncoms, warning Charladora not to translate all that shit from Thieving Wolf about white stockmen stealing the best grazing lands of Dinetah when they were allowed to come back west from New Mexico. Thieving Wolf had just said himself they'd never owned clear title to half their present holdings, and the Hopi for one were mad as all get-out about that.

Longarm showed the mounted Indians the way up the box canyon to the grazing herd. They told him they'd mill the sheep and goats all together, and send Charladora to tell him when they were ready to head the stock out. The gal stayed there to translate, lest any blue sleeve suspect them of stock raiding without a permit.

Trotting the buckskin back to where Granville and his staff were starting to break camp, Longarm reined in and called out, "While I got the chance, you gents had best gather round and listen tight! I told a mess of other Navaho to stay south of the river. But once we cross over there'll be no way to keep 'em at a safe distance without gunning 'em, which would likely upset General Sherman a mite."

Granville asked, "Are you saying my men and me may be in danger?"

Longarm replied, "Not physical, as long as nobody acts really silly. I'm trying to tell you all while there's time. The nation we may be spending quite some time with plays by different rules than we and a heap of other Indians live by. Remember, I said *different,* neither more nor less strict. A Navaho would as soon cut his own throat as mess with a second cousin thrice removed or even talk to his mother-in-law. He's forbidden to fish for mountain trout or harm half a dozen other critters our kind shoots for sport. He thinks whupping a child for any reason is a cowardly sin, and considers a rapist a weakling who can't charm a gal worth spit."

He saw that newspaper gal drifting over to join them afoot, and decided to tell her more about Diné morals in private. He told the gathering of uniformed men, "On the other hand, they don't share our views on bragging, begging, or stealing, and whoever told you no Indians ever lie was surely an Indian. For

201

they're every bit as smart as we are. Tell your men to watch the females and kids more than they may have to watch the menfolk. Navaho husbands brag on their wives walking out of a trading post with a hogshead of flour under their big floppy skirts. But men consider it unmanly to steal anything less valuable than a pony. That's how come Indian traders let the men browse inside but ask their wives to stay out on the porch. So in sum, guard your guns and riding stock from the men, and don't let the gals get a crack at your pocket combs or, God forbid, canned goods."

Granville's literally girlish adjutant asked if it might not be best to simply forbid all Indians to enter their night bivouacs.

There was at least one real lady present, but it had to be dealt with. So Longarm calmly said, "Your enlisted men won't go along with that. One of the notions Navaho gals don't share with Queen Victoria is whether it's right or wrong to make love with most anyone for fun or profit. Messing with a Navaho gal against her will can take fifty years off a man's life. It's usually her uncle, not her husband, she runs crying to. But after that, as George Washington found with squaws of another nation, it's nigh impossible to keep troops far from home away from giggling young gals."

Not looking at the blushing brunette, he added, "Don't call these Navaho gals squaws, by the way. That's all right for Cheyenne, but their own word is *istsa,* sort of. It's best not to try unless you're ready to try making swallowing sounds."

Captain Granville allowed he wasn't interested in Navaho women.

Longarm believed him. As the soldiers got back to breaking camp, Longarm dismounted to walk his buckskin back to the remuda and switch mounts. Grace Weatherford tagged along, asking, "What's the story on you and that moon-faced young squaw, Begochidi?"

He laughed incredulously and assured her, "She's with old Thieving Wolf. Tagged along to translate as well."

He didn't feel it would be wise to add he didn't think Charladora was all that moon-faced. He'd thought her high cheekbones set her big sloe eyes off sort of pretty.

The pretty white gal asked what her rival's name might be. Longarm said he'd forgotten, and warned her, "It ain't smart to play the game of Real Bear with a man about another gal, honey."

She said she didn't know that one. So he explained how the Lakota said a young man could gain great medicine, enough to have everything he wanted, if only he could go up on a mountain alone and spend a whole night under the stars without thinking once about Real Bear.

She said she didn't follow his drift.

He said, "Asking a man not to think about a certain totem, or a pretty gal, is almost certain to make either stand out in his fool head. So when you don't want a rival, don't name her as one."

It wouldn't have been smart to add he was already starting to wonder what little Charladora's legs looked like under all that calico.

Chapter 18

Moving the herd south of the San Juan was a bitch. They lost a goat and almost a dozen sheep to the swirling brown river. They'd have doubtless done worse if they hadn't had all those Indians, on horseback or afoot, helping the poor dumb brutes across.

Longarm had to agree when Captain Granville opined they were as well off without those two sullen Basques, although Longarm felt the two of them had had plenty to sulk about, and it was simple arithmetic that allowed almost two dozen Indians to move sheep better than two skilled sheepherders and a handful of green-ass drag riders.

Getting rid of those spring wagons had served to speed things up before the Indians took over. After that Longarm had to allow the Navaho sheepherder and Churro sheep seemed made for one another and Dinetah.

The sometimes steep-walled but broad grassy bottomlands they were moving south through, averaging better than twenty miles a day, had enjoyed plenty of spring rain and not too much grazing from the far smaller herds they passed from time to time. Charladora explained how different clans or extended families spread out along the Chinlé so as not to overgraze or compete for firewood. They had to burn wood, scarce as it grew in the bottomlands now, because neither horse nor sheep shit burned as handy as the cow chips of the High Plains over on the far side of the Divide.

Thieving Wolf still insisted there wasn't near enough grass for his poor people. He held that the Diyini had meant all the grass from, say, the Valley of Mexico to the Peace River

Range of Canada for the Diné and their Chiji or Chiricahua cousins.

He said, "We do not have enough grass if you expect us to live without raiding richer people. My poor people put a lot of effort into having children and increasing their herds. You Belagana keep saying you need more land. So do we. How are we to survive on this little patch of our world you have left us?"

Longarm didn't figure Thieving Wolf had ever heard of West-by-God-Virginia, and the *rico* would just call the Hopi a passel of sissy farmers if a well-meaning stranger pointed out how well Hopi made out with a much smaller reserve. So he quietly asked whether any of the younger Diné might have been talking another war with the blue sleeves in the hope of gaining some more elbowroom.

Thieving Wolf said he'd heard about those sniping incidents, way off in parts of his crowded range he'd never seen. He repeated what he'd said about it being dumb to risk your life for what you might be able to get for the begging.

He used the Spanish verb *mendigar*, which meant just plain begging with no small print about tributes or peace offerings. So Longarm was sure he was talking straight. Like bragging or buggery, begging was not considered shameful by most Indians. A *lying* brag was a mistake few Indians would ever live down, if they were caught. Corn-holing a Nádlé, or Diné sissy, was considered common courtesy to the confused soul, as long as one's wife wasn't jealous, and begging was just a way one got something from a fool too selfish to offer.

A Navaho of any substance who neglected to offer and made his pals beg for something they needed was the one they considered a total disgrace. Unlike Cheyenne, Comanche, or Lakota, none of the Na-Déné-speaking nations considered it an honor to die fighting, and they considered a hero a total asshole unless he was one of the immortal Diyini, like the Hero Twins of Changing Woman. For a *real* person who took chances like that could wind up *dead*!

Longarm knew how they felt about death. So it was left to another Belagana, his good pal from the *Washington Globe*, to get into that with the English-speaking Charladora.

205

The two gals had started talking friendly the first day out, as gals who suspect one another of bitchery are prone to. Nobody with a lick of sense rode drag when they had so many willing helpers. So both Thieving Wolf and his pretty translator naturally rode up at the head of the column with Granville, Grace Weatherford, and the others. Longarm tried to steer the conversation elsewhere, noting the uneasy expression in the Navaho gal's dark eyes. But the white brunette kept at her, saying she wanted to explain Charladora's people to her own readers. So the Indian gal finally said, "We don't look at what you call death the way you do, Grace. You picture death as a *something*, but we picture *life* as something and death as *nothing*. No eating, no singing, no laughing, no screwing, ever again!"

The white gal blushed red as sunset on a snow-peak, and whispered there were gentlemen present. Charladora nodded innocently and said men didn't get to screw after they were dead either. Longarm tried to smooth it over by horning in. "What she's trying to say, ah, Miss Weatherford, is that they celebrate life with all its ups and downs as a gift from that Changing Woman I told you about. They can sing by the hour about all the interesting things that us living folks get to go through, from pain to pleasure. They don't sing much about Mr. Death. They'd as soon not think of such a dull cuss."

The white girl persisted, asking the Indian girl if she wasn't a sort of atheist, seeing she didn't believe in any hereafter. Longarm had to laugh. He asked, "What did they put in your coffee this morning, Miss Weatherford? These folks have more gods than you can shake a stick at. Not having anything writ on stone, or even paper, they can give you a different count every time you ask."

The newspaper reporter nodded and said, "All right. Let's start with who the most important Navaho god might be."

Charladora looked confused and asked, "What do you mean? How can any one of the Diyini be more important? Is the mountain you know as Mount Taylor more important than Mount Humphreys? One is fastened to the earth by a great stone knife. The other is held in place by sunbeams. Which is more important, or marvelous?"

Longarm muttered, "Never argue religion with an Indian—or anyone else, come to study on it!"

So they dropped the subject for the time being, and later that night Longarm explained the more democratic pantheon of the Na-Déné spirit world, the so-called Apache bands holding to many of the same views. He and the newspaper gal were in his bedroll at the time, even though they'd finally located her baggage aboard a mule pack, so she didn't want him to go as deep into Indian lore as she wanted him in her.

After a couple of nights spent the same way, moving up the Chinlé bottomlands, she commenced to feel less suspicious of the younger if less-refined-looking Indian gal.

All the whites, including Longarm, were starting to worry more about faint but persistent drumbeats way the hell off amid the canyon-cut cliffs to either side.

When they asked the Indians with them, Thieving Wolf said it was nothing to worry about. It was up to a full-fledged *rico* to say so for certain, and Charladora, being female, had no say in drum chants at all. But Longarm tended to believe it when she lightly explained her folks were always banging drums somewhere in Dinetah.

She said, "I have heard there have been women with the *biji* to be chanters. But I have never met one. Girls are not allowed to attend some of the chant-way rites. But we always hear the drums. None of the beats we have been hearing sound like the War Way or Curse Way, if that is what you are worried about. The drums sound Blessing Way more often than not. Blessing Way brings good *alil* whether someone is sick or just having a hard time getting the beans to twine up the cornstalks the right way."

Captain Granville, who'd been listening off to one side, piped up to say he'd heard Indians could send messages by drumbeat, noting those drums on all sides seemed to be keeping pace with the column.

Charladora seemed sincerely puzzled. Longarm said, "Talking drums are African, Captain. I read that in a book. Indians signal more with smoke, and so far, knock wood, I haven't seen any smoke talk along the rimrocks to either side."

Charladora demanded, "Why would anyone be signaling ahead that we were coming? Thieving Wolf sent his nephew,

207

a good rider, to tell everyone to the south we were coming, with many sheep, many!"

So they let muttering distant drums mutter, broke trail for noon dinner, and got a further lesson in local religious notions later in the afternoon.

A roadrunner broke cover out ahead to proceed them on its long skinny legs till the captain's pretty adjutant, maybe to prove how manly he was, blew its feathery ass off and its liver and lights out with a well-placed round from his Schofield .45.

Longarm was only disgusted. Thieving Wolf had a fit. He rode off into the chaparral, bawling fit to bust. Charladora turned on the first john, black eyes blazing, and snapped, "I reproach you as a cruel child, Lieutenant! Natsedlozi is one of the few beings who never does us harm, whether in his animal or *yei* existance!"

The baby-faced officer protested, "For Pete's sake, it was only some kind of big bird!"

Longarm said, "It was a roadrunner. White folks out this way like 'em too. They eat scorpions, rats, and rattlesnakes, and like you just heard, they never do a bit of harm to anyone or anything we might like better than, say, a sidewinder. What she meant about its *yei* or spirit is that Roadrunner, with a capital R, is one of their good spirits. So don't go shooting at things you just don't understand, hear?"

The adjutant looked hurt and turned to his captain, asking, "Sir?"

Granville said, "We'll talk about it later, Bobby. Meanwhile, try to control your impish impulses."

Thus it came to pass that Longarm got to confuse all the whites near the head of the column later that same afternoon when, following the riverside trail through a patch of dense prickly pear, they met up with an old dog coyote, staring them down bold as brass from the center of the narrow passageway.

Longarm knew what made the old coyote so bold, even before Thieving Wolf, who'd rejoined them a mile or so back, reined in to point and wail, "*Carramba!* We must turn back!"

So Longarm whipped out his .44-40 and let fly, nailing the sassy coyote between its bold yellow eyes for a clean kill.

As they all steadied their mounts Thieving Wolf marveled, "It was only a *mai*, not Atse Xacke. But how did you know, Belagana?"

Charladora called, in an admiring tone, "I told you this one has much *bixo*, maybe even *biji*!"

Longarm explained to the confused whites gathered around, "She's saying I have good medicine. She and her folk neither fear nor harm ordinary coyotes. It makes some of the critters mighty bold, knowing any Indians they meet around here will circle wide around 'em lest they turn out to be Coyote, with a capital C. Since I somehow suspected the one yonder was just a garden-variety coyote, I chanced my life blowing it out of our way so's we could just keep going. Sometimes an old dog coyote will play a sort of game with sheep, popping in and out of sight to spook both them and the Indians herding them."

He saw it seemed up to him. So he dismounted, strode over, and picked the dead coyote up by the tail to heave its limp form out of sight and hence out of any Indian's mind in the prickly pear.

As he remounted, Charladora said in Spanish, "You are very brave. I would want you at my side, in the dark, if I ever met a Chindi!"

He was glad she'd said that in Spanish. He just wasn't up to telling a newspaper reporter how folks who didn't believe in any afterlife were still so afraid of haunts.

The topic came up again the next day as they seemed somewhere near the mouth of Canyon de Chelly, which was really a canyon maze running back into the foothills of the Chuska Mountains between the Chinlé and Chaco bottomlands. Just where the canyon mouth might be was sort of mysterious. That was why the Navaho had used that hideout with such success for so long.

When he asked Charladora whether her people still scampered back and forth through the Chuskas, she sighed and said, "Not as much as they used to. People who want to move between the Chinlé and Chaco ranges feel safer using the trails that pass near Fort Defiance. The blue sleeves, for all their faults, don't allow our enemies to lie in wait for us among our own rimrocks. The old trails, further north, are not used as often. People say they have met Chindi, even Nayé, where we used to hunt deer and bighorns amid the sky-reaching rocks."

Longarm rode on with eyes slitted, trying to draw a clearer map of the vast and still largely uncharted reserve in his mind. He knew that further south, lacking such natural boundaries as the San Juan, the official boundaries were string-straight but nipped and tucked to allow for judicious mining claims, grazing rights, and other land grabs north of the Little Colorado. Thieving Wolf hadn't bullshitted entirely about more than one white Arizonian feeling his or her own need for elbowroom.

He saw how Fort Defiance, located near the reservation line although in a sort of notch in what would have been a neater square southeast corner, *did* offer some protection to anyone crossing the greasewood flats of the Defiance Plateau. Passage into the Chaco bottomlands would be blocked from the north by that Ute Strip. He opened his eyes and firmly declared, "Canyon de Chelly is where I'd set up to distribute them sheep back there fair and square."

Charladora repressed a shudder and insisted, "It's better to stay out of the Chuskas and even the Chaco Valley now. I told you why, and despite what Thieving Wolf says we still have plenty of grass, plenty, on this side of our reserve, where there are not as many ghosts and monsters."

That was about all he could get from any Indian, even though old Thieving Wolf confirmed they'd been having problems with spooks to the east.

Longarm was making mental X marks on his invisible map when Grace Weatherford insisted, on his other side, there was just no sane way to believe in ghosts but not life after death at the same time.

He dryly asked, "Since when have haunts been all that rational? I've never been able to follow how a Good Book saying everyone goes to Heaven or Hell afterwards allows for dead folks to moan or blow trumpets in a haunted house or spiritual meeting. It all falls apart as soon as you demand some common sense. Meanwhile, these Indians are scared of stars and Lord knows what else. Now what if somebody had a good reason for keeping others, white or red, out of them Chuska Mountains to our east?"

She asked why anyone would want to do that. He shrugged and said he didn't know, but added, "I tracked down an evil spirit on another reserve one time. Turned out to be a spooky white rascal working for a land grabber. When and if we make it to Gallup, I mean to look into any recent mining or grazing claims that might hinge on more Indian trouble than any Indians around here were really planning."

The white girl stared off across the dramatic scenery to the east as she softly said, "You're an odd one, Custis Long. A body could take you for an Indian fighter or an Indian missionary. I can't decide if you could be described as overly strict or awfully generous in your views on Indian policy."

He said, "I ain't nothing but a lawman, sworn to uphold the laws and constitution of These United States as the Lord gives me the powers to follow their drift."

Before she could answer they all heard a distant rifle shot. The captain was the one who asked what it was. It seemed too obvious to answer. Longarm rode wide of the column to gaze back along the trail, standing in his stirrups. He could make out an antlike cluster amid the dust kicked up by the herd back there. He said, "Looks as if we had some kind of accident with a gun back on the drag. I'll ride back and see what happened."

He did so, loping the length of the stalled column as troopers called out questions he had no answers for. The Indians behind the first two platoons had allowed the sheep to mill. As Longarm swung wide he met a white trooper coming the other way fast. Without so much as slowing down, the cavalry rider wailed, "It's Corporal Brown. Picked off by a sniper in the chaparral and dead as a turd in a milk bucket!"

Longarm whistled and heeled his black barb into a full gallop. When they slid to a stop near the dusty drag riders kneeling around their fallen squad leader, Longarm saw that other trooper hadn't lied. Nobody had ever looked deader than the late loutish Corporal Brown. Another noncom, glancing up from the dead man's bloody blue shirt, opined, "Big Fifty buffalo round. Took him under the right shoulder blade and blew his lung and half his heart out the front of him."

Longarm had no call to check the pulse of anyone that thoroughly killed. Drawing his own long gun from its saddle scabbard, he said, "I'll circle out for sign. Anyone have any notion which side of the trail that shot might have come from?"

A dazed-looking trooper said, "Sounded like it come from directly behind. Must have passed right betwixt me and Kellerman here to hit Arkansas so low!"

Longarm nodded, and headed out into the greasewood and rabbitbrush at an angle, making for a patch of higher cover to the northeast.

He swung wide to circle the sticker brush at tricky range and cut off retreat to the red cliffs to the east. He felt mixed emotions as he spied no sign in the open patches of soil on the far side. For his duty was his duty and backshooting the U.S. Army had to be a federal offense, but he'd *liked* those old boys.

He heard hoofbeats, and glanced over his shoulder to see Charladora loping his way on her red roan, a lot of leg showing between her high-tied moccasin boots and the hiked hems of her calico skirts.

She called out, "I think they rode the other way, west of the trail. It is hard to be sure with so little dust rising after all that rain."

He started to tell her to go back. Then, way behind her, he spied the platoon Captain Granville had sent riding lickety-split for those same cliffs to the east. So he said, "This is your range. You seem to know it better than some of us. Is that a Spencer rifle stock I see riding with you?"

The Indian girl patted the buckskin saddle boot of the repeater she'd lashed to the front fork of her simple rawhide saddle, and told him it was loaded to fire seven times.

He nodded grimly and said, "We might do better if we fanned out and circled some for sign. Meanwhile I'll rally them misguided troopers and meet you west of the trail, hear?"

She was already loping off. He raised the muzzle of his Winchester and fired. Way off in the distance that squirt lieutenant heard the rallying shot, waved his fool saber, and kept charging the wrong way.

212

Longarm shrugged and wheeled his mount to head west. Fair was fair, and east was the logical way he'd expected pissed-off Basques to ride. There was no mystery as to why even an asshole like their gallant captain had figured that much out.

Charladora was waving him over from a couple of furlongs north, just west of the trail. As he joined her she pointed at the ruined remains of a harvester-ant mound and said, "Steel-shod mount. Bigger than what most of us ride, but headed that way, toward Black Mesa."

He dismounted, hunkered down for a closer look at one clear imprint, and grunted, "They stole more than one army mount as they lit out. But Black Mesa? Why would Mex Basques be headed for them Hopi pueblos over yonder?"

As he remounted, Charladora suggested, "Maybe they just want to get out of Dinetah as quick as they can. I think I know the way they will choose. Come."

He was tempted to argue as the Indian gal led him what seemed the wrong way entirely to judge by those hoofprints beelining west by northwest. She pointed much more southwest, shouting, "There is a canyon over that way. I helped my aunts gather wild plums there when I was little. They said not to stray too far up it because sometimes our Hopi enemies entered it from the far side. If I had just shot a blue sleeve and wanted to get away to the west, I think that is the way I would ride!"

"If you knew the country," Longarm grunted more to himself as he rode after her. Neither Hernan nor Ramon had ever said they'd been this way before. On the other hand, anything was possible and if he didn't catch them, at least he could say he'd tried. A killer who did know the country could be expected to attempt a false trail. He'd leave the hoofprints he had to leave across the bottomlands as far as the rocky scree along the base of those distant cliffs. Then he'd hairpin back to make for that canyon mouth only a local Indian could be expected to know as well.

The same sandstone formation that rose blood red to the east rose dark purple in the west against the late afternoon sky. With the sun in their eyes Longarm had to take Charladora's canyon on faith. But it stood to reason the killer or killers

213

would want to get off the wide open bottomlands of the Chinl
some damned way.

As they rode into the wide band of deep shade cast b
the cliffs as they approached them, Longarm could see bette
how the weathered sandstone looming high above had bee
fluted in horizontal grooves by the once-more-mighty Chinl
River and carved even deeper, although at much wider-space
intervals, by tributary streams in a once-wetter West.

Charladora reined in, studied the rocks ahead, and decidec
"We are too far north. This way."

They rode south along the very edge of the shattered scree
spread a good fifty yards out from the bases of the cliffs
Longarm just had time to spot the swarm of flies above
streak of lighter brown debris when the Indian girl calle
back, "A pony shit there. A lot. They do that when they hav
been ridden hard and you rein them to a walk."

He didn't tell her the flies meant fresh horseshit. The prett
little thing was damned good at reading sign. He knew th
so-called Navaho allowed womenfolk more freedom than ever
their Chiricahua cousins. So this one had likely played witl
the boys some while growing up.

When they got to her canyon, he knew for certain tha
those Basque boys had been holding out on him. For h
thought she was joshing him as they seemed to be ridin
smack into a big blank wall, till they got close enough t
see the slit of sky cut into the rimrocks above. The canyor
mouth was as narrow as the gates through the high walls o
a mighty private estate owned by a rich recluse. There wa
just room for them to ride side by side along the winding
rocky bottom in most places. There were bottlenecks wher
house-sized boulders had fallen from the cliffs above and they
had to ride Indian-file.

He asked her if there were any cliff dwellings up this one
She shot a glance at the streak of sky above and answered
"No. Nobody has ever lived up this one. I hope nobody ha:
ever *died* in it. As I told you, there used to be wild plum:
further up, where the walls stand farther apart and Fathe
Xactce can smile brighter on higher ground. But nobody ha:
ever used this canyon for more than a place to gather fruit or
my aunts said, sneak through Salahkai to raid the Hopi."

214

He didn't ask what a Salahkai was. He'd seen the map. They seemed to be cutting right through the big Salahkai mesa that rose west of the Chinlé bottomlands as a flat-topped counterpart to the Chuskas to the east.

They came to a stretch where fine sand had placered in the lee of a flat patch of slickrock. Two neat lines of pony tracks, fresh ones, told them how smart Charladora had been. Modesty was not considered a virtue by her kind. So when she didn't brag he knew she was worried. He said, "I'd best take the lead. This Winchester packs sixteen rounds, even if you do know your way through the pumpkin better."

She let him ease his pony around her roan, but murmured, "I am not afraid of those stupid killers out ahead of us. It will soon be getting dark. This is no place to be caught in the dark by *sq* and Chindi!"

He told her to turn back if she cared to. He knew lots of her own menfolk would have by this time. Some held the so-called Navaho had given up raiding and split off from other Apache types because they were too afraid of the dark to raid as well. Most everyone was afraid of haunts, or Chindi. The Navaho were almost alone in thinking the *sq*, or stars, were evil spirits.

They got over the slickrock, rounded a bend, and found themselves in a grand ballroom inhabited by giant chessmen, or maybe bowling pins, once you considered all the monstrous bowling balls of weathered granite imbedded in the pumpkin-colored sandstone. Charladora pointed at some green treetops peeking over a fallen column of rock the size of an uprooted cathedral tower and said, "The wild plums are taller now. The way out to Black Mesa is somewhere just beyond them."

Longarm reined in and said, "You'd best stay here whilst I scout some afoot. They may have run, or they may have figured what a swell spot this would be for an ambush!"

Behind him, she almost sobbed, "I don't want to stay here alone in the dark!"

He assured her there was at least an hour or so of daylight ahead, and moved on with his saddle gun at port, calling out in a louder tone, "I see you there, Hernan. Don't you reckon we ought to talk this over before someone gets hurt?"

There was no answer. With any luck, there was nobody there. He made it to the fallen cathedral tower and found a cleft to wedge himself higher. He put his hat on the muzzle of his long gun and raised it to see what might happen. When nothing did, he took a deep breath and peered over the top to see that, sure enough, an inviting grove of wild plum nestled in a granite bowl. He thought he'd spotted movement up yonder among the elephantine boulders. He called out, "Come on, boys. You know I got to take Ramon in, but I'll testify at his trial it was self-defense. Sort of. Ramon might have thought the big bully would come after him."

There came no reply. Longarm worked his way on through the cleft and dropped down the far side, insisting, "Aw, come on. We can work something out, *companeros de me vida!*"

A shot rang out, and Longarm didn't suspect any *bee* of buzzing so close to his right ear. So he made it to a waist-high boulder in two zigzagging bounds and dropped behind it, shouting, "Now cut that out, *pendejo!* You're already in enough trouble over that soldier you just shot, with a lot better reason! Can't you see I'm trying to be *nice* about all this?"

Another rifle shot spanged off the top of his boulder. He yelled out, "*Cono, no me friegues!* I'm getting mighty tired of this shit!"

His reasonable request was answered by another ricochetted buffalo round. So there it was. They meant to make a fight of it, and they had him pinned down like a greenhorn behind the only cover within suicidal reach.

He tried peering around the rock low to his right. Whether the rifleman peering down his way from that granite rise ever saw him or not was moot. For another shot rang out, the higher-pitched bark of a Spencer, and suddenly a male figure rose, arms flung wide, to dive forward into the plum trees below.

Charladora, bless her, appeared atop the boulders up yonder to wave her Spencer and call out, "Watch your back! I don't know where the other one is hiding."

Longarm did. He fired as yet another total stranger rose from a cleft in the granite rise to aim at the Indian gal's pretty behind. From the way the rascal's hat went flying

216

Longarm knew he'd hit him right where the hangman would have placed the knot.

He took time to examine the one who'd fallen into the plum grove before he scrambled up the granite, where Charladora was already at the pockets of the second one. He hunkered down beside her, told her to cut that out, and rolled the dead rascal face up.

Por nada. He'd never laid eyes on the ugly son of a bitch before, as far as he knew. He heaved a vast sigh of relief and said, "Hand me that wallet. You've no idea how glad I am to say I didn't know either one of these old boys. But now I'm supposed to try and find out who they might have been."

The contents of the wallet didn't help much. He handed the six dollars back to Charladora, saying, "Anyone can get a library card just by asking, whether he's named Tom Jones or not. Crooks do that a lot for the edification of small-town lawmen. The fact that this card was made out over in Gallup might mean something. Then again, it might not. They were headed west, not southeast."

Charladora said, "It's getting late. Could we get out of this dark canyon before we celebrate our winning with our clothes off?"

He gulped and said, "The captain will doubtless want to know who gunned Corporal Brown. I ain't sure we ought to dance around in front of him with our duds off. It ain't a regular Belagana custom and they might not understand."

She shot him a puzzled look and asked, "Who said anything about dancing? Don't you want to screw me?"

He gulped again, harder, and said, "Any man would. But I ain't so sure I ought to, Charladora,"

She asked, "Why? Because you have already been screwing that other woman every night? I don't want to screw you to take you away from her. We have just killed two men, *two*! They are lost to Changing Woman for all time. They will never sing, or laugh, or screw again. Unless we do something to make this a happier place, the plum grove where I gathered fruit as a child will be a sad place, where only the Chindi of these murderers might want to sing, or laugh, or . . . do you think Chindi screw?"

He laughed and said it sounded more silly than spooky. Then, since he knew neither of them would ever forgive him for refusing to be a good sport about local custom, he led her down among the plum trees, found a patch of orchard grass out of sight of that one dead cuss, and kissed her good before they both stripped buck naked and flopped down in the grass to take the curse off the whole canyon as if her odd method depended on having lots of fun.

He didn't ask where she'd learned to do it so much like a white gal. He didn't really want to know, and her English was just about as perfect, although her hip movements were even finer.

Chapter 19

Despite some of the civilized habits she'd picked up, Charladora didn't make a romantic pother of a friendly screw, and so Longarm's white gal never suspected a thing later that night. For like most men, Longarm felt mighty romantic with a guilty conscience. She said they'd surely get caught together in his bedroll if he didn't calm down a mite.

The captain was feeling far from calm about the triple shootings. He had picket fires all around, and his lover-boy adjutant posted double guard. For Granville was sure Longarm had only nailed part of a rebel guerrilla band. Both the dead killers had worn border spurs and Texas hats. Granville hadn't been in favor of the recent ending of the postwar Reconstruction regulations. He said this was the thanks President Hayes got for trying to make up with unreconstructed rebels, and would have told a long tale of Texas raiders out to seize the Colorado gold fields for the South, had Longarm not explained he drank a heap with old-timers from the First Colorado Volunteers.

He kept his own mind open. Those two he and Charladora had tracked down worked as well a dozen ways. It was true most such sniping at army columns had taken place along the western reaches of the vast reserve. After that it was only a relief they'd been neither Indian nor Mex Basque. So who in blue blazes had they been, and how come they'd smoked up soldiers but left the Indians alone?

Next morning, as they were breaking camp, Thieving Wolf's nephew rejoined them. After coffee and a heap of discussion in Na-Déné, old Thieving Wolf announced, in Spanish, that the Indian agent from Fort Defiance was meeting with most of the important *ricos* at Ganado, on the Red Pueblo, which was hardly where Longarm felt like going.

Captain Granville didn't want to go there either. Studying his government survey map he declared, "That tribal center called Ganado is a two days' drive west of Fort Defiance."

Longarm said, "Two days for sheep. You and your troop could make them forty-odd miles in one day's ride if you put your minds to it."

But Granville demanded, "Why should we want to? Our orders are for Fort Defiance, not yet another blasted sage flat with Lord only knows how much slickrock between."

Longarm insisted, "If you forge south-southwest instead of around the southeast bend of this here valley, you'll wind up among them very rimrocks snipers were sniping from them other times."

He suspected that was what the gallant captain had been thinking about already when Granville all but stamped his foot and insisted he was only following orders.

So they all followed the Chinlé flats together, as far as it was possible. Before noon Charladora called out, "Hear Thieving Wolf. He says we have to drive the herd up that side canyon over by those blue oaks if we want to move them over the mesas to Ganado. He says there is no better place, and anyone can see how far east this bottomland has to go."

Captain Granville didn't even rein in. He told the Indians to just report to their white agent as soon as they reached Ganado and tell him the relief column had gone on to Fort Defiance as ordered.

Longarm fell in on the captain's other side, protesting, "Damn it, Captain. You got them two rascals who shot Corporal Brown wrapped in tarps back there. But how do you know there ain't others waiting for us up among them cliffs ahead?"

Granville shrugged and said, "They haven't shot one Indian to date. I frankly thought they *were* Indians until just now. I mean to deliver those bodies to the provost marshal at Fort Defiance and let his M.P. investigators figure out who they might have been."

Longarm said he'd rather take one of the bunch alive and ask *him*. He insisted, "General Sherman only wanted an investigator like me to tag along in hopes of finding out who was behind all this sniping. He ordered you and your troop to beef up the defenses of Fort Defiance under the mistaken impression they were Indians. Last time these old boys attacked Fort Defiance under Manuelito they almost *took* it."

Captain Granville said they had Gatling guns and fourpounders at the fort these days.

Longarm sighed and said, "Doing nothing, unless somebody takes the field to track . . . *somebody* up to something. It's true no Indians have been directly molested. But they tell me somebody's been spooking them. They're afraid to move betwixt the Chinlé and Chaco ranges, save by way of them open flats around Fort Defiance."

Captain Granville seemed to think that was a grand idea. He said Navaho wandering all over through uncharted canyons made him proddy. Longarm saw he was getting nowhere with the faint-hearted soul, and dropped back beside Grace Weatherford to fill her in on the imminent parting of the army column from the government herd they'd been escorting. She agreed Granville was likely scared of busting a fingernail amid the rimrocks dead ahead. But when Longarm asked whether she meant to attend the big powwow at Ganado with him, she sighed and said her assignment was to cover the army's response to the current Apache scare. She asked why he couldn't let the old Navaho worry about their own sheep now that they were almost there.

He said, "Honey, they never sent me to see them almost there. They sent me to make sure they got to the folks they were meant for. As for the Apache scare, Granville's scared, all right. But Victorio is way to the south, and them soldiers blue mean to hole up at Fort Defiance till further notice. You'll see more action in Gallup this Saturday than you'll ever see with this outfit."

He swung them off the trail so they could talk as the army column began to swing one way, following the trail, while the

221

Indians drove the herd straight ahead.

It wasn't easy. The bellwether and other goats could see what the Navaho herders wanted. But the sheep seemed to think they were being asked to run smack into a rock wall. The Navaho made up in numbers for what they lacked in dogs. Indian dogs were seldom asked to tag along on any important errands for the same reasons white settlers didn't spend too much time training pigs or chickens.

Longarm told the newspaper gal the real story likely lay ahead at the big powwow he just had to attend. He said at least a few B.I.A. officials would be there, along with all the important folks of the Navaho Nation.

He said, "There'll doubtless be singing, dancing, and all sorts of colorful stuff to report to your readers. All they ever do at a peacetime army post is run the flag up, run the flag down, and screw each other's wives."

She smiled wistfully and said, "*Bego, bego!* You know I'd rather go on with you, Custis. But I just can't. What if I wait for you in that town near the fort, Gallup?"

He shrugged and said, "Don't wait too long. I won't know which way I'll be headed off this reservation till I figure out what's going on here."

She shot a nervous glance at the last army pack mules passing them and said, "I have to ride on, dear. Maybe Gallup?"

He said, "Sure, maybe Gallup," and rode after the Indians riding drag behind the dusty ass-end of the herd.

He passed them at a lope, since nobody volunteered to ride drag, and began to cheer up once he'd chased sheep and Indians up that canyon passage to fall in between Thieving Wolf and Charladora near the head of their own column. Charladora said they'd sent scouts out on point, and calmly asked where his other woman might be. When he told her he was glad Thieving Wolf didn't speak much English, Charladora told him in an innocent tone, "*I'm* glad. We didn't get around to all the positions I know yesterday. But I don't think we ought to screw tonight up on the mesa. My people poke fun at others they catch screwing, and there is a hogan I can borrow for us at Ganado."

He felt no call to argue. He rode on ahead, once they'd followed the ever-climbing canyon up to the flat mesa top.

There were widely scattered clumps of juniper and piñon up there in the cloudless but windy sky. But it would have been suicidal to fire on that large a party from any cover within rifle range, with no place to run to, so nobody did.

As he'd told the captain, sheep moved far slower than riders or even legged-up infantry. So while the ride to the other drainage basin would have taken him and his Indian pals less than a full day, they had to spend another night under the evil stars high up, where the spooky things looked close enough to scoop into your hat if you stood in the stirrups and stretched a mite.

Being a white man, Longarm sort of admired the Milky Way and maybe Mars, if that was what that big bright red star was. But he had only admired the night sky from his bedroll an hour or so when a small, scared voice begged to join him under his stouter-looking canvas tarp.

As he welcomed her between his cotton flannel summer blankets, it turned out she'd crept over wrapped in no more than her trade blanket. She agreed it made more sense to leave it outside on such a warm night, but explained she didn't want anyone to spy the familiar pattern. When they hauled it in after her, he asked how come she didn't use a regular Navaho blanket since it was so famous.

She said her people could get more for a hand-woven blanket than it cost to buy a less-scratchy version at the trading post. So that doubtless explained why they now wore head bands of bright bandanna cotton instead of their old-time beadwork headbands. He asked her if that perfume she seemed to have on was store-bought as well. She snuggled her warm young naked body closer to his, and said she'd scrubbed her tawny hide with soap-weed lather and scented it with wild rose petals so he'd want to screw her instead of just talking, talking, like a noisy *djogi*.

When he asked her what a *djogi* was she hissed, "Jaybird, you big silly. Do you want to talk or do you want to screw?"

He taught her not to ask stupid questions by hitting bottom, more than once, as he taught her a couple of positions she'd never thought of despite her mighty vivid imagination.

• • •

223

That big powwow Longarm had told Grace Weatherford about was as colorful, and noisy, as he'd promised. Navaho were cautions for long drumrolls and way-chants. Most every important thing they decided seemed to call for considerable way-chanting. They had the Blessing Way that made sure nobody in town was going to get struck by lightning, get bit by a snake, or catch the clap. But after they'd made everybody healthy, wealthy, and wise, they felt obliged to use the Upward Reaching Way to discourage any evil spirits, and once the chanters heard of those evil Belagana losing to Longarm and such a brave real woman, they had to chant the Big Evil Star Way to excuse the two of them because they'd been close to dead men at twilight.

Longarm was too polite to tease old Thieving Wolf when Charladora explained there'd have been a longer Going Back for Scalps Way if they'd taken that particular chance with the fickle spirits.

They wound up in that hogan she'd mentioned, since the pounding and chanting figured to go on a spell. She stuck a couple of *ketans* or prayer sticks in the open doorway to keep spirits and nosy kids out. As they reclined on blankets smoking afterwards, they were still going at it out yonder, and he had to say one way sounded much the same way as any other way to him.

Charladora handed back the cheroot and said, "That is because you only hear the repeated drumbeats. You do not know the words. Some of our ways are frightening. Others are beautiful."

He said he didn't doubt that. But he did, till the pretty little thing sat up, her naked nipples perky in the romantic gloom, to chant in English:

> In beauty may I dwell.
> In beauty may I walk.
> In beauty may my kindred dwell.
> In beauty may my kindred walk.
> In beauty before us, may it rain.
> In beauty behind us, may it rain.
> In old age
> The beautiful trail
> May we walk in beauty.

He hauled her back down, kissed her, and told her that had sounded mighty beautiful. He meant it. But after a night of beauty they were still pounding on those goddamned drums. So he got dressed and went out to see if he could find that Indian agent.

He could. The other white man answered to Vandenberg. He was a heavyset middle-aged and bored-looking cuss from New York State. The gal serving him breakfast and adoring glances in front of another hogan was young enough to be his daughter, but not half as pretty as Charladora. She spoke neither English nor Spanish. Longarm's respect for the older man went up a notch when Vandenberg dismissed his play-pretty, not unkindly, in her own lingo.

Longarm said, "I've tried to learn Na-Déné that good. But it sure gets confusing when you're not sure whether you're talking about a piss pot as its maker would describe it, a piss pot as someone pissing in it would describe it, or the inner soul of piss pots in general!"

Vandenberg chuckled and said, "You're talking about Do'tsoh, or Big Fly, the spirit who reports to the other spirits on pissing and more important subjects. The trick is to stop translating in your head and try to *think* in the lingo."

Longarm looked dubious. The Indian agent agreed it wasn't easy. He said, "Our ways of thinking are full of contradictions too. I never saw how many till I tried thinking like an Indian. How would you explain the Trinity, or who the children of Adam and Eve married if incest is an unforgivable sin?"

Longarm smiled thinly and said, "Missionaries have told me what a time they have convincing Indians why Wakan Tonka would let his only begotten son be tortured to death if his medicine is supposed to be all that strong. But I never looked you up to argue religion or even learn to conjugate Na-Déné verbs. What can you tell me about the tales of spooks amid the canyons of the Chuska Mountains running north from the flats around Fort Defiance?"

Vandenberg shrugged and said, "I said I *tried* to think like them. I don't really believe in Chindi. Do you?"

Longarm said, "I never believed in the Windego that devils

225

the Algonquin-speaking folk. I still caught one trying to scare Blackfoot into acting foolish."

He got out two cheroots and offered one as he continued. "That particular haunt was a white man working for a land grabber. You'd know better than me who'd come out ahead by drygulching soldiers in the western reaches of this reserve and scaring Indians over to the east."

Vandenberg grimaced, lit the cheroot, and let out some smoke to give himself time to think before he decided, "Nobody. Nobody I can think of anyhow. Prospectors have found seams of coal on Indian land over toward Black Mesa. Can't see anyone sniping at soldiers to keep a coal mine a secret. The government already knows the coal is there, and the B.I.A. is not about to allow another Tombstone grab of mineral rights. That was Grant's Indian Ring, giving away Apache rights to all that silver. We don't do that anymore in the B.I.A."

Longarm figured he was probably right, as long as the currently honest Administration stayed in power. He asked about land claims.

The Indian agent insisted, "Won't work. Those bastards running the bureau under Grant already gave away the really good grazing along the Little Colorado. The Painted Desert forms a natural buffer for us down that way. The Gallup grab was pretty raw. But so was that Santa Fe Ring President Hayes just cleaned up. That new territorial governor, General Lew Wallace, won't stand for anything like that."

Vandenberg flicked cheroot ash thoughtfully and added, "Even if he would, the Chuskas are smack dab in the middle of my reservation. So what good would it do an outsider if the Indians were scared out of them? They don't really exploit a tenth of all the land we've ceded them as it is. There were only eight thousand Navaho left back in '68, when they were given more than twenty-five thousand square miles to live on."

Longarm let smoke trickle out his nostrils and quietly observed, "I've seen many a square mile of it that ain't so grand, and I'll bet you got more than eight thousand of 'em out there now."

Vandenberg shrugged and asked, "Is that our fault? If I give you a big fine canoe and you overload it, is it my fault when it sinks?"

Longarm sighed. "Let's hope we never live to see it. Mayhaps they'll learn more trades. What can you tell me about all them new sheep and goats?"

The Indian agent grimaced. "They'll doubtless distribute them fairly among the established family flocks, once they get done drumming about it."

Longarm asked how long that might take. Vandenberg said, "At least the rest of this week. They haven't even begun the sand paintings as yet. They don't start evoking the kinder holy people until they drive away or appease the mean ones. I confess I have a time telling their good spirits from their evil spirits."

Longarm said, "Oh, I had that explained to me by a sort of pretty Chiricahua a spell back. They're the same spirits. All but Changing Woman. The Chiricahua call her Painted Woman. She's the only one you can always count on to be nice to you. The others are like fire or water. The good or bad depends on whether you're cooking dinner or trapped in a burning house. Or drowning instead of dying for a cool sip. I sure could use a map showing the locations of your different family fields and flocks, sir."

Vandenberg snorted, "So could I. We can only *hope* we're not being suckered into issuing the allotments more than once to the same fool Indian! They don't stay put, like Pueblo. If you'd like an educated guess, I'd say most of them right now could be found in a sort of V, with the lower point based on Fort Defiance. They like to get in for salt and matches, and despite your fears of overpopulation they don't really have much call to range too far north on either side of the Chuskas."

Longarm asked if there were more flocks grazing north along the Chaco or Chinlé. When the agent decided there had to be twice as many along the route he'd just followed, Longarm said he'd figured as much and they parted friendly.

He thought about parting friendly with Charladora. But all parting felt as shitty. So he just drifted over to where he'd left

227

his two ponies, saddled up, and rode, not looking back.

It didn't feel good. But it could have felt worse. He didn't know how to say anything really beautiful in Na-Déné, and a gal who walked in beauty deserved no awkward bullshit.

Chapter 20

Longarm had meant what he'd said about Fort Defiance being smart day's ride from Ganado. He got in before sundown, and would have made it sooner if he hadn't tensed up negotiating more than one likely stretch for an ambush.

There were fewer of those stretches as one approached the army post on the Defiance Plateau. For they'd sited it slick, back before the War Between the States, and the Navaho had lost a heap of ponies and their riders the only time they'd attacked at all seriously.

Situated near but not too close to the Bonito Canyon, on flat but well-watered grass flats the Indians had always admired, the isolated army post had suffered stock raids from the beginning, and had paid the Navaho back, with interest, by razing the hogans and shooting the stock of suspected Navaho *icos*.

Through the late winter and early spring of '60 the Navaho had gone all out to wipe the pesky place out. The famous Manuelito, known as a *xastoi* with much *bixo*, and many who listened to him hit the army remuda and its guards with close to five hundreds riders as they were grazing out on the flats. So that was when the Navaho first learned how dumb it was to go up against Colt Dragoons, or even single-shot rifles, with bows and arrows in broad-ass daylight. The lesson had cost Manuelito more than thirty brave *xastin* who would never listen to him again.

Manuelito and his powerful ally, Barboncito, had naturally tried again under cover of darkness, despite their inborn fear of stars and spooks.

The army had taught them how dangerous the dark could be as well. Two hours before a cold gray April dawn the Navaho had poured down Bonito Canyon like a spring flood to hit the fort on three sides as a howling horde of a thousand or more.

The howling had been a mistake. Some few actually made it in over the glorified fence the army engineers had dubbed perimeter defenses. The army took a handful of casualties in the time it took the sleeping troops to wake up, grab their prewar guns, and proceed to make good Indians out of their unexpected visitors.

The Indians, having taught the blue sleeves a good lesson, they said, declared the end of their good fight. That was when they learned how tough it can be to let loose of a bear's tail once you grab it.

Six troops of cavalry and nine companies of infantry marched out into Dinetah to "pacify" the Navaho. After playing hide-and-go-seek in the canyonlands for over a year, the Navaho declared peace some more, and the bored and weary army built another fort about thirty miles to the southeast, on even better grazing land that the Navaho had used for years as a winter gathering.

So that was where the official Navaho War broke out, after what had commenced as a friendly horse race between the soldiers and the band of Manuelito turned into a riot, with each side accusing the other and most of the casualties women and children.

Everyone knew how Kit Carson and his Ute scouts had calmed things down after the general hell-raising that had followed.

So despite all the recent scares, Longarm found the gates of the fort lightly defended when he rode in just after suppertime. The neighborly young officer of the day ordered Longarm's ponies rubbed down as well as watered and oated before they were stabled. Then he led Longarm to the officer's club. where, suppertime or not, soup and sandwiches could always be managed at short notice by the enlisted staff, and better yet, they served real Maryland Rye for the asking at the bar out front.

The post commander was in his quarters with his handsome wife. It seemed safe to say the same could be said for Captain

Granville, in a way. But it seemed the outfit had arrived safe and sound the afternoon before. But only one of the junior officers killing an evening in their club had ridden in with Granville. He was the shavetail who led the second platoon. He didn't know much. But others who'd been there longer were able to answer most of Longarm's questions.

The two bodies he'd sent on to the fort with the outfit had been identified pro tem as locally known but Texas-bred saddle tramps, if not the actual stock thieves some had said they had to be. In the past, both had been seen in Gallup, drinking with a more certain suspect known only as Red. No further description save for tall, red of hair, and with a red walrus mustache.

Longarm didn't mention someone called Red who'd ambushed a sheepherder and tried to get *him*. A man could waste a lot of wind chewing the fat with others who knew even less.

He asked about that newspaper gal in a desperately casual voice.

It was the shavetail who knew her who piped up. "Oh, Miss George rode out this morning with that heavy patrol."

Longarm frowned and demanded, "Patrol?"

The shavetail nodded and said, "I wanted to go with 'em, but at least a third of the outfit had to stay here in reserve. The major gave Captain Granville a chewing for coming in with only those two bodies after losing Corporal Brown. Then he sent the more experienced Captain Flannery out with a troop-strength patrol and a couple of our tame Navaho to scour that Salahkai Mesa good. The major says he's had about enough of this sniping shit!"

Longarm nodded, but asked, "What about the Chuska Mountains, just to the north? The Chuskas are a devilish maze of goat trails and uncharted canyons. So that's where trouble in these parts has always come from."

Another officer explained, "Our tame Navaho don't think so. They'd be the first to agree with you on all the fighting and fussing those higher hills have seen. For they were on the losing side. But they say none of their own people have been sniping at any blue sleeves and that, even if they were, the Chuskas have been bad medicine for their nation."

A first john attached to the garrison offered, "Ghosts. All the Navaho Colonel Canby and Kit Carson killed between them due north in those haunted hills."

Longarm agreed the Indians had already told him about some folks being spooked by stars and haunts up yonder. He asked if the army had a handle on the Chaco bottomlands to the northeast. They told him things had been quiet on that front, with only a few Navaho up that way and no incidents of any kind to report, despite the Jicarilla Apache Reserve to the east and Ute Strip to the north.

A somewhat older lieutenant who'd been listening more than he'd been talking, opined, "We know now the snipers have been white men all this time. Seems to me a white man with a hard-on for soldiers would feel safer sniping at them from over there along that western side of the reserve. Only Indians they'd risk bumping into, hitting and running, would be harmless Hopi and helpless Diggers off to the west."

A more opinionated younger shavetail said knowingly, "I'd hate to risk meeting any Apache doing anything this spring. The Ute can be mighty sullen as well. I vote for those snipers having some hideout over to the west as well."

Nobody had asked him to vote on it, and the post commander had told the patrol he'd sent out to scour the canyons over yonder. Longarm doubted his boss, Marshal Billy Vail, would want him retracing his own fool steps, no matter what that pretty reporter gal and a gal who walked in beauty might think of the notion.

He slept on it overnight in the handsome guest quarters a club orderly finally showed him to. But in the morning, sober, he still felt he'd done about all he'd been sent to do by Billy Vail and even General Sherman. The sheep and goats had been delivered. It seemed the Navaho didn't figure to ride with Victorio after all. There were still a heap of unsolved puzzles. But Longarm had yet to figure out whatever happened to the Lost Tribes of Israel and it hadn't killed him.

So after a good breakfast he rode out to the east, mounted on the buckskin and leading the barb. There were some really swell loose ends left up Durango way. But he knew Billy Vail would fuss like hell if he wasted the time it would take to

232

work his way that far north by even the Chaco bottomlands on horseback.

He figured it would be best to go through Gallup and over the Zuni Pass, to put him on the stage route down the San Jose to the upper Rio Grande, as fast in his own saddle as by stage. He knew he could get himself and the ponies on home from, say, La Joya by rail, aboard the Denver and Rio Grande.

It should have worked out that way. He enjoyed a swell noon dinner in the dusty mushrooming town of Gallup and rode on, past old Fort Wingate, where that Navaho War had gotten ugly. The Navaho didn't get to winter there anymore. The swell grass all around was grazed by the stock of the winners these days. He was planning on supper and a sleep over at the trail town of Crooked Tree just his side of the Zuni Pass over the Continental Divide. That was where things got mighty odd.

It was Longarm's usual custom to pay a courtesy call on the local law before he wandered about a small town spooking folks as a mystery man packing a .44-40. So when he came to Crooked Tree he asked directions, tethered his stock to the hitch rail in front of the town lockup, and moseyed in to see if a federal lawman passing through could get free overnight livery for a couple of well-behaved ponies.

The town constable turned out to be a somewhat older and good bit shorter cuss called Feathers O'Foy. He kept gulping as if he had a feather down his throat as he allowed they'd been expecting someone such as Longarm to show up and sent an owl-eyed deputy to get some cuss called Whitey. That left Longarm talking to just two of them.

When Longarm asked how come they'd been expecting him, O'Foy said something about that shooting up Durango way. Longarm said he could have nailed at least some of the rascals who murdered that poor sheepherder, and asked if they wanted to see his badge and identification.

The remaining deputy asked what sheepherder they might be jawing about. O'Foy hushed him with a warning look and smiled, like the cat in that book about Miss Alice, as he said he was sure the credentials of such a famous lawman could hardly be in doubt.

They both listened goggled-eyed as he filled them in on all his recent adventures. He was tired and hungry, and how come he had this feeling that they didn't believe a word he was saying?

The other deputy came back in with Whitey, who turned out to be an aptly named giant with snow-white hair, another brass badge, and a Merwin Hulbert .44-40 riding low in a *buscadero* rig.

Longarm's first mistake was taking the big paw Whitey held out to him as they were introduced. The giant gripped his gun hand hard with both his own, and hung on tight as the others threw down on him, save for the son of a bitch who lifted his own side arm from behind.

His second mistake was resisting, more by instinct than design, as he yelled, "Have you all gone *loco en las cabezas?* I'm on your side! I'm the law. Federal, you assholes!"

That was when somebody smacked him good with a gun barrel on the back of his skull.

So that was when he lost track of this old world for an indefinite period. He only knew it was dark outside and not much brighter inside the dinky cell he found himself locked up in, with a scared-looking Anglo kid dressed sort of Mex, when next he could get his eyes to focus.

That wasn't easy. His head still throbbed like hell, and had a bump on the back of it big enough to hatch a sidewinder at least. But he swung his legs to the floor off the fold-down bunk they'd put him on, and commenced to cuss, loud and inventive, as the kid tried to warn him the deputies were likely to get sore.

He said he was sore too, and asked what the sons of a triple-titted one-eyed whore and a clapped-up turkey buzzard had charged either of them with.

The kid claimed to be innocent, just passing through with horses he'd come by as honestly as most. Longarm was inclined to believe the sad story this time. The kid said, "They told me you were the one who backshot a famous lawman up Durango way. Are you really the man who shot U.S. Deputy Custis Long, mister?"

Longarm blinked owlishly and said, "Not hardly." He rose to move over to the bars and ring them good with his boot heel as he roared, "Somebody get me a lawyer back here, goddamn you all as total assholes! How in the hell could I have killed

234

myself when any fool can see I ain't dead!"

One of the deputies who'd jumped him finally came back, swearing softer but just as mean. From his side of the bars he said, "If I was you I'd keep it down. Too many folks know we got you rascals locked up back here as it is and, well, we don't have us an opera house in Crooked Tree."

Longarm growled, "Your town's well named. The first part, I mean. I see you've even swiped my tobacco and matches. So surely by this time even your illiterate constable must have noticed my papers and federal badge!"

The deputy nodded and said, "We got all the late Deputy Long's stuff in a desk drawer for safekeeping. We figured his killer had to be carrying his wallet and badge when they never found neither on him up in Durango."

Longarm forced himself to seem calmer as he got the dumb story out of his captor. The best way he could work it out was that some cuss about his size and build had checked into a Durango hotel as U.S. Deputy Custis Long for some fool reason. If it had been meant to throw somebody after him off his trail, it hadn't worked. He'd been shot in the back on the streets of Durango within twenty-four hours of his arrival in town.

Longarm told the local deputy, "I see what's going on now. I can prove some imposter got himself killed up Durango way and that I'm the real Custis Long easy. I just rode down from Durango with a whole cavalry troop, and spent last night as a guest of the army at nearby Fort Defiance. So since you must have a telegraph office here in your fair city . . ."

"You'll be a guest of Crooked Tree, Lord willing and the night riders let you, at least till our circuit judge gets back. I ain't got the wherewithal to send telegrams for no backshooting owlhoot riders who might have told them army men most anything. You come in here bold as brass with your whoppers, didn't you?"

He looked past Longarm at the younger prisoner to say, in a less surly tone, "We wired Lincoln County about you, Billy. They said a couple of deputies will be coming for you. Let's hope they get here soon enough."

The kid sobbed, "He's right! You *are* a bunch of total assholes! How many times do I have to tell you I've never

235

been anywhere near Lincoln County or even laid eyes on Billy the Kid!"

The deputy replied, not unkindly, "You can say it all the times you've a mind to, Billy. You still answer to the posted descriptions of William H. Bonney alias Billy the Kid, worth five hundred dollars dead or alive."

Longarm said, "No, he don't. That other kid's real name is Henry McCarty or McCarthy, and he'd be at least twenty right now. Anyone can see this kid ain't started shaving regular yet. How old are you, son? About fourteen, fifteen?"

The kid looked away and muttered, "I guess I can be be free, white, and twenty-one if I want to."

Longarm snorted in disgust and said, "That's what I get for trying to help a fool runaway. But getting back to the real Billy the Kid. I suspect we met up in the flesh one time, and I've seen a tintype they say he posed for. Neither the boy I met nor the stupid kid who posed for that notorious tintype looked anything like this young squirt. And I repeat, he's too young, no matter what he says."

The town deputy said, "I don't care what either of you say. I got a spicy magazine story to finish. So keep it down back here if you want any damn breakfast, hear?"

Chapter 21

For someone free, white, and twenty-one who'd been locked up longer than Longarm, the kid sure seemed to be taking a night in jail mighty seriously. Way after ten, the kid was still fretting about the injustice of it all, and refusing to let Longarm sleep off his headache. When the kid shook him and jarred him wider awake just as he was dozing off again, Longarm growled, "I'm going to smack some sense into you if you don't simmer down, boy. I told you they have to stand us before at least a justice of the peace sooner or later, and once I prove who I am I'll tell 'em you ain't Billy the Kid."

The kid said, "Somebody just rattled the front door. I don't think Waterman's out there now. I was *afraid* they might leave us to night riders."

Longarm rose and went over to kick the bars some more, even as he joshed, "Necktie parties are usually reserved for someone who's done something mean to someone local, kid. Why would a mob be coming for a pair of owlhoots wanted in other parts?"

The kid seemed right about the deputy out front deserting his late-night post, unless he was deaf or just didn't give a shit. The scared-looking kid said, "I heard them talking before. Seems folks around here are all het up about stock stealing. Lots of stock stealing with nary a head recovered. Maybe they mean to torture that out of us before they string us up. They say stolen stock has to be sold *somewhere*, and they'd know better who was doing it if they could figure out

237

what they were doing with it."

Longarm moved over to the single small-barred window high on the back adobe wall. As he grasped the stout steel bars, the kid shuddered and said, "I can't abide much pain, and I just don't *know* how a thief might go about selling purloined beef in these parts. There's no use fooling with those bars, mister. I've thought of that. They're set in walls almost two feet thick."

Longarm heaved, not feeling any give, as he answered, "That's a foot each way. A foot of *'dobe,* after an unusually wet spring."

The kid said, "Maybe so. But you ain't that strong. Nobody human could be. It would take a team of plow horses at least to yank one bar loose."

Longarm said, "One bar ought to do it, skinny as your ass is. If there's nobody out front, and you manage to get at the keys, and our guns and such . . ."

The kid insisted Longarm was wasting time and effort as he moved to the bunk beds and began to strip the mattresses of their unbleached linen covers. When Longarm proceeded to tear the linen into strips the kid marveled, "Oh, Lord, they'll beat us both for certain!"

Longarm muttered, "Not if we ain't here," as he knotted and twisted the linen to form a long if clumsy rope. The kid asked, "What are you doing that for? The ground outside is almost level with this floor. We're on the first story!"

Longarm looped his improvised line around a window bar, threaded the ends through the bars of their cell door, and tied a solid square knot to form a taut double line. Then he pried a wooden slat from a bunk, and wedged it between the two coils of linen as he told his mystified fellow prisoner, "I read somewhere how the old-timers out to fire one of them catty-pulps could build up a heap of catty this way. They call it torsion. See how tight that linen's getting as I twist with such fine leverage?"

The kid said, "Listen! I think I hear hoofbeats outside and it's close to midnight!"

Longarm put some back into it as the torsion got tougher. The kid had ears at least as good as his own. He wondered numbly who'd put the locals up to such shit. Someone always had to. The average cuss hardly ever thought about busting prisoners out of jail and lynching them. That one deputy, at least, was either in on it or scared of a bunch he likely went to church with, the son of a bitch.

Longarm felt something snap. He couldn't tell if it was 'dobe or just linen. He twisted harder. Then it really snapped and he had to laugh.

He twisted some more and the kid laughed too as the window bar held firm and the whole front of their cell leaned inward. Nobody had ever expected that much force to be used against those bars from that direction. So they'd been installed with a big old roof beam intended to keep them from being pushed *out*.

Longarm grabbed hold with his strong hands to pull them further in. So he didn't have to trust the kid after all. He just followed his slimmer escapee out through the wrecked front of the cell, and led the way out front where, sure enough, they found the office dark and deserted. The kid started to strike a light. Longarm hissed a warning and said, "Don't tell anyone out there what we're up to. Let them guess!"

They rummaged blindly through desk drawers, found their rolled-up gun rigs and manila envelopes stuffed with their pocket possibles, and eased over to the door, side arms in hand.

Through the dusty glass, they could see the ominous figures on the far side of the dark deserted street. Longarm said, "They must be waiting for a leader, a battering ram, or a rope. Let's see if we can find another way out. Do you know where they might be keeping our ponies, kid?"

His fellow escapee said, "At the public livery down the way. I heard them talking about the owner being an honorary deputy. But I don't see any side door. That one by the gun rack leads into their toilet. I know because they let me use it, handcuffed to a pipe, as they brought me in."

Longarm grabbed a Greener riot gun from the rack as he said, "I saw some boxes of ten-gauge on yonder desk, kid. Grab 'em whilst I see why they felt they had to cuff you in there."

The answer was simple. There were no bars on the narrow window. Better yet, it opened on a narrow breezeway. So a few minutes later, as someone up the street was shouting, "What are we waiting for?" Longarm and the kid had Longarm's two tested ponies saddled with their own rigs rescued from the tack room of the livery stable. But as they were tiptoeing out the back of the stable to the alley, reins and guns in hand, a door popped open inside the stable at the top of a flight of stairs, and a sleepy female voice called out, "Is that you, Melvin? What are you doing down there at this hour, you fool man?"

Longarm whispered, "Here, get them both down the back alley a ways. I'll cover you."

The kid gasped, "You're not going to kill her, are you?" But he did as told when the noisy gal came clumping down the wooden stairs, preceded by wild shadows cast by the candle stock in her hand.

Longarm flattened against a stall near the foot of the stairs. As she got there he saw she was older than him, but built much nicer in her flannel nightgown. Before she could make him out he blew out her candle with a wild wave of his hat brim and yelled *Bego! Bego!* goosed her good, and sent her dashing out the front way screaming, "Help! Help! I'm being attacked by Injuns!"

So it wasn't long before the whole town was awake and Longarm was riding out of it with the kid as if their lives depended upon it. For their lives doubtless did, judging by all that fussing close behind.

A Greener ten-gauge, fired at random on the run, could do a lot in the way of slowing headlong riders down. But every time Longarm reined in for a listen, they heard hoofbeats back yonder, in growing numbers as word spread. Longarm knew the mob would hang back out of range as long as they couldn't make out any targets of their own in the starlight. But as near as Longarm could make out, he and the kid were following a contour line across fairly open range on the western slopes of the Zuni Ridge. Come sunrise, not too distant in the future, they'd be riding like two ants across a crumb-specked tablecloth, too far from from any possible help to matter.

When the kid urged him to at least trot his damned buckskin some more, Longarm muttered, "Every time we ride sudden, they ride sudden. Every time we stop, they stop, lest we get the drop on 'em in this tricky light. Shut up and let me figure out some way to make that work more in our favor."

The kid said, "If you're really who you say you are, wouldn't we be safe once we made it far as that Indian reservation?"

Longarm snorted, "We would. It's too far to reach before dawn, and I can't see either Navaho or troopers from Fort Defiance down this way."

Then he laughed harshly, and chortled. "Bless you, my child. It may not work, but it's worth a try!"

The kid asked what he was talking about, of course. Longarm said, "Ride on at a trot and pay no mind to unusual noises back here. Rein in, say, four furlongs on, and don't throw down on anyone loping to join you. It'll be me. What are you waiting for, a pat on the ass?"

The kid rode on. Off the other way, Longarm heard the cautious pursuit gather speed again. He fired the Greener, emptied his six-gun into the ground, and whooped like a Comanche with a toothache as he steadied his spooked mount.

It wasn't easy. The buckskin kept trying to bolt out from under him as he wailed, "Don't leave me, pard! They got me pinned by one leg under my pony and . . . No! Jesus! Not my eyes, you damn savages!"

Then he whooped some more as he reloaded, hoping someone in the crowd back yonder would know an old Ute charging yell when they heard it. He didn't know what a Navaho warwhooping sounded like.

Ute yells remembered from unhappier times seemed to do it. He let fly more pistol shots and lit out after the kid. He thought about letting the kid go on his way, but decided against it. He was glad the kid was still with him as they rode on to the north together. For that mob would have likely caught such a babe in the woods, and doubtless strung him up before he could convince them he really wasn't Billy the Kid.

This other one answered to Bascom, Pat Bascom out of Tennessee by way of the Texas Panhandle and some bullshit about family trouble there that Longarm didn't have the time for.

He said, "Never mind why you had to get to Flagstaff, Pat. Unless we get away, our final destination figures to be

241

betwixt Mother Earth and a handy tree limb. They might have bought that ruse back yonder. Even if they have, they're likely to edge in, come sunrise, to view my mangled remains. We'd best be somewhere else when they do, and our mounts are only mortal."

Pat said he sure painted cheerful pictures in the dark.

Longarm said, "So do them stars, and a late moon's rising to guide our way better. So despite the risk of trespassing on more settled land, we'd best swing a tad to our left and see about picking up some spare ponies."

Pat demanded, "Are you crazy? How are we to steal horses with the whole county on the prod for us, and don't you know what they do to a horse thief, Custis?"

Longarm chuckled and asked, "What did you figure they aimed to do to us innocent wayfaring strangers, kiss us on both cheeks?"

So they rode on, with the kid still talking too much, as scared or nervous folk are inclined to. The late moon finally rose, a thin new crescent that could have stayed on that Turkish flag for all the good it did them as a night lamp. You could sort of make out the moon-frosted tops of the sage and still-sprouting tumbleweed all about. But only for a few yards out, with lots of inky puddles of darkness in between.

Longarm said, "They've sure overgrazed down this way. You say there's a bunch of new spreads raising heaps of stock?"

Pat said, "I rode through this country some before they picked me up for looking like Billy the Kid. Saw lots of cows first. A few calicos, some of that black stock we call Cherokee longhorns in the Panhandle, but mostly pure Andalusian, fresh from Old Mexico."

As Longarm was digesting that, the Texas kid said, "They say they would have way more if someone wasn't running stock off wholesale. I reckon that's why they were so het up about outlaws in general."

Longarm said, "I've noticed being robbed can make folks surly. I don't think that big low star a tad to our right is really a star. Looks more like someone left a lamp in the window for someone out late at night. We're out late at night. So let's go see if they have any good riding stock."

242

Pat said Longarm was fixing to get them both shot from cover, but came along anyway as Longarm asked if anyone had considered where that stolen stock was being unloaded.

Pat replied, "They kept asking me, as if they thought I ought to know. They say the real Billy the Kid runs lots of stolen cows down to a secret spread he has in Old Mexico."

Longarm snorted and said, "They told me he was washing dishes in a beanery in Shakespeare. This would be a piss-poor time to try for a border jump with stolen cows. Both the U.S. and Mex armies are out in force along the border right now, with Victorio and at least four hundred Bronco Apache likely to pop out at you most any place, and I wouldn't be too sure about the even meaner Yaqui down that way!"

Pat said, "Well. They've been running the stolen beef to market *some* durned way. There was talk about the Navaho to the northwest earlier. But both the army and their agents say they haven't seen so many cows up that way."

Longarm nodded and explained, "The Navaho cotton more to sheep or goats. They ride better than they rope, and I just came down through Dinetah without meeting all that many cows or cowboys. Let's both just hush and see how close in we can get before they notice."

They didn't get too far. They were still a couple of furlongs out in the dark when a pair of yard dogs commenced yapping and Pat hissed, "Let's get out of here!"

Longarm kept riding. When the window lamp winked out and somebody cracked the back door to demand, "Who's out there at this hour?" he yipped, *"Heyakikikikihey!"* and fired the Greener at the other white man's voice.

It spooked his pony almost as much. But he didn't want to be too near his own muzzle flash in any case. He'd known to begin with that the buckshot from his stolen riot gun wouldn't do much damage from that far out. But as his buckskin crow-hopped in the moonlight, the cuss in the remote house was busting out a window pane with his own gun barrel, wailing, "Injuns! Everybody in here with me ahint these thicker walls!"

So young Pat was laughing like hell and whooping like a Kiowa as they watched four hands scooting from the bunkhouse on the far side of the barn to hit the back door at the same time in a wailing tangle of arms, legs, and pleas for mercy.

Shortly thereafter, of course, those in the house commenced to peg wild shots at nobody in particular as they enjoyed an Indian uprising their grandchildren were never going to hear the last of. It naturally never occurred to them to fire blind at their remuda, penned between the bunkhouse and the barn. So with Pat covering him, Longarm used the throw rope from the kid's Texas stock saddle to select a pair of ponies inclined to run more than they bucked as they circled him in the tricky light.

He had to cut the Texas kid's fairly new genuine manila to make hasty halters. But Pat was laughing more than fussing as the two of lit out with four ponies and a demonstration of pistol shooting and improvised war whoops.

But as they rode out of earshot Longarm grumbled, "We got to find us something to drum on. You have to let a cuss get too close before you can spook him by just yelling."

He went on to explain how spooked those soldiers blue had acted about harmless way-chanting by distant Navaho. He said, "They make those noisy drums by stretching green rawhide over big hoops of wood and letting them dry as taut as, well, drums."

The kid said, "I got a fringed deerskin jacket wrapped in this possibles roll with my slicker and blankets. Got it off a Comanche who needed drinking money. I reckon it's half brain-tanned, but it ought to shrink if we soak it some first. I know it gets stiff as pasteboard when it dries after getting damp. You have to knead it like dough to soften it up again."

Longarm said they'd study on it after they put more distance between themselves and anyone out to do them dirt.

So morning found them in a secluded brushy draw, still short of the reservation line, with no guarantee those pissed-off stockmen wouldn't just keep coming.

Longarm and the kid changed their saddles and bridles to the cow ponies they'd stolen for any breaking that needed to be done while they had the time and place.

But both ponies, a bay and a paint with one blue eye Longarm just hadn't seen in the dark, behaved like perfect

ntlemen, or nutless geldings at any rate. The blue eye staring
ut of a white patch didn't seem to run the paint sideways after
ll. It only stood to reason they wouldn't have a poor cow pony
the remuda of a working spread to begin with.

Fashioning a big Navaho drum took longer. It was simple to
ut a springy digger willow limb and lash it into a hoop about
ght for a smaller kid to roll. But the Texas kid's deerskin
cket wouldn't be big enough, even stretched on the hoop
ter soaking.

When Pat said, "I'm sorry I never thought to buy a big-
er one," Longarm replied, "It's the thought that counts. We
ot the hoop. So now all we need is a critter big enough
skin."

Looping the big hoop over the upthrust butt of his Win-
nester and packing the Greener in his free hand, Longarm
aid it was time to move on, and forked himself aboard the
lue-eyed paint. The kid got on the bay. But as they rode up
he draw, leading their more jaded but unsaddled buckskin and
arb, Pat asked, "Wouldn't it be safer to hole up by day and
de by night, Custis?"

Longarm explained, "Let's hope they feel the same way. I
now how you ride in Indian country during a rising, kid. But
e're the only Indians that have riz up this way."

Pat murmured, "You hope," as they moved on, trying to
ay below the skyline as they followed the same level along
he Pacific slope of the Continental Divide.

In this corner of New Mexico Territory the spine of North
merica really snaked from the southwest to the northeast
t almost a forty-five-degree angle. When Pat pointed out
heir course was taking them ever more east of Fort Defiance
s they moved north, Longarm replied, "Beelining for the
ort could get us killed. The country over that way is too
ettled, and by now most every asshole with a gun will be
ut looking for Billy the Kid, the man who shot Longarm,
nd at least one good-sized war band. I remember how silly
got around Dodge the time Dull Knife jumped the South
heyenne Reserve. A well-known bullshit artist called Bat
Masterson is still bragging about how he led that big posse,
kely half the whores from the Alhambra, out to save the
vorld from all them homesick Indians."

Pat laughed and said, "I remember that scare. It was close to home in Tennessee. But how are we to reach the safety c that army post if you figure we're cut off from it?"

Longarm said, "By riding farther and wider, of course. I we just hug this high country another thirty miles or less, we'l be amid the headwaters of the east branch of the Chaco. Onc we are, we can follow the ever deeper canyons down acros the line into the eastern bottomland of the reservation. Dinetal used to extend all the way up through the Chaco Canyons t the Divide. But don't start a war with Uncle Sam if you wan to hang on to all you started with. Los Estados Unidos D Mejico had already found that out when the Navaho and the Confederate States of America got to learn the same lesso at about the same time."

Pat said something about losing a favorite uncle with Hood' Texas Brigade. Longarm said they'd all been young and fool ish back in those days. When Pat asked which side he migh have ridden with, Longarm muttered, "I disremember. You jus heard me say it was all mighty foolish, and I don't want to tal about it."

That first boy he'd killed at Shiloh had been about as youn, and wide-eyed as this one. Was there any other resemblance It got hard to say after you'd killed another, then another, a young and scared shitless as yourself, till after a while you go too tired to feel more than sick and sleepy as the killing got t be more like *work*.

Later that morning, as they were swapping saddles again ir yet another mountain draw, Longarm shot a big bitch coyote staring at them boldly from the next rise.

As he reloaded his pistol Pat marveled, "Good Lord, you're fast! I was just fixing to say, 'Look at yon coyote!' when you' drawn and killed it!"

"It's a knack you pick up," said Longarm. "Scoot up tha slope to our south and see if that shot attracted anybody whils I skin the critter out. He must have mistook us for Indian pals Hoped a pistol shot would keep his demise more private."

As the kid climbed out of the draw, Longarm moved up t where the coyote lay on one side, staring up reproachfully with one dead yellow eye, and got to work with his pocket knife.

He naturally had a sewing kit in a saddlebag. So he

246

stitched the still-warm skin to the willow hoop, hair side down, with stout waxed shoemaker's thread. The result didn't sound impressive when he hit it with a stick. It would have to shrink some first.

He called up to the kid, "Anything off to the south, kid?"

When Pat said the range looked empty as far as the eye could see, Longarm built a small brushwood fire up the draw from their tethered stock. When the kid complained, "You're sending up smoke, a heap of smoke, in broad daylight, Custis!" Longarm just laughed.

He said, "Ain't you never heard of smoke signals, you wild-ass Kiowa? It would take too long to sun-dry this coyote-skin drumhead. Got to toast it over these hardwood sticks a mite if we expect to worry anyone at a distance."

Pat laughed and said, "Between smoke signals and Navaho drums, we figure to have the whole U.S. Army chasing us as well before you ever get us out of this fix!"

Longarm started to say something soothing. Then he chuckled dryly and said, "Bless you again, my child. For a punk runaway lying about his age and Lord knows what else, you sure keep coming up with swell ideas for me!"

Chapter 22

It was late in the afternoon, topping a rise between draws that likely led down to the Chaco canyonlands to the west, when Longarm spotted dust less than five miles behind them. The kid was ready to make a run for it. Longarm warned there was too much daylight left, and added, "As green a spring as we've had, you got to ride hard in good numbers to kick up that much dust. They might not have spotted us at all yet. So like the old bull said to the young bull, let's just mosey on nice and easy and screw 'em all."

So they did. But next time they rode high that dust to the south seemed closer. The kid said the lynch mob was gaining on them. Longarm said, "We don't know who it is. Could be the army. We'd best see if we can find out the safe way."

He reined in on the brushy bottom of the next draw, and handed his reins and lead rope to the kid as he explained, "Army keeps on coming when they suspicion Indians. Most others tend to back off."

He swung down from his saddle, Greener in hand, but laid the more noisy than useful shotgun aside as he gathered dead brush and laid out a windrow, maybe fifty feet long, in line with the draw and so more broadside to those others in the distance. Then, as the kid watched bemused in the saddle, Longarm piled greenwood and silvery fresh sagebrush on his windrow, in separate piles about a yard from one another. When the kid asked why, he said, "You'll see." He moved to the uphill end, and hunkered down to light one end of the odd-looking creation before he scooped up the Greener, remounted the blue-eyed paint, and said, "*Vamanos, chivato!*"

we want to watch what happens next from someplace else!"

So they did, from their bellies, atop a handy hogback out-cropping a couple of miles to the north. The kid thought it was pretty slick, the way each pile of salad greens sent up big white mushrooms of "smoke talk" in turn, at slow intervals, as the windrow burned down-slope, not as fast as it would have burning the other way.

Longarm was more interested in dust above the high chap-arral to the southwest. When the kid said there didn't seem to be any, Longarm grunted, "I was afraid they might not be the army. They may keep after us at a walk. They have to have at least one good tracker with 'em. I hope we've confused the shit out of him. We'd best keep going the same way till sunset. After dark it ought to be safe to swing down any of these draws we've been hitting. They all lead down to the Chaco bottomlands of the reservation. We ought to feel a whole lot safer there."

They crawled back down to the ponies, and rode on at as fast a pace as they dared, walking their mounts where it was dusty and trotting them across thicker sod. The range got less abused as you got further away from the new spreads to the south.

When they found themselves on the bottom of a really deep draw just after sundown, Longarm said, "This must be the place," and led the way northwest. The kid said the sides sure rode steep as they got ever deeper below the regular grade of the Pacific slopes. Longarm said, "I keep forgetting you're new in these parts. You'll see steeper side walls than them as we go deeper into the pumpkin."

The meltwater channel he'd chosen didn't make a liar out of him as it was joined by others to dig itself ever deeper till it was a full-fledged arroyo. Longarm had to correct Pat when the kid called it a canyon. He said to just wait a few miles and they'd really see canyon walls.

But of course, they couldn't really see much in such dim moonlight when Longarm finally reined in to say, "I make the sheer walls on either side a good sixty feet or more above our innocent heads. I don't see how anybody can get at 'em, save from up or down this old crack in the ground. So we'd best find some browse for our ponies, share the fresh beans

249

I picked up in Gallup, and get some rest. We could have a long day ahead of us, kid."

Pat said they'd already had one as they rode on. When Longarm heard a cheerful trickling up a side cleft, he swung into it and, sure enough, they found another tiny Eden, off to one side of serious sudden floods, but watered by a baby waterfall spring out of the rocks two thirds of the way to the starry sky.

They had to build a small fire near a limpid little pool to find all that out. Pat declared it a swell hideout. Longarm said it was likely safe to camp there overnight.

They both knew enough about horseflesh to see to the four ponies before they worried about their own empty guts and weary bones. For only human beings were strong-willed enough, or dumb enough, to keep going when they were hurting. Horses were far stronger, but there'd be no reasoning with their crybaby minds when and if they just had all the pushing they could abide.

Longarm let the fire die down to glowing coals once he'd warmed the beans some in the opened cans. They didn't need coffee, wide awake as they still felt despite the hours of scared riding. Tomato preserves would wash the beans down as well and leave nicer tastes in their mouths to sleep on.

So they lazed side by side on their spread-out bedding, sharing an after-supper cheroot as they talked about this and that. For a kid too young to shave, Pat seemed worldly enough about the comings and goings of older folks. When Longarm got to that blue bottle he'd found in that other canyon on the way down the other side of the Chuskas, Pat asked if he still had it. Longarm got up and fetched it from a saddlebag. When he hunkered back down, Pat took it, held it up to the dim red light, and sniffed it good before deciding, "Hair rinse. Can't tell if it's henna or black. They both use the same soapy solvent."

Longarm frowned thoughtfully and said, "I thought it smelled a mite like another bottle I stumbled over in a redhead's dressing room. You're saying that bottle started out full of hair dye?"

Pat said, "Nope. Rinse. Coloring less fast than dye. Ladies use a rinse instead of a dye when they only want to change their hair coloring for some special occasion, say an important party or maybe a fancy ball in town."

250

"Or a cattle raid in parts where you might not be as well known by witnesses!" Longarm said. "I told you about someone, a pal called Red, ambushing me and that Mex Basque, remember? How do you like that tied in with someone down this way called Red associating with suspected stock thieves?"

Pat handed the bottle back, saying soberly, "It sounds wilder than a natural mousy blonde wanting to be the belle of the ball. But I guess it's possible. Say a stockman known and respected on his home range wanted to lead an outlaw gang in other parts. Folks would be inclined to remember flaming hair more than other features, and he could shampoo his hair back to its natural color any time he needed to!"

Longarm said, "You can buy a fake mustache of any color in many a joke shop too. But hold on. Poor old Mauro was gunned by a gang led by a so-called Red way up north, where nobody's been missing any cows. So why would anyone be playing tricks with henna rinse up that way?"

Pat asked to hear some more about that rich widow with a stranglehold on Indian beef up Durango way.

Longarm said, "Already thought of that. Can't get it to work. Say some gang was stealing stock south of the Indian country to sell to the government as honest Flying W beef. The Indian agents would surely notice the registered brands of recently stolen stock."

Pat asked, "Didn't you say that cattle baroness buys stock off other spreads, or says she does, before she slaps her own brand on for the road?"

Longarm nodded. "First thing I considered when I spied some green hides at a trading post. But the purchasing agents handing out government money for beef on the hoof only do so after checking every brand they see against a nice thick brand ledger. The lists of run or otherwise suspicious brands is mighty long, thanks to the way the price of beef's been rising since the depression of the '70s. But there's no way you could hope to slip by a federal buyer armed with a federal brand book, kid."

Pat said quietly, "Not unless you bribed somebody."

Longarm shook his head. "Thought of that too. Know the old boys buying beef for the South Utes, by rep at least. We cleaned out a lot of crooked Indian agents after President

251

Hayes took over. I'll allow this mysterious Red seems to be all over creation, if you'll agree he's up to something slicker than I've been able to figure out so far. You up to another smoke, kid?"

Pat declined and murmured something about turning in.

Longarm said, "Go ahead. I ain't sleepy. So I'll just set and smoke a spell. If it'll set your mind more at rest, you got my word as an enlisted man and gentleman that I won' pester you in your bedroll."

There came a long thoughtful silence. Then Pat quietly asked him, "How long have you known, Custis?"

He lit his second cheroot, not looking at her, as he quietly said, "Didn't take me as long as it might have some others. As a man living a more active life, I've met up with other adventurous ladies out to pass themselves off for boys in a man's world. Most gents ain't used to the way female hips fill out male pants, no offense. Like I said, I've encountered the phenomenon before."

It would have been offensive to mention that time, back along the trail, when he'd wondered how come old Pat squatted down to piss up the draw a ways. But he had to ask, "How come you let them hold you as Billy the Kid back there when all you had to do was, ah, open your shirt a mite if you didn' want to drop your drawers, Pat?"

She laughed bitterly, and asked, "Would you want to prove your female nature to that monster Whitey? I *did* explain I was a girl the first time I was picked up on suspicion in a West Texas trail town. Have you ever been screwed by eight men in a row, Custis?"

He managed not to smile as he replied eight sounded like a mite more than good clean fun. She said something about hating men in any numbers, and he told her to just go to sleep because he didn't care.

But of course, now that it was out in the open, she had to go on and on about some husband who'd been a drunken brute, and then a lover who'd run out on her after she'd run off with him and all the jewels she'd inherited from her sainted momma.

He said, "Stuff a sock in it, will you, kid? I've heard your sad story many a time. You ought to hear the ones my side

252

ells about false-hearted women. They're likely all true. Men and women surely deserve something nicer than each other, but I ain't the Lord, so I ain't the one to complain to."

By this time she was under her covers, but still bitching in a sleepy whine that inclined him to suspect he knew why that other cuss had run off on her.

You couldn't tell exactly how a gal might be built with her in loose-fitting manly duds. But he knew she was small, yet stronger than most gals of any size. Her features were regular. She'd look downright pretty with a little powder, paint, and longer hair. By the time she'd dozed off, the fire had died completely. He just sat there smoking as the springwater gurgled at him in the darkness and stars only a Navaho could call spooky smiled down into their little hollow. So once he'd finished the second smoke he hauled off his boots, put his rolled-up gun rig in his upside-down hat, and finished undressing under the covers of his own bedroll, lest she strike a match and call him a durned old dirty thing.

He quietly called himself some dirty things as he lay there in the dark with a hard-on, trying to fall asleep as he heard her soft breathing teasing his old organ-grinder for him.

Cocks were sure independent thinkers. It was a caution how many otherwise sensible men had gotten themselves killed following the instructions of their cocks instead of their brains.

Gals seemed to have more control of their privates. That might have been why they seldom made such total fools of themselves. He found his fool mind following his cock's throbbings to picture that petite brown-headed gal so close to him taking on eight men, one after the other. He hadn't asked if she'd enjoyed at least the first few prongings.

He knew lots of gals daydreamed about taking on a whole gang of horny rascals. Gals could do that better than men. He'd have never been able to keep it up for that many gals in a row. But it sounded as if it might be fun to try. Gals seemed to feel different about an unexpected surprise from a stranger of the enemy gender.

He didn't know what he was going to do with that old organ-grinder when Pat suddenly moaned and groaned, "Oh, Custis, that feels so . . . Oh, Lord, I seem to have been dreaming just now."

He said, "Seeing we're pals, you can go on just calling m
Custis."

She was too sleepyheaded to get it. She asked, "Was
talking in my sleep just now? I surely *hope* not!"

He gallantly assured her she hadn't said anything unseem
ly.

She said, "Men are disgusting, and I never mean to fall i
love again. But I was married a good three years, and th
first two weren't so bad. That false-hearted traveling man
ran off with treated me all right at first too. Why do yo
men always play a woman false as soon as she says sh
loves you?"

Longarm gently explained, "Men have had the same experi
ence with fickle ladies. Everybody gets along well at first
That's why they call that first grand month the honeymoon
I won't say I love you if you don't say you love me. Coul
we both go to sleep now?"

She agreed. But a few minutes later she giggled and said
"I'd just die if you knew what I was doing under these cover
right now."

He sighed and said, "I'm fixing to start jerking off mysel
if you don't drop it."

She gasped, and asked if he had to talk about what she calle
the universal secret vice so crudely. He said, "You was the on
who brought it up, and now that it's up, don't you think it'
sort of silly for us two adult folks to jerk off side by side lik
a couple of horny kids?"

She didn't answer. She was breathing too funny. But just a
she was really starting to pant she giggled and asked, "Wha
on earth are you doing to yourself? I can heard the groun
shaking all the way over here!"

Longarm was already sliding his own naked flesh out from
under the covers as he answered urgently, "That ain't me. It'
hoofbeats, a whole lot of hoofbeats, coming down the canyor
suddenly!"

He tossed his rolled-up gun rig, hat and all, to thud beside
her as he leaped up bare-ass to gather up his Winchester and
the ten-gauge Greener, husking, "They may not know abou
this spring-hollowed side branch. Move back by the ponies
and hope I can stop 'em if they do!"

254

He padded barefoot to the narrower opening, armed and dangerous, to hunker down with a long gun in each hand. Then Pat was huddled against his bare back with her naked cupcake tits hugging the nape of his neck as she aimed his six-gun over his right shoulder, asking, "How could they have cut our trail in the dark?"

He whispered, "Let's hope they never did. They could be headed down this natural route to the Chaco bottomland for the same reasons we were both picked up back yonder in Crooked Tree. It's natural to just follow the natural lay of the land. Now hush, and if you want to be useful, go back and fetch me that last box of shotgun shells. You'll find 'em in my left-hand saddlebag. My saddle's near the head of my bedroll. *Move* it, girl!"

She moved it. But before she got back he heard loud yips and the slapping of coiled rope against chaps, along with the considerable bawling of cows that just didn't like to move that much after dark.

Pat came back to poke his bare shoulder blades with her turgid nipples this time as she hissed, "I couldn't find the durned old box."

He whispered, "Don't matter. They seem to be going right on by. They ain't that bunch after us. It's a cattle drive! Fair-sized herd, from the sounds of it. Wonder where in thunder they could be headed at this or any other hour!"

She whispered, "I'll bet it's that gang of stock thieves the folks to the south are so sore at!"

Longarm whispered, "I just said that. Their hoofprints will blot our trail out betwixt here and the east end of this canyon. But you know, we could likely use a posse of sore losers about now. Must be at least a dozen riders out yonder and even if we trail after them, I don't see how I'll ever get 'em all in one place long enough to get the drop on 'em. Be still. I think I hear the drag coming!"

He did. As the drag riders passed, cussing and spitting, none of them said anything Longarm could use. Pat whispered, "What are we going to do now, Custis?"

Longarm said, "Nothing. They'll surely leave a trail a schoolmarm could follow, and it's pure suicide to go up against unknown numbers, positioned unknown ways, in the

255

dark. So our best bet would be some well-earned rest and an early start come sunrise. If that's really that outlaw gang of the mysterious Red, you can see now why they call such gents owlhoot riders. They'll be holed up in broad day. I doubt it'll be out in the open. Wish I had a more educated guess as to where in blue blazes they mean to move that herd!"

She shivered in the cool shades of evening, and asked if it was safe to get under the covers again. "You said yourself we were headed down this canyon for the Chaco bottomlands."

He said, "I know. Go on back to them bedrolls. I'll just make sure they rode on to wherever they think they're headed!"

His bare shoulder blades felt lonesome without her warm tits up against them. He told himself to worry about more important matters. That couldn't have been an honest market herd headed down into the Navaho reserve. The Navaho had no call for that much beef. A drive north along the Chaco bottomlands would wind up in that South Ute Strip. But that Widow Donovan from Colorado had a lock on beef sales to the Ute. Their white purchasing agents would record all sales from any direction, brands and all, while the Ute themselves didn't have the wherewithal to buy at discount. And even if they had, it would be a mighty stupid Indian who'd pay for a cow when he could have one as good gratis from the B.I.A.

Moving stolen cows south off the reservation, to be sold as Navaho stock in the very country they had been stolen from, made even less sense. So Longarm stepped out into the canyon, put his bare foot in a fresh cow pie, and still made himself listen tight till he was sure they'd moved on down the canyon.

He cussed his way back, hugging the rock wall till he could swish his bare foot in that springwater and wipe it on grass before he groped his way back to the bedrolls. He set the two long guns to one side against his saddle, and started to feel his way into his own roll. When he found it full of naked lady he gulped, and said he was sorry but he'd thought this was his bedding.

When she shyly confided it was, he started to ask a stupid question. But he never did. As he slithered his own naked goose flesh down under the covers with her now-warmer curves, she soberly warned him not to seduce her just because she was trying to be practical.

256

He assured her he wouldn't as he hugged her naked nipples to his bare chest and proceeded to rock the little man in her wet canoe to warm her up. But she hugged him back, and rolled him atop her as she moaned, "I've already been doing that and I'm fixing to come, feeling mighty empty, if you don't . . . Jesus H. Christ! What are you trying to stuff me with down there, you brute?"

It was a dumb question. So he didn't answer, and once she got to moving her horsewoman's hips in time with his thrusts, it was tough to remember this was all supposed to remain platonic.

Chapter 23

Come morning they were still just friends, and somehow found the strength to mount up and trail after all those night-owl cows. Cows couldn't move much more than twenty-four miles in the same number of hours, even if you ran some meat off them. They walked more than a mile an hour, and trotted even faster, of course. But you had to let them rest a mite and graze a heap, or they'd just lie down and die on you. So Longarm and Pat caught up easy. The mysterious herd was grazing around another spring in a box canyon off the main trunk of what the maps called *the* Chaco Canyon, which was more like a pint-sized version of the Grand Canyon, with the same side canyons and islands in the sky forming a hell of a maze. Longarm never would have thought to look for cows up that one box canyon if he hadn't been following them and paying attention. The mysterious herders had run the stock across miles of slickrock and cobbles before swinging off the main canyon. But that many cows drop a heap of shit, and a sharp eye could make out swarms of hover flies in the noon sun from farther off than he could spot fresh olive-drab spattered across cobbles.

They didn't follow the cow-shit trail right up the side canyon, of course. Once they knew which way the cows had been run, they rode back as far as another side canyon, then followed it back into the pumpkin as it narrowed to little more than a slit. Longarm asked the gal to mind their ponies as he slithered topside for a look-see.

Getting up to the flat rimrocks was no chore. So he was more pissed than surprised when Pat popped out of the crack as he was crawling off with his Winchester and that improvised Navaho drum. She said she'd unsaddled the ponies they'd been riding and tethered all four to the grounded loads. He said he hoped it would work, and crawled on. She asked why they were crawling when there was plenty of flat rim-rock to stand on, and how come he'd brought along that drum.

He said, "It ain't the fall down an unexpected crack that kills you. It's the sudden stop at the bottom. I ain't sure why I dragged this drum along. Wouldn't have made it if I hadn't thought it might come in handy."

She gasped, and allowed she followed his drift about sudden stops, when they got to the rim of that other canyon and peered over the sheer drop.

The cows were sunlit, grazing grama and peppergrass around the half acre or more of springwater. A remuda of about a dozen-and-a-half cow ponies had been hobbled to graze closer to an abandoned dwelling built into the cliffs across the way. Longarm pointed at the old cliff dwelling with his chin and said, "That's where the riders will have forted up for the day. I told you about finding that hair-rinse bottle in another such place. Aside from the thick stone walls and handy loopholes, they know the Indians living in these parts today never go near those haunted cliff dwellings. That's how come white folks still find so much pottery, baskets, and such. The leader of that gang knows a thing or two about local Indian customs."

He levered a round in the chamber of his Winchester, laid the gun aside, and hauled the big flat Navaho drum up between them as he grinned and said, "I've been studying up on the subject as well."

He drew his six-gun and began to beat the drum with its steel barrel, trying to remember how that Beauty Way went so he could keep the same beat. Pat marveled, "My God, that's loud! You're going to have them coming at us like a swarm of bees, you maniac!"

He sort of sang in time with his booming drum, "I hope so. No way I'd ever get at 'em unless I can smoke 'em out of that cliff dwelling."

She protested, "They'll have us treed up here! There's no

way we can get to our ponies again without going back down to their level!"

He assured her, "They can't tell just where I'm drumming from. Hear all them echoes? Even if they do guess which side slit we went up, how far up it do you reckon they'd get with me aiming down at them? We could hold 'em off till the army gets here just with serious *spitting*!"

She gulped and answered, "If you say so. What makes you think the army may be coming, Custis?"

He said, "They're supposed to. They've been alerted to Indians off the reservation. This canyon used to be a Navaho stronghold, much as Canyon de Chelly got to be after everybody knew about this one. But it ain't on the Navaho reserve no more. They lost their lands this far east—till just now, I mean."

He saw movement across the way. Pat did too. She said, "I see what you're up to. You're not a maniac. Those drumbeats will carry for miles, and someone's sure to report them to Fort Defiance, if they can't hear them there themselves!"

He said that was barely possible, but it was stretching the powers of his drumming to carry more than ten or twelve miles. He allowed that the trading post at Mexican Springs, halfway to the fort as well as on the reservation, might hear the drumming. If the trader there didn't, some Navaho was sure to drift in from the Chaço bottomland, way closer, and just tell him.

She asked how much time they were jawing about. He glanced up at the midday sun and decided, "We've got seven or eight hours of daylight left this early in the spring. To answer your question, I doubt any help will get here that soon."

A denim-clad figure in a big gray hat appeared in a doorway of the distant cliff dwelling, shaking a fist in their general direction. Longarm only meant to keep the sass pinned. But as long as he had to expend a round he'd paid for, he took careful aim with his Winchester as he asked Pat to keep beating their drum. She wasn't able to make as much noise with her smaller fist. So Longarm fired, then blinked in astonishment when he saw his target jackknife around his belt buckle, bounce off a stone jamb, and somersault down the steep grade below the cliff dwelling to send up a mighty cloud of dust and send some cows bawling in all directions.

Longarm muttered, "I could never do that again in a million years. But let's see what I can do about them cows!"

He spotted one chongo horn that looked old enough to be a natural leader, and sent up a geyser of dust and shredded grass to indicate the path to even greener pastures.

His ploy worked. When the chongo bolted he took a dozen with him, stampeding back along the only exit path he knew. A few more well-placed rifle shots soon had half the herd on the move. That was far more of the herd than the gang across the way wanted moved. But another shot at the first sign of movement up among the ruins discouraged any bolt for unsaddled as well as hobbled ponies a long way off. That lucky shot had doubtless persuaded them someone had them covered with a scope-sighted buffalo rifle.

He took the drum back and began to beat it some more as he told Pat between beats, "Reminds me of the famous last words of an otherwise obscure Union general. When they warned him about Reb snipers with scoped sights, he laughed and said they couldn't hit an elephant at that."

"At that what?" she asked.

"He likely meant to say at that range," said Longarm. "He never got to finish what he was saying."

She said, "Oh. I see why they're acting so shy across the way. But won't they be able to get to their ponies after dark, Custis?"

He sighed and said, "Nope. But I hope I don't have to shoot their hobbled mounts. We got all afternoon before they're likely to make a bolt from them ruins. How do you feel about going back and fetching us some grub and water. Bring that ten-gauge too, if you're woman enough."

She said she was. So he reclined there, whamming away on the drum and wondering why he was thinking of a dusky gal who walked in beauty after such a swell morning with ivory flesh and light brown hair all over.

Poor Pat was likely right about the fickle nature of menfolk. Some womenfolk seemed to enjoy novelty as well. Longarm had never figured out whether it was the sameness of the pussy

261

or the sameness of the gal wrapped around it that inspired a man to wonder what that next gal down the road would be like. Most all pussies felt about the same while actually coming, bless every one of 'em. So it was likely the same stories, the same jokes, the same naggings about the same things that got a man to wondering what he'd ever seen in such a tedious gal.

By the time Pat was back it was getting hot up there in the sun. When she said so, he pointed at some wind-tortured piñon further along the rim and said, "I noticed. I was waiting so you wouldn't think I'd run off on you with a buzzard bird. If we haul everything under them scrubby piñons, we'll have the mouth of that box canyon covered just as well or better."

The move naturally involved an interval of silence for the drum. So the next time Longarm peered over the edge one poor simp with a throw rope was sliding down the rocks in the open. It took Longarm three shots to drop him, halfway over to the shying ponies. Longarm sighed and said, "Likely the kid of the outfit. Kids always get to wrangle and ride drag."

She said, "I never would have known that as a Texas Panhandle girl. I think he's still alive. Isn't that him calling out like a lost calf?"

Longarm picked up the drum to resume his drumming louder as he tried not to listen. But sound carries upward, and the wounded kid did sound something like a calf bawling for its momma as he begged and pleaded for someone to help him, or at least shoot him all the way dead.

A white kerchief on a rifle barrel appeared atop the walls of a roofless ruin across the way. Pat said, "I'll bet they want to come partway and parley, Custis!"

Longarm said, "I know what they want. They want to pick up their dead and wounded. But they mostly want to get a better handle on who we are and what we're up to."

He fired on the parley signal, growling, "Let 'em guess. They must know Victorio is out, and us Bronco Apache don't parley when we have our enemies pinned down. We keep 'em pinned until dark. Then we move in to finish 'em off. We paint them white stripes across our eyes to recognize one another in a night fight."

She laughed and said he likely had the gang scared skinny. He said he hoped so as he beat the drum some more. By this time almost all those probably stolen cows had departed for a quieter range. He found he could move the hobbled ponies some with carefully placed shots. But he saw he was in danger of running low on ammunition if he wasted that much pity. So he let them be for now, and went on drumming.

When Pat said it was awfully hot up there, even under the shade of the pine-scented branches, he agreed they might as well shuck their sweaty duds and let the faint canyon breezes get at their poor hides. It wasn't as if they were strangers to one another's naked bodies, even if they were just friends.

That did feel a lot better, and Pat laughed like hell when he proved he could beat a drum while braced across her shoulder blades as he pounded her dog-style.

He had to drop the drum and fire the six-gun past her bobbed head as they were fixing to come. He came in her just as the sneaky cow thief across the way ducked back inside another slot.

But all good things must come to an end. So they were dressed some more against the coming sunset breezes, and he was reluctantly making ready to execute some innocent cow ponies, when off in the distance they could just make out the tinny sound of an army bugle.

So Longarm told Pat to keep drumming as he blasted away at the sky with all the ten-gauge shells they had left.

The poor desperate bastards pinned down in that cliff dwelling had the same great notion. At least one of them had a Big Fifty to blast away with. So just after sundown, with the light still fair in the gloaming, a troop of U.S. Cavalry, riding column of fours, tore round the bend into view to rein in and mill some as they spotted the remuda and some half-dozen remaining cows.

A voice from the ruins across the way shouted, "Take cover and watch them rimrocks to the east, soldiers blue! There's Apache up yonder! Already got two of us and we thought we was goners!"

But as the troopers dismounted and began to fan out, Longarm got to his feet, tossed his drum aside, and fired his six-gun for attention before he shouted down, "I ain't Apache. I'm U.S.

263

Deputy Marshal Custis Long, and I've been holding them rascals till I got me some backing here. If you'll be good enough to disarm and hold on to 'em for me I'll come down and arrest 'em!"

So the soldiers only had to shoot one of the gang who tried to make a run for it in the tricky light. Then Longarm came down and got to talk to the survivors, who kept telling him to go fuck himself because they'd never heard of anyone called Red.

So Longarm asked the troopers if they'd just lock the rascals up at Fort Defiance long enough for him to get a mite more on them.

After that lucky break with a chance patrol, things proceeded to go to hell in a hack. For they only had the underlings found in possession of stolen stock on that one charge, and the well-coached rascals knew it. There was no deal anyone could offer a man facing a few years on grand larceny that could convince him he was better off tied in to the premeditated murders of all those federal men, civilian as well as military.

So Longarm parted somewhat friendlier from his platonic pal Pat, and got himself back up to Durango faster than he'd come down, the long way round by rail.

Things turned out sort of disappointing in Durango too. When he asked at the livery about that blue roan he'd loaned a lady in distress, they said they'd never seen Nancy Slade or the pony he'd trusted her with.

He asked at the other liveries just in case, and got the same answer. At the railroad station they recalled selling a train ticket to that flashy piano-playing redhead after all this time. But if old Nan had ever been by, her ash-blond hair and mannish attire had failed to leave any lasting impression.

He went next to the security office next door to ask how they'd made out with the mystery of his murder. A bearded railroad dick in charge that afternoon said the joke had been on them when a couple other deputies called Smiley and Dutch had come down from Denver to view the remains, and identified them easy as those of the notorious Monte Matt Gray. Asking around town more carefully had soon explained the mix-up. The slicker had been pretending to be a lawman he barely resembled in the hopes of avoiding those Fuller boys. So Smiley and Dutch had just gone on up to Leadville and arrested Fullers till they had the one who'd backshot Monte Matt. Smiley and Dutch were like that. Marshal Vail didn't like to send them on delicate missions because their methods, while effective, tended to be bloodthirsty.

Since that mystery was no longer a mystery, Longarm went on over to the Western Union and got off a heap of wires. As long as he was there, knowing some were reluctant to answer embarrassing questions, he asked the telegraph clerk when the town law, or railroad law, had put out that all-points alarm about a killer running wild with the badge and identification of a murdered federal deputy.

The Western Union clerk recalled no such traffic. He said the railroad dicks had wired the Denver District Court about one of its deputies being on ice if they wanted him, and suggested the *Rocky Mountain News* might have spread the alarm while covering the story.

Longarm shook his head and said, "Nope. Way I was told, the law down around Gallup . . . Hold on. I passed through Gallup and a lot of other places before I got to Crooked Tree, where someone keeping tabs on me, who knew I was still alive, would figure I'd be headed next!"

The telegrapher allowed he'd recall sending any sort of message to a town with such a name, and suggested they might ask the night man. Longarm shook his head and said, "It would have been sent to someplace like Gallup, in code, for a scoundrel there to relay as a fake message from some real lawman. So I'd be obliged if you'd just get them messages from me off far and wide. I'll be back later to see if anyone has some answers for me."

He went next to have some chili con carne over a T-bone steak, with such swell apple pie that he ordered a second slice. The pleasantly plump Swedish lady who ran the place said she admired a man with a healthy appetite, and allowed she got off work around nine. Longarm said he'd remember that, finished his black coffee, and left a whole dime tip lest she feel totally unwanted.

Having the time to kill, he decided to see who'd replaced Red Robin at that Blue Danube up the street. The scrawny old gal who had didn't play enough better to make up for those rotted-out front teeth.

So he was relaxing with his back to the bar, beer gripped with his left fist, when just around sundown Whitey, that big deputy from Crooked Tree, came through the door. He spotted Longarm, smiled with his teeth, and sashayed over to say, "They told me you might be here. I reckon you think me and the boys down in Crooked Tree were dumb as hell, taking you for your own killer, right?"

Longarm smiled back just as friendly and replied, "Why, no, I never said you were dumb. I suspect you knew exactly what you were doing, Whitey, or should I call you Red?"

The white-haired giant was as lulled by Longarm's awkward position for drawing as Longarm had been hoping someone might be. When Whitey went for his own low-slung Merwin Hulbert, faster than most men might have, he caught a bullet with his paunch that set him on his ass in the sawdust gut-shot, as the piano stopped with a whimper and folks cleared the premises hollering for the law.

Longarm stepped away from the bar, putting his derringer away and drawing his more serious six-gun casually, as he sipped some beer and said, "That was stupid, Red. The boys you coached down around Gallup never gave you away. I was only guessing smart. How does it feel to be the one shot for a change?"

The painfully shot gunslick groaned, "Awful, you mean-hearted son of a bitch! We both know I'm done for. So can't you at least give me some liquor for this searing agony?"

Longarm didn't tell him what raw liquor was likely to do when it hit internal injuries. He said, "I'd be proud to spring for Maryland Rye if you'd care to answer me some last questions, Red. We found an empty bottle of the hair rinse you used to be two gents. I just now proved how fast a gent can move betwixt north and south of Dinetah the long way round by rail. But I'll be switched with snakes if I fathom the profit motive in all this double-dealing bullshit!"

The white-haired Red said he'd talk if only Longarm would fetch him a whiskey, a big one. So Longarm hunkered down to disarm the dying deputy, moved back to the bar, and set his beer aside to roll over the zinc top and fetch a brown bottle of house liquor. Nobody seemed to be there to stop him.

He went back, hunkered down, and handed the redeye to Red as he said, "I'm waiting. What have I been missing up to now?"

As the dying man raised the bottle to his lips and guzzled deep, a pair of railroad/Durango dicks came in, their own guns drawn, to freeze and stare thoughtfully down at the grim tableau.

Longarm told them who he was, and added their boss could vouch for him down by the depot. One of them said they knew who he was, and asked who the cuss he'd just shot might be.

Longarm explained, "He's a part-time town deputy and full-time crook from down Gallup way. He and his boys tried more than once to kill me. Then he had me locked up as my own killer and organized a lynch mob to avenge my death. Now he'd fixing to tell us why. Ain't that right, Red?"

The white-haired giant spread out in the sawdust just lay there, a drunken grin on his face and a glazed look in his eyes. One of the local lawmen opined, "No, he ain't. How come you called him Red when he's so white-headed?"

Longarm growled, "He deserved to last longer than that, the big sissy. It's a long story and, damn it, I can only tell you part of it so far!"

He told them all he knew as things got more back to normal there in Durango. After they had Whitey, Red, or whoever the hell he was safely stored for now at the undertaking parlor across town, Longarm went back to the Western Union.

He'd gotten answers to some of his wires. There were other questions still to be answered. So figuring he was stuck in Durango at least the night, he went back for more coffee and that swell apple pie.

The pleasantly plump gal was pleasantly surprised to see him again after all, and once they got up to her place on the hill, he found she was mighty sweet but tart in bed as well.

She sure made an interesting contrast to anyone he'd been this close to lately, and he'd warned her before taking her home that he was a useless tumbleweed who'd be long gone before she ever got the chance to ask him why he couldn't find a safer job and settle down, for heaven's sake.

Chapter 24

The next day, around noon, a yard dog yipped at the Flying W just as Widow Donovan was fixing to pour for her houseguest, Mr. L. M. Endicott of the D&RG Railroad.

The still-attractive young widow arose with a frown to peer out from behind her lace curtains. When she saw who was riding in she sighed and said, "I was afraid of this, Larry. You'd better let me do the talking till we know what he wants."

Longarm had to admire the neatly sprawling spread as he rode down into the sheltered hollow it occupied to the northeast of and somewhat higher than Durango. The surrounding hills were still sprinkled with piñon and juniper a more hardscrabble settler might have cut by now for firewood. The cows he'd passed, riding quite a ways, wore their well-known brand with an almost smug look of contentment. None of them were Cherokees or Andalusians, and he was sure any older brands would indicate honest sales. For he'd been studying some since old Inga, that pleasantly plump gal, had fed him a fine breakfast in bed.

The yapping yard dog was securely chained. So he dismounted close to the front door. As he stepped up on the veranda the oak door swung open, and the familiar but better-dressed lady standing there smiled sheepishly up at him to ask, "Did you figure it out or did you have some other business with the Flying W, Custis?"

He smiled back at the ash-blonde he'd known as Nan Slade and told her, "Both, ma'am. I wondered how come that cowgal I loaned a pony to never left it at the livery like she promised."

She said, "Your blue roan is safe with my remuda. I was trying to come up with a graceful way to return it when they told me you'd been killed in town."

He said, "That might hold up in court at that. Are you going to invite me in, old pal?"

She sighed and said she was too flustered to remember her manners. As he followed her inside she started saying something about a scandalous love affair gone awry down in the Ute Strip.

He said, "I wired Red Wash, ma'am. It's true that blond daughter of the Slades run off over a year ago. You'll be pleased to learn her folks have forgiven her since she's been married up out Odgen way."

She laughed weakly and confessed, "All right, it so happens I like Indians. Don't *you* like Indians, you picky thing?"

He didn't answer. As they entered her parlor L. M. Endicott got to his feet near the cold fireplace. He was a familiar figure too. He said, "Glad to see you again, Deputy Long. For a while there, we thought you'd been murdered."

Longarm asked, "How come? I was talking to you in the flesh at that Blue Danube before another cuss entire was backshot in my name. You've doubtless heard by now of the other so-called lawman I met in the same joint? He said he'd been told I hung out there. Who do you suppose might have told him that, Mr. Endicott? I hadn't mentioned I might be there to anyone in town. Had to be someone who'd seen me there before. The gal I know who was working there left town before Monte Matt was backshot in another part of town."

The ash-blonde in the expensive summer frock of ecru silk warned, "Don't let him goad you, Larry. I see what he's trying to do here."

She turned on Longarm to demand, "Why are we playing cat and mouse in this ridiculous vertical position, Custis? If you think you have something to accuse us of doing to a living soul, spit it out!"

Longarm said, "All right. I'm saying you and this gunslick have been working with cow thieves. I'm saying you were in on murder most foul to cover your tracks, or the tracks of a mess of cows at any rate."

As Endicott began to coil like a spring she hissed, "No! I

270

said *I* had a handle on it!" Then, more sweetly, she asked Longarm, "Do you have any evidence one cow bearing my brand has ever been stolen from anyone, Custis?"

He smiled sheepishly and said, "I doubt I could even make a horse-thieving charge stand up in court. I know you've been selling lawful beef to the Ute Agency, ma'am. I was hoping you could tell me what else you've been up to with this two-faced sewer rat."

Old L. M. must not have liked to be described that rudely. He went for his gun, even as the blonde screamed, "No!" and wailed like a banshee calling hogs.

Longarm won, just as she'd warned. Her business partner, if not part-time lover, staggered backwards to back-flip over a big leather chesterfield with Longarm's round just under the heart. It would have been dumb to risk wounding a son of a bitch who moved that fast.

As he thudded limply to the clay tiles on the far side, the widow started screaming, "Help! Rape! I'm being raped by a murderer in here, boys!"

Her screaming stopped as Deputy Smiley of the Denver District Court came out through a beaded curtain to mildly ask, "Don't rape the poor gal, Longarm. Hasn't Billy Vail told us all how bad that can look in court?"

Smiley was the morose-looking breed's real name. Nobody had seen Smiley smile in living memory, despite his dry sense of fun.

Longarm asked, "Dutch and the other boys have all her hired hands on ice?"

Smiley nodded and replied, "You told us to. It was simple to move in and get the drop on everyone whilst they were so interested in *you*. You had to gun the railroad dick, huh?"

Longarm said, "Oh, that's all right. Miz Donovan here is fixing to tie up all the loose ends for us now. Ain't that right, ma'am?"

She suggested he do something mighty disrespectful to his mama. So he pushed her gently but firmly down on the chesterfield and said, "I reckon you ain't grasped this situation yet, ma'am. We've only had to kill a half a dozen of your gang. We've got a whole bunch in the army stockade down to Fort Defiance."

He turned to Smiley and asked how many Dutch and the others had the drop on out back. The lanky breed said, "Eight. All innocent, to hear them tell it."

Longarm said, "There you go, ma'am. We'll be questioning all your surviving underlings separately. They'll naturally be told who's dead and offered the usual deals for turning state's evidence. When even one of 'em sees he's facing the rope dance should even one other talk first, well, we won't need to offer the rest of you much, will we?"

Smiley had moved around behind her to hunker down and search the dead man's pockets for clues, loose change, or whatever. So she had to really work on her poker face when Smiley remarked, right in her ear, "I talked to an old boy who was there when they hung that other widow after Lincoln was shot. He said he never wanted to take part in such a hanging again."

Longarm said, "The federal hangmen use a five-strand rope of fancy Eye-talian hemp, three quarters of an inch in diameter. They knot it behind your left ear. They'll drop you a tad farther than they might a man, lest your lighter weight not snap your neck clean when you hit the end of your rope."

Smiley said conversationally, "The boys felt sort of sorry for that Widow Surratt. It was a hot sunny day. So they gave her a chair up there on the gallows platform, and held an umbrella to shade her as the death warrants were being read aloud. Someone tied her skirts secure around her ankles lest they fly up and embarrass her modesty when she flew through the air at the end."

"You're making me sick," the ash-blonde protested.

Smiley got back to his feet, muttering, "He sure packed a modest roll for such a big-time crook. Anyway, as I was saying, they stood Widow Surratt up and put the hood over her head. That's to spare the feelings of the witnesses. The prisoner don't need to see what's going on when they spring the trap. Everyone wanted to see Widow Surratt and the other plotters hang all at once, so instead of dropping them through trapdoors, they fixed it so's the whole front half of the big long platform swung down on hinges."

The rich young widow stared down aghast at the serpentine trickle of blood that had followed the tile cracks clean under her chesterfield to emerge near her feet. Longarm pretended not to notice as he asked, "What happened then, Smiley? Did the lady die with dignity?"

Smiley said, "They never die with dignity. She may not have felt it. But she naturally wriggled and jiggled at the end of her rope, and the old boy who was there said, despite her bound skirts, she let fly twice as much piss and shit as the others hanging with her that day."

Longarm smiled thinly down at the pale-faced blonde and suggested, "If I were you I'd wear those tight jeans you had on when first we met, ma'am. I'd go easy on that last supper too."

Smiley said, "Aw, it don't make no never mind after you're dead. If they were hanging *me* in the morning I'd order all I could ever eat and let *them* worry about cleaning up after me."

"You're just saying all that to get me to confess to crimes I'm not guilty of!" she sobbed, covering her face with her hands.

Longarm said, "Aw, mush. We'll take your word you never gunned anyone personal, if you'd be good enough to help us with the fine print."

She didn't answer.

He insisted, "Look, cowgirl, you're going to prison no matter what you say on the face of the evidence we have so far. Should we get any more out of anybody, those who ain't cooperated are the ones our old Judge Dickerson is sure to nail with accessory to murder in the first."

Smiley said, "Old Hanging Dick is sure a caution with culprits who want to act like clams."

They could both see the little wheels going around in those big blue eyes. Longarm said gently, "It's over, ma'am. Might as well make it easy on yourself."

So she did, with Longarm taking notes. He had to write it down a second time to make it read clearer. For they'd sure gone to a whole lot of trouble just to cheat the U.S. Government.

Later that same week, up in Denver, Longarm reported for work at the federal building no later than usual to find Henry, the kid who played the typewriter out front, all het up.

Henry said, "It's about time you got here. Marshal Vail is in a snit over that report you had me type up and, oh, yes, there was a gal who says she writes for some newspaper asking for you. She was pretty too, you dog."

Longarm considered, shook his head, and decided, "Tell her I had to go up to Fort Collins if she comes back."

Henry asked, "Why? There's nothing going on up that way right now, is there?"

Longarm grinned and said, "That's why no newspaper reporter, male or female, is likely to head up that way. I got a supper planned at Romano's this evening with Miss Morgana Floyd of the Arvada Orphan Asylum, see?"

Henry grinned and said he surely did. So Longarm went on back to the oak-paneled office of his boss, Marshal Billy Vail.

The somewhat older and far shorter and fatter Billy Vail shot a disgusted look at the banjo clock on one oak wall, and bared his teeth without removing his pungent cigar from between them as he said, "It was good of you to come all this way before noon. I've been straining my brain with this confusing report you handed in. Even though Henry seems to have tidied up your spelling, this one's sure a tangled tale!"

Longarm said, "That's because my official report had to start at the beginning and go on to the Donovan woman confessing. Put it all aside, save for what they were pulling with Indian beef sales, and it all falls in place neat enough."

Vail leaned back in his swivel chair and said, "Why don't you go ahead and do that very thing, old son?"

So Longarm sat down in the one leather chair on his side of the cluttered desk and reached for a cheroot as he began. "Once upon a time there was a handsome young widow who'd inherited a thriving cow spread. She was so handsome that by screwing some and bribing others she soon had an exclusive contract to supply beef on the hoof to the South Ute Nation."

As he lit his smoke Vail grumbled, "Got all that. But the federal prosecutor ain't about to charge anyone with political favoritism."

Longarm shook out his match and mildly observed, "The scare will do 'em some good. So anyhow, once she'd made friends in high places, she was getting a good price for her cows. She was even able to buy stock off her neighbors and resell it at a profit. The only limits to her budding beef empire was biology. You can only breed cows so fast on any range, and most of her grazing rights were marginal. She said it was Endicott, a more worldly well-traveled man, who led her down the primrose path. Maybe he did. Endicott, as a railroad dick and part-time crook, knew one Whitey Mullins, a born thief, working as a lawman down around Gallup because he hadn't figured out where a cow stolen in such a remote part of New Mexico Territory could be sold."

He flicked ash on the rug. It was likely good for carpet mites, and old Billy's own fault for not providing ashtrays. Vail was so interested he forgot to fuss as Longarm continued. "They couldn't just steal cows from down south and run 'em up north to be sold as Flying W beef to the B.I.A. The white government agents didn't like young Widow Donovan *that* much. So every now and again she and her boys drove a herd of lawfully acquired cows down to the Ute Strip and got a B.I.A. bank draft for 'em, all nice and legal, with both her bank records and the B.I.A. records tidy."

He took a drag and let some out his nostrils to organize his own thoughts. "Meanwhile, Whitey Mullins, disguised as the mysterious Red, would gather a herd of stolen stock down the other way. He and his owlhoot riders would thread them north through the canyonlands of Dinetah, scaring off any Indians they met in the haunted Chuskas."

Vail nodded and said, "I'd feel sort of morose about some of them hills if I was a Navaho too. But where were they aiming to drive a stolen herd? You just said the Donovan woman only bought documented beef to flesh out her own increase."

Longarm said, "They couldn't sell recently stolen cows to anyone for cash. The Ute didn't have much cash to spare in any case. But a Saltu cow is a Saltu cow to your average Ute. So some of their band leaders were more than willing to swap two for one, on remote parts of the Ute Strip. They got two stolen cows for one documented cow. After that the gang only had to drive the documented Flying W stock the long way home, through canyons measureless to most white men, and their boss lady was set to sell the same cows, again and again, to the same Indian agents. Not all of the Indians themselves were in on it. That's how come some sold honestly branded hides to that trader to their northwest."

Vail nodded and said, "Right. Indians who'd wound up with twice as much beef wouldn't have been dumb enough to sell their hides. I hope you told the B.I.A. all this in your report to Washington that General Sherman asked for so urgently?"

Longarm said, "I did. Some Indians are likely to get a good scolding. But when you study on it, all they really did was trade with white men taking advantage of poor Mr. Lo."

"Get to all that gunplay," Vail demanded.

Longarm said, "The widow herself says she just can't say whether all those patrolling troopers were gunned because they were fixing to cut cow sign in sheep country, or just to get them all patrolling far from crooked cattle drives. She says Miss Charladora and me, betwixt us, nailed their main assassins. She might have been telling it true."

Vail said, "Let's not roil the waters. A deal is a deal, and she's still going to be too old to corrupt politicians when she gets out of prison as it is."

Longarm muttered, "You ain't seen her ass, or some politicians, but be that as it may, now that she's come clean, we got enough to put the others away for the rest of this here century."

He blew a sober smoke ring and opined, "It's a shame, in a way, the pretty little thing couldn't have been content with the handsome profits of an honest monopoly. Her chief lieutenants were greedy assholes too. If they hadn't behaved so wild with those poor troopers, I'd have never in this world been asked by General Sherman in the flesh to ride with that dumb asshole Captain Granville. Granville wouldn't have known a stolen cow if it was farting in his face. But as a more experienced rider, inclined to find the best ways through canyon country, I just naturally wound up catching the old boys with stolen cows from the south."

Vail said, "I'm not too clear as to how you caught on to the less crude operation at the north end of the field of action."

Longarm said, "I wasn't sure just what was going on, before we got Widow Donovan to confess. But that was greed and guilty conscience as well. When Endicott found out a deputy

276

with my modest rep was fixing to horn into their operation, he should have just told the widow and his other pals to pull in their horns and leave me be. But they were too greedy, and I told you all they done to be rid of me. Had the gal I had down as a runaway left that pony I lent her where I asked her to leave it, I'd have assumed she'd gone on before Monte Matt was gunned in my place by old boys who knew who he really was. A gal who'd never left Durango and still needed a mount should have attended the viewing at least. But she never did, so I started looking around Durango to ask her if she was blind or just disrespectful. You only have to describe a good-looking gal in some detail in a small town before somebody figures out who you might mean."

He enjoyed another drag and continued. "Hearing nobody working for the D&RG had recognized my corpse as somebody else sort of cinched it. L. M. Endicott had made a point of coming up to me, in fair light, to ask who I was and what I was doing in his town. Didn't take long to find out which railroad dick that had to be, or pick up some dirt about him spending the night now and again out to the Flying W. But I must confess I was hoping I'd guessed wrong about the gal, till she invited me right in and tried to brazen it out."

Vail said, "Yeah, yeah, I got all that about you waiting for some backup and riding out there to distract them out front whilst others worked around to the back through the trees. You're right about them going to a whole heap of trouble just to share some dishonest bucks. She'd have been better off paying more for her extra stock and taking a less greedy profit."

Then, grudgingly, the older lawman growled, "Most of all, they'd have been way better off if they'd never messed with my senior deputy! You done good, Longarm. Now get out of here before we blubber up all over each other. It's almost noon, you lazy rascal, but don't take too long with them pickled pig's feet at the Parthenon, hear?"

Longarm promised he'd tell them not to needle his beer either, as he rose to amble back outside, grinning around the cheroot between his teeth.

He told Henry he'd be over at the nearby Parthenon if anybody robbed the bank across the way. Henry said, "I take

it you don't want me to tell that newspaper reporter? She
was here again just now. She seemed anxious to see you
Said she'd only be in town over the weekend. You haven'
gotten that pretty blond lady in trouble, have you?"

Longarm said, "Nope, she's likely just romantic and . .
Hold on, did you say blond just now? Not brunette?"

Henry shook his head and said, "I guess I know a blonde
from any brunette. Said her name was Sparky something, from
Omaha. Said to . . ."

But Longarm was on his way out. For sultry Miss Morgana
Floyd would be there indefinitely, while that acrobatic blonde
from Omaha had just now said she wouldn't!

If you enjoyed this book, subscribe now and get...

TWO FREE

A $7.00 VALUE—

If you would like to read more of the very best, most exciting, adventurous, action-packed Westerns being published today, you'll want to subscribe to True Value's Western Home Subscription Service.

Each month the editors of True Value will select the 6 very best Westerns from America's leading publishers for special readers like you. You'll be able to preview these new titles as soon as they are published, *FREE* for ten days with no obligation!

TWO FREE BOOKS

When you subscribe, we'll send you your first month's shipment of the newest and best 6 Westerns for you to preview. With your first shipment, two of these books will be yours as our introductory gift to you absolutely *FREE* (a $7.00 value), regardless of what you decide to do. If

you like them, as much as we think you will, keep all six books but pay for just 4 at the low subscriber rate of just $2.75 each. If you decide to return them, keep 2 of the titles as our gift. No obligation.

Special Subscriber Savings

When you become a True Value subscriber you'll save money several ways. First, all regular monthly selections will be billed at the low subscriber price of just $2.75 each. That's at least a savings of $4.50 each month below the publishers price. Second, there is never any shipping, handling or other hidden charges—*Free home delivery*. What's more there is no minimum number of books you must buy, you may return any selection for full credit and you can cancel your subscription at any time. A TRUE VALUE!